SOLITAIRE,
A Dog Story

Candice L. Martin

Candice L. Martin

Copyright © 2015 Candice Martin

All rights reserved.

ISBN: 1519610335
ISBN-13: 9781519610331

DEDICATION

With warm gratitude to my husband, John, for the years of patience he needed to help me get through this.

CONTENTS

CHAPTER 1 1

CHAPTER 2 5

CHAPTER 3 18

CHAPTER 4 24

CHAPTER 5 37

CHAPTER 6 43

CHAPTER 7 47

CHAPTER 8 57

CHAPTER 9 64

CHAPTER 10 69

CHAPTER 11 75

CHAPTER 12 85

CHAPTER 13 97

CHAPTER 14 110

CHAPTER 15 119

CHAPTER 16 124

CHAPTER 17 132

CHAPTER 18 138

CHAPTER 19 148

CHAPTER 20 153

CHAPTER 21	170
CHAPTER 22	178
CHAPTER 23	188
CHAPTER 24	195
CHAPTER 25	206
CHAPTER 26	215
CHAPTER 27	220
CHAPTER 28	240
chapter 29	255
chapter 30	266
chapter 31	276
chapter 32	285
chapter 33	306

Preface

The main canine character of SOLITAIRE, A Dog Story is based on the Akita breed standard as it is accepted in the U.S. and Canada today. In many other countries of the world, this type of dog is known as an *American Akita* and it is differentiated from the *Japanese Akita* in size, coat and to some degree, temperament. Both types are also known as *Akita Inu*, but 'Inu' only means 'dog' in Japanese, no matter where the animal is from. I have chosen not to go to great lengths to highlight these differences in the hopes of keeping my novel a more flowing narrative for all people to enjoy, regardless of their knowledge of the dog world. I hope this difference doesn't negatively affect your enjoyment of SOLITAIRE's story.

CHAPTER 1

Molded gray plastic surrounded the big dog closely on three sides, supported her massive weight off the ground, and formed a low ceiling above her head. An open metal grate that was the door and fourth side of the travel kennel allowed light and air to enter, but there was little room for circulation of either, so the interior was stifling.

The dog, a fully-grown Japanese Akita, lay nearly senseless in the front of the kennel, her breathing ragged and shallow. Her square muzzle was pressed tightly against the criss-cross of metal wires, as if she meant to inhale any passing breezes before they had a chance to mix with the stale air inside the kennel.

She never turned away from the door, not even in sleep, because she understood that her only chance for freedom would come when somebody on the outside opened its latch. But if she was to have the strength to help herself, the day of her deliverance would have to come soon; the unhealthy fogginess that had clouded her mind for so long was beginning to take a heavy toll on her body as well.

The Akita had no awareness of how long she had been traveling. Strange clouds had begun to fill her head while she was still at her home kennel, before the traveling had started. When they first manifested themselves, she had welcomed the soft relief that the mists brought, for they padded the jagged edges of painful memories that had become too difficult for her to live with. She had been despondent, unable to eat, drink, or even sleep. But as the clouds thickened, her dulled mind had given up battling the physical needs of her body so that she was able to go on living, though in a twilight world of swirling fog.

After a time, the memories themselves had begun to fade into the haze. But no matter how all-encompassing that fog seemed to be, now and then a puppy's sharp cry of alarm would cut through it like a knife, bringing the great dog raging to her feet inside her kennel, knowing she was desperately needed but not able, in her muddled state, to remember why.

During those rare moments of wakening, she had become blearily aware that her surroundings were changing. The people who had always taken care of her were gone, replaced by others, giants with strange-sounding voices and rough hands.

The Akita moaned, her ears flicking in annoyance as a new sound breached the borders of her consciousness. Slowly, unsteadily, she raised her bear-like head, blinking her eyelids repeatedly in an effort to part the sticky film that covered them and blotted her sight. The rude clacking noise of boot heels hitting a smooth concrete floor got progressively louder, as though the wearer was passing through a long corridor. She searched through the mists of her mind to find a thread of coherency, a clue as to why that sound should mean something to her. What was the reason her fur bristled in such a discomforting way when she heard the approach of booted feet?

At the same moment that she picked up the less ominous and barely audible swishing of a second pair of shoes, two human shapes rounded the corner of the kennel room and into the mucous blur that was her vision. Both men were very tall, as everyone here seemed to be; both were strangely pale of hair and skin; one was thinner than the other. She sensed a hideous familiarity about the thin one, the one who was wearing boots, but she was unable to recall why she should feel that way.

The heavier man didn't come any further into the room, but turned into a side closet where the Akita could hear him tinkering with small items. She forgot about him altogether when the thin stranger approached her kennel and squatted down to peer into her face with eyes that reminded her so much of the sky on a clear winter morning that she began to tremble from their chill.

The man's cold gaze remained unblinking while he took a long draw on the short, misshapen cigarette he held in his hand. Then he leaned forward to place the stub on top of her kennel.

The black leather of the Akita's nostrils flared to gather his scent, a subconscious reaction that she immediately regretted as he exhaled the foul-smelling smoke in her face. The sweetish reek combined with the odors of his aftershave and leather boots to greatly increase her feelings of nausea. When her stomach began to heave, the Akita's sense of discomfort turned to fear and any hope of forcing an escape was forgotten as she tried to back away from the offensive stranger.

But there was no room for retreat in the small kennel. A low growl was the only defense she could muster as the man flung open the door and thrust his hand inside to grope for a thick cord that had been left hanging around her neck.

She was rewarded for her efforts with a brain-jarring punch that smashed her head against the side of the box. Stunned by the ferocity of the blow, she didn't growl again, but was docile while the man wrapped his fingers around the rope and yanked her from the kennel.

She hadn't expected to be treated so cruelly, and lurched forward, unable to stop herself from falling untidily onto the concrete at the thin man's feet. She attempted to pick herself up, but the man stamped his booted foot on the section of rope that lay slack between them, simultaneously pulling up on his end of it and using the leverage to force her chin back to the floor with a crack. This time, the confused dog remained sprawled helplessly before him, unable to even lift her head.

The man called to his companion in a harsh accent that was unfamiliar to her ears.

"Johan! Bring the horse blanket along with the syringe. This one's feeling quarrelsome today."

If the Akita didn't understand his words, she was cognizant enough by now to realize that she wouldn't receive any mercy from this human. Her fear left her in the face of hopelessness.

The other man hurried into the room carrying a thick, dark blanket, which he threw over the dog's head, pitching her into sudden blackness. She felt his weight drop heavily on her shoulder, and pain lanced through the area. Struggling to adjust her position in an attempt to relieve it only caused him to tighten his hold, so she was forced to lie still, her heart beating a wild rhythm.

The second man's voice sounded far-off and fuzzy through the densely-woven cover when he spoke.

"Mr. Trident, shouldn't you take it easy with those injections if you're going to ship her on tonight?"

Trident! The name-word paralyzed the Akita with fear and loathing. She began to pant, even more terrified.

"I would have rather not used anything at all, but this bitch is still as wild as ever. I hoped she would have calmed down by now, but I'm already late in shipping her and I can't take any more chances. I have to get her out of here before this customer changes his mind, too. When those last people refused her, it put me in a real bind. Hopefully, I'm shipping her far enough this time that I won't get her back!" The man called Trident paused before he took a firm grip on the Akita's thick foreleg and dragged it toward him. "But the only way the airlines are going to accept this crazy bitch for transport is if she's whacked out of her mind the whole way."

The Akita was in utter panic now and would have fought the men, but the weight on her shoulder and the awkwardness of her position did not allow for any resistance. She felt the sharp prick of a needle, and her muscles involuntarily began to relax, though she remained conscious enough to hear the regret in Trident's voice as he murmured, "I wish I never would have started with this one."

CHAPTER 2

Lying in the ditch by the side of the dusty Kansas highway, Johnny felt the air so heavy on his chest that he seriously doubted whether his lungs would be able to rise and fill with his next breath. It seemed to the teenage boy as though all life on the prairie was being held in suspension, so silent were the small creatures; almost as though they were waiting for something important to happen. He waited, too, at the bottom of his breathing cycle, strangely comfortable with the thought that he would die if he didn't force his indolent body to breathe soon. He closed his eyes and enjoyed the unusual sensation of total relaxation.

Too soon, the turmoil returned. Distant grumbling from a heavy diesel motor brought Johnny to his elbow with an audible gasp that seemed to bring the rest of the world back to life, as well. A small bird that had been dozing nearby was obviously startled and took off in a wide arc, its wings beating movement into the still air. Similarly agitated, a large bumblebee heaved itself from a blossom next to Johnny's ear, buzzing so loudly as it dipped and skimmed by that the boy thought about recommending a good muffler shop. Beside Johnny, a small black and tan terrier that had been snoozing peacefully sprang to sudden, riotous life, yapping deliriously as it sprinted past on the way to the highway.

"Jack! Get back here! You'll get yourself killed!" Johnny made a half-hearted attempt to stop the dog. He must have said those words to that dog a million times over the past six months, but Jack hadn't gotten himself killed yet, so Johnny gave up and roused himself instead.

Johnny would turn fifteen that summer, but was maturing quickly as a lot of farm kids do. His legs were still too long and thin, his feet too big. His arms were skinny also, but his shoulders were broad and already had a muscular hardness from years of helping out with farm chores. Light brown shoulder-length hair that was his only egocentricity, and the bane of his father's existence, was swept back into a casual ponytail.

Standing now, Johnny had to squint to make out the undulating form of a semi-truck approaching through waves of heated air. The highway it traveled on sliced a straight line through the prairie, separating drab, open fields on one side from equally dismal fields on the other. Deep ditches formed the only barriers between tarmac and grass and were filled with a mixture of both. Just behind the ditches, and parallel to them, stretched miles of stringy barbed wire that was the preference for fences in this area. At odd intervals, those parallel lines were broken by white gravel driveways that set off at sharp angles to the highway before meandering out of sight over the low horizon.

Johnny turned to ponder the entrance to the driveway where he waited. A weather-beaten sign that was strung in the center of the wood-and-wire gate informed the unknowing that this property belonged to Welsely Farms and Kennels, Inc. Below it, a new, larger sign with bold black lettering warned: ABSOLUTELY NO VISITORS! In all this emptiness, he thought, why would anyone feel the need to post a sign like that?

Welsely's foreman, Fleet, had explained that the property was posted to discourage peddlers and nosy tourists from stopping by, but Johnny didn't believe that; there weren't that many day-trippers in this part of the world. Abel, the other boy who had been working in the kennels a lot longer than Johnny, said it was because Welsely's was a puppy farm and they wanted to keep the government inspectors out. Johnny figured that was probably closer to the truth.

Johnny had come to work for old Ms. Welsely last winter, when things were pretty quiet on his family's farm. He yearned for the independence that making his own spending money would give him, so he had begged his father's permission to get off the school bus a few stops early in order to take this job. He had begun by mucking-out the dog kennels each afternoon, but his duties had grown in proportion to his willingness to learn. For several weeks now, he had been helping Abel with the dogs' afternoon feeding and whatever grooming he could fit into his short hours. To his surprise and his father's disgust, he had found that he liked working with dogs better than he did dusty earth and inanimate objects, so when Fleet had asked him to help out on weekends, he had readily agreed.

That was when the trouble with his father had begun. The elder Wales needed his son's help, too, and was insistent that Johnny's job didn't excuse him from chores at home. Johnny was defiant, however. He didn't want to leave his paying position at the kennel and thought his father should be more understanding of that, since he was the one who was always complaining about the family's poor finances. But the only thing his defiance had gotten Johnny was more work. Now he found himself responsible for the chores on both farms, and his schoolwork as well. For the past month, his days had started before five in the morning and didn't end until well after dark. In spite of his youth and enthusiasm, Johnny's body was beginning to wear out. He couldn't even look forward to the day when school would finally let out because he knew there would be another argument with his father about which farm was going to get the benefit of those extra hours he would have available.

The uneven whine of the semi's motor as the driver geared down brought Johnny's attention back to the job at hand.

"Morning, son!" the driver called cheerily once the hissing air brakes had brought his rig to a full stop. "You from Welsely's?" When Johnny nodded, the driver seemed dubious. "Well, I hope you brought some transport, son. This package ain't exactly the right size for tucking under your arm."

Johnny pointed at a battered white three-quarter ton Ford parked just inside Welsely's gate. Satisfied, the driver set his brakes and opened his cab door to climb down.

"How come they let you drive that pickup, boy? You ain't old enough to drive yet, are you?"

Johnny cracked a sideways smile. "You don't see that pickup outside the fence, do you?"

He had found answering one question with another was the best way to keep out of trouble sometimes. The truth was, he had been driving farm vehicles around his family's property since he was old enough to reach the pedals, and was often asked to drive Welsely's pickup in the course of his job here. However, he had been warned sternly about staying on the back roads until he was old enough to apply for his license.

When the driver turned to back down the steps of his cab, Johnny couldn't help but notice that he had the look of someone who spent long hours behind the wheel with little or no exercise. He had looked meaty enough while he sat in the cab, but once he got out, his legs were surprisingly thin in denim jeans so tight that they had to be buttoned below his paunch. Johnny hid a chuckle as the man made a futile effort to pull his pants higher before turning around.

Jack seemed to take the driver's odd squirming actions as his cue to rush his ankles, barking shrilly. Instead of being alarmed by the terrier's attack, however, the man only chuckled and bent over to try to make friends. Acting like he was insulted by the offer of friendship from a stranger, Jack stayed just out of reach of the man's big hands. When the driver finally gave up and walked to the rear of the truck, the unfriendly terrier fell in behind him, still barking ferociously.

"Jack doesn't like many people," Johnny said in the form of an apology as the beleaguered trucker passed in front of him.

"Yeah? Well, neither does the fella in the back of my truck – and he's a heck of a lot bigger! He nearly ate my dispatcher back at the dock!" When Johnny looked questioningly at him, the driver was quick to add, "Not that I blame him, I guess – he's come a long way, and he's probably not real happy about his traveling accommodations. But he makes me real nervous. I'll be a lot happier when this one's off my truck and on yours!"

Johnny was still puzzled. The animal being delivered was a champion Japanese Akita bitch, a show dog used to strangers and unfamiliar surroundings. The driver must be exaggerating about her aggressive behavior.

"Well, maybe she just doesn't like being called a he," Johnny teased weakly, not knowing what other excuse he could offer for the dog's strange behavior. "Anyway, I reckon she'll be fine once she's settled in her run."

The trucker sniffed doubtfully.

"I'd still rather keep my distance, if you don't mind. I've got a forklift on board. Give me a minute to lower the elevator and we'll unload her kennel the safe way. Then once she's in the back of your pickup, you can do whatever you like with her. Okay?"

They reached the back of the truck and Johnny waited while the driver climbed onto the bumper of his semi and gave the heavy roll-up door a shove, revealing a large gray travel kennel. The kennel's grated front door was facing the dark interior of the trailer, so Johnny wasn't able to see the animal within. However, he gave more credence to the driver's tale of horror when he saw the sturdy plastic box rock with the weight of the creature and heard its claws scraping the hard plastic floor as it circled to keep the driver in sight. There certainly was no mistaking the harsh warning in the dog's throaty growl.

While the driver started up his forklift and maneuvered it into position, Johnny cleared the bed of Welsely's pickup to accommodate the large box. Some wooden stakes and wire bundles that were used for emergency repairs around the property were taking up a lot of room, so he unloaded most of them by the side of the driveway for pickup later, after the new dog was safely offloaded into a run.

While he worked, Johnny pondered the Akita's aggressive response to the truck driver's presence. The man was obviously frightened of such a big dog; was it possible that the Akita was simply reacting to that fear? Johnny had heard that dogs can smell a bad odor when somebody's afraid of them. He decided to ask Mr. Lorch what he thought about that.

Ken Lorch was Johnny's boss and the newly-installed manager of Welsely's kennel operations. He used to be a professional show handler, and had impressed Johnny right away with his extensive knowledge of dogs and dog lore. It seemed like Mr. Lorch had noticed Johnny's enthusiasm, too, because he often talked with him about his plans for the future of Welsely Farms and Kennels, Inc. and made the boy feel like he could be a

SOLITAIRE, A Dog Story

part of it if he wanted to.

On the day Welsely Farms' offer to purchase this Akita bitch was accepted, Mr. Lorch had been very excited. He had proudly shown Johnny an advertisement from a glossy magazine that featured a photograph of the Akita-Inu, taken at an exhibition in Japan. The picture was of a spectacular Nordic-type dog in a regal pose, looking aloof while her proud young Japanese handler accepted the silver trophy awarded for "Best Dog In Show."

Mr. Lorch had told Johnny that the Akita was the largest member of the ancient Spitz family of dogs, which included the white Samoyed, the wolfish Siberian Husky and the faithful Norwegian Elkhound. Johnny's first glance at the dog in the photo took in the pricked ears, large furry tail curled over the back, and straight hind legs typical of the Spitz breeds. But as he studied the photograph further, he got the feeling that those physical traits were probably all the Akita had in common with her brothers and sisters in that canine family. There was nothing of the 'laughing' Samoyed or gentle Elkhound apparent in this dog's demeanor.

When he voiced his thoughts, Mr. Lorch had complimented Johnny on his well-formed conclusion. The Akita, he explained, unlike other spitz types, had long been used by its Japanese masters in the sport of dogfighting and was known to not only hunt, but to savagely kill, the Yezo bears of the region, which could weigh upwards of 800 pounds. Johnny figured that would account for the formidable personality apparent even through the eye of a camera, as well as the Akita's impressively greater size.

This was obviously a huge female, even for the breed. Mr. Lorch had bragged that she weighed an amazing one hundred and forty pounds, which was probably why she had been sold outside of Japan; they preferred a more compact dog over there.

Johnny was amazed by how much the Akita's broad head, with its powerful squared-off muzzle, seemed more like that of the great bears her ancestors hunted than like a dog. It was strongly supported by her thick neck with its 'stole' of rippling muscle accented by coarse guard hairs that lay across her shoulders, tapering down to her proud chest. Her hips and flanks were also well muscled and she stood straight and firm on stout legs that terminated in large, rounded paws.

The bitch was gazing at the camera with serious, fairly small eyes, triangular in shape and deeply set in the front of her head. Johnny remembered thinking that the slight wrinkles he could see on her forehead only accented her intelligent expression rather than imply any worry or nervousness.

Her small, thick ears were also triangular, slightly rounded at the top and held forward at an angle that suggested that the photographer had her total, undivided attention, whenever he was ready to snap the shot.

Of all the Akita's striking qualities, Johnny had decided that her luxurious coat was the most intriguing. It was characteristic of the Nordic breeds in that it was actually two coats. The undercoat was the color of blonde mink, while the overlaying guard hair was black as midnight and so thick that you could barely make out the gold beneath it. The combination of colors gave her a warm burnished glow. The hair was much shorter on her head and muzzle, where it darkened down to solid black velvet. Also short and thick, the hair on her sturdy front legs and paws was white from just below the elbows, matching the trickle of white down her broad chest and on the last third of her bushy tail, which lay quietly on her flank.

Mr. Lorch had told Johnny that dogs of the Akita breed are even now considered a national treasure of Japan, and that he thought their popularity in the U.S. would explode once people here realized what a truly noble breed they were.

Johnny had been impatient to meet this member of dogdom's 'royalty' in person, but now that she was here, he was feeling slightly abashed. Mr. Lorch had told him so much about the nobility of the Akita breed – but noble dogs don't try to bite people, as this one obviously had. He'd have to report that, he guessed, when he got back to the farmhouse.

The forklift, with the huge kennel hefted in its metal grip, approached the back of the pickup truck and slowly lowered its live cargo into the bed. Any aggressive tendencies the Akita might have shown during the off-loading seemed to have been subdued by the roar of the machine, and she hunched fearfully in the back of her box while Johnny tied the ropes that held the kennel in position.

Before he raised the tailgate, Johnny glanced inside the travel kennel. Pressed against the back wall of the box like she was, the Akita didn't look as big as she had in the photo. She didn't look aggressive, either. In fact, the poor dog looked downright pitiable to Johnny, and his heart did a rapid turnabout as he realized that the Akita might just need to be shown a little compassion. What did they expect of the poor dog, anyway? She had already spent too much time stuffed in that smelly travel kennel – was it any wonder she was in a bad mood? He told himself that, once she could relax in the comfort of her own run, the Akita would return to grace.

"Don't worry, girl." His voice was low and soothing. "You're going to like it here. I'm going to take care of you, and you and I are going to be real good friends." Confusion was all he could read in the Akita's dark eyes.

The driver had finished loading his forklift and called his good-byes before he climbed into the cab of his truck. Johnny waved in return, grabbed Jack before the terrier could run off, then took his own seat behind the wheel of the pickup.

The ride over the dirt road to the kennel area of Welsely Farms was bumpy, but not long. Just over a slight rise, the road dipped suddenly, winding down into an old river valley that formed a cool gray-green nest for the farm buildings and dog runs, hiding them from the view of the main road.

Six generations of the Welsely family had lived out their lives here in the valley. Johnny's employer, Ms. Anna, was the sole remaining member of that family. She had once told him that when her great-grandfather had tilled the fields, the river had flowed on top of the land. But that was before the burning sun of the central plains drank too much of its strength, leaving it no choice but to seek cooler, darker passages below ground. She said the ancient trees that shaded the long dirt drive leading to the house had once stood along the banks of that river. Driving through the cool shadows cast by those hoary giants now, Johnny imagined their roots plunging deep into the earth, drinking from the waters of their birth.

He honked as he approached the main house to let Mr. Lorch know he was back with the 'Japan Package', as the Akita had come to be known, then took a cut-off track just before it that led directly to the new quarantine area. One of Mr. Lorch's first projects had been to erect these runs, and he had made it firm policy that every new dog spent the first two weeks of its confinement here in solitary until it was declared free of communicable diseases and could join the healthy dogs in the main sections of kennels. The last occupants had been a pair of English Cocker Spaniels that had been removed to their new quarters earlier that morning.

Johnny reversed the truck up tightly against the opening of a 12 x 15-foot dog run fully enclosed by galvanized steel mesh. The floor was concrete for ease of cleaning, and a small wooden hut stood in the center as shelter from foul weather. It was the middle run in a row of five, all of which were empty.

Johnny opened the door and waited for Jack to bolt across his lap before getting out himself. He watched the terrier scamper off after one of the yard cats and disappear into the barn just as a lean, knotted-rope of a man emerged from it.

Fleet paused for a moment outside the barn, long enough for Johnny to take in his appearance. He was one of those people whose age is always a mystery. Although his brown skin was desiccated and wrinkled from the strong winds and merciless sun of the plains, he had intense blue eyes and moved with the lithe grace of a man in his prime. His straight, medium-length hair was the color of old hemp; a light sandy-brown kept from brightness by the dull gray streaks that ran through it. Faded blue jeans that hugged his long legs and a pale cotton shirt, long sleeves rolled above his forearms, was his normal way of dressing. His customary footwear was a pair of snakeskin cowboy boots that looked old enough to be comfortable. Today, he was wearing a lightweight leather jacket, as well. That was Johnny's clue that the foreman was heading somewhere off the property.

He fervently hoped Fleet was in a hurry.

Johnny circled around the back of the pickup, loosening the ropes that secured the shipping kennel along the way. He kept one eye on his foreman while he talked to the frightened Akita bitch.

"This is going to be your home for a couple of weeks, girl. It isn't much, but it's a lot better than the place you're living now." A private groan of disappointment escaped him, making the Akita tense in anticipation of trouble. Johnny was immediately apologetic. "It's okay, girl. It's just that Fleet is headed this way."

In Johnny's opinion, Fleet was the only bad part about working for Ms. Welsely. The foreman had been unpleasant enough before Mr. Lorch arrived, but now he never seemed to miss an opportunity to express his disapproval of the new manager's policies. He may have been right about some things, but Johnny hated to hear about it because he liked Mr. Lorch. Besides, he figured 'sour grapes' was the real reason behind Fleet's animosity. In the six short months he had been working as a kennelboy here, he had seen Fleet taking advantage of Ms. Welsely's age and frail health to usurp more and more control around the farm. Johnny had often felt the tension between the two adults, which led him to the conclusion that, although Ms. Welsely seemed to need Fleet, she really didn't like him very much. In spite of that, it had been a shock to everyone when she had brought in the new overseer, putting an abrupt end to Fleet's ambitions.

Why Fleet bothered to stay on when he was so full of bitterness had been a mystery to Johnny until the day he was so tired of hearing the foreman's complaints that he asked him straight out. Fleet had looked at him like he was pitifully naive, and sneered, "You don't get it, do you, kid? That guy isn't going to stay around here long, believe me. He's city-bred and used to being at the center of attention. And when he leaves, old lady Welsely's going to beg me to take over this place again. You wait and see." Johnny had vowed that would be the day he finally quit this job.

"That the Japan package? Took long enough."

Johnny nodded dumbly, hoping to avoid further conversation.

"I'll give you a hand getting her out of there, then I need the truck to pick up the old lady in town." Fleet opened the latch of the tailgate, then allowed it to fall so that it jarred the whole truck. "Jesus! She is a big bitch!" he remarked as he stepped closer to peer into the travel kennel. The dog was still hunched in the back of the crate, so he shook the steel closure to get her attention. Suddenly, the air was filled with growls and curses as fangs ripped through flesh.

"Sonuvabitch!" Fleet cursed between clenched teeth, backing away and holding his bloodied hand.

Johnny froze, stunned by the sudden turn of events. He hadn't taken the trucker's warning seriously enough to expect this attack on Fleet. Guilt, as much as pity, made him rush to help. He left Fleet leaning against the truck's bed while he rummaged behind the seats in the cab for a rag to wrap around the wound.

He could still hear the dog's rasping growls from inside the cab and thought that Fleet must be bothering her again. But when he glanced out the back window, he saw that the man had moved away from the pickup and it was the Akita who was doing the taunting, daring Fleet to make another careless movement that would bring his flesh close enough for a second attack. Worried that matters could get worse, Johnny hurried back with the rag.

Fleet was seething.

"They sure don't teach these brutes any manners in Japan! This bitch is going to need a whole lot of education before she's going to do us any good," he spat angrily and, Johnny thought, nervously. "Lorch is an idiot, bringing in a vicious animal like this! I warned him against trying to breed the giant types. We don't need this one any more than all those other fancy breeds we got in here the last few months!"

He grabbed the rag proffered and bound his wound tightly. Then he picked up one of the wooden stakes that Johnny had left in the truck bed and pounded the top of the travel kennel in sheer frustration.

Johnny physically flinched, knowing the tirade that was about to be launched at him but helpless, now, to avoid it.

"None of what that man does makes any business sense to me. As far as I can see, he's just throwing good money away on bad. And don't I know this business as well as anyone? Hell, who does he think was running Welsely Farms for the last two years? The old lady? Not bloody likely. And I did it without any exotic new breeds or fancy quarantine area!" As he spoke, he punctuated every angry statement with a bang on the plastic kennel.

"And now we've got a damned Japanese Akita, of all things. Who's ever even heard of an Akita outside the show ring? Where's our market? The dealers aren't going to touch any pups they can't move quickly, and I sure don't see anything special about this bitch."

With the last statement, his anger got the best of him and he jabbed the stake into one of the side openings on the crate. Johnny jumped to stop him, concerned about the dog inside, but the Akita already had her teeth on the stick and worried it away from Fleet. As she tore it into splinters, the ferocity of her roars startled both of them into a quick step backwards.

Now Fleet was embarrassed as well as frustrated. He kicked at the truck's side with a booted foot, adding another dent to the already bumpy fender.

"Come on, kid." He was still breathing huskily, but making an effort to calm himself. "My hand is hurting like a sonuvabitch! Let's just get the bitch out of there so I can go get Anna. I'll take care of this problem later."

The trucker had loaded the travel kennel close to the back of the pickup's bed so that all they had to do was lift it down to the ground, but the weight of his end was still too much for Fleet to lift with one hand. Johnny suggested they wait until he could bring Abel to help. He sprinted off and moments later was back with the other kennel helper, a lanky, tow-headed boy a few years older than himself. Between the three of them, they were able to unload the unwieldy kennel and manhandle it into the run.

Once the crate was situated, Fleet motioned the two boys to leave the run. When they were safely outside, he unlatched the door to the travel kennel and gave the box a lurching kick that sent the dog inside sprawling.

"That's just so you'll remember who I am when I get back," he snarled at her. "The quicker you realize who's the boss, the quicker we can start re-educating you in proper manners."

When the Akita made no sign of leaving her traveling den for such a hostile environment, Fleet glanced up at the boys waiting by the fence and sniggered knowingly.

"That's what I figured. Just because she's big and noisy doesn't necessarily mean she's brave. Get a high-pressure hose, Abel. We'll have to force the bitch out."

Abel glanced at Johnny, unsure of what he should do. Hoses located at various places around the kennel grounds were fitted with high-pressure nozzles that were meant to facilitate the cleaning of dog runs, but Fleet often used the stinging jets of water on the animals themselves, as discipline if they broke any of his rules. Neither boy wanted to take part in tormenting the Akita, but they knew that if they refused to help Fleet, the foreman would get angrier and she would probably suffer more for it.

Johnny used another approach.

"Aw, Fleet," he said, trying hard to make the disgust in his voice sound more like boredom. "Why don't you give her some time to adjust? She'll probably come out on her own. And your hand looks pretty bad...."

Fleet looked doubtful, but Johnny had noticed how he was cradling his right hand protectively.

"Right now, we should go up to the office and ask if Mr. Lorch can drive you into town. He could pick up Ms. Welsely while you have your hand doctored," he continued in his most persuasive tone. "The dog's not important. You can take care of her when you get back, like you said."

Fleet's injured hand, wrapped in the bloody rag, was throbbing painfully now, making him more biddable to suggestion than usual.

"All right, but I don't want her getting too comfortable in there," he said. "Scared dogs are nothing but trouble, and fear-biters like her are the worst."

He turned his back on the crate, satisfied that his judgment of the dog was correct and that she would think twice before she ever tried to bite him again.

Like a whirlwind, the Akita was on him. Her first leap took her out of the kennel and onto Fleet's back, where her tremendous weight unbalanced him and pulled him backwards to the ground. He rolled once, twice, but she would not be shaken off. She gripped the leather collar of his jacket between powerful jaws and shook him viciously, tearing at the extraneous skin so that she could reach the softer, more vulnerable man-skin underneath.

Abel was surprised by the dog's rush from the kennel and stood gaping stupidly at the violent scene until he felt Johnny shove the hose end into his hands.

"Keep the hose on the dog!" Johnny shouted. "We've got to help Fleet. Keep the hose on her, Abel!"

Belatedly, Abel sprang to life. He turned the nozzle to full blast, aiming a jet of water between the Akita's eyes to blind her, in her mouth to drown her, against her chest to force her backwards, away from her attack.

The pressure turned the water into icy needles that shot up the Akita's nostrils and into her slitted eyes. She choked as water filled her mouth and rushed down the back of her throat. While she gagged, Fleet was able to pull loose and rolled onto his back, one arm raised to protect his face. He stumbled to his feet, but didn't seem to know what to do.

"Get behind the water, Fleet!" Johnny called from outside the fence. Abel's hose seemed to be working to keep the Akita at bay. "We'll protect you!"

Hopefully, the Akita had had enough, but if she did attack again, Johnny thought that the force of the water might unbalance her enough to allow Fleet to deflect her to the side and make good his escape.

In his terror, Fleet was obedient. He backed up carefully until he stood against the fence in front of Abel, and behind the hose's torrent. He kept his arms upraised defensively, in case the dog dared to brave the rush of water and strike again.

"Make your way over here, Fleet," Johnny coaxed from a few yards to the left. "The door's open, and I'm ready to close it behind you."

He found he was holding his breath along with Fleet, willing the man to take the sideways steps to the run's opening. But Fleet seemed mesmerized by the huge dog pacing just on the other side of the water, and he didn't move quickly enough.

Howling like a demon, the huge animal threw herself directly into the gush of water that shielded Fleet. Her mighty leap took her over his braced forearms and she hit his chest like a fur cannonball, throwing him violently backwards against the steel mesh enclosing the horrifying arena.

She fell backwards, as well, but recovered her footing quickly and jumped again, clamping powerful jaws around Fleet's right biceps. This time she drew blood. She stayed up on her hind legs now, tugging madly on Fleet's arm, utilizing the heavy muscles of her well-developed neck and chest in an effort to yank him away from the fence.

Johnny watched, horrified, while Fleet clung desperately to the wire with his left hand in order to stay upright. He was petrified that if the Akita dragged Fleet down again, he would not be able to rise. Fleet must have known the same fear, for he began to fight as madly as the Akita now.

He risked letting go of the fence long enough to grab a fistful of coarse hair on the back of his attacker's shoulders and ripped her away from his body. She allowed him to throw her, even seemed to help by jumping away from his side in the same instant, but she kept her jaws clamped tightly around her pound of man-flesh.

The combination of her weight and his panic-driven strength was enough to enable the powerful Akita to tear muscle and tendon away from the bone of Fleet's arm. She landed on the ground with a jolt that loosened her hold on his jacket and the mangled flesh beneath it. Fleet landed on top of her and held her down while he pounded her with his good left fist, screaming in pain and fear. The torrent from the hose was still spraying them both, blood and water mixing on the concrete floor.

Abel stood open-mouthed at the gate, his water hose pointed in the general direction of the combatants, not knowing what more he could do.

Johnny couldn't just stand by and watch any longer. He knew he would have to take some more aggressive action if he wanted to help Fleet. He ran to the pickup, which was still parked nearby, and grabbed a wooden stake from the bed. As he threw open the door to the run, he yelled to make sure Abel understood what he was to do.

"Don't take that hose off her until I tell you!"

Johnny ran to where Fleet was struggling to hold the maddened dog down. He was straddling her, his face just out of reach of her snapping jaws, his left forearm across her throat. But Johnny noticed that the man's breath was coming in desperate gasps and he didn't seem to have the strength to finish the fight. As Fleet weakened, the Akita fought harder.

The boy crouched beside the two and waited for his opportunity. It came when Fleet pulled back a bit and Johnny was able to kneel heavily on the dog's chest, momentarily driving the breath from her lungs. He slipped the stout wooden shaft across her throat beside Fleet's arm and held both ends firmly against her insane struggling.

"I've got her, Fleet! Get out of here and be ready to close that gate when I come through."

He waited interminable moments while Fleet lunged toward the gate. But what about his own escape, he wondered. Would he be quick enough to escape this monster once he let her go? Surely, she would be slower now and close to exhaustion after her battle with Fleet?

After an eternity, he heard Abel's voice.

"Okay, Fleet's out, Johnny. Make a run for it!"

Johnny's arms were trembling; his knees felt weak, but still the dog writhed angrily beneath him.

"Okay, girl," he whispered tightly. "Relax, now. . . I don't know what got into you, but we've only just met, so you know it wasn't my fault. . . I promise I'll find out what happened, if you'll just let me get out that gate with all of my skin intact!"

If the boy's soothing talk had impressed the beast at all, she didn't show it. Instead, she fought with renewed hatred, trying to rid herself of his weight. When he thought the moment was right, Johnny sprang backwards to his feet, stake in hand and at the ready to use as a club.

The Akita righted herself, involuntarily shaking out her coat as if his very touch had violated her. She refocused dull eyes on his face and growled low. Johnny held steady, sure that the dog was simply taking his measure before charging again, but then her eyes brightened perceptibly and she raised her black lips in an ugly grin before turning away from him. Johnny had the strange feeling he had just been excused, the Akita showed so little interest in him. He watched, astonished, as the dog lowered her head and scanned the steel enclosure until she had Fleet in her vision again.

Fleet paled the moment the awesome beast's gaze found his face. Though he was safe behind the steel mesh, he instinctively tried to raise his bloodied right arm to protect his throat, but it wouldn't respond. He looked down stupidly, as if wondering why this should be so. Shiny white bone showed through a gaping rent in his jacket, while the flesh and musculature that had been his biceps hung limply out of the ragged hole, dripping blood down his sleeve.

Johnny used the instant of the Akita's indecision to duck out of the quarantine run, locking the door tightly behind him. He ran to Fleet, past Abel who stood as if dumbfounded, still holding onto the hose with the water digging ineffectually into the ground at his feet. Johnny swallowed hard when he saw the gore covering Fleet's jacket and it was only the urgency of the moment that kept him on his feet. He guided the injured man to the passenger seat of the pickup truck.

"Oh God, Fleet," he sobbed through taut white lips. "You've got to get to the hospital. Sit here in the truck while I get help from the house."

"I'll kill her," Fleet whimpered, still staring at his arm. "I'll kill the bitch."

CHAPTER 3

Ken Lorch had been closing up files and straightening his office desk before enjoying his first look at the new Akita when he heard excited shouts from the direction of the quarantine runs. Hurrying from his office, he was just pushing open the screen door of the farmhouse when Johnny barreled up the back steps, nearly running him down. His curiosity turned into shocked concern as the kennelboy blurted out the details of Fleet's injury, then he leaped off the porch and led the way back to the scene of the savage attack.

When they got there, Ken paused to stare for a moment in astonishment at the patches of dark, red blood that were spattered all around the quarantine runs. The monstrous, water-drenched Akita bitch was pacing around and around the steel mesh enclosure as if she was demented. Abel was standing slack-jawed in amazement with the water hose lying by his feet. Fleet, barely conscious now, was slouched in the truck where Johnny had left him, his left hand holding a ragged red hole in his jacket closed.

Both boys were impressed with the way Ken took control of the situation. They watched as the older man stripped his leather belt from his pants to make a tourniquet around the top of Fleet's shredded arm, slowing the gush of blood to a less hideous ooze. Though he moved quickly, by the time Ken moved around to the driver's side of the pickup and got in, Fleet was showing signs of shock.

"We've got to go quickly," Ken told the boys. "Fleet's lost a lot of blood. You two try to hose the area down before Anna gets back from town. I'll pick her up and let her know what happened, but I don't want her getting any more upset than necessary.

I don't think I have to tell you boys to stay away from that animal," he visually checked the steel and concrete enclosure again to satisfy himself that it was secure, "but stay away from that animal!"

"Yessir, Mr. Lorch," Johnny nodded in agreement. "We'll stay away."

He stood back to allow the truck room to maneuver, then shouted as if in afterthought what had been uppermost on all their minds. "Mr. Lorch, do you think she's rabid?"

"I don't know, Johnny. Just be careful, eh?" He wagged his head uncomfortably and drove off down the dusty drive.

Once Ken left, taking Fleet with him, the Akita stopped pacing. She stood quietly against one wall of the run, her head low and weaving from side to side like a Spanish bull trying to get a fix on a matador, until the pickup had gone out of sight over the rise. She was thoroughly soaked with a mixture of water and blood that made her look hideous and was going to look worse later when her fur dried to a stiff, bristly mat, but her anger seemed to be dissipating along with the clouds of dust showing the truck's passage.

Not knowing what else to do, Johnny picked up the high-pressure hose, adjusted the force, and turned it on the dog. For some reason he didn't want anyone else to see her that way. What was he afraid of? That people might think she was vicious?

"Yeah, right," he let out a small, derisive snigger.

The Akita's black eyes shifted at the noise to take him in, but there was no sign of further aggression. Indeed, she stood so still under the gush of water that it seemed to Johnny as if she was eager to be rid of the manblood as well.

"Well, I ain't never heard of a mad dog wantin' a bath before," Abel declared from a safe distance away.

"Me neither, Abel. Do you suppose she really is? Mad, I mean? Fleet was picking on her awfully hard. Maybe he did something mean to her when I went to find you."

"Come on, Johnny," Abel shook his head and moved a little closer, still keeping a watchful eye on the fearsome beast in the run. "You always take the dog's part against Fleet. He ain't so bad. He says you got to keep 'em in line or else somethin' like this happens. Maybe he shoulda kept an eye on her and give her a good kick when she came out of her crate. Teach her a lesson so she'd think again 'fore she tried to bite a person."

"That's stupid and you know it. Fleet just uses that as an excuse to be cruel. What about that poodle that died last winter? I guess it was trying to tear his arm off, too?"

Both boys were silent as they thought about that unfortunate victim of Fleet's temper. Ms. Welsely had been told that the puppy had fallen from his crate when Fleet was taking him out to medicate him, but Johnny knew differently.

That afternoon he had been on his knees behind one of the rows of small dog kennels, cleaning out a clogged floor drain, when he heard Fleet come striding into the building, obviously agitated and mumbling something about some pigheaded man not knowing his business. Oops, Johnny had thought, another dealer complaint. They seemed to be pouring in these days and it was making Fleet very difficult to get along with. He had stayed quiet, hoping he wouldn't be spotted. He had problems of his own and didn't need to listen to Fleet's.

The tiny black poodle puppy had been isolated in a separate cage from his littermates earlier that morning because of an eye infection. He wasn't happy about it and was letting the whole world know it with his shrill little barks. Johnny heard Fleet bang on its cage and yell at it several times to 'shaddup', but the pup was defiant. Johnny could tell Fleet was reaching the end of his patience and was about to get up to see if he could help the situation when there was the sound of a cage door springing open, then a strangled yelp from the puppy. Immediately after, he heard a dull thud that sounded ominously like something soft and fragile hitting the concrete floor, then silence. Fearing the worst, he had hurried around the wall of kennels to confront a cursing Fleet.

"Sonuvabitch! Just jumped right out of my hands, he did," Fleet raised an eyebrow and stared at Johnny, daring him to contradict his story.

The kennelboy had kept his secret, only sharing his doubts with Abel, who reminded him that Fleet was in charge, and it would be Johnny's word against Fleet's should he decide to go to the old lady with his version of the story. Johnny had only been part-time back then, hoping for full-time summer hours, so he had agreed to keep quiet against his better judgment. He had soothed his troubled conscience with the justification that he hadn't actually seen Fleet do anything wrong, anyway, so how could he prove his story to Ms. Welsely?

Since that day, Fleet had made a concerted effort to befriend Johnny. He tried to let the boy know through lightened workloads and more relaxed supervision that he valued his loyalty, but Johnny was not so easily won over. It still felt bad inside whenever he thought about the puppy, and he hated himself for his indecisiveness in not reporting the tragic episode. He wondered when he was going to be able to stand up to people like Fleet and get some control over his own life.

After Johnny gave the Akita a thorough rinsing, he continued soaking the quarantine area with the hose until there was no sign remaining of the bloody battle that had taken place. Ms. Welsely would be distressed enough about Fleet's arm without having to see the grisly evidence for herself.

He left the shipping kennel in the run, mindful of his promise to Mr. Lorch not to take any chances with the new dog. All the while he had been washing her quarters, she had stood against one side watching him, moving nothing but her ears and small, bright eyes. Now she lay down in a semi-dry patch and stared at him coolly while he contemplated her.

Watching the newcomer, Johnny felt his rational fear melting away, replaced by an illogical tangle of emotions. Despite her cruel deeds of this afternoon, the Akita bitch was a compelling creature.

He couldn't help but admire her proud bearing and sheer physical beauty. At once menacing and elegant, the huge bitch seemed to know that no one would dare to disturb her further that day and lay like a big cat in the sun, her coat quickly drying to its full luxurious thickness. She held her alert ears well forward, accustoming herself to the normal kennel sounds, none of which seemed to particularly alarm her. Head high on her thick neck with its great mane of fur and muscle, she sniffed the light breezes and seemed satisfied that the object of her hatred was gone, even his blood washed away.

When she lowered her muzzle again to take in Johnny's smell, the heavy dewlap protecting the front of her neck and chest puffed slightly, a long, furred cushion under her chin. It was no wonder that his earlier attempt to disable her with the wooden rail across her throat had little effect: her kind was born with natural shields of fatty tissue around all of their vital areas.

Even her eyes were surrounded by 'pillows' of fat and thick fur that hooded them, protecting them from fang or claw. Located as they were in the front of her skull, those eyes allowed the Akita to focus directly on the opponent ahead of her. One of the few breeds able to look comfortably and directly into a man's face, she would never back down to an aggressive stare like so many other dogs must. Johnny could almost forget how malevolently those eyes had shone such a short while ago. Now that the great bitch was at rest, they seemed to him nothing more than honest windows to a strong personality, but he understood that they gave nothing away that the Akita wished to remain hidden. Respectfully, the boy had to concede that this was a dog well bred for the perilous exhilaration of battle.

Abel had become bored with watching the new dog and had wandered off long ago to finish his chores, but Johnny was intrigued and stayed close by for the rest of the day. He noted that she did not drink any water at all, though there was plenty available, and felt an inexplicable hope rising. An animal with rabies feels a terrible, unquenchable thirst. But he also realized that a healthy dog would have required some water after an exertion like she had experienced that afternoon. He felt himself wavering between wishing she would drink and being glad she didn't; and wondering why he cared. His confusion grew along with his concern for the Akita's well-being. She seemed perfectly calm and healthy now, but she didn't move. As the afternoon wore on, she lowered her head, but she didn't close her eyes.

The next day was the same. And the day after, though the Akita was sleeping almost constantly by then. Johnny knew she was in trouble and his kind young heart went out to the forlorn creature. He passed close by the quarantine runs at every opportunity and stopped to talk to her, but elicited little response other than a heavy sigh now and then, as if she wanted to let him know how boring his attentions were to her.

Early on the fourth morning when he arrived to work, he was alarmed to see the Akita lying stretched out full on her side. In that position, the extent of deterioration of her once powerful body was painfully apparent. Through the thick fur, dull and brittle now, her bones stuck out where smooth flesh should have been. Her muscles were noticeably flaccid and hung from her frame like an old blanket. Her head, always oversized in comparison to her body, now seemed hideously large. Filled with a trepidation that overran his common sense, Johnny quickly unlocked the door and rushed to kneel beside her.

The startled bitch scrambled to her feet in alarm and took a defensive posture, all signs of weakness disappearing for the moment as she turned her snarling countenance on the boy. Johnny froze in place, scant inches away and eye to eye with the dreadful beast. His vision was full of her great, round bear-head with ears laid back tightly against her skull, eyes drawn to slits of dull charcoal and a horrifying array of strong, white teeth; and he was stunned by the ugliness of her monstrous expression. How could he ever have thought such an evil face was anything like beautiful?

But once again, the huge dog did not attack him. Though her eyes never left his, their murderous glint softened as she recognized her young caretaker. She slowly relaxed her defensive posture, brought her ears forward and smoothed her wrinkled muzzle. Then she looked over his shoulder at the open kennel door and tensed slightly as if she might bolt.

"Oh! Don't do that, girl," Johnny pleaded, bringing the dog's attention back to him. His heart banged fearfully in his chest as she turned those cold black eyes on his once again and raised her lips in a quivering threat. He was fully aware of how dangerous his position still was, but he couldn't let the Akita escape – for many reasons.

"They'll shoot you for sure if you get loose! They won't have any choice, girl. Just stay here. . . take it easy. . . It's a lot safer in here. . . There's nothing out there for you, anyway." Johnny's voice was steadier now and he hoped he sounded convincing.

The Akita stopped snarling. She still stared at him, but her anger had gone again and with it, it seemed, her strength. Her hindquarters sagged and she allowed her body to fall heavily back to the ground.

Johnny was shocked by the wave of grief and anguish that washed over him then. It was impossible that a dog could feel such strong emotions, let alone impress him with the depth of those passions. He stayed on his knees beside her, desperately wanting to touch her, to share her burden of unhappiness, whatever it might be. Tears filled his eyes and his heart grew incredibly heavy until it felt as though his chest would burst, but he couldn't make his hand reach for her. It was as if she had commanded him and he couldn't disobey. He knelt helplessly on the cold concrete of the run as the sadness overwhelmed him. When he could take no more, he quietly rose to his feet and walked out of the enclosure, leaving the Akita in peace.

For the next few hours, Johnny went about his chores without talking to anyone. He couldn't shake the mood from his early encounter with the new bitch and certainly couldn't explain it to anyone else. He tried to put his strange emotions down to that old catchall, 'puberty', but knew in his soul that they had emanated from the Akita. Somehow, she had 'allowed' him to feel how miserable she was. Why? Did she want him to help? But he got no sense of 'wanting' that way. Perhaps she had just let her defenses down long enough to let him understand that there was no hope left for her so that he would leave her alone.

But Johnny wouldn't believe that. He made up his mind right then that he would do anything he could to give the Akita the time she needed in order to heal herself. The first thing he would do was speak to Mr. Lorch.

CHAPTER 4

A droplet of light morning rain rolled down the Akita's slanted forehead to her squarish muzzle, then tickled her whiskers on the way to the hard concrete that was her bed. She twitched unconsciously and changed positions, moaning softly all the while.

"You aren't even smart enough to go in out of the rain."

One ear moved like a tiny radar cone to pick up the boy's voice, but otherwise the dog showed no signs of life.

"See what I mean, Mr. Lorch? She hasn't eaten or even drank since she . . . since she arrived. I know you don't want anyone in there until you decide what you're going to do with her, but she's going to die unless we do something pretty quick." The youngster begged with his eyes as well as his voice, but his boss was unmovable.

"She's not going to bite anyone else like she did Fleet. She stays here in quarantine for ten days to make sure she doesn't show any sign of rabies. Fleet has enough problems with that arm. He doesn't need to worry about those injections as well."

"But Mr. Lorch, today she let me put her food in without even growling at me. She's getting used to me. She isn't mad, she's sick! It's like she doesn't care what happens to her. If we don't do something, she'll die before the ten days are up, and then Fleet will have to have the shots."

Ken smiled at his helper's enthusiasm. Three days ago, this beast had tried to kill the boy, and now he was begging for her life. Ken believed that Johnny was going to be one hell of a dog-man someday, but there was no sense getting worked up about an animal sentenced to death. The boy was right about one thing, though: if this animal died, Fleet could have a very unpleasant time ahead of him.

"Okay, Johnny, tell Doc to have a look at her when he comes to do his rounds tomorrow. He'll know what to do. But don't you be spending all of your time back here," he admonished the kennelboy lightly. "We've got a lot of other dogs to take care of around here."

Striding off toward the house and his office, Ken went over the whole incident in his mind for what seemed like the thousandth time. He still didn't know how to explain the dog's strange behavior. That Japanese Akitas were aggressive with other animals was well known, but an unprovoked attack on a human was highly unusual, and Ken wanted to know why it had happened.

Maybe the bitch was rabid, but he didn't think so. Seeing her lying in the drizzling rain this morning, he had felt her sorrow like a weight on his own heart. Her life had been disrupted, of that there was no doubt, and she had flown halfway around the world in two days, but most animals adapted to new situations quickly. What had gone wrong with this poor, miserable creature?

Whatever it was, it had become her death warrant. Doc could keep her alive for the next six days, but then she would receive the lethal injection that would protect other people from her rage.

Ken didn't have much hope that the dog agent who had brought her to his attention would give him any answers, either. He would be too busy protecting his own behind for sending an obviously vicious animal to the Welsely Farms kennels. But Ken had placed a call to his service anyway, requesting that he get in touch a.s.a.p.

He had also emailed the kennel in Japan, where the Akita had been bred, for an explanation right after he got back from taking Fleet to the hospital. Two days later he was still waiting for a reply, hoping it would provide him with some kind of rationale for what had happened.

Ken entered the old farmhouse by the side screen door and turned right immediately, into his office. He poured a cup of this morning's black, lukewarm coffee and settled wearily into his chair.

Funny the way things turned out. A year ago he would never have believed that he would be managing a puppy farm surrounded by the vast wheat fields of Kansas. But a year ago he, Kenneth J. Lorch, had been an international celebrity in the dog business, a professional show handler at the zenith of his career who had his pick of the best dogs in America to grace his kennels. It took a lot of style to get to the top in every kind of show business, and Ken liked to think that he had the formula down to perfection. He had mixed just the right amount of suave showmanship with sufficient breed knowledge to be able to display any dog to its fullest potential, then topped it off with the single-minded ambition of the true winner.

During twenty-five years, his career as a handler had taken him thousands of miles to fabulous locations in seven different countries where he had exhibited the greatest dogs of the time at the top shows in the world. He had rubbed elbows with all types of people; rich and poor, sophisticated and ignorant, those who just loved dogs and those who just loved 'the show'.

He was retired from the show ring now. A small lump still formed in his throat whenever he thought about that. He had loved his life on the circuit and had worked hard for many years to be the best dog handler in the business.

Maybe too hard, he reflected now. Maybe he had lost sight of some of the important things about winning and losing. For whatever reason, a year ago he had made a mistake and been caught out by a rival who threatened to take advantage of the opportunity to ruin his reputation and have him dishonored in professional circles. Ken had no alternative but to retire gracefully.

Not to be able to exhibit dogs at a professional level, the only thing at which he had ever truly excelled was immensely frustrating for him. Ken would do anything to be able to turn the clock back and erase his mistake, but he knew that wasn't going to happen.

Instead, he had devised a plan that he hoped would one day allow him to reenter the glamorous world of dog shows through a different door. His rival had agreed not to make any formal complaints about his wrongful action as long as Ken withdrew from the show ring as rapidly as his contractual responsibilities would allow, thereby removing himself permanently from the competition for the lucrative fees paid to the favored few handlers at the top of their profession. However, nothing had been said about Ken's coming back to exhibit his own animals. He could return with a clean slate in the "Bred-by" classification as an owner-handler.

Ken knew as well as anyone that it took years to build a string of winning show dogs, and in order to compete at the level he was used to, he needed financial as well as physical backing. He also needed a regular job. All of which had led him to apply for the position as manager of Welsely Farms and Kennels, Inc.

He had met Anna Welsely at ringside several times when he was still a winning handler. From their conversations, he knew she was an experienced breeder, though he had never seen any of her animals being shown, which had made him wonder what kind of kennel she ran. The elderly woman definitely had an eye for a winner, though she wasn't always impressed with the judge's opinion as to which dog that was, and Ken had enjoyed her country witticisms about what a dog should and should not be.

Once, when he had time between classes, he had invited Anna for a little friendly conversation over coffee. Even then he had been curious about her background. But although she had been her usual loquacious self while standing at ringside earlier that afternoon, Ken had some difficulty bringing her out once they were seated in the cafeteria, away from the barking and press of the myriad canines anxious to be judged. To use one of her own euphemisms, Ken thought she seemed as nervous as a 'long-tailed cat in a room full of rockin' chairs'. She rose from her chair often on the pretext of needing more sugar, checking to see what kinds of pastries were available, wanting to see who was judging the Chihuahuas – anything but sit still and face him in direct dialogue.

Ken was patient. He had met many longtime breeders who had the same problem. Having given their whole lives to dumb animals, they were at a loss when confronted on a one-to-one basis by other human beings. He tried handling her like he would a timid animal, using his most soothing voice and warmest smile to gain her trust while carefully approaching her from angles that didn't startle. But when she still seemed tense, he brought the conversation around to a favorite old subject between them, inquiring what her opinion was of the Black & Tan Coonhound he was taking to the next class. That provoked the response he expected and he grinned with self-satisfaction as she sat down abruptly, facing him directly with a disbelieving look on her face.

"You call him a Black & Tan? I'd call him a Black & Black. Where's the tan on that dog? Just those two thumbprints over his eyes?" The tiny woman lost all signs of coyness as she warmed to her topic. "I ain't even sure if he's a Coonhound. Dog's Dinner! That animal's the size of a cow. How's he gonna chase a little varmint through the ground cover? And what happens if he gets one treed? Does he bark or say 'moo'?"

Two cups of coffee later, Ken had finally been able to lead the talk away from dogs again. He wanted to hear more about Anna Welsely. Much more forthcoming now, Anna told him how, when her father died many years ago, leaving his 32-year-old spinster daughter as the last surviving Welsely and sole heir, she had gotten away from farming which she knew from experience was endless toil for little profit. She leased the majority of her acreage to neighboring farms and invested the small amount of cash she received in pedigree bitches of the most popular breeds at that time. She transformed her barn into a kennel with wire cages for the small breeds and outdoor runs for the larger ones. At first, she had found it more economical to send her bitches out for mating, but over the years she had acquired her own stud dogs for most of the breeds. Through her own hard work and careful business management, Welsely Farms and Kennels, Inc. had grown to be a chief supplier of puppies to pet shops all over the United States.

Anna had thrown this final declaration out with bravura, almost as a challenge to Ken, then sat back to await his reaction. She knew that most of his peers would be horrified to realize that he was openly associating with the owner of a 'puppy farm', as they called her type of kennel, and she wanted to know how he stood on the issue. Show people often made Anna feel like an impostor standing at ringside, making judgments on their prime quality animals, but she stubbornly refused to be ashamed of her life accomplishments.

Ken had already picked up a few clues from their previous conversations as to the type of breeding she specialized in, so was not too surprised by her admission. Unlike his associates, he felt that categorizing all kennels as 'show' or 'pet', 'good' or 'bad', with no room for even the most compassionate and knowledgeable non-show breeder in between, was wrong. He had realized a long time ago that not everyone felt the competitive thrill that he did on entering the ring, but that didn't mean they loved or respected their breed any less.

He admitted to Anna that the way a lot of his friends simply dismissed all pet breeders with adjectives like 'ignorant' and 'inhuman', and would not dirty their fingers with what they felt was the messy end of the business, sometimes irritated him. That left the breeding of the American family pet either to private individuals, 'backyard breeders' he called them, who had little or no knowledge of what they were doing when they allowed their little "Ginger" to mate with the dog down the road who *looked* somewhat the same and *seemed* to have the proper papers; or to unscrupulous puppy mills.

Though they might call themselves kennels, Ken knew these cruel puppy factories seldom had the interest of any dogs in mind. From his experience, he estimated only two out of ten puppies born in these places actually lived long enough to make it into a loving home, and even less were able to struggle through their first year, so weak were they from the ravages of disease brought on by their filthy early environment. It amazed him that so many puppy mills were still able to operate freely in the U.S. with so remarkably few controls.

In turn, Anna applauded the various dog clubs for their efforts in educating the public as to the dangers of buying a 'petshop puppy', but she felt they were still leaving a large void in the market that they weren't willing to help fill: where was the average Joe going to buy a purebred Cocker Spaniel puppy for his 10-year-old daughter? Certainly not from those same show breeders who warned him off the corner pet shop. Most of them 'designed' their litters around their own show strategy and had few, if any, pups that they were willing to sell to pet homes. Even if there were a puppy available, the cost would be more because of the higher expense in running a small kennel, paying retail for food, veterinary care, etc., not to mention exorbitant stud fees, than it would be for a larger, wholesale operation. The puppy would probably be well worth the extra money, but could Joe afford it?

These and other points were the subjects of many a lively exchange between Ken and Anna whenever they met after that. Now that she was semi-retired and had more time to indulge her passion for the dogs themselves, Anna seldom missed an opportunity to attend any Midwest show where there was a large entry in the Hound Group, her first love. And she always looked Kenny Lorch up, no matter what ring he was exhibiting in.

To Ken, seeing her on the sidelines during one of his last appearances in the ring seemed very opportune. From their prior conversations, he knew that Welsely Farms was old enough and profitable enough to provide him with the means to realize his plans. If he was to believe Anna, the breeding stock, though hardly Westminster quality, were good, healthy specimens of each type, and their papers were honest. He would have something to work with. The kennel was properly licensed and inspected regularly with minimal problems.

Most of all, during their ringside chats, Ken had recognized in Anna Welsely a burgeoning desire to make a mark in the field she had labored at in obscurity for more than thirty years. He thought they could help each other.

At coffee that day, Anna had listened to Ken's ideas quietly. As she confided to him later, she hadn't actually been looking for a manager until he spoke to her, but when she realized that there might be a solution there, she was suddenly able to acknowledge that she had a problem.

She had admitted that her arthritis was getting worse every day. Many mornings she could barely get out of bed at 6 a.m. like 'honest workin' folk do', let alone oversee a large kennel operation single-handed. Because of this, she had let much of the management of Welsely Farms rest on the shoulders of her kennel foreman, and she wasn't happy with the results. At first she had rationalized that Fleet's inefficient manner of doing business was due to his lack of experience and that he would get better at it. But the plain truth was that profits were down, the puppy mortality rate was steadily climbing and the other kennel personnel were not their usual boisterous selves. It was a prime example of the Peter Principal, and she blamed herself for the resulting problems more than she did Fleet.

Ken had more experience running a big kennel than Fleet did, that much was true. But she still worried that, by replacing one manager with another who had no vested interest in the kennel, she wasn't really solving her problem.

"Kenny, I admit I need help. I'm gettin' too old for cleanin' up dog poop and playin' mid-wife to a Schnauzer. And I just ain't got the fight for sparrin' with ornery customers like I used to. But I've already tried hirin' in a manager and that don't seem to work too well for me." Her firm gaze held his attention. "I ain't got no family to leave the farm to, so I've thought about sellin', but I ain't willin' to give up everythin' my daddy left me and everythin' I've built on it just yet. What I need is someone to take a real serious interest in the place. Here's my proposition."

When Ken had frowned nervously, her features buckled into a toothy grin and she had comforted him.

"Don't worry, I ain't gonna' to ask you to put up any money. You said you need an income, so it makes sense that you probably can't afford to buy into Welsely Farms, anyway. That's no problem. I'll pay you what you need for managin' the kennel for the first year.

Then, if we're still gettin' along after twelve months – me bein' the decidin' party on whether we're gettin' along or not – I'll sign over a half-interest in the business to you and you can pay yourself what you think you're worth.

In five years, if I live that long, you can have the whole place. After that I only want to spend the rest of my days livin' in the house where I was born. But the business will be yours, and the land will be, too, when I die."

Ken couldn't believe what he had just heard. Anna had provided him with the trickiest part of his future plans – the 'owner' part of 'owner-handler'. And it would all happen in just one year! He promised himself he would try very hard to get along with Anna Welsely and to repay her faith by thinking of nothing but Welsely Farms' success. That and building a string of show dogs the envy of all of his old colleagues of the ring!

Two weeks later he had driven his forty-two foot motorhome, containing all of his worldly possessions, into the driveway of Welsely's Farms and Kennels, Inc. and was made welcome as the new general manager. The vehicle was still parked on the side of the house, waiting for the day when he would load it with cages and dogs and head back out on the show circuit.

Remembering his elation of that day, Ken looked around his cozy office and mused about how much he would miss the place when Anna told him she didn't think they were 'gettin' along' so well anymore after this gargantuan foul-up.

The room was furnished with old, though he didn't think antique, wood furniture that was probably locally crafted. The upholstery was worn and needed redoing, but he had been procrastinating about that because he didn't want to chance losing the comfortable feel of the old cushions in a trade for the neatness of new. The walls were painted a medium tan and trimmed in ivory. On two of those walls hung his personal collection of paintings and prints of famous show dogs, mostly of the hound and working types. In the corner of the other two, diagonally opposite the entry door, was a tall bookcase filled with classic works by such dog-lovers as Jack London, Albert Terhune, and Fred Gipson, as well as specific breed books for most of the American Kennel Club varieties. The floor was polished hardwood with one large oval rag rug centered in front of Ken's bulky old mahogany desk. Current work files rested neatly on one corner of the large desktop and an old telephone occupied another, with his laptop sitting neatly between them. Anna often commented on the tidiness of his desk, worried if it was truly a sign of a warped mind like they said.

The office might have been dark if it were not for the two large windows on the south and east walls that allowed lots of fresh prairie air and Kansas sunshine in. Two armchairs, one on each side of the south window, matched only in that they were both faded beyond color recognition. Between them was a low table covered with the latest issues of several dog magazines. On top of a file cabinet which held the breeding records for every dog on Welsely Farms sat the all-important coffee machine.

As his office was in the southeast corner of the old farmhouse, he was perfectly situated so that he could look out one or the other of his windows and see that all was running smoothly in the kennel yard.

From his east window, Ken could see the training ring that had been one of his first planned additions to Welsely Farms. He believed that dogs need practice time under realistic conditions in order to show to their best potential. Since there was not much in the way of a show hall out here in the middle of the Kansas prairie, he had suggested to Anna that they build their own enclosure. The end result was a fairly small, open-roofed structure with solid plank walls so that the dogs wouldn't be distracted by movements outside the ring.

The idea was a hit with everybody. Anna had been so delighted with the idea of having a private 'dog show' right on her own acreage that she insisted he add a small viewing section with tiered seats so that she could spend her time there more comfortably. The kennelboys who trained the dogs enjoyed playing 'handler' in the ring, and the dogs got the benefit of experience in an enclosed area as well as good exercise.

Beyond the training area, further to the east, was the old monstrosity of a barn that was home to about 200 small to medium-size breeding bitches, their puppies, and the stud dogs. They were strictly pet stock, worth nothing in Ken's grand scheme of things, but they were healthy specimens and made up the economic backbone of Welsely Farms.

The barn had remained Fleet's territory by mutual agreement, and Ken seldom visited there. He felt slightly guilty about this omission in his responsibilities and would have liked to remedy it, but standing up to Fleet, as he had found out early on, was like trying to walk on quicksand. The man seldom argued outright, but he had an insidious way of pulling you down to his level and suffocating your righteous objections with his own complaints.

Ken knew he should have fired the foreman the day he took over as manager at Welsely's, when Fleet's welcome had been strained to the point of sullenness. But he had thought it was only fair to give him a chance to find new employment before letting him go. Besides, he was convinced that Fleet would soon leave on his own, rather than suffer the humiliation of taking orders from his replacement.

Four months later, Fleet was still an annoying thorn in his side. His excuse was that there were few jobs in this area that didn't include farm labor, something that he was not interested in doing. Ken was beginning to think that he stayed out of sheer stubbornness.

Just to the north of the training ring were the five quarantine runs. As he sipped his coffee, Ken angled his chair so that he could see past the training ring to study the tiny figure of Johnny Wales clinging to the galvanized fencing of the run where the Akita bitch, the embodiment of all of his present problems, lay waiting for death. He wouldn't hassle Johnny about the time spent with her. The poor kid was taking this whole thing very hard for some reason. Ken guessed that was his fault, too. He had shown too much enthusiasm for the dog when he ordered her and had given Johnny his books and articles detailing the Akita breed. He liked the youngster and was trying to motivate him to do more than settle for a lifetime job as a kennel cleanup boy or field hand. Handling top show dogs could be a fascinating career for someone with Johnny's talent for getting along with animals.

Ken, himself, had started out in 'Junior Handling' when he was little more than twelve years old. Like Johnny, he had come from a small town where people were born, lived out their lives and died without ever traveling more than a few hundred miles from their homes. Possibly that was the reason Ken felt so strongly about sharing his knowledge and experience with the boy. He wanted to inspire Johnny to follow in his footsteps, to realize his full potential as a professional handler. He worried that this whole ugly incident could turn the boy off of dogs as a business, and Ken wouldn't blame him. But this was a business, he reminded himself, and Johnny had to understand that there were down sides to it just as in any other enterprise. It wasn't only playful puppies and elegant show dogs; it was also dirty kennels and heartbreaking accidents like this one, and the one that had brought him to Kansas.

Ken shook his head abruptly to clear his mind of those uncomfortable memories and switched his attention to the office's other window, through which he could see the new building that housed the large dogs and Ken's 'specials', the champion show dogs he had brought with him to Kansas. It was also home to the new show stock that he had been carefully purchasing over the last few months from breeders all over America. He kept these special animals as far from the quarantine area and the barn as he could. He had a lot of Welsely Farms' money tied up in those animals, more than the operation could comfortably afford, and he was taking as few chances as possible with their health. With one unavoidable exception.

Not even bothering to adjust his position so that he could look at it, Ken thought about the rusted mesh pen that leaned against the far side of the specials kennel. It was always littered with bits of rug, old bones, and gnawed pieces of the planks that used to form a sunshade for the half-dozen hounds who now lounged happily on top of the whole wreckage, exposed to the elements.

Anna Welsely's pack of hounds was a constant aggravation to Ken, especially housed so closely to his specials, but neither the old woman nor her hounds would be budged on the matter. The hounds had always had their home on that spot and nothing Ken could say would convince her to move them. His concerns that the free-ranging hounds would bring all manner of infectious pests back from their daily jaunts were brushed aside by Anna, who just laughed and offered her favorite quote by David Harum: 'A reasonable amount of fleas is good for a dog. They keep him from broodin' on bein' a dog!' So, when the foundation for the new building was laid, it was situated a few yards east of center and the hounds' rickety enclosure stayed exactly where it had always been, albeit with a fine new structure to lean against.

Turning his chair back now, Ken leaned forward to open the top drawer of his desk. He took out a tan file that contained a photo advertisement torn from a world-class dog magazine. Leaning back once more, he sipped his cold coffee, put his feet up on his desk and studied the dog in the picture. He would have liked to find some answer for his dilemma there, but unfortunately the same conclusions he had reached three days ago came back to plague his thoughts. He knew he had no one to blame but himself.

"Well, whatever your name is, you sure fooled me." Ken couldn't address the dog by name as the whole advertisement was in oriental script, and although his agent had rolled her pedigree off his multilingual tongue, for Ken it would have been unpronounceable anyway.

He had always bragged that he knew dogs so well that he could tell by their eyes, even in a photo, what their character was going to be like. He chided himself that that was where having a big ego can get you. And he, of all people, should have learned that by now.

He examined the picture more closely, but his final verdict didn't change. Ken could find no trace of viciousness or anger showing in that Akita's gaze. Even in retrospect, he thought that she looked like a well-adjusted animal that knew her place in the world – and that place was center stage. She exuded quality and showmanship like few animals Ken had ever encountered. Was it even the same dog that had attacked Fleet so ferociously? He could have wished it wasn't, but his experienced eye told him it was so.

"How could I have been so wrong about you?" he groaned. He closed his eyes and thought back to the first time he had looked at this advertisement. It had come to him with a note from an international dog agent who said he had heard through a mutual associate that Ken was building a new show kennel and that he might be looking for a top-quality dog at a good price. Ken's ambitious plans required a sensational dog, not just a good one, and he had been willing to commit a great deal of Welsely Farm's money for the right animal. This Akita had seemed like the one.

Perhaps he had made his decision too quickly. He had picked up the office telephone right then and dialed the agent in Holland, Leonard Trident. An answering machine had connected after the fourth ring and gave a short message in Dutch, then French, then English. Although the voice was heavily accented, Ken had been relieved that at least he could make himself understood. Like most Americans, he had no second language and was in awe of anyone who spoke differently than he did. After leaving his name and reason for calling, he had found himself waiting impatiently for his telephone to ring again.

Looking back now, he realized that he had wanted that dog so badly that he hadn't even bothered to ask why the Japanese were willing to sell such a magnificent animal to an American kennel. He knew that it was normally very difficult to export an Akita from Japan because they are considered a national treasure in their homeland, and the government as well as the breeders did everything in their power to keep the best dogs at home.

Most of the early Akitas to come to the U.S. were brought back by American servicemen after WWII, when the Japanese people were starving and couldn't possibly find food enough for their huge dogs. Even then, the dogs the soldiers were allowed to take out of the country were not good quality animals. Now, fifty years later, Ken felt that the Japanese dogs were still far superior to the Akitas in America.

Trident had returned Ken's call about two hours later and jumped at Welsely Farms' offer. Even then Ken had been so smug about purchasing a great bitch for half her market value that he didn't question why she was being sold for such a ridiculous price.

Ken grimaced in shame at the memory and threw the page back into his drawer. He was sorry he had ever seen that photograph, or talked to Trident, though he was mighty anxious to talk to him now.

He turned his thoughts away from the dog and considered the plight of her victim. Fleet would be released from the hospital tomorrow but would remain home on bed rest for another few days. He was a lucky man to still have his right arm and it didn't look like any major paralysis would last. But it hurt. The doctor on duty at the hospital emergency room said he had never seen a wound like it. The nurse had vomited. The uneven tear could not be sewn up because of the risk of infection, so the muscle and torn skin were bound to the bone with cloth bandages that had to be removed twice daily and the wound cleaned. The first time the doctor unwound the old wrappings, Fleet had become so nauseated with pain that he had almost passed out. After that he was given tranquilizers an hour before the doctor's visit to help him through the ordeal.

Now the wound was looking better and only had to be cleaned once daily. It was still incredibly painful, but Fleet had learned to endure it without sedatives. Every time the bandages were changed he swore another oath, vividly describing what he was going to do to that bitch when he had both arms again.

Ken had just hung up the telephone after listening to one of Fleet's more descriptive oaths not half an hour ago. He winced again as he remembered the brutality of that promise. He hoped it was just Fleet's reaction to the pain of his wound and wished he had something more to say to the man than 'I'm sorry'. He felt so helpless, waiting for answers.

The telephone finally announced a call, breaking into Ken's thoughts. He set his coffee cup down and reached for the receiver, his pulse racing. He was surprised at the emotion that he felt. This situation was ruining his self-control. If it wasn't Trident, someone else was going to get an earful. Ken was in no mood to spare anyone's feelings.

It was Trident, at last. Ken didn't bother with the niceties of a 'Good Morning'. He angrily described the events of the past four days, blaming the agent for his part in shipping an obviously vicious animal. When at last he stopped talking long enough to take a deep breath and listen for an explanation, he found he was shaking. With some satisfaction, he heard the man on the other end of the line clear his throat uneasily. Good. He had meant to put Trident on the defensive.

Trident began discreetly.

"Look, Mr. Lorch, I really don't know what you are worried about." The w's were pronounced as v's, but otherwise his English was better than a lot of Americans'. "Most of my people just care that the dog looks good. The Akita looks great. She's healthy. She isn't rabid; I would guarantee that. For one thing, rabies is unheard of in Japan. For another, she had to have had all the shots for contagious diseases before she could be shipped.

It sounds to me as if she didn't exactly get along with one of her handlers, that's all. It was probably just the traveling. Once she gets used to her surroundings she'll settle down."

"Super, Trident. And if she doesn't, I've paid a lot of money for a bitch that I'm going to have to put down in less than a week. You should see the mess of my man's arm! I can't trust her not to do it again and certainly wouldn't breed such a bad-natured beast!" Ken was having a hard time controlling his temper.

Trident switched to a more persuasive tone.

"Sure you can breed her, Mr. Lorch. Just keep her caged and shoot her with a little morphine when you need to handle her. I don't have to tell you how to do that, I'm sure. Once she comes into season, throw the dog in. She won't eat him. And in a couple of months you'll have a very valuable litter that will more than pay you back for the trouble she's given you."

Ken clenched the receiver in both hands in order to resist throwing it across the room. How dare the man intimate that he would rely on drugs to control an unsuitable animal? He tried to calm his voice but found he was shouting anyway.

"A litter that will grow up as vicious as their mother? Are you crazy? We're trying to run a high quality kennel here, which is the reason we paid so much for this bitch. Japan owes me an accounting, and if you knew the dog was mean when you bought her, you owe me as well!"

Ken was incensed at Trident's care-less attitude. He banged the telephone back onto its base and rubbed his forehead with both hands – hard.

Now what was he going to do? He had to agree with Trident that it would be pretty far-fetched for the Akita to have rabies. According to her paperwork, she had been given the proper injections and was showing no signs of the disease after four days. It was against U.S. law to put her down until ten days of quarantine had passed, proving she was free of the disease; but even after that, if he ordered her destroyed without the consent of her Japanese breeder, Welsely Farms would take a big loss that they couldn't afford. Ken worried that Anna would not risk another large investment if this one failed, and that would end his show-breeding program for good.

The thought of being stranded off-circuit for the rest of his life was a grim one, indeed.

CHAPTER 5

One small puppy's voice cried out weakly in pain and sorrow. What had happened to warmth, to softness, to Mother? Everything had changed from comfort and security to a terrible, cold void. As the first moan came quietly to an end, another baby's cry took its place, then another and another, until finally the sad song was ended and there was silence. . . .

Now, other voices, harsh and excited, brought the Akita out of her troubled sleep. She raised her eyelids and wearily focused on the young man moving cautiously toward her. It was that boy again. Why wouldn't he stay away like the rest of them? She had no reason to live and no will to fight – and no need of friendship.

"Watchit Johnny! She's awake again!" Abel shouted.

Johnny glanced back to where Abel stood outside the fence, fingers clutched around the handle end of a sturdy web lead, and face pressed close to the steel mesh in nervous agitation.

"What're you trying to do, Abel, set her off again?" he snapped angrily. "Just try and stay calm, will you?"

Welsely's veterinarian, old Doc, was crouched beside Abel, poking another length of line through the holes of the wire, getting ready to tie the Akita securely if Johnny was able to coax her over. His 'tool kit', as he liked to call his medical bag, was open on the ground next to him, needles and various solutions of his own invention readily available.

While he waited anxiously for them to finish their preparations, Johnny soothed the pathetic animal at his feet with his voice.

"It's okay, girl. . . We're only trying to help you. . . No reason to panic. . . I'm not going to hurt you. . . We just want to give you a shot to perk you up a little bit. . . preferably without you taking someone else's arm off."

He slipped the noose of the nylon kennel lead over the Akita's head without her seeming to notice, but when he knelt to slide the loop back over her ears, she breathed a cranky growl that ended in a moan of solemn frustration.

Johnny rubbed her furred neck with gentle hands, tears blurring his eyes. Over the past few days he had often felt tears threatening, as if the Akita's depression was slowly overwhelming him. Indeed, the whole farm seemed to have gotten quieter as the miserable dog weakened and lost the will to fight whatever was destroying her.

He found it difficult to believe this was the same creature that had arrived so ferociously only five days ago. What could have happened to reduce such a magnificent animal to this sad pile of fur and bones? It wasn't only the lack of food and water. There had to be more of an explanation. Would he ever know? Or would she die with the secret locked inside her?

His mouth hardened into a straight line. He was going to do everything in his power to return this dog to health, and he was going to keep her alive no matter what Mr. Lorch said. Fleet's arm was healing well and aside from a ragged scar, he would be no worse for the attack. Johnny was of the opinion that it was true justice, anyway: Fleet getting a little of the pain back that he dispensed so readily to those who couldn't, or wouldn't, fight back. Surely they would give the Akita another chance?

Johnny glanced over again to check on Doc's progress. The old man was sitting on the ground now, unhurriedly searching his bag for some elusive instrument.

Sighing in exasperation, Johnny turned his attention back to reassuring the Akita bitch. She seemed so close to death that he couldn't help being frightened for her and wished Doc would move a little faster than his usual snail's pace. He stroked her velvety black head, the first time he had been able to touch her so intimately, and felt a small enjoyment as his fingers ran down the deep furrow of her brow.

He didn't know the cause of her sorrow or the incredible anger she had displayed that first day; but sitting close to her like this, he knew in his heart that this was a creature whose life was worth sacrifice. How had he come to feel so much compassion for this strange dog? Was it just his eternal curiosity that wanted satisfying, like his father always said?

Doc's voice broke through Johnny's reveries, bringing him back to the moment. "All ready, son. Let's get her over here. Careful, now. We don't want anybody else hurt."

As Johnny took his hand from scratching behind the Akita's ears and began to straighten, the dog allowed her head to roll to the side and she looked up at him through glazed eyes. Johnny was surprised to recognize a small flicker of regret in her questioning expression.

He bent over her and whispered soothingly, "No, girl, I won't leave you alone, don't worry."

The great dog sighed with a fatal heaviness and closed her eyes.

Panicked, Johnny leaped to his feet. He had to get the Akita over to the fence where Doc could help her. Now!

"Abel! Hold onto that lead! I'll help her to stand if she needs me while you pull her to the fence. Slowly, now. Just keep the lead tight in case she decides to fight."

"Okay, Johnny, I've got it. But, be careful, huh? I don't think she's as weak as she looks, and we know she's a killer!"

"She's no killer, Abel, and I don't want to hear you say things like that about her anymore." Jeez! That kind of talk would almost certainly seal the poor dog's fate. He'd have to work at getting the other kennelboy on his side first, if he ever hoped to be able to convince Mr. Lorch to spare the Akita's life.

Luckily, Abel would be easily swayed. Though he was slightly older than Johnny, he was a little slow-witted and normally could be talked into agreeing with anything Johnny proposed. The only difficulty would be figuring out how to convince Abel that the bitch was deserving of their sympathy.

"God, don't let her act up today," he prayed fervently. "For sure she'll be put down if she hurts anyone else."

As the noose around her neck pulled slowly tighter, the Akita opened her eyes a little wider and they cleared slightly. She tensed her muscles and was able to drag herself to a sitting position, but it was no use; she didn't have the strength to resist the tug of the lead. With a groan, she fell over on her side and closed her eyes again, willing to be dragged.

"Come on, girl, get up. We can't do all the work. You still weigh plenty and we can't lug you the whole way." Johnny crouched by her side, forgetting about his own safety, and tried to pull her onto her belly again so that he could help her to stand.

She opened one eye, sighed, and rolled upright. This time when she rose onto her haunches, Johnny helped by lifting her hindquarters, and the Akita was standing. Weaving pathetically, she obediently followed the lead. She didn't seem to care where she had to go or why, only that they would leave her alone once she got there.

When the big, rangy dog neared the fence, Johnny gave her behind an extra push that sent her crashing into the wire. Doc was able to reach his long, thin fingers through to grab her tail and held onto it until the boys had securely tied off her neck lead and fastened the other line around her midsection just in front of her hind legs. They worked hastily, but she offered no resistance.

Once the Akita was safely bound, Abel couldn't contain his excitement.

"Whew, Johnny, you sure've got a gift!" he gushed, uncharacteristically. "If I hadn't seen it myself, I wouldn't have believed it. You just talked that crazy bitch into followin' you! I thought for sure, when you pulled her up like that, she was gonna take your face off! But you just kept talkin' and she didn't do nothin'."

"This poor animal couldn't hurt her own fleas right now," Doc cut in. "You were right, Johnny. She may be too far gone already to save her life, but we have to try for Fleet's sake." He picked up the closest foreleg and began snipping the hair away on the front side near the elbow. "Now, if we can just find a vein that'll take this needle, we'll start the fluids going."

It was necessary to apply a tourniquet before enough blood swelled the vein so that Doc could insert a needle. He quickly attached the I-V tubes that led to a bottle tied onto the galvanized fencing about four feet up. In the bottle was his special mixture of necessary fluids, energy-giving natural sugars and vitamins, as well as cortisone; a mixture that he had found to work well in bringing animals out of deep shock.

As he watched the level of lifesaving fluids in the bag lower, Johnny thought about how many times he had watched Doc struggle to save a life and lose. Most of those animals had wanted to live; had clung to life tenaciously while the old vet dosed them with medication, stuck them with needles, opened their frail bodies with his scalpel. Now this poor bitch seemed to want to die and maybe deserved to, but they couldn't let her.

It was Doc's turn to stroke the Akita's broad, flat forehead.

"Lousy life, huh girl? Well, it'll all look better tomorrow." He looked up at the boys. "Johnny, make sure there's plenty of water in her bowl at all times. And put this in it." He handed the kennelboy a large brown bottle of liquid vitamins. "Two capfuls every time you fill her dish. And see if you can get this paste down her as often as possible. It'll give her a little boost so that maybe she'll feel like eating. Feed her some of that canned stuff the puppies like so much. It smells good, and if her nose starts to quivering, she might try a bite.

"Water's the main thing, though. She's a big strong girl. If she drinks on her own soon, she has a chance of making it."

Johnny wasn't fooled by what Doc didn't say; that he thought that chance was a slim one.

"Thanks, Doc. I'll take real good care of her," he choked.

Doc turned to see tears streaking the boy's cheeks. His own eyes softened as he remembered a time when he had felt as deeply about every animal's well-being. It was a long time ago.

"Johnny," he said gently, "don't get carried away about this dog. She's weak now, so no danger to anybody, but as soon as she gets some strength back, she's going to be trouble again. I've seen animals that are just plain nasty. Thank goodness not many of them get this big."

"She isn't nasty, Doc! She didn't hurt me yesterday when she could have!" He caught himself before he blurted out the details of yesterday morning's bizarre encounter and quickly changed the direction of his

SOLITAIRE, A Dog Story

defense. "I think Fleet scared her that first day and she was only protecting herself. And I don't blame her! I felt like punching him myself when he was hammering on her kennel like that! And who knows what else he did to her when I was away getting Abel! You know how mean he can be. You even said he was gonna get his own back one day!" The boy was vehement now. Any appeal to Mr. Lorch would be useless if Doc opposed it.

The veterinarian turned his back on Johnny, brusque again.

"Well, Fleet doesn't need anybody to wish any more evil on him right now. I don't think the dog's rabid, though. Has Ken found out anything about her?"

"No, Mr. Lorch hasn't said anything about the Japanese guy calling, yet," Johnny started, then brightened as a new thought occurred to him. "Hey! Maybe that's her problem! Maybe she feels uncomfortable with our way of speaking. American would sound totally different to a dog than Japanese, don't you think? Maybe that's what made her think Fleet was a 'bad guy'! You can't blame her for protecting herself!"

Abel gave a hoot.

"Well, then, America had jest better watch its ass if that dog ever gets loose 'cause they ain't many Japs in Kansas t'hold 'er back!"

Even Doc had a chuckle at that idea.

"Johnny, my boy, I think you're grasping at straws. Why don't we just wait a little longer and see what turns up in her history? Could be, though, that her old kennel did neglect to tell us that she's attack-trained or something. Then you'll have to go to Japan for us and learn how to give her commands in her native tongue."

Another idea occurred to Doc.

"Say, maybe she's been trained not to eat or drink until she's given a specific command, as well. I've heard of people doing that with their animals, but never agreed with it, myself, for just this reason. I don't think many dogs would starve themselves for the sake of the right command, but it's possible."

This was more like what Johnny wanted to hear.

"Do you think so, Doc? Could we go to Mr. Lorch and tell him right now?" The boy felt hope rising for the first time in five days.

"Easy, lad. I was only thinking out loud. Anything's possible, the Lord knows, but this dog did a lot of damage to Fleet and I don't think either he or Ken is going to forgive her that easily.

"Besides, son," he continued more solemnly, "I've done all I can, but I really don't have much hope that she'll live through the night."

Johnny was crestfallen. Even Abel was squinting and biting his lip in an effort to keep his emotions under control.

Doc wanted to say something more comforting to the kennelboys, but could only add, "If she does make it to tomorrow morning, we can talk about all this again. And I promise I'll try to help, Johnny. But she has to show some desire to help herself, first."

CHAPTER 6

Even after she opened her eyes, the Akita could hear whines of abject misery, but now they were accompanied by dull scratching sounds and seemed close by. She raised her head and slowly looked around to find the reason. There, just outside the steel mesh of her run was a tiny monstrosity of a dog, dirty black and brown with uneven knotty hair and huge pointed ears – and it was winking at her! She lay quietly, too weak to get up to investigate, and watched dispassionately as the hairy little ogre dug furiously at the foot of the wire, stopping every now and then to wag his ugly stub of a tail at her, then to whine his frustration at not being able to get closer. He seemed to know, however, that no amount of crying was going to help his situation, so he soon resumed his fervent digging.

The bigger dog's forehead wrinkled in the first amusement she had felt for a long time as she watched the crazy antics of the little prospector. His tiny paws worked quickly, burrowing down to a depth of about six inches, then along for a foot or so, making a shallow ditch in which to lie while he pulled more dirt out from the other side of the fence. He ducked down into the trench until his whole body was lost to sight and only his wagging tail was above ground, then he dug a little further into his tunnel and carefully moved the earth back with his front paws to where his hind feet could kick it up and out of the hole in a veritable sandstorm. Soon the thin border of earth just inside the door of the run began to crumble and give way, then out popped his tiny black and tan head. He snorted loudly, sneezed to clear his nose of excess dirt, then scraped and clawed at the hard ground until finally he pulled his whole nine and a half pounds into the Akita's kennel.

Now his tail really started to wag, so fast it seemed it would surely break loose and fly off into a corner of the run. He laid his oversized ears back in an overtly friendly gesture and showed by the twinkle in his one good eye that he was happy to make the acquaintance of such a grand lady of the canine world.

The Akita bitch watched in wide-eyed disbelief. How dare this tiny creature enter her quarters? And why wasn't he afraid of her? She squinted her black eyes and growled.

You are in the presence of Akita-Inu, mouse. I desire no clown to amuse me, so if you value your flea-ridden hide, you will take it back down that hole from which you came.

The terrier's tail stilled for just a moment before it began wagging even more furiously, and he approached on dancing feet. As he came closer, the Akita growled another warning.

Your fearlessness may well cost you your life, mouse. Begone! Leave me to my misery.

The little dog whined in an ingratiating way before lying down inches from her gigantic muzzle. He rested his own tiny nose on his paws while he tried to control the insane movement of his tail, but only succeeded in slowing it down a bit.

His audacity shocked the Akita, who was used to having her presence respected, but she was too feeble to hold the weight of her own head for long and soon lay back down as well. The terrier's whole body trembled with the effort of lying quietly where he was.

The Akita bitch studied him with lidded eyes. She was still so weak that it exhausted her to concentrate long enough to separate dreams from reality. She wasn't sure if she cared to try, but this scruffy little dog with the permanent wink intrigued her. Where had he come from and what did he want with her?

Her splayed nostrils took in the terrier's smell and found no fear there. Surely, if he meant trickery, he would have shown some nervousness. Her gaze fell on his scrawny body with its black and tan shag of coarse hair. How could such a tiny animal have so little fear?

Focusing again on his face, she found his saucy expression disconcerting. With him looking at her like that, it was difficult not to feel her heart lighten, and she felt her whiskers tingle slightly. But it was too late for friendship now. She was dying. With a long, drawn-out sigh, she allowed her eyes to close.

Johnny found the two dogs lying nose to nose when he came to check on his charge after lunch break. His first concern was for Jack, that the Akita had hurt or perhaps even killed him, but then he realized that the tiny dog was wise enough in the ways of the world never to get himself into an indefensible position. Courageous the terrier was, but smart too! Johnny searched for the inevitable pile of dirt that would show where Jack had entered.

The crew of Welsely's joked that it was because Jack was an Australian

Rough-coated Terrier that he was always 'Down Under' – down in the dirt and under the fences. But although Jack was a resourceful escape artist, he wasn't without his scars. Digging around the sharp fencing had cost him one of his eyes already. That painful experience seemed to have taught the spirited little fellow the hard way to be cautious, but it hadn't taught him to quit. As Ms. Welsely said, "You gotta remember that Jack's a terrier, and a terrier's gonna dig! He'll dig for rats, he'll dig for foxes, he'll dig for rabbits – and he'll dig to escape!"

In fact, Jack had gotten so good at figuring out ways of getting out of his cages that Anna had long ago given up trying to contain him, and he was normally left to run freely on the farm. Johnny thought that was just. Most of the dog breeds didn't seem to mind being penned up; but to Johnny's way of thinking, a terrier just wasn't a terrier in a cage. Unfortunately, now Jack was proving to be ingenious at getting into other dogs' kennels, as well.

"Darn you, Jack! I'm tired of filling in your holes! How do you know where every run has an opening?"

But Johnny was more relieved than angry and the terrier seemed to sense that. Though he didn't understand most of what humans talked about, he was sensitive enough to get the general feel of the situation from their tone of voice. Now he looked up sleepily, his tail resuming its normal chaotic rhythm.

At the sound of Johnny's voice, the Akita struggled clumsily to her feet, where she swayed tenuously but still managed to look foreboding. She growled throatily, and Johnny was stunned by the menace that had returned to her glowering stare.

Astonished as well by the Akita's threatening demeanor, Jack jumped up and prepared to run – or fight! But her abrupt movement had sent the Akita's head reeling once again, and she lost her struggle to maintain her balance. As suddenly as she had risen, the big dog collapsed. Weak and shivering, she whined softly when Jack came to her to lick her muzzle.

"Looks like you've made a friend, Jack," Johnny said. In spite of his concern for the Akita, the picture was just too ridiculous not to smile. There lay the immense bitch, weak but still majestic of bearing, while hopping all about her in delirious enthusiasm was a patch of black and tan ego affectionately known around Welsely Farms as 'One-eyed Jack'.

It seemed that all the excitement had created a thirst for Jack so that, as soon as he could stop leaping long enough, he headed for the water bowl. He didn't seem the least bit disturbed when he was joined a few moments later by his mammoth kennelmate. She lowered her head and drank long and well. Johnny's grin remained as his throat tightened.

"That's it, girl. Drink deep. That water will give you a chance to live long enough to sort out your problems. And Jack and I are going to help all we can!"

CHAPTER 7

This was Fleet's fifth beer since he had arrived at Earl Kell's farm this afternoon, and it was time he made another run 'to pay the rent'. He wobbled a little as he rose from his seat at the kitchen table and banged his head on the overhead light, causing it to sway dizzily.

"Careful, son. You wanna end up back in the hospital?" Earl's comment was meant to amuse, but Fleet didn't think it was funny in the least.

"It's this damn stupid arm," he grumbled. "Seems like I can't do anything without it causing me problems. I never realized how much having your arm in a sling messes up your balance."

Earl puffed rudely, mocking his partner's incessant complaining of this afternoon.

Fleet turned a baleful glare on him, contemplating whether it was worth wasting his last swig of beer for the pleasure of pouring it over Earl's semi-bald pate. He had been released from the hospital earlier in the day and had come to Kell's place looking for solace in a little comradeship and a few beers. The more beers he drank, however, the more sympathy he felt he was entitled to, and Earl didn't seem at all interested in commiserating with his injuries. In fact, he seemed to think the whole situation was one big joke.

Earl noticed Fleet's dour expression and realized he was sorely trying his drinking buddy's patience. He averted his eyes and pretended to study something very interesting in the bottom of his beer can, in an effort to hide a drunken smirk, but his hunched shoulders began to shake with silent mirth and he wasn't able to hold his tongue for long.

"Purty soon yer gonna be cussin' that arm fer drawin' up yer manhood an' makin' it too small to pee with," he sniggered, still peering into the hole on the top of his beer can.

Fleet scrutinized his friend and concluded that Earl Kell had to be the ugliest man on the prairie. He was a few years older than Fleet and a few inches shorter, with beefy facial features and a stocky build that came from his unslakable thirst for domestic beer. Rather than be bothered with the necessity of a comb or brush, Earl kept his fine reddish-gold hair and beard shaved to the same short bristle all over – with the same shaver, as Fleet had discovered. His eyes had the paleness of a deep cavern creature, neither blue nor green, though right now they were quite bloodshot. His skin always stayed brilliantly sunburned where it was exposed to the weather; probably white as a fish's belly where it wasn't, but Fleet didn't want to know about that.

To someone unfamiliar with him, Earl's large paunch belied his brutish strength. Fleet knew otherwise. His partner had been raised in a backwater town in the low country of the Carolinas and was tougher than any of the alligators you could meet in the swamps there.

Heaving a resigned sigh for his only friend's mocking ways, Fleet decided that Earl was too soused to bother insulting him with a beer shower, so he downed the remnants of his can and toddled off in the direction of the toilet.

Earl and Fleet had known each other for many years. They had met in Florida while working in the same illicit trade: running exotic animals and birds in from South America. When that profession heated up and the authorities had caught on to their cruel, if innovative, methods of transporting live contraband, they had both been forced to leave the state. Fleet went to New England to manage a retail outlet for a guy he knew who owned a string of pet shops, and Earl went 'down home' to the Carolinas. They hadn't met again for a few years until Earl called Fleet to ask how much his store would pay for a litter of purebred Rottweilers – sans papers. Fleet's price was right, so Earl had stolen the pups that night and delivered them across a few state lines by the next morning. It was a simple matter for Fleet to register false papers for the good-looking brood and sell them on at great profit. The boys were back in business!

Things might have gone on that way for years if it wasn't for the fact that Fleet's employer turned out not to be the entrepreneur they thought he was. He had gamely looked the other way as long as he got his share of the profits without taking any of the risks, but he got very nervous about a year later when he was tipped off that the police were considering searching his establishments to look for stolen property. He hastily sacked Fleet, throwing him out into the street with a carload of his pilfered puppies before there could be any more trouble.

Earl had really gotten on Fleet's butt that day! Not knowing what else to do with all those puppies, and without crates to put them in, Fleet had driven straight through to Earl's warehouse. By the time he arrived, his whole back seat was a stinking mess of doggy-doo and vomit from carsick puppies. He was ready to drown the whole wailing lot, but Earl hadn't wanted to give up the easy money they were making. Instead, he talked Fleet into a slight modification of their current business structure.

That's how they had landed on a rundown farm in Kansas. And that was why Fleet had cultivated the job on the Welsely Farms property next door.

Earl might sound like a yokel, but he was smart about some things, so Fleet had listened to his partner when he suggested leasing a parcel of land somewhere with an established farm on it and keeping the farm as a legitimate front while they ran their own breeding kennel in secrecy. There was good money in dogs the way they did it, but they sure didn't need any do-good inspectors crawling around telling them how to run things, he explained. The boys needed to rent in an area where they could afford enough acreage to locate a kennel structure far from any roads and out of their neighbors' hearing. Kansas, with its sprawling landscapes and slight population, was perfectly suited to their plans.

There was another issue that needed to be resolved before they could begin operating big-time: a breeding kennel was going to require large amounts of dog food, injections, and other items on a regular basis, and the boys needed to be able to purchase these supplies without any of it being traced back to the farm. Otherwise the animal inspectors would surely get wind of it. It wouldn't do to have these doggy products delivered to an address where there wasn't supposed to be any dogs, either. So while Earl maintained relative anonymity, taking care of the 'farm', Fleet had moved down the road, becoming the front man of their operation, in charge of routing their supplies through the licensed kennel of Welsely Farms and Kennels, Inc.

This system had worked well in the beginning, but the number of dogs in their kennel grew and soon Fleet was having difficulty hiding the increasing overabundance of supplies from Anna Welsely. He had been working hard to gain her trust so that she would accept his purchase orders without question, but in the end it was her failing health that had forced Anna to put her full confidence in Fleet, and he finally came to the position he had strived for: that of running the day-to-day operations of the kennel, unsupervised.

Fleet was delighted to find that this presented even more opportunities where profits could be made. Now he was able to arrange shipment of Kell's litters along with those of Welsely Farms to avoid paying shipping expenses, and he was able to use Welsely's kennel paperwork on those pups to avoid suspicion. He gained access to Welsely's long client list and was able to offer customers the breeds they wanted at a highly discounted cost, never mentioning that they were not buying best-quality Welsely puppies.

At one time, when Kell's kennel had become overpopulated and the dogs were complaining about it, Fleet had noticed that the animals at Welsely's were listening, some answering the far-off barks. That was when he had decided to board up the windows on that side of the barn, complaining about human intruders. While he was at it, he convinced Anna of the necessity of privacy and got permission to install the 'Absolutely No Visitors' sign. He told her it was for the security of her dogs, but in truth he was afraid that one day some health inspector might drive into Welsely Farms unannounced and, without his guidance, stroll off to investigate just how many dogs that farm next door kept.

All in all, things had become very easy for the boys. That is, until the arrival of Ken Lorch. Fleet hadn't been able to hide his dismay when Anna told him of the appointment of a manager, but not for the same reasons she might have thought. This new man was going to upset his whole scheme! How could it be otherwise?

Earl, always the practical one, hadn't been upset. He just figured they had to be smarter than this Lorch was. He had calmed Fleet down by telling him that their operation had outgrown the original plan anyway. It was getting time-consuming and dangerous, shuttling the supplies back and forth in the small pickup. He suggested it was time that Fleet befriend one of the regular truckers from the big supply houses, one he knew well and who might be willing, with a little extra consideration, to drop certain shipments off at Kell's farm after he was finished with his normal run. Fleet could call the orders in to him directly, bypassing the office help. It worked. The trucker was very agreeable. And he even gave the boys a better discount.

Fleet had found out early that his natural surliness was a good weapon against the new manager's polite curiosity, one he had used liberally over the last few months so that now Lorch avoided any contact with him, leaving him alone in the barn with almost as much freedom as he had before.

But now there was this latest problem. Fleet's being away from his job on Welsely Farms with a bad arm was going to pose a slight dilemma for their business. Earl had reminded him earlier that afternoon that they had several litters ready to ship. As if Fleet needed to be reminded of that. But so what if a few of the puppies were going to be too old to be accepted by the retailers? Earl knew well how to use his 'kennelman's bucket' to keep the population under control, and the boys would be able to pick up shipping again with the next litters.

Right now, Fleet was more concerned with how Ken was going to react when the calls started coming in from retailers with complaints of infectious puppies and there was no sign of illness in Welsely Farms' kennel. Normally those callers would ask for Fleet if they had any problems – he had made sure they understood that a long time ago, when he was still in charge, and hadn't bothered to inform them of any changes when the kennel came under new management. That way, he could handle problems before Ken or the old lady ever suspected there were any. They might suspect something if they ever looked at Welsely's dwindling client list, but Fleet had made sure to keep that conveniently out of their sight.

While he was away from work, Fleet's only hope was that Ken's honest ignorance while dealing with these complainers would divert the blame. Hell, Welsely's was known to run a clean kennel, and theirs were probably not the only pups received by the stores this week; possibly the dealers would blame one of the other litters from a less reliable kennel for carrying the disease. He was probably worrying over nothing, like Earl said. Still, he'd feel better when he was back taking care of things over there.

By the time Fleet came back into the kitchen, Earl was lifting the pop-tops on two more beer cans. All animosity was forgiven between the two pals as they both pulled heavy swigs from their brews.

After lowering his can, Fleet reached for the dirty ashtray in the middle of the table. He picked around in it until he came up with a tiny butt, which he put between his lips. It was too short to ignite without burning himself, so he took it back out and set it on the table before he stood to search his change pocket for a clip. That task required a fair bit of effort since he had full use of his left hand only, but he was finally able to pull the small silver holder out of his pocket. He sat back down and concentrated on pinching the clip onto the unlit end of the roach. Earl watched him intently, mesmerized by his actions, which brought a smile to Fleet's clouded features. When he had finally succeeded in locating the roach clip to his satisfaction, Fleet held the stub just in front of his taut lips, flicked his lighter, and sucked hard.

"You gotta have a whole lotta patience to smoke that shit," Earl pronounced, grabbing his pack of Marlboro's. "Regular cigarettes're a lot easier."

Fleet nodded in agreement.

"True," he choked, keeping his throat closed to prevent the smoke from escaping. "But those don't help with the pain in my arm like these do."

That seemed to remind Earl of something.

"So, what're y'all gonna do if'n they don't put that Ay-kita dog down, son?" he asked, his low country accent only slightly more slurred than usual.

"They'll put her down, I'm not worried."

"But if'n they don't?" Earl prodded, watching for Fleet's reaction.

Fleet wondered what the man was trying to do, badgering him like that.

"I don't know, kill her myself, maybe." He knew that was a stupid boast, but his friend seemed to want to hear it.

Earl smiled a slow grin that exposed more gum than teeth and his eyes lost a little of their dead look.

"That'd sure make that new boss over there think twice before he bothered y'all agin, huh?" He leaned closer across the table. "I got a idea, buddy. I'll be needin' a big, nasty-lookin' dog soon for somethin' I'm settin' up. Jest wait a liddle while 'fore you go wastin' that varmint. We may be able t'make it look like a accident – and make a little money on 'er, besides."

"What are you talking about, Earl? That bitch is too traceable to sell her out from under Lorch and old lady Welsely – leastwise and make any money on her. And she's too big to hide here if you're thinking of breeding her. Besides, that would mean bringing another Akita in to sire the litter, and I don't care if I ever set eyes on another one of those Japo mutts."

"No, son, this is even better. Come'n see what I mean." Earl pushed his chair away from the table and beckoned for Fleet to follow him as he led the way out the back door.

Instead of heading for the main kennel building as Fleet expected him to, Earl took a path that lead directly to one of a group of outbuildings that encircled the yard. Earl wasn't into farm work – or much work of any kind, for that matter – so these sheds, that had once been used for the storage of everything from tools and small farm machinery to animals and excess produce from the vegetable harvest, had long ago been left to deteriorate at their own slow pace.

As they came closer, Fleet was slightly surprised to see that the door to one of the sheds was bolted and had a brand new, heavy-duty lock hanging on the outside of it. Earl fumbled with a set of keys he had brought with him and soon had the door open. It was dark inside the shed and it smelled fetid, like maybe an animal had died in there a while ago.

"Sonuvabitch, Earl! What've you got in here? It smells disgusting." Fleet couldn't even breathe in the rancid atmosphere and started to retreat, but Earl hissed at him to wait.

"This'll be good, buddy. Really good," he promised as he hurried over to unlock a wooden shutter and threw it open to allow more fresh air to circulate through the dank storehouse. "It'll be better soon," he assured Fleet, though the other man remained dubious.

Their eyes were becoming accustomed to the low light now and Fleet warily looked around the small building. He wasn't sure if he wanted to discover the source of the terrible stench too suddenly. After a whole joint and a six-pack, his stomach wasn't feeling all that reliable.

"Look here, son! Ain't he a beaut?" Earl was really excited. "Fleet, y'all come over here and meet 'Gatorbait'."

Fleet peered into the corner stall indicated by Earl. The first thing he noticed was that the wooden railings had been strongly reinforced with steel bars like those used to cage lions or bears or some other kind of wild creature like that. There was a heavy metal grate that looked like it could be a lid, but it wasn't mounted at the top of the bars. Instead, it was fixed inside the cage at about a foot and a half off the ground, which led Fleet to believe that whatever was in there couldn't be very big anyway – or maybe it could.

He jumped away from the suspicious stall and swore nervously.

"Jesus, Earl, you don't have an alligator in there, do you?" He wasn't familiar with such things and didn't want to take any chances.

Earl's laughter was an obscene, choking gurgle in his throat. He shook his head 'no', but it was some minutes before he could pull himself together to respond verbally.

"They ain't no gator in there, Fleet. But, son, if'n y'all coulda seen yor face! Maybe I will get a gator next time!"

He went on sniggering while Fleet gingerly approached the stall again. This time his eyes were working well enough to make out the shape of a rather large dog lying prone at the bottom of the cage. Its coloring was dark and mottled, but that was about all Fleet could tell about it in the gloom. The dog didn't acknowledge their presence. In fact, it didn't move at all.

"You sure it's still alive?" Fleet questioned, thinking he may have found the source of the odor.

Another gurgle of laughter, then, "Course, he is. But ol' Gatorbait, here is one helluva mean varmint, so I hafta keep 'im sorta well-confined 'til I finish trainin' 'im. I built this cage m'self. It's my own invention fer trainin' fightin' dogs. Keeps 'em quiet so's they don't hurt themselves – or me – 'til the time's right."

Fleet looked at his friend incredulously. He knew that Earl had been experimenting with breeding what he fancifully called 'alternative' breeds of dogs; purebred crosses produced for specific reasons for special customers. He seemed to think they were going to make him a lot of money, but Fleet had never fathomed his intention. The discovery that his buddy was involved in the bloodiest of sports came as a total surprise to him.

Earl took Fleet's silence as evidence of how impressed he was. He grinned that gummy grin again and signed for Fleet to watch while he showed him how the cage worked.

He untied a rope from its anchor high up on the wall. Fleet traced the line with his eyes up and over one of the heavier ceiling rafters, then about halfway down to where it hooked into a one-inch metal chain. The chain continued the fall and was, in turn, fastened to the metal grate covering the lower half of the dog's pen.

Earl leaned into the pull and the grate shifted noisily, then lifted until it locked into place about three feet up from the floor. He tied the rope back on its bracket and came to stand beside Fleet.

"Y'all don't go too near the pen, now," he cautioned. "I don't like 'im gettin' too worked up 'til he's fully roused. Cramps the muscles."

Fleet gave Earl a long sideways look. What was the idiot talking about? The man had always displayed a callous attitude when it came to dealing with the breeding stock, that part was nothing new. As he often said, "If'n y'all can't think of dogs as livestock, like a cow or a pig or a chicken, you ain't never gonna make any money in this business." Fleet agreed that sometimes what most people would call hardheartedness could be justified by a hefty profit, but this new training cage idea was really sick.

This whole fighting thing was crazy, and Fleet didn't want to know anything more about it. He was ready to go back to the kitchen and roll another joint and forget all about dogs right now. But curiosity made him crouch down for another, closer look. He peered into the far recesses of the cage where his gaze was arrested by the sickly yellow eyes of the wakening dog inside.

"Sonuvabitch, if he doesn't have the eyes of a gator," he breathed.

"Awesome, ain't he?" Earl was gratified by his partner's reaction. "I found 'im in the Everglades, y'know, down there in Florida. They got some mean folks down there in those swamps, I'll tell y'all!" He smirked in remembrance. "I felt right t'home.

Know what they was doin'? Besides drinkin' and gamblin', I mean. They was fishin' for big gators and usin' live pups for bait! They stick two great big hooks just under the skin on both sides of the pup, back of its front legs, and throw it out in deep water, then wait for a gator to come along and grab it. If'n the pup swims in too quick, they jest pick it up and throw it back out agin. Normally, they don't hafta throw 'em out too many times before. . . Bang! The gator's hooked and the boys jest reel it in."

Fleet was appalled, but he couldn't take his eyes off the incredible beast in the cage. He watched as it slowly rose from its flattened position, never blinking, and pressed its spine against the cage top in a backbreaking stretch. The heavy grate creaked in its slot, but stayed put.

The dog approached the front of the cage and just stood there, staring at Fleet like some evil necromancer. Apart from its ghastly eyes, the dog was colored in motley shades of bluish-gray, ranging from the dirty-white flecking on its lower legs through blue irregular blotches on its back, to slate gray around its drooping ear leathers. Even its nose, in this light, was only dull gray, not black and glisteny as a normal dog's should be.

"He looks like a rainy day," Fleet mumbled.

"Well, he fights like a demon from Hell!" Earl bragged.

Fleet slowly averted his eyes, not wanting to alarm the frightening hound, and asked, "Earl, what are you doing with a fighting dog? There aren't any matches around here. Nothing worth pitting him against, anyway."

Earl's ugly features took on a cherubic glow.

"That's t'other part of my idea, son. We could use that fair bit o' wooded property real far back off the road. It's four-wheel drive country only; ain't gonna be no cops back there. I seen the way the good ol' boys back home set up a ring. Dead easy. And in dogfightin', they ain't no set of rules to memorize: jest put 'em together and the last one standin', wins!

Oh! and Fleet, you oughta see the money they rake in from those fights! Thirty, forty grand in a weekend! Not to mention that a good time is had by all, 'cept mebbe the hound that loses. They don't gen'rally get another chance t'embarrass their masters, if you catch my meanin'."

The mention of easy money – lots of it – was just the balm for Fleet's outraged sense of morality.

"Okay, now we've got a ring, but we've still only got one dog."

The angelic glow came back to Earl's face.

"Yeah, like I said b'fore, I'll be needin' a big, nasty-lookin' dog soon. . . Y'all got any ideas where we might find one?"

Fleet scrunched his leathery features into a frown of disbelief. Hadn't the stupid redneck been listening to him all afternoon?

"Earl, this dog may be Champion Ugly, but he's no match in a fair fight with that Akita bitch. I told you, she's a monster; another half as big as him, and even meaner. And she knows what she's doing, too. If we pit them against each other in the ring, she'll eat him up – those long ears first – and we'd lose our dog and our betting money, too. Then we'd still have to figure out what to do with the Akita."

Earl's mouth tightened into a pout. He threw a scornful look at Fleet, then walked determinedly over to another stall and pulled out a large club and a burlap sack.

At the sight of the club, the hound in the cage growled so intently that the noise sounded more like a hiss. He slid stealthily back into the darker recesses of his cage so that once again the only visible parts of him were those serpent-yellow eyes.

Earl got about halfway back across the shed when the dog suddenly rushed out and threw himself like a maniac against the bars of his cage. Fleet watched in fascination as the dog tore thick chunks out of the wooden rails surrounding his cage, salivating and roaring in a frenzy of murderous anticipation that became more deafening as Earl approached.

Fleet flinched, unable to contain a shocked gasp when Earl crashed his club down onto the raging animal's skull with a heavy 'thwack!' that sent him sprawling. Quickly, before the dog could get up, Earl opened a small door at the bottom of the cage and threw the burlap sack inside, then backed off a step or two.

The hound scrambled to his feet and lunged at the bars again, his long muzzle reaching between them to catch his tormentor. But his balance was off and he missed Earl's fat nose by mere inches. Knowing he wouldn't have another opportunity today, Gatorbait sat back on his haunches, pointed his nose toward the low ceiling and howled his frustration in one long, bloodcurdling wail.

Fleet was amazed that any animal could live through that bash on the head. The brute could take intense physical pain, that was for sure, and he still looked like he wanted to carry on the fight!

"I'll chop his ears tomorrow," Earl offered, shakily. He looked over to Fleet, who was still mesmerized by the sight of the wild dog tearing into the burlap bag and whatever bloody thing it contained, devouring everything in his voracity.

Earl cackled in relief to see that Fleet was even more afraid of the dog in the cage than he was.

"Besides, son," he laughed slyly, "who said anythin' about a 'fair fight'?"

CHAPTER 8

The next morning, Doc pulled into the kennelyard even later than usual. He had prepared himself for the sure disappointment of the Akita's death with a few extra glasses of brandy last night, and now his head was pounding like a kettledrum.

For most of his seventy-odd years, Doc had enjoyed a drink, but he never felt he had a problem with it until his retirement from full-time practice, when it seemed like brandy was the only thing that could dull the aching loneliness he felt. Just about the time he realized that his pleasure had turned into an addiction, Anna had asked him to help her out part-time with the routine vetting of the dogs at Welsely's. The two had been casual friends for many years, and he knew that Anna was well able to administer shots and medicate her dogs against the common kennel illnesses, so he had worried that she was offering him the position out of pity. He would have refused, but she had insisted that the work would be easy, not requiring him to keep regular hours, so if he was a little under the weather early in the day, or couldn't make it at all, there would always be tomorrow. When he admitted that his hands weren't as steady as they used to be, she had been philosophical: if an emergency came up that required that much close work, there was always the county vet's office in town. So Doc had taken the job, and though it hadn't stopped him from drinking, it had kept the loneliness at bay for at least part of the day. He was always cognizant of how much of his sanity he owed to Anna, and strived to do the best he could by her. He wished he could have done more to protect her investment in the Akita.

Before leaving his car, Doc drew a deep breath to fortify himself. He collected his black bag from the trunk, then headed toward the quarantine runs at a slow amble.

Johnny was hanging on the fence of the middle run, his shoulders slumped as though he was watching something painful, when Doc came up behind him and laid a comforting, if shaky, hand on his young shoulders. To his surprise, the boy whirled to greet him, intense joy radiating from his young face. The vet's lined countenance lit up as if by reflection, and he followed Johnny's nod to grin stupidly at the two dogs inside the quarantine run.

Both dogs were relaxed, lying fully stretched out on their sides, enjoying the warm sunshine. Now and then, Jack raised his head to wink solicitously at his new friend and waggle his tail comfortingly. The terrier's whole body was not as long as the Akita's foreleg, but he radiated self-confidence and she seemed to be soothed by his presence.

Doc realized he had given in to grief too early and now felt oddly elated by the big dog's miraculous recovery. Though he tried to be sensible, reminding himself that his efforts would come to nothing, anyway, because the Akita was slated to be put to sleep in four more days, he still couldn't help feeling good about giving her those four days. Maybe it was Johnny's absolute faith in the animal that had affected him so that now he found himself hoping she would live long enough to prove herself. Maybe he was just taking pleasure in the return to health of a beautiful animal, a joy he hadn't allowed himself to feel for a long time.

He slapped the boy's back heartily and winked at him.

"Well, well, Johnny. Looks like we've worked a miracle! I didn't give that poor animal much of a chance of making it through another night, but she's looking pretty darned good now! Has she tried eating anything yet? Aside from the kennelboys, I mean!" Doc guffawed at his own humor.

The Akita had eaten this morning, though Johnny had been worried at the start about whether she was going to. He had prepared a very appetizing meal for both dogs, but little Jack, always the gentleman, had backed off to allow the lady to eat her breakfast first. The Akita had held off also, possibly worried that there might be something wrong with the food if the terrier wouldn't eat it.

Jack had sat patiently for a while, whining encouragement to the Akita, but when she still wouldn't touch the delectable meal, he had jumped up and run across to his tunnel, which Johnny left open in case the little fellow needed a quick escape route. Down the hole he went and immediately scampered out on the other side of the fence. He hadn't stopped to look back, but sped off around the back of the barn. Minutes later he reappeared, still running, and struggled back through his hole. Johnny was revolted, but didn't intervene when Jack swaggered over to where the Akita lay and deposited a rather large, still-trembling rat under her nose. Then the terrier had wriggled all over in a silent 'You're welcome!', fairly danced over to the stainless bowls of dog food and began to eat heartily, as if he were sure that now his ladyfriend had just the breakfast she desired.

Johnny had held his breath as the Akita watched her small companion eating, glanced down at the rat, and seemed to decide even poison was preferable to that! With some effort, she had risen to her feet, padded to the other bowl, and delicately tasted its contents.

Johnny's grin widened at the memory, but Doc took the boy's smile to be in appreciation of his humor.

"Speaking of kennelboys, where is Abel, anyway? I haven't seen him around this morning."

The happy light left Johnny's eyes. He looked down at the ground, then up again at the two dogs. His lips firmed into a straight, resolute line and the corners of his eyes crinkled slightly in distaste.

"Abel's gone to pick up Fleet. He got out of the hospital yesterday and says he wants to come by today to make sure the Akita's going to get her proper punishment."

The boy turned his face to the old man.

"Doc, why does she have to die? There's nothing wrong with her. Look how gentle she is with Jack. It's only Fleet that makes her crazy! Can't you talk with Mr. Lorch? Or maybe Ms. Welsely? Can't we do something for her?" Johnny's eyes pleaded as strongly as his words.

Doc cleared his throat uneasily before answering.

"Johnny," he said gently, "why are you defending this animal? She's nothing to you. She only arrived last week and right off she showed herself to be extremely dangerous to people."

"That's not true!" Johnny cut in. "She hasn't hurt anyone besides Fleet. I've been in her kennel a lot the last few days without any problems."

Doc's quick look of surprise forced Johnny to alter his defense slightly.

"You treated her yesterday and you didn't get bitten." He lowered his eyes as they threatened to overflow again. How could he explain to the old man what had happened that afternoon two days ago when he felt he had been 'touched' by the Akita? Johnny wasn't quite sure he believed it himself – it hadn't happened again – so how could he make Doc understand? He only knew he had to try.

"Besides, Doc, there's something special about her. She's so beautiful and so sad. . . I've never seen a dog so sad. . ." He raised his eyes to the veterinarian's face. "Maybe she's sad because she hurt Fleet, I don't know. But I want to help her. She's starting to perk up a little, now. Can't we give her a chance?"

"Well, she's got four more days, Johnny. There's not a lot I can do to change that under the present circumstances. But maybe we can help her if we can show Ken that her attack on Fleet really was a one-time occurrence. I know Ken isn't the kind to willingly kill any animal, especially one that he's made such a heavy investment in."

I'll give you some advice, Johnny. Now, don't be stupid and get yourself hurt, but try to win the Akita's confidence. Talk to her, feed her, water her as usual. Routine is important for instilling confidence and trust in any animal. I'll see if Ken can find out whether she was being specially trained like we talked about yesterday.

But Johnny,"– Doc grasped the boy's shoulders firmly – "don't try to handle her without someone standing by with the hose. Promise me. I'm not only worried about you getting hurt, but if you do, that dog will never get another chance."

As he looked sternly into the boy's eyes, Johnny's stubborn will slowly resolved into meek cooperation.

"Okay, Doc," Johnny mumbled. "I'll be careful, but I still don't think she'd hurt me."

"That's because you've never been hurt before, youngster. Wait until life deals you a few cruel blows; then you won't be so sure of your invulnerability." Doc stiffened and seemed to become an old man again. "Hope doesn't guarantee fairness in this life, you know," he added lamely.

Johnny felt as though he had just been slapped, and it stung. He knew the kindly vet wouldn't have reprimanded him so sharply if he hadn't pushed him to it. He felt he should apologize, but was afraid he wouldn't be able to control his tears if he tried to speak, so he turned back to stare at the dogs in their run instead.

"Dogs' Dinner! What's all this mournful conversation?" The loud, croaky voice of Anna Welsely sliced through the morning air. As usual, Anna was accompanied by a half dozen of her snuffling, baying hounds.

"Consarn it!" she yelled at them. "Why do you have to talk whenever I do?" The frail woman kicked mildly at the dogs to quiet them, but they easily avoided her boots and kept on barking.

At the sound of her voice, One-eyed Jack bounced to his feet inside the run and continued springing two feet off the ground in the same place until his mistress acknowledged his presence.

"What're you doin' in there, Jack? You look like a dee-ranged rabbit, jumpin' up and down like that."

As if he accepted that as an appropriate invitation, the little terrier hurled himself against the steel mesh, yapping and whining excitedly.

"Don't tell me they finally found a kennel you couldn't get out of," Anna teased affectionately. She lowered herself to her knees so that she could stroke the honey-colored hair on Jack's head, but found it almost impossible to do with him leaping and twisting like a freshly hooked bass.

"Who's your friend, little guy? Ain't she a pretty? I hear she ain't too friendly, though. Maybe she don't speak the language?"

Doc and Johnny waited while Anna exchanged greetings with the dog. She always said her hello's to her four-legged friends first, and she said them loud enough for any humans in the area to hear. She was fairly reclusive, and this was her way of letting people know what she was thinking about before the conversations started.

At one time Anna Welsely had been a larger, more robust woman, but her illness in combination with a certain amount of age had melted her body into its current diminutive form. Her hair was almost the same honey-gray color as Jack's topknot. However, she kept hers a little less disheveled than he did by pulling it back into a tight bun at the nape of her neck.

While attempting to pet Jack through the wires, Anna appraised the Akita bitch with a knowing eye. She was amused to see that the animal was returning her gaze with solemn interest. There was no hostility in that gaze, only curiosity.

Ken had, of course, shown Anna the photographs of the Japanese 'investment' and explained the breed's nature before the final deal was signed. Like Johnny, she had been impressed by the nobility of the animal in the pictures, but she still wasn't prepared for the awesome aura of dignity surrounding the Akita in real life. Though she was the one in the cage, the huge bitch showed no sign of defeat. Indeed, it seemed as if she was holding some sort of court, albeit an unhappy one. If she was dying, she welcomed death. If she was to live, it would be on her own terms.

Satisfied that the Akita did not seem to have sustained too much damage to her spirit during this last unfortunate week, Anna visually assessed the harm done to her body. She noted that although the dog had lost fluids and subcutaneous fat, her muscle hadn't deteriorated too much yet, so that while thin and weak from her recent ordeal, the Akita was still a powerful specimen and would probably recover quickly. But why had she gone downhill so quickly in the first place?

"Is she sick, Doc?" Anna asked without taking her eyes off the object of her scrutiny. She could see that whatever infirmity was causing the dog's poor physical condition had dulled her dark outer coat and left it dry and coarse, without the resiliency it needed to lie smoothly along her body. Instead, the hair stuck out at odd angles, exposing the softer gold fur underneath in ugly patches along her flanks and at the bony joints of her elbows and knees. The once luxurious 'shawl' of muscle around her shoulders showed almost all faded yellow now and was beginning to sag, adding volume to the already heavy dewlap beneath her chin. Still feeble, the Akita was carrying her tail far too low for Anna to be able to appreciate that thick coil of black hair with its tip of frothy white.

But if Anna's years of experience showed her all too clearly how sad the dog's current state was, they also allowed her to envision how beautiful the same animal would be with proper diet and grooming, when the natural sable highlights of her body coat would shine, a delightful contrast to the pure white of her paws and a warm compliment to the deeper ebony of her facemask. The old woman was slightly taken aback to realize how much she looked forward to seeing that curled tail riding gaily atop the Akita's back one day.

Doc broke into Anna's thoughts to answer the question she had posed earlier.

"It's odd, Anna, but I haven't found anything wrong with her yet. I've done some tests, but so far they all come out negative for disease and parasites. Lack of food and, mainly, water is all I can come up with as a reason for her poor shape. Not bad health." He cast a sidelong look to the kennelboy standing beside him. "Maybe when she's a little stronger we can take her to Doc Hill over to town. His clinic's better set up for in-depth testing."

Anna didn't seem to have heard the last remark. She was studying the Akita's unusual profile, noting how smoothly the line ran from the base of her shoulders, up the back of her neck and over her forward-slanted ears as she turned to keep track of the hounds' explorations. How catlike and lovely that gentle slope was!

Catlike also, but more like those of the wild mountain lion, were the Akita's small, well-protected eyes. Anna thought she could understand how a mouse must feel under the benign scrutiny of a well-fed cat.

"You don't think she's rabid, then," the old woman spoke again. "Neither do I. And I've seen a lot of mad dogs and other varmints 'round here in my long lifetime. Nothin' recently, thank the Lord, but once you've seen the disease, you don't forget it!

How long d'you think she's been without food? She couldn't have been on route long enough to explain this kind of damage, could she?" It was obvious that the bitch was very feeble now, yet when she had arrived only six days ago she had possessed enough strength to half-kill a grown man. And Fleet, at that.

"That I can't tell you, Anna. She wouldn't have been able to live without water for more than five or six days, but it may be that she hadn't eaten for a while even before she left Japan and that could account for her failing so quickly once she got here."

Anna reflected on the fact that the Akita was unusually tall and big-boned for a bitch and decided that perhaps that was part of the reason she looked so gaunt after only a short period without food.

"Possibly, possibly. . . I guess we'll know that when and if her old kennel ever gets in touch with Kenny."

Anna smiled at the combination of sensations she was getting from the Akita. Elegant, yes; feral, undeniably; compelling, yet frightening. The one thing she didn't sense was any rancor in the animal's makeup.

"Solitaire," she mouthed softly.

SOLITAIRE, A Dog Story

Doc leaned closer.

"What's that, Anna? Are you talking to me or your dogs?"

"I'm talkin' to that dog over there," the old woman nodded in the Akita's direction and smiled. "She's far above the rest of 'em, ain't she, Doc? She's playin' her own game by her own rules. She's playin' Solitaire. Now I know why Kenny paid the money he did for her."

Anna sighed admiringly and attempted to rise from her crouched position, holding tightly to the wire fencing. Both Johnny and Doc leaped to assist her, but she shrugged them off.

"You boys relax," she said. "I'm supposed to be out here for exercise. I just ain't as good at the knee bends as I used to be. Gettin' down's the easy part!"

"How is the arthritis today, Anna?" Doc asked with genuine concern. Over the many years he had known Anna Welsely, he had watched her physical condition deteriorate steadily as the result of the relentless disease inhabiting her joints. But she never complained about the pain. Instead, her nature seemed to have mellowed as her body weakened, and she smiled a lot more now than she ever had as a younger woman. Her mind remained as sharp as ever, though.

"The arthritis is doin' great, Doc. It's my knees that ain't doin' so well!" She chuckled ruefully, then turned her attention back to the kennel's occupants. Jack had returned to the Akita's side and lay there quietly, his one bright eye still watching the little group outside the run with interest, his tail wagging whenever Anna spoke.

"Well, our Jack likes her. And I like her. We'll call her Solitaire."

Johnny couldn't contain his rush of excitement.

"You mean we don't have to put her down?" he blurted, then caught himself, "Ms. Welsely, ma'am."

Anna chuckled more merrily this time. "Now, you know I don't stand on formalities, Mr. Wales. Fact is, I don't stand too well at all."

At that, Doc insisted on helping his friend to her feet. When they saw her get up, the hounds came leaping and bounding back to their mistress, each one eager to receive a touch from her hand.

"Well, I reckon she's more peaceable than this pack. But I don't have the say, Johnny. First, of course, Doc has to clear her for rabies. Then it's up to Kenny. His decision is final. I won't go against my manager. That's why I brought him here to run this place."

Johnny's face showed his disappointment that it was back to Mr. Lorch again. They all knew that Fleet had been on the phone to the boss every day this week to make sure he was seeing things from the 'poor' victim's point of view. Fleet meant to see this dog dead, and though Ken Lorch was likable enough, he hadn't yet shown the strength of character he would need to stand up to Fleet in an argument.

CHAPTER 9

The roar of a fast-moving truck was accompanied by a loud beep from its horn as it passed the farmhouse on its way to the quarantine area. The three people standing by the dog runs turned to watch it approach, each with a different sentiment.

When Fleet climbed unsteadily from the passenger seat of the Ford pickup, Anna's first impression was that the foreman was drunk, but then she realized that Fleet was probably just heavily medicated for the pain in his arm.

"Sonuvabitch!" Fleet gushed, elbowing the truck door shut with his left arm, the other being in a sling. "That bitch is even bigger than I remembered. And, believe me, my memories are pretty vivid!"

He flashed a confident smile as he strode toward the quarantine runs and the group standing beside them. Anna's hounds clambered over each other in their eagerness to lick his one free hand, but Fleet ignored the noisy beasts and they knew him well enough to stay to the side, well out from under his feet in their pointy-toed boots.

When he reached the wire mesh of the middle run, he leaned on it heavily and leered at the dog inside.

"Well, my lovely," he whispered, grinning. "I made it, no thanks to you, and it looks like I'm going to be around to do you the honor of escorting you out of this world in a few days' time." He clenched his teeth and lowered his voice even further. "And I'll be sure Doc makes it as slow and painful as he can, just to pay you back for all the trouble you've caused me."

The hairs on the back of the Akita's neck raised slowly until the hackles all along her spine and across her broad shoulders stood straight up, making her look twice her already impressive size. She laid her ears back flat against her head and narrowed her eyes until they were thin slits of dull black onyx. As she glared at Fleet, a mighty rumble began deep down in her throat.

"My Lord, Fleet!" Anna moved quickly to intercept the deadly challenges being thrown out by the two combatants. "You sure do have a way with this dog – I can tell she's real taken with you!"

Fleet blinked rapidly and ran his good hand down the nape of his neck as if to flatten his own guard hairs. He stood back from the wire a pace and cleared his throat self-consciously, flushed by a sudden rush of nervous adrenaline that made his heartbeat pound loudly in his ears.

"We'll all be better off when that bitch is dead," he muttered, mostly to himself, then rubbed the back of his neck again before looking to the others for support. "You can see she's crazy mean. Hell, all I was trying to do the other day was make her feel at home, and look at the thanks I got." He massaged his crippled biceps for effect. "I just thank God it wasn't one of the boys she attacked."

Fleet put on a mournful expression, wagging his head to impress his audience with the unpleasantness of that concept, then continued in a stronger, but still pleasant voice.

"That is one crazy bitch, I'm telling you. She's a killer and she's never going to let anyone or anything get near her." He glanced at first one then another of his listeners in order to gauge how his performance was affecting them.

Doc had lowered his eyes as if to stare at his own belt buckle, noncommittal as usual. Fleet was comfortable that the old vet wouldn't dare go against him directly; he would sooner crawl back into his bottle of brandy.

Johnny stood with his arms crossed in front of his chest. His lips were drawn into a straight line and he was shaking his head slowly from side to side. In Fleet's subjective state, he preferred to think that the boy's actions were meant to show appreciation of the nasty picture he had just conjured, rather than disagreement with his conclusions.

But when Fleet turned to face Anna, he couldn't overlook the fact that the old woman wasn't trying very hard to hide a mischievous smile, and his temper exploded.

"That bitch is a born killer, Ms. Welsely! You mark my words: if she isn't shot soon, she's going to attack somebody else. I say she's too damn big to take another chance with!" He kicked at the steel fencing in his customary gesture of exasperation.

Solitaire was on her feet in an instant, lips pulled tightly over gleaming white fangs. The air reverberated with the echoes of her menacing growl as her hatred of the man poured forth.

I know you, Hateful One! You are the personification of all things evil and I challenge you to come to me and accept your destiny. Escort me from this world? Yes, but we will leave it together, you and I! Only enter my domain and we will have an end to suffering — yours as well as mine!

Anna jumped as though she had been struck by a physical object. She grabbed the fencing to steady herself and stared questioningly at the creature she was sure had spoken, her eyes open wide and her jaw slack.

"Solitaire?" she gasped, "That you, girl?"

Now it was the dog's turn to be jolted. Her ears flicked forward and her mouth snapped shut as she turned to examine the old woman.

But Doc had moved just as quickly to support Anna, who was looking as if she might be having a heart attack.

"Just relax, Anna. You're going to be all right. Where does it hurt? Your chest? Come and sit over here for a while and tell me how you feel. Where are your pills?"

"I'm all right, you old fool! Leave me alone now!" She shook his gentle hands off her thin shoulders. "I just thought for a minute there that I heard her say somethin'."

"Who, Anna? The dog?"

Anna looked around at the incredulous faces surrounding her and realized that she had better amend her story or they'd have her committed for sure.

"I guess it musta been the wind or somethin'... I don't know...," she mumbled unconvincingly and stole a glance at Solitaire, who was looking as dubious as the rest. "Mebbe I'm just gettin' a little senile, huh?"

But she was sure it was the dog she had heard — not heard, exactly, more felt. She had lived with dogs all her life and sometimes it seemed as though she could read their minds. She knew when they were hungry or thirsty of course, or when they needed a friendly pat, but this was the first time she had known a dog to use words with so many syllables that she needed a dictionary to understand them.

Doc insisted that she sit down and rest. He reminded her that the hot sun in Kansas can boil your brain if you stay out in it too long; he'd seen it before with elderly people and Anna's mumbling was a bad sign.

"Talking dog or no," Fleet broke in impatiently, "we've got a date on Saturday morning, right Doc?"

Doc looked up from his unwanted ministrations of Anna and shook his head wearily.

"I guess we do, Fleet, unless Ken changes his mind before then."

"Well, we don't have to worry about that, do we?" Fleet sniffed. "She just showed all of us here that she can't be trusted." He glanced into the run, but though the weak Akita had lain back down, she hadn't relaxed her posture, and he found he had to look away quickly or be drawn into another battle of wills with the unholy creature.

As he turned his head, a small movement that seemed too jerky to be caused by the bigger animal seized his attention.

"What's Jack doing in there?" His surprise showed in his raised voice.

Anna snorted loudly and raised her hand to scratch her neck just below her left ear. A smile still played about her lips like a bad child.

"Looks to me like he's takin' sides, Fleet," she teased and gave Johnny a sidelong glance.

The boy caught her message and grinned widely as she continued in a mocking drawl.

"What was it you was sayin' about that big, dangerous beast in there layin' next to our Jack? Somethin' about her killin' anythin' that tried to come near her?"

Once again, Fleet had to clear his throat, which was still unusually tight, but he forced a thin smile for Anna's benefit. Taking sides? No, he wouldn't allow it to go that far. He had his own reasons for wanting to stay on at Welsely Farms, and the success of his plans depended on receiving a certain amount of sympathy from Anna. He couldn't afford any 'contests' with her right now. Much as he would have enjoyed putting a bullet in the Akita's thick skull right then, he might have to back down on his demands – publicly, anyway. But if he did, he wouldn't let her forget that she owed him something in return.

"A whole lot of good those quarantine runs are, with Jack running back and forth between them and the main kennels," he began slickly, but Anna had been waiting for that one and was ready with her retort.

"Now, Fleet, you can't have it both ways. Either the Akita's vicious and we have to put her down or she's sick and we have to quarantine her. Make up your mind."

Fleet's eyes were shooting daggers, but he kept his voice sounding amazingly nonchalant.

"Well, the decision isn't mine, anyway, is it?" He shrugged off the responsibility. "I'm not the one in charge around here anymore. I guess we just have to wait to hear what our new manager has to say about it."

His sarcasm wasn't lost on anyone in the group, though no one cared to leap into that breach. While he savored his little victory in having the last word, a new idea dawned on Fleet. How could he have overlooked it before? The tightness in his throat was disappearing now and he smiled a real smile again as he recalled his discussion with Ken Lorch that morning. The new boss was a fool, but he just might turn out to be Fleet's ace-in-the-hole. Unlike old lady Welsely, who sometimes seemed to revel in adversity, that man would do anything to avoid a confrontation, and Fleet had made sure that his new boss knew just how upset he would be if the bitch wasn't put down. After all, Ken was wholly to blame for ordering the vicious brute in the first place; he owed it to Fleet to take care of the problem in the proper way.

"Maybe I'll go on up to the office and let Ken know what's happened this morning. That dog isn't getting any better, as far as I can see." He turned to Anna. "Ms. Welsely, can I help you to the house? I think a cold lemonade would do you a world of good. And maybe you ought to take one of your naps this afternoon. You look awfully pale."

That patronizing tone was a warning to Anna that, although Fleet may have altered his course slightly, he still had the same end in sight. She had figured out Fleet's disturbing personality swings a long time ago and they didn't bother her much; she could give as good as she got. But she could see that Johnny was hard put to keep his contempt of Fleet's mockery hidden. She decided it would be a good idea to set the boy a task before tempers flared.

"Johnny, put the hounds in, will you? Those critters have had enough exercise this morning, and so have I." She waited for his respectful nod before continuing in an upbeat manner. "Okay, Fleet, I'll hitch a ride up to the house with you and Abel – if you think there's enough room in the front seat of the truck for a poor, wizened little old lady?"

She gave Doc a quick wave of her hand, then strode off as uppity as her crippled legs would let her, leaving Fleet to follow behind. The pack of hounds bolted ahead of them both, sniffing the same path they had just come down as seriously as though they really believed some new game may have stolen by when they weren't looking.

Johnny whistled sharply to call in the small mixed pack before they could follow the truck, then walked with them bounding alongside in the direction of their large communal run.

CHAPTER 10

From her sunny spot in the quarantine run, the Akita watched the people disperse. She was content to be alone once more. Well, almost alone. The little beast that the humans called 'Jack' had succumbed once again to the soothing rays of the warm midmorning sun and was stretched out, snoring softly by her side. She idly wondered why he stayed around when she had not given him the least sign of acceptance other than allowing him to remain in her company if he so wished. Perhaps that was enough for one such as he. For the present, she couldn't be bothered to discourage him.

The old man who smelled to her of medicaments and drinking alcohol was still puttering around outside the run, but she dismissed him as harmless – and useless, no doubt.

Keeping her head raised in a seemingly vigilant posture, the Akita tucked her chin in and down, allowing the weight of it to balance squarely on her strong neck, then half-closed her eyes against the bright sun. Twitching ears showed that she was still on the alert and listening for sounds of alarm, but her breathing slowed and became more regular as she allowed her conscious mind to relax into a meditative mood.

She inventoried her physical body and realized that she was feeling slightly stronger this morning. The early meal, though light, had gone far toward reviving her starving musculature and she was surprised by how much better she felt. She curled and uncurled her big rounded paws, checking that her extremities were in good working order as well, and was satisfied.

The unhealthy fogginess that had clouded her mind for so long was finally dissipating so that she was able to ponder the events of the last week. Or weeks. She still wasn't sure how much time she had spent in that plastic crate. That dark time was represented in her mind more as a bad, unfocused dream than as an actual occurrence. She could remember cold fear and a terrible, wrenching ache in her heart, but beyond those emotions, there was nothing. Even the fires of her anger had sputtered out without the substance of real memories to kindle them. It seemed like her soul, itself, had been taken from her by callous humankind, and she was empty.

When she had finally regained full consciousness, it was in this new land with all its strange sounds and smells, and she had been completely bewildered. Needing time to figure out what had happened to her life, she had kept any humans she encountered away from her box. Most of the humans had almost instinctively given her the respect she deserved and she had been able to study them from a comfortable distance.

Unlike her previous caretakers, the people in this place were very difficult to read. More often than not, they talked before they thought about what they wanted to say, a strange turnabout that confused her and made separating their jumbled expressions into understandable forms a slow process. Her first impression had been that there would be little hope of finding anyone gifted with the ability to listen in this country, but then she had encountered the old female who had come by for the first time this morning.

Was it really possible that the woman had understood her? No. It was more probable that she was emotionally perceptive and had only felt the strong anger in the Akita's growls. She had not listened to what was actually being said – or had she?

The Akita knew the woman was different from the others, but how so? Besides the obvious matter of her sex, the human they called 'Anna' seemed significant, somehow. Clearly the other canines on the property, including the little terrier, adored her. Even the other man-things showed her respect above what they gave to each other.

The woman moved with the slow grace of someone afraid of hurting herself, so she must be infirm. Solitaire had seen older kennelmates nurse bad or dysplastic hips the same way and had felt their despair. However, although this female was the guardian of many years, she didn't seem in need of pity. Her lively eyes shone with good humor and keen interest in the world around her.

Anna's voice, when she talked to the other humans, was rough and grated on the Akita's sensitive ears. Yet when the woman had looked at her and called her that name-word, 'Solitaire', an amazing feeling of tenderness and understanding had suffused the lonely dog's spirit. She had felt a strong urge to go to the woman. She knew she would be treated with respect. Only the presence of so many other strangers, two and four-legged, had reminded her to be cautious.

She had enjoyed Anna's scent, which brought to mind wildflowers and open spaces. For the despondent Akita, remembering that scent evoked a vivid memory of an outing she had been taken on, long ago in happier

SOLITAIRE, A Dog Story

times, to an open park. Content for the moment, Solitaire allowed her subconscious mind to explore that memory once again in a daydream.

She was very young. She could feel the clumsy gait that comes with a puppy's overlarge paws. To her inexperienced eyes, the park was a sparkling mass of darting movements just begging to be chased; and to her inquisitive nose, a plethora of strange new aromas beckoned to be explored.

Young ears don't always hear what they don't want to, so when she somehow became free of her handler she just 'missed' his call to return.

She ran and ran across the sun-drenched lawns chasing little motions that fluttered by on the breeze, stretching young muscles that never seemed to tire. She stuck her curious nose into the warm, damp earth left open by the gardeners and snuffled the sweet fragrance of the flowers.

On she galloped, from one brightly colored garden to another, until she was giddy from lack of breath. Then she threw herself into a cool, leafy glade near a stream and lay there until her breath — and her handler — returned to her. Instead of punishing her, as she might have expected, the young man patiently laughed at her innocent gambol. Together, they explored the pleasures of the fast-moving rivulet and spent the rest of the afternoon playing along its shady banks.

Solitaire's thoughts returned to the present, and she sighed heavily. It was difficult to believe that there was a time before this cruel present when she had respected — even loved — her owners and the caretakers who had guided her life. She supposed that had only been puppyish naivety, though. Surely they had been no more admirable in spirit than those people who had controlled her days since she had grown to maturity.

Like this new one, Fleet. The Akita's nostrils widened in distaste as she recalled the unique, sickly-sweet odor that lay on his body. It didn't seem like a natural human redolence to her, and based on that smell alone, she had responded to him with the same ferocity she would show to a mortal enemy. She knew it was against the Teachings for a dog to lay teeth on any man for the purpose of damaging him, but Fleet's aura had been too provocative to ignore. Besides, although his outward appearance was certainly different from those human caretakers she had left behind in Japan, Solitaire was sure she 'remembered' him as a dangerous foe, and felt justified in her attack.

Her fur lifted in agitation as she recalled how Fleet's words had sounded so slurred when he spoke to her this afternoon. She couldn't remember why she should know it, but she had been positive that his inability to speak clearly was a side effect of the hated smell, and she had become even more upset. She wasn't sure whether it was the man, himself, or the state of the man that angered her, but she was sure of one thing: *One day, Craven One, we are destined to discover who is the more powerful. It seems neither of us have anything to lose, so it will be an honest contest.* This time the big dog's growl was more of a purr, so soft that even Jack dreamed on, undisturbed.

Johnny was on his way back, having fed and watered Anna's pack. Solitaire couldn't see the hounds from her run, but she could hear them as, satiated now, they squabbled quietly over their favorite locations for a morning nap.

Dismissing the hounds as unimportant to her, Solitaire returned to watching the boy's approach through slitted eyes. She tried to feign disinterest, but as he came closer, her nostrils opened wider and trembled to the rhythm of her quickening breaths. She had to admit that she was intrigued by Johnny's scent, though it was almost imperceptible beneath the other kennel odors he 'wore' throughout the day. His was a clean, youthful aroma not unlike that of a just-weaned puppy that hasn't developed any bad habits yet. She relaxed her stern expression, letting her mouth fall open a little and pulling the corners of her lips back in a show of good humor. Even in these troubled times, she could still find joy in the young of any species.

Doc called for Johnny to assist him, and the boy swerved obediently away from the quarantine area with only a glance in the Akita's direction. Her lidded eyes followed their path to the barn before she finally dropped her head and gave in to peaceful sleep.

By the time Solitaire woke, the sun was becoming uncomfortably warm and she was panting. She didn't get up right away because Jack was still stretched out along her side and she hesitated to disturb him, unconsciously clinging to his small company while consciously acting cold and indifferent. In the end, it was the dripping saliva that rolled off the end of her tongue and bounced off his shaggy head that woke the little terrier.

First he shook his head vigorously, then he pawed at his face and ears as if to chase off a horde of buzzing flies, and snorted loudly. He wagged his stub sleepily at his gigantic friend and yawned widely and comfortably, with a quick shake of his whole body at the end. Then he stalked off to the water bowl.

Solitaire watched his antics with mirthful eyes. The cocky little terrier was able to lift her spirits in a way she hadn't thought she would experience again. Maybe it was a good thing to be in a new place where her broken spirit had a chance of healing. Maybe, with new friends to help her, she would be able to let the memories go and forget about the self-destructive search for revenge that had taken such a strong hold on her life. Maybe she didn't have to die after all.

The sound of someone approaching caused Jack to jerk his head up for a look around. He whirled to see if Solitaire had heard the sound and what his fierce companion might do about it. In the process, he dragged his scraggly beard through the water and it dripped down his chest.

The nervous, questioning expression on the tiny dog's wetly-bearded face was too much for Solitaire's reserve. Though she tried mightily, she couldn't control the quivering of her own bushy tail. Finally she dropped her ears straight out to the sides of her head, creased her eyes and allowed her enjoyment to show.

Poor Jack looked thoroughly confused, now. The Akita's odd facial expression must have seemed very un-doggy to him; for a moment he looked worried that perhaps she was going to attack somebody again. But when he saw Solitaire's jerkily waving plume, he began to run all about her, yapping in excitement, as if to let her know that if that was the way a Japanese dog shows her pleasure, who was he to say it looked weird? A friend is a friend and a terrier accepts everyone exactly the way they are!

By the time Johnny returned to see what Jack's excitement was all about, the two dogs were sharing another cool drink. With every energetic lap of her tongue, the Akita was soaking the smaller dog with excess water that fell from her huge maw, until a dripping Jack finally gave up and stood back from the bowl, waiting for his friend to finish. The look on his tiny face, full of dismay at the lady's table manners, made Johnny laugh out loud.

"You be careful, Jack, or that Solitaire's going to slurp you up with her morning drink."

Jack glanced up and wagged his tail in Johnny's direction, then returned to worrying about whether there was going to be any water left for him.

The Akita cocked an ear at that new name-sound, but continued drinking. After so many days without liquids except those that Doc had forced through her veins the morning before, her body was parched for the sweet taste of water above all else. Only when the large bowl was empty did she raise her head. Jack snorted disgustedly and slumped to the ground as heavily as his minuscule frame could manage, evoking another guffaw from the newly-lighthearted kennelboy. Johnny was enjoying the sight of the Akita acting like a dog on the road to recovery, with Jack providing the comic relief.

"I'll get you more water, Jack, and colder, too," he said aloud.

But the little fellow had obviously had enough. With a sniff, he was up and darting across to his tunnel. Another instant and he was gone from sight, lost in the tall grass of the surrounding fields.

Solitaire blinked as if she didn't believe what her eyes had just seen.

"You'll get used to it, girl." Johnny chuckled softly and went about refilling the water dish from a nearby hose. "That little dog is always in a hurry. Now you see him – now you don't. Mostly you don't when it's time for shots, or grooming, or placing blame, as Ms. Welsely says."

The Akita lay back down, this time in a shadier spot, and listened to the boy's gentle voice droning on about who was who at Welsely Farms. During the days she had been semiconscious, she had taken more comfort in the sound of that sympathetic voice than she cared to admit, even while rejecting the speaker. Now she willingly allowed Johnny's meandering dialogue to lull her into a deep and dreamless sleep.

CHAPTER 11

Ken groaned when he heard the pickup's door slam and the voices of both Fleet and Anna as they came into the house by the front entrance. They were probably on their way to his office, and not for the first time, he wished he had the nerve to escape out the back way. It was always an effort to cover his apprehension in the presence of those two strong personalities. So often he felt like they were using him as 'rope' in their ongoing game of tug-o-war.

Ken tried hard to keep his patience with Fleet, but it seemed like the foreman took his reluctance to argue as weakness and he was becoming somewhat of a bully, delighting in searching out more ways to add to his boss' discomfort.

Anna, for her part, was supportive enough of Ken's position, always referring to her manager when it was time for a decision to be made. The trouble was, Ken felt the way in which she presented her side of the arguments was often designed to let him know that she had already made her mind up and only expected him to concur. Even though he did agree with her opinions most of the time, and might have come to the same conclusions without her subtle prodding, Ken found he was often reticent about committing himself because he felt like he was being manipulated by her as well.

So there he was, in the middle of every conversation between Anna and Fleet, not wanting to side with either party for fear that he might be considered weak. As it was, everyone just thought of him as indecisive.

The 'middle man' complex was sneaking up on him again, Ken realized. All his life, he had been unable to shake his feelings of inferiority that stemmed from being only 'average'. The 'middle' child in a family of five children, he was always 'average' height for his age, 'normal' weight, 'medium' brown hair and eyes, 'fair' complexion. It seemed no matter how hard he tried – or whether he tried at all – his schoolwork ended up with a 'B+' grade average. Now here he was, a 'middle-aged' man in a 'middle-income' job at a kennel deep in the 'mid-west' of America.

The only times in his life that Ken Lorch had ever felt anything like 'exceptional' was when he was in the spotlight at a dog show, handling an outstanding breed champion on its way to winning the 'Best in Show' trophy. Unfortunately, that was a feeling he hadn't known for a long time and might never feel again if his lofty plans for Welsely's kennels backfired.

Ken heaved a sigh of resignation, then steeled his nerves and waited for his fellow antagonists to come through the door.

"Mornin', Kenny!"

Anna sounded particularly cheerful this morning. Either her arthritis was in remission or she was ready for a grand battle, Ken thought bitterly and, he knew, a little defensively.

"Good morning, Anna," he responded, standing politely. "How are you feeling this morning? Looks like you've been out?"

"Yeah, sure was! I gave those hounds a good run, too! 'Course, they did all the runnin'. All's I did was wait for 'em." She chuckled at the recollection.

Anna was in a fine mood. That made Ken even more anxious. This was going to be a real contest, he decided, but about what?

It couldn't be the Akita problem again. It was pretty much a foregone conclusion that they would have to put the bitch down, the only question being when. He knew Fleet would like to put a .22 to her head right now, and Ken couldn't really blame him, but there were other things to consider besides Fleet's satisfaction; like whether Japan would take any of the responsibility for the dog and return his purchase price, at least. The shipping fee, which was grotesque in itself, was going to have to be Welsely's loss. He was certain that prospect was not contributing in any way to Anna Welsely's cheerfulness this morning.

Ken turned to greet Fleet cautiously, noting his drawn expression. Had the two of them been at it already?

"Good to see you, Fleet!" Did that sound warm enough? He came around his desk and clapped Fleet on his good shoulder in an effort to seem more convincing. "Welcome back. We missed you around here. Hey, you look good, Fleet." Ken scolded himself for such a foolish remark, considering that the great bandage around Fleet's whole right arm could not exactly be overlooked. "I mean, at least better than the last time I saw you . . ." He reddened with embarrassment, realizing that perhaps Fleet might not want to recall that bloody encounter.

Fleet cut into Ken's flustered greetings. "I missed seeing you at the hospital, Kenny. But then I didn't get many visitors. I guess people don't like going in those places in case one day they have to stay, huh?" His sideways smile put the point home.

"I'm sorry I didn't get by, Fleet. Really. But with you gone there was a lot more work to be done around here." Ken's lips formed a smile of apology. Why was he always on the defensive with this man? To cover his embarrassment, he got up and made a show of pulling chairs closer to the desk for his visitors to sit in.

Fleet slumped into one. Anna, as usual, preferred to wander around the office, looking at the books, the artwork, out the window; anything rather than sit face-to-face for a conversation. It was another of her idiosyncrasies that both men were used to.

When Fleet was settled, Ken continued. "So when does the doctor say you can come back to work?"

"Oh, I'll be here to see that Akita bitch shot, you can count on that." Fleet rubbed his right shoulder and stared at Ken, mutely challenging him to dispute his right to retribution.

Ken had no reason to argue. He only wished Fleet wasn't so obviously relishing thoughts of the bitch's untimely end. He squirmed under the man's demanding gaze, not wanting to pronounce the words that would seal the Akita's fate just yet.

"Well, we're still waiting to hear from Japan on that," he temporized, "and Doc says he's waiting for a couple of blood tests." Ken's voice trailed off weakly. He pretended to study the graffiti on his desk blotter in an effort to avoid Fleet's scornful expression, but he could feel those icy blue eyes boring holes into his forehead. He tried changing the subject slightly.

"Besides, you're going to have to take it easy for a while yet, Fleet. An injury like yours doesn't heal overnight, I know. Of course, you don't have to worry about your paycheck. Anna and I have discussed that. And Welsely Farms is already taking care of your medical costs."

Fleet made no reply, so Ken kept on talking.

"Why don't you take a little time off, Fleet? Do you have somebody you'd like to visit? Something you'd like to do? We still have four days of quarantine to go before we can be sure the Akita isn't rabid, so I thought maybe—"

"That bitch is not rabid!" Fleet's indignant bellow bounced off the walls of the small office, making Ken wince involuntarily. It was unlike the man to show such passion, and Ken wondered again what had gone on between Fleet and Anna this morning.

"I'm telling you, that dog's just plain vicious! She was every bit as mean this morning as when she arrived, too, in front of Ms. Welsely and Doc and everybody. And for no good reason! All I did was look at her and she like to tore my head off as well as my arm. Ask Ms. Welsely, she'll tell you. There's something wrong with a dog's brain when it behaves like that!"

Too incensed to remain in his seat, Fleet rose and began to pace the floor in front of Ken's desk, muttering peevishly.

"She nearly tore my whole goddamned arm off, for chrissakes!" He stopped abruptly and pointed an accusing finger at Ken.

"Look, you brought that animal here, Lorch, and you're going to have to take the responsibility for her!"

Fleet had stunned Ken with his vehemence, and now he went in for the kill – straight for the gentler man's bleeding heart. He slumped back into the chair, carefully cradling his injured arm.

"I don't even know for sure if I'll ever be able to use my right arm properly again," he whimpered. "The doctor says it'll always cause me pain, and arthritis is bound to set in later. Who knows how long I'll be able to work for a living?" He massaged his right shoulder protectively. "Don't take the satisfaction of seeing that bitch punished away from me, too."

Though he tried to make this last sound like a plea, it came out more as a threat.

Ken was well aware that Fleet was taking flagrant advantage of his compassionate nature, but if the Akita was acting aggressively again now that her strength was returning, he might have no other choice than to give in to the angry man's reasoning.

Anna's voice, oddly placating, drifted from the far corner of the room where she had been studying one of a series of 'Fox & Hounds' prints.

"Now, Fleet," she began slowly, indulgent as a mother to her small and backwards child. She never took her eyes from the artwork she was examining while she talked. "You know the law says we got to hold the dog in quarantine. It's for your own protection. You'll have to take all those nasty shots in your belly if they autopsy her and find any traces of that virus."

She whirled suddenly to face the men and switched to her normal, brassy tone of voice.

"I had 'em back in '52, you know, when that durned fox got into the chicken yard and gave me a nip just before I whacked him with a shovel. They ain't much fun."

Both men turned quizzical expressions in her direction, but Anna didn't explain further. She enjoyed dropping hints of some of her experiences and then waiting smugly while those around her clamored for further details. But today Fleet wasn't going to let her change the subject.

"Ma'am, they don't give gut shots for rabies anymore, and I already had to have two of the new kind – one in my arm and the other in my buttock. That was pleasant. But you know as well as I do, that bitch isn't rabid. She's going to have to be put down sooner or later, so why not sooner? She's just a really bad investment." He shot a poisoned glance in Ken's direction before going on. "And I don't see why you're throwing good money after bad with all these tests that Doc's doing. The only injection that animal should get is the killing kind."

"Oh, Fleet, a couple o' days ain't goin' to make any difference to anybody." Anna made another effort to appease him. "Leastwise then you'll be sure there ain't no reason for another shot in the butt, won't you?"

The merry look in Anna's eyes hadn't faded a bit, and for an instant Ken caught the impression that she was imagining sticking the hypodermic into Fleet's backside herself. Then, before a confused Fleet could compose himself for another outburst, she turned her total attention back to examining the print on the far wall. The matter was concluded as far as she was concerned.

Ken was as confused as his kennel man. Why was Anna stalling for time in favor of this dog? He was heartened by her unwillingness to rise to Fleet's taunts about the financial losses pending, and whose fault it was, but did she really think there was a chance to save the Akita, or was she just playing her old game of 'Devil's Advocate' with Fleet?

Whatever her reasoning, Anna seemed to be on Ken's side about waiting out the quarantine period before making a final decision. Ken figured relief must be showing on his own face as surely as the disappointment he saw etched into Fleet's hard features. He took his employer's cue and ended the discussion quickly.

"We don't really have much choice, Fleet. I'm sorry, but it is the law. The dog stays alive for four more days. And as long as she's here, she will be treated humanely. If she needs veterinary attention, she'll get it."

He stood abruptly when it looked like Fleet wanted to argue further.

"You really ought to be resting, Fleet. You're looking awfully tired. I'll call Abel back to drive you over to the bunkhouse, if you like."

Fleet knew he was being dismissed. He was seething, but he stood and started for the door.

"Don't bother. I think I can walk that far."

When she heard the screen door banged shut, Anna turned to Ken with an unrepentant smirk on her face.

"Whew! That's one bent-outta-shape individual!"

Ken couldn't resist returning her grin, though he felt a little guilty doing it. He had been dreading Fleet's return, but now that the fireworks were over, he had to admit that it had felt good to get the upper hand with his foreman for a change. This time he was thankful for Anna's interference. Still, he was curious about her motives, especially in light of her unusually sunny disposition.

The woman was fairly twinkling with good humor as she crossed to the door, still chattering.

"That Fleet! The only reason I've kept him around this long's because he don't dare cross me – he knows my bite's a lot worse'n his! Now you sit down, Kenny, and relax for a bit while I get us some cold lemonade. It was Fleet's idea, actually, but I guess he forgot. When I come back, we'll talk serious about this new 'Solitaire' dog of ours. That's her name, by the way." She tossed this in casually, as though he really ought to have known it already.

Ken waited until he heard her in the kitchen, then got up and moved the chairs back to their original positions by the window. He sat in one of them and stretched his legs out. Anna was right; a little relaxation was just what he needed right now.

A short time later, Anna came back into the office pushing a cart on which a frosty jug and two glasses were riding. She didn't trust her weak joints enough to carry trays anymore.

"Ain't nothin' like lemonade on a hot day," Anna declared as she poured for both of them. She lowered herself into the armchair across from Ken before picking up her glass and taking a long sip.

Ken showed his appreciation of the icy beverage by draining half of it in one gulp. Then he refilled his glass before he leaned back comfortably in his chair. They sat together quietly for a while. Every now and then a stray breeze blew in through the open window to cool their sweltering skin, much as the lemonade refreshed their parched throats. All was tranquil in the kennel yard as noontime approached and the work slowed to a halt.

"Anna, I'm curious." Ken let his confusion show in a lengthy pause. "We both know that the Akita doesn't have rabies, and since Fleet hasn't pressed charges, we probably could put her down safely now, rather than wait another four days. We've already wasted a lot of time and money on that dog." He stopped short of reminding her that finishing it right now would also save everybody from another four days of Fleet's haranguing.

"If you're thinkin' it's only the money I'm tryin' to save, you should know me better 'n that by now, Kenny Lorch," Anna scolded. "The decision to buy that dog was made a long time ago and the money's been spent, for better or worse, so we had best move along and make the most of what we got for it. Unfortunately, what we got is a sick Japanese Akita and she's the one I'm thinkin' about now.

"Besides the fact that the law says we have to keep her the full ten days, I think she's an interestin' bitch. I sure don't see any madness in her. Anyways, I was thinkin'... It's obvious she's been drugged up for a long time, ain't it?"

Ken nodded.

"Mmm. Pretty heavily, I would say. But in light of the temperament she showed when she first arrived, it's easy to understand why."

Anna repeated herself.

"I mean a real long time, Kenny. If that kind of dopin' was done just to help her travel, they oughta get a new vet over there. That poor dog's muscles are so atrophied she can hardly stand, and her hair is fallin' out in handfuls. It looks like it's been snowin' dog-hair in that quarantine run!"

Ken's eyebrows rose and the corner of his mouth turned down as he explored the meaning behind Anna's statements. If it was true that the Akita had been kept drugged for an extended period of time before she got here, then the kennel in Japan should have to answer for that. There might be a chance Welsely Farms could not only be reimbursed the money they had paid for the dog, but also what they had paid for shipping; possibly even damages. All they had to do was prove the Japanese had misrepresented the Akita's condition before the sale.

"That might be the way out for us, Anna. We could sue the old owners if Doc's test results support your theory. Then it wouldn't be such a blow to our program when we have to put the bitch down."

Anna grimaced. Ken had only grasped a part of her meaning. She needed to make Ken understand what was on her mind, but that was going to be difficult because his age and background were so different from hers. She was sure he could never fully comprehend why she kept a man like Fleet on as an employee, let alone why she would approve of keeping a dog like Solitaire in her kennel. Sometimes she wasn't too sure of her reasoning, either, except that she had lived by the doctrine of 'live and let live' all her life and couldn't change now if she wanted to.

"I ain't thinkin' about puttin' her down right yet, Kenny," Anna started firmly. "Heck, I've seen dogs act a lot stranger than this one. So has Fleet, though he never threw a temper tantrum about it before." Ken already appeared confused, so she decided now might be a good time to fill her manager in on some cold, hard facts about Welsely's kennels.

"Look here, Ken. Nobody gives their prize pet away to a 'puppy mill', as you insist on callin' this place. 'Til you got here, most of the dogs we took in had been passed from home to home. Some of 'em stolen. Most of 'em with problems that the dealers weren't about to tell us about, even if they knew." Anna had expected Ken's dismay and went on regardless.

"We always tried not to buy any stock that'd been illegally got," she explained, "but as long as they come with papers, who can tell? Unless, of course, they've been tattooed or micro-chipped. It's real easy to make up false registrations, but awful tough to remove a tattoo or one of those new chipie things. Wish more breeders used them…" She realized she was rambling and came back to her point.

"Normally, it only takes a few days before you can tell whether a dog's behavior problems are from the stress of travelin' and new surroundin's, and which are from a lamentable past. Sometimes it takes longer, say a week or two, for a real belligerent dog to calm down. It's been my experience, though, that if they're left alone for a while, they always do quiet down and life returns to normal and we never have any problems with them after that.

Now, I know I said that I wouldn't question your decisions concerning the animals or the help here, and I'm not," – she sat up very straight in her chair – "but if you're interested in my opinion, I think Fleet's got you all wound up over nothin'. He's supposed to be an experienced handler, but he made a mistake and picked on the wrong dog, that's all. To my way of thinkin', it's about time he got his comeuppance!"

"Anna, surely you don't mean that," Ken mumbled, appalled.

"I do too mean it!" the older woman snapped and sat back haughtily in her chair, eyes blazing with righteous indignation. "Fleet didn't get hurt so terrible bad th'other day, except to his fool pride. The man's been askin' for somethin' like this for years. He never could figure out that it just makes sense to treat the animals you depend on for your livelihood with a little respect!"

Anna was fuming now, and not just about the problem with Fleet. She had noticed that Ken was worrying his lower lip again, and it rankled her more than it should. Sometimes the young man sitting in front of her could be infuriating in his insecurities. Over the last several months she had come to respect Ken's abilities in the field of canine husbandry as well as his judgment in most aspects of running the business of Welsely Farms, Fleet excluded. She was sure that he was the right man for the job and had tried many times to let him know that it was only his own self-doubt that was holding him back from full management, and herself from full retirement. She kept trying to hand Ken the reins of Welsely Farms and Kennels, Inc., but he just wouldn't pick them up.

"And now you're gonna compound Fleet's bad judgment by lettin' him have his way at the expense of that noble animal out there. We ain't never put a dog down at Welsely Farms just for protectin' itself in a strange situation, and just because this one came out on top in a struggle with Fleet, instead of givin' in to fear, ain't no reason to have her destroyed."

Hearing Anna describe the events surrounding the Akita's arrival in those terms made Ken feel ashamed of himself. He should have been able to see both sides of the story as clearly as she had; he was supposed to be the sympathetic dog man around here, yet he had been prepared to go along with Fleet's wishes just to keep the peace. After a few more moments of guilty introspection, he sighed and let his disappointment with himself show.

"I guess I just hadn't thought of it that way, Anna."

"Of course you didn't," Anna was unrelenting, "because you let Fleet's rantin' bother you too much! He's always goin' on about somethin' or other – you take that man seriously, and he'll be a yoke 'round your neck! Stand up to him while you can, or mark my words, he'll run you into the ground with his selfish demands!"

Ken ran his hands through his hair and groaned, "I know that, Anna. He just always seems to know what buttons to push to get the right reaction out of me."

"Yeah. He's a sly one, all right," Anna commiserated, softening a little when she saw the pained expression on Ken's face. "Come on, Kenny, loosen up a little," she coaxed. "It ain't too late to do the right thing."

When he didn't brighten up right away, she leaned toward him conspiratorially.

"Just between the two of us, Kenny, you know what I've been thinkin'? If that bitch had the heart to put up a fight like that when she's in such wretched condition, imagine how much presence she's gonna have if we ever get her to the show ring!"

Ken's eyes cleared. Watching him, Anna had a hunch that he was already imagining the troublesome Akita in the role he had bought her for, that of a Best-In-Show winner. She was pleased that she could tell what her manager was thinking so easily; an honest man shouldn't have to hide what is on his mind. Ken's open nature was part of what had attracted her to him at the first, but she hadn't realized when she hired him how vulnerable it would leave him when he was confronted with the baser human behavioral traits such as Fleet's jealous bullying.

"Already hankerin' after her first big win, ain't you Kenny?" she teased.

Ken writhed in his chair and altered his dream-like expression to one more serious, which let Anna know that her guess had been spot on.

"Oh, stop lookin' so guilty, Kenny!" Anna cajoled some more. "There sure ain't nothin' wrong with wantin' to see a beautiful animal like that do well. We all have different dreams that drive us, and that ain't a particularly bad one."

The screen door down the hall slammed as the boys arrived in the kitchen to prepare their lunches. Anna started to rise from her chair to join them, but Ken stopped her in mid-motion with a soft touch on her arm.

"Wait. There's one more thing I need to know. What was it about the Akita that makes you want to defend her so strongly? Frankly, after all the years you've been in this business, I would never have believed you'd get so emotional about any dog here – except maybe One-eyed Jack."

The urgency in Ken's expression caught Anna off-guard, and it was her turn to cringe. His question was sincere; she didn't want to brush it aside, but how could she explain the voice she had heard – or rather felt – this morning? The people who were right there didn't believe her, so how could she expect Ken to? She told herself that she would be better off to keep her mouth shut and let Ken think she was an old fool than she would be to speak up and prove it to him, but he was demanding an answer.

The office telephone rang, and Anna slipped off the hook for the time being as Ken reluctantly left her to answer it. At that point, she would have been thankful for any reason to postpone their discussion, but she was thrilled when Ken covered the receiver to inform her that the man on the other end of the line had an unmistakable Japanese accent!

She watched, excited as a schoolgirl, the emotions that crossed Ken's face as he first went through the pleasantries of a greeting, then the sterner task of telling his caller about Solitaire's current condition. Anna got the impression from Ken's lengthy explanations that the Japanese man was both surprised and upset.

But then it was the other man's turn to talk. Ken listened carefully for a while, then all color seemed to drain from his face and his side of the conversation became very stilted, consisting mainly of phrases like "You don't say...." or "No, I didn't know that...." Eventually, he thanked the man for his trouble and hung up the receiver.

"Anna," he said, pale as a ghost now. "That was Mr. Asaki, the manager of the kennel that bred the Akita. He said he was very sorry about what happened, but he doesn't feel his kennel shares any liability for Solitaire's condition because they didn't sell her to us. They had already sold her over a month ago to a private individual – to the agent, Leonard Trident!"

CHAPTER 12

One-Eyed Jack arrived back at the small-dog kennel just in time to chase the last of those annoying cats up into the rafters of the old barn. The cheeky felines took advantage of every opportunity when he was away to lie in the sunny spot by the open door, ignoring the frenzied barking of the caged dogs behind them. However, Jack always put a stop to that brazen behavior the instant he returned to the barn, much to the delight of his imprisoned comrades.

The little terrier was proud of his ability to keep the barn cats in line. After all, even Anna's pack of hounds was known to back down when faced with one of those spitting, puffed-up balls of fur and claws. What he never realized was that it was his piercing yap that moved the cats to seek quieter quarters when he was around. They weren't really afraid of him, but they knew from experience how persistent he could be. Once he found one of them out, he would perform a dizzying dance around and around the unfortunate victim, shrieking in its ears until the poor thing finally gave in and hastily relocated to the upper beams, well out of the little dog's sight.

These days, as soon as the cats heard the brisk padding of terrier paws on the hard dirt drive, they readied themselves for a prompt departure. Being felines, however, they never actually left their places in the sun until they were sure Jack was aware of their insolent behavior, which served to drive their tiny adversary to new heights of indignation every time. For a terrier like Jack, though, the more aggravation he endured, the stronger his feeling of satisfaction when the job was accomplished.

Now his little chest was puffed with pride and he sneezed disdainfully every few steps as he made his way back down a row of kennels. Those stupid cats ought to have learned by now that this terrier took his duties seriously! The excitement outside may have kept him a little long in the quarantine area this morning, but he was back on the job now and woe betide the barn cat who tried to push its luck on his turf!

As Jack trotted between the six-high rows of wire cages, he stopped here and there to exchange greetings with a friendly beagle or to jump up and touch noses with a congenial dachshund. This section of kennels held stud dogs and the breeding bitches when they weren't in season.

There were no solid dividers between the kennel sides or tops and bottoms here. That had been one of Fleet's brilliant ideas to save on labor costs. He claimed that one hosing-down by Abel with the pressure sprayer was all that was necessary for daily cleanliness for dogs and cages alike. The theory was that the animals should then dry quickly after their shower, due to the fresh air circulating on all four sides of them.

The fact, however, was that the lack of dividers between the kennels allowed more than water and air to circulate. Any dropped food or slopped drinking water, as well as urine and feces, simply fell through the wires of the upper kennels onto the unlucky occupants of the lower ones. Nothing short of a firehose was going to get rid of every particle of filth from those poor animals' coats.

Air drying seemed like a good idea, but that didn't work either because the atmosphere inside the barn was always charged with humidity from wastewater that lay in mucky pools beneath the larger sections of kennels. The Australian Terrier's lively sense of smell had been letting him know for some time now that the septic system installed to take care of the residue that washed out of the cages was not doing the job. Things were rotten in the back corners of the barn where humans might never go, but little dogs did.

There were opening windows down the full length on both sides of the barn, but the ones on the north side, where most of the kennels were located, had been nailed closed on Fleet's orders and boarded up. For most of the dogs housed in this dark area, Jack was their only contact with the world outside their pens, which explained why they were so excited to see him every morning. To Jack, their enthusiasm was proof of just how necessary he was at Welsely Farms. Though he never really doubted the importance of his position, he enjoyed having it reinforced at every opportunity, so he made the effort of calling by here at least once daily.

After the fervor of his mates was exhausted and those who could had returned to watching the barn door in the hopes that some newer, and therefore more interesting, entity should appear, Jack proceeded to the next stop on his morning rounds.

This was a smaller section of kennels located between the infirmary and the area where the bulk dog food was stored and prepared, about halfway in on the south side of the building. The windows on this side of the barn had been left uncovered, much to Fleet's chagrin, because the boys and Doc claimed they needed better light in their working spaces. Happily, the sunlight didn't stay only on their worktables, but spilled over to flood the cages located here with brilliance and warmth. There were solid floor pans between these kennels, so all four levels were cleaned individually, as were their inhabitants.

Mostly, these cages were full of young puppies that had been recently separated from their mothers. After the frightening experience of their first real bath, the youngsters were caged in groups of five or six to await the trucks that would come to take them away from Welsely's, never to be seen again.

The puppies were of many diverse types, from Bulldogs to Basenjis, but to Jack they all might as well be littermates; their freshly-cleaned coats, be they smooth or fuzzy, curly or straight, were so perfumed that even he couldn't tell which pup came from which brood bitch. As all young things will, the puppies rolled and tumbled with one another when the opportunity arose; but in between times they sat quietly, dewy eyes full of bewilderment, not understanding changes some of them wouldn't prove old enough to endure.

Whenever Jack passed by their pens, he feigned dramatic surprise to see such big, scary puppies! That piqued the babies' bountiful curiosity and buoyed their flagging courage so that soon they were all gathered at the front of their cages, tails wagging furiously. Jack would crouch down on his elbows, stubby tail sticking straight up in the air, then jerk his front paws backwards and forwards across the floor, yipping playfully. This would send the puppies into paroxysms of ferocious barking. When the terrier, who was scarcely bigger than most of them, acted frightened again and started running around, nose to tail in tight circles, the puppies would climb all over each other in their efforts to get out to play with the wonderfully strange dog! By the time Jack pranced off, even the youngest of the pups felt elated and much surer of himself.

At the end of this row of kennels was a utility table that the boys used for food preparation, stopgap grooming, and miscellaneous odd jobs. Though it towered above him, the Aussie wasn't daunted by it in the least. Without any adjustment to his normal jaunty gait, he sprang up and landed lightly on the top. He gave a quick whine of greeting to the Westie bitch who lived there, then made an heroic blind leap to a wall-mounted shelf above the table. This was a bit dangerous for him because the kennel boys were constantly leaving odd things in the way, like pill bottles, prickly pin brushes, or one time, a slippery magazine that had sent him sprawling back down to the table top.

Now Jack was level with the fourth tier of cages, the uppermost line on this side of the barn. The occupant of the first kennel was his dearest friend, a tiny apricot Toy Poodle. Like the West Highland White terrier in the cage below, and a few other dogs further along the rows, she lived here permanently because her constitution had proven too delicate to endure Fleet's daily showers.

The humans called her 'Amber'. She was even smaller than Jack was, only six pounds of canine pulchritude covered all over with silky pinkish-beige curls. Her ears were long and full, resting on her tiny shoulders like a fluffy shawl. Dark brown eyes sparkled hugely in her exquisitely chiseled face. Jack thought she always smelled good, not perfumed like all the animals did right after a grooming, but clean and pleasing, somehow, and his brisk disposition always softened when he was in her company.

Amber had been sleeping on a soft blue rag that she liked to bundle in the back corner of her cage, but now she uncurled herself and stretched dreamily before rising to greet Jack. She had to pick her way daintily across the cage because her paws were so tiny that they could slide through the wire inner floor if she wasn't careful.

Jack thought that only made her appear more fragile and worthy of his patronage. Not that he wouldn't like to see her running freely one day, but part of the reason the little poodle was situated so high up was so that Jack couldn't release her from her cell again.

He had helped her to escape once, last autumn when it was unseasonably warm in the barn and he was disturbed by his tiny friend's feverish panting. Poor little Amber had been clipped short in the beginning of the summer and housed in a ground floor pen on the north side of the barn. Over the next two months, while her abundantly curly coat was growing out, it had become glued together like a felt mat by the filth that rained on her constantly from the kennels above. By autumn, her soft curls were more like a dirty pelt that effectively prevented any fresh air from reaching her skin. On this particularly hot day, her tiny pink tongue was just not able to do the whole job of cooling her body on its own. Jack had been convinced that his friend was in trouble and he took it upon himself to get her out of there.

Once Jack had put his agile mind to the problem, he found it was a simple matter to open Amber's cage door from the outside. All he had to do was jump against the metal lever, pushing it upwards, and bounce hard against the door wires until the two actions came together and the door sprung outwards. Voila! Another escape was accomplished!

The tiny fugitives had made a quick dash for the wheat fields to the north of the barn, but their escape was too exciting for the dogs left behind to keep quiet about. The furor they rose brought the kennel boys running from their chores just in time to see two little furry bottoms go under the fence and disappear into the tall grass.

The boys had called out to Jack to come back, but the terrier wasn't about to return until he helped his companion to enjoy at least a small taste of freedom. He knew they would have to go back sometime – the barn was the only home they knew – but first he would show poor, deprived Amber a little of his exciting world.

Jack had raced gleefully along, glancing over now and then to encourage Amber to greater speed, but he soon noticed that she was having a problem keeping up. As a matter of fact, she had begun to fall way behind and appeared to be limping. Jack slowed his pace to match the poodle's, worried that she had hurt herself somehow. He had watched anxiously as Amber's limp quickly developed into a stagger, then was astonished to see her suddenly reel uncontrollably off-course, to finally collapse in a small, disheveled heap beneath the towering shafts of wheat.

Jack was horrified, watching his little friend's frail body shudder in convulsions. What had he done? He worried that Amber was going to die because of his silly antics unless he got her the kind of help only humans seem able to give. As he charged off in the direction of the barn, he shrieked his loudest, most attention-getting yaps in the hope that the boys hadn't given up looking for them too easily and were still outside in the kennel yard.

When he was only halfway back across the field, Jack had heard the voice of Anna from somewhere to his right, calling her hounds in. He changed direction in mid-leap and ran toward that voice until he bumped headlong into the gnarled shins of his mistress. Immediately, he was sorry because Anna gave a small yelp of pain and surprise, but he didn't have time to make a formal apology. He had circled the bewildered woman, jumping up and down and yapping until she had to put her hands over her ears.

"Okay, okay! I get the message, Jack. What's got you so upset? Dogs' Dinner! What's goin' on?"

The sudden, excited baying of Anna's pack had caused the Aussie to stop his hopping momentarily while he listened, trying to locate where the hounds were in relation to his friend. Too close! He turned his terror-widened eye back to Anna, beseeching her to understand the urgency of his dilemma.

Anna had been listening to the hounds as well. She was very familiar with the sound the pack made when they found quarry, and was quick to put two and two together. They had probably found whatever it was that Jack was carrying on about. She had started off as rapidly as she could manage in their direction, but Jack raced far ahead of her.

The hounds had circled in to surround the spot where tiny Amber lay insensate, tongue lolling out the side of her mouth, eyes glazed. Now and then a convulsion shook her body, which both excited and confused the noisy pack so that they were being careful to maintain a safe distance until they could work up the collective courage to strike.

Jack could have wished for wings to fly over the hounds' backs and rescue his friend; but being a sensible terrier, he had opted to run like hell between their multiples of legs and under their taut bellies until at last he stood at their center, alongside his unconscious companion.

At first the hounds had been taken aback by this new creature that had miraculously appeared in their midst, but they had recovered quickly once they realized who it was, and continued their deadly encirclement of their prey. By then, the animals' excitement had built to such a frenzy that they were virtually incapable of stopping of their own free will. They were slaves to the primeval instincts of the pack and were driven by its bloodlust to savagely destroy their downed victim; or victims, if that was the way the one-eyed Aussie wanted it.

Jack had taken a defiant stance over Amber's crumpled body, ready to defend his friend with his life. But he wouldn't be taken easily! He bristled with rage to think that these brainless creatures would dare to harm a fellow canine for no other reason than the bloody pleasure of the kill.

Jack had known these hounds, and the ones they had replaced, all his life. Taken individually, he was sure that they would never attempt such a loathsome deed, but he was witness to the fact that nothing was beyond them when they were running together as a pack, immersed in the thrill of the hunt.

Anna called her dogs to 'Off' as she made her way too slowly through the tall grass, but the hounds were in the spell of their ruthless game and wouldn't be distracted by her commands, if they were even able to hear them above their own clamor. Jack was on his own, and he readied himself for the lopsided battle to come.

Growling fiercely, he screwed his tiny face into the most horrific expression he could manage in a last-ditch attempt to scare his adversaries into retreat. He laid his oversized ears back against his head, squinted his good eye, and wrinkled his button nose, pulling his lips upward under his scraggly moustache to expose small spiked fangs.

But his efforts were wasted, as the first advance came from behind him. Jack's sharp ears had picked up the movement when it began, giving him time to spin around and clamp his teeth onto the bigger dog's leathery nostril. He heard a satisfying pop when the surprised hound jerked its muzzle out of his grasp and its nose snapped abruptly back to its normal shape.

One of the younger dogs saw its opening and leapt forward in an attempt to grab Jack's spine in its powerful jaws. Instinctively, it knew that one violent shake would snap the tiny line of vertebrae running down the terrier's back, ending his fight. But Jack whirled again, like a dervish, too fast and aggressive in his defense for the inexperienced animal to gain a proper hold. The hound had hastily withdrawn to the sidelines to watch its elders and wait for the next opportunity.

Jack fought valiantly to keep the hounds' circle from closing, but Anna's pack was trained to work so closely with each other that all of them together made up one offensive animal; a many-headed gargoyle that the Aussie knew he had no hope of conquering. His situation could not have been more desperate when the hounds tensed themselves for the final attack.

Suddenly, a pained yelp erupted from somewhere deep in the pack and ferocious snarls turned to confused whines as hound after hound began to back away from their feisty quarry.

Jack had been momentarily confused until he realized that Anna had finally gotten close enough to make an impression on the hounds, and they were on the run. But he was still too full of the fighting madness to let the cowardly beasts get away unpunished. He went on the offensive. He charged, growling, through the retreating hounds' forelegs, then doubled back to deliver sharp nips to the sensitive wrist area behind their pads, which caused the surprised animals to lift their feet high in the air as they continued to back away. It was a sight Jack would have found laughable were he not so enraged.

On the other side of the mob, Anna waded into their sea of bodies, using her walking stick as a cudgel and hollering like a banshee.

"You Hoary Hounds from Hell! I shoulda drowned y'all as pups! Get outta here and 'Go Home' 'fore I have your tongues for clappers! Get outta here, now! Git!"

Whining in pain and disappointment, the hounds had grudgingly dispersed. Anna made sure the last of them was slinking homewards contritely before she turned back to assess Jack's condition.

"Jack, you little scrapper. What unearthly troubles have you been gettin' yourself into now?" Fear had made her voice even gruffer than usual, but Jack knew she was mortified to think that her hounds might have hurt him.

He had looked around guardedly to satisfy himself that none of the hounds had lingered on. His heart was beating too fast from the abundance of adrenalin still coursing through his body and he began to pant. The fight over, he had suddenly felt afraid. And not only for himself. He sniffed cautiously at Amber, who made no movement at all.

"Who's this, Jack? Oh my! Jackie, how did this little girl get way out here?" Anna's voice had softened to a croon while she gently checked the toy poodle for any wounds or broken bones. Once she had satisfied herself that whatever was wrong with Amber had not been caused by her hounds, she lifted the little dog tenderly to her bosom. Jack was beside himself with worry, but all he could do was cling to his faith in humankind as he followed Anna back to the barn.

Once there, the kennel boys had filled her in on the details of the escape. She had nodded her understanding before walking briskly by them, past the dog kennels, and into the grooming room located along the south side of the barn. There, Anna had laid the seemingly lifeless poodle in the big tub used for bathing kennel dogs, and soaked her with cool water from the hand shower.

Jack was left to search for a way to get onto the grooming counter so that he could see what was going on. It wasn't a place he generally cared to go, so it had taken him a few minutes to figure out the best way to climb up. Once he reached the top, he peered over the edge into the deep tub. Amber had seemed a long way away from him and he didn't like it, so he did something he never dreamed he would ever do willingly – he jumped right into the bathtub.

Jack's concern was so obvious that Anna hadn't had the heart to laugh at his antics.

"It's okay, little feller. Your friend's gonna be all right. She just got a little too hot, is all. Lookit this messy coat. Lord! She shoulda been clipped weeks ago. And today is too darned hot for runnin' around the countryside like a pair of idiots, especially when poor Amber ain't used to it! You oughta know better'n that!"

Jack understood that he was being scolded for Amber's poor condition. He adopted his most mournful facial expression in an attempt to convince Anna of his sincere remorse, but she hadn't seemed very impressed. In fact, she had aimed the shower nozzle at him, soaking his coat as well. Being as he was still panting pretty heavily and the water helped to cool him down, Jack hadn't minded too much – just as long as there wasn't any soap in it!

Amber had improved rapidly once her body temperature was brought down to normal, so Anna rubbed her dry as gently as she could with a rough kennel towel and took the poodle back to her old compartment. Once there, she must have realized how simple it had been for Jack to free his friend and decided some changes were necessary, because since that day the kennel boys had been instructed to wire-lock all of the pens on the bottom rows.

As for Amber, she had been relocated permanently to the sunny side of the barn where she could be watched more carefully, and Anna had warned all concerned of what would happen if the grooming chores fell so far behind again – no excuses!

Jack was pleased that Amber's new cage was high enough for her to comfortably see out of the windows. She seemed to enjoy gazing out over the sunny fields. It caused him a little more effort to visit her, but he didn't mind that as long as she was happy. Besides, their mistress had been intuitive enough to locate Amber's kennel on the nearest end of the row, where Jack could sit by her side and they could content themselves with visiting through the bars.

Amber was beside Jack now. She stuck her soft muzzle between the wires and gave him a loving lap on the side of his face in warm greeting, as she always did.

Bonjour, Little General! I heard you playing with the babies and knew you would be by my side soon.

Jack gave an involuntary little shudder to make his hair lay back down along his spine. Amber's kiss always gave him goose bumps, which both pleased and embarrassed him. He wasn't sure if a terrier should let his weakness for the gentler gender show so readily, but Amber had never betrayed his emotions. Besides, she was a French Poodle, and everybody knew there was no stopping one of them from openly displaying their affections whenever and wherever they felt like it!

Amber, m'luv, I can't understand how you stay so sweet and beautiful, living in this prison. Don't you miss the adventure? I would starve myself to death, rather than live in a cage!

Amber's tail fluttered happily and she lowered her long lashes like the born coquette she was.

But Jacques, I live your adventures with you. It's better that way, you know. I would never have the courage to chase one of those enormous cats like you do! Besides, I prefer the view from my window to actually being outside. I get too exhausted to run very far. You remember.

Jack knew what she was going to say and cut her off before she could finish her thought.

Nonsense, darlin', that was only weakness from being locked away in this cell all your life. A few weeks of freedom and you'd be as fit as I am!

He sat up a little straighter to emphasize his athletic form.

Amber lifted her aristocratic nose and shook her pretty pink ears away from her face to let him know that it wasn't worth discussing, then changed the subject back to him.

You've been very busy the last few days, Jacques. What interesting news do you have for me?

Jack was never reticent when it came to relating a tasty bit of gossip. He leaned closer to the kennel bars, his nub of a tail wiggling happily.

Ah, Amber, there's been some strange goings-on going on outside!

Amber knew from his conspiratorial tone that there was a story forthcoming, so she padded back across the kennel to make herself comfortable on her rag bed and listened, enraptured, while Jack told her of the new arrival who came from a faraway place called 'Japan'. Of course, he embellished his tale with many accounts of his own cleverness and heroic actions, to Amber's delight. Only when he was finished his story did she speak again.

Ooh! That Fleet makes my French blood boil! But are you sure that this Solitaire made herself understood to our mistress, Jacques? I don't mean to imply doubt, but there are so few of us who can communicate wholly with each other anymore, and I have never believed those old fables of dogs talking with humans. I mean, it has never been proven to be possible.

Jack was adamant in his response.

Darlin', when that new bitch threw her challenge down to Fleet, I know our mistress understood her! And Solitaire was just as flabbergasted as I was! I don't think she's ever been 'listened' to before.

Amber jumped up quickly and made her way across the floor grid, a concerned expression crowding her tiny features.

Jacques, you didn't let this Solitaire know that you are a 'communicator', did you?

Jack didn't like to see the poodle even mildly upset and he hurried to soothe her.

No, no, little one, no worries! I've kept to myself until I can consult with The Owl and The Pussycat. Their ancestors were from that side of the world as well, you know, so it's possible they'll know more about this Japanese Akita and her breed family.

Amber visibly relaxed.

That's a wonderful idea, Jacques. They are very wise. Are they together at this time?

Jack assured her that they were and that he would be able to confer with them later that evening. Right now, though, he had a few more duties to perform around the farm, so he bade Amber a fond farewell and hopped down from his high perch, landing first on the desk, then on the concrete floor at a full run. His terrier appetite was telling him that it was lunchtime for the kennel help and they usually needed a little assistance from him to clean up the scraps when they were finished, so he raced off toward the farmhouse kitchen.

"Hey, Jack!" Abel called when the terrier hit the outside of the kitchen door with a bang and began scraping insistently for someone to open it. Without getting up from his seat at the table, the kennel boy leaned over and gave the screen door a shove. "Just in time, as usual. I swear I can't figure out how you do it every day."

The terrier made straight for Abel and gobbled up the piece of ham he offered. Not bad! He turned to find what Johnny was going to treat him with, but the boy wasn't even looking at him. He was reading one of those books again. Jack could never figure out why Johnny bothered reading about dogs in books when he had the real thing right in front of him! He sneezed a derisive sneeze and sat at the boy's feet to wait.

"Maybe this is the problem," Johnny spoke at last. "It says here, Abel, that Akitas don't like to be manhandled and will actually hold a long-term grudge against a person if they're treated roughly."

"Don't sound right to me," Abel shook his head. "Dogs don't hold grudges. Ha! If that was the case, none of 'em in our kennels would have anythin' to do with old Fleet, that's for sure."

"But that's what I'm saying, Abel. I still think it was Fleet's fault for

SOLITAIRE, A Dog Story

aggravating Solitaire, and that's why she went for him and why she hates him now. There can't be any other reason. If she was just vicious like Fleet says, she'd be vicious with everybody, but she's being real good with me now. She hardly even growls anymore."

Abel broke in, "Yeah, well I ain't goin' into her run without the hose, that's for sure. And I don't think you oughta, either. You remember what Doc said about gettin' her into even more trouble."

"Jeez, Abel, how much more trouble can she be in? Fleet's still carrying on about putting her down; and you know him, he won't stop until he gets his way. Well, anyway, Ms. Welsely seems to like her. And Jack does, too. Right little guy?" He had finally noticed the Aussie by his feet and deposited his lunch plate on the floor for him to lick clean.

Anna's coarse shout preceded her into the kitchen.

"Of course Jack likes her. Our Jack'd make a friend of a bear with a thorn in its paw!"

Jack hurriedly bolted the last of Johnny's sandwich and ran to dance around in front of Anna's knobby knees. It was obvious to anyone who saw them together, that Anna Welsely was the one human being the little dog truly adored.

"Well, Twitchin' Terrier Tails, what have we here? If it ain't the little devil, himself."

The boys watched Jack's ecstatic welcoming performance for Anna as she bent over carefully to give him a pat. She didn't look up when she asked, "Has Doc gone yet, or is he still out in the barn?"

Johnny piped up with the answer.

"He's gone, Ma'am. Left about noon and took Fleet with him." The enthusiasm left his voice when he added, "Fleet said he'd be back tomorrow afternoon."

Anna ignored the rancor hidden in the boy's remark and went on stroking Jack a while longer before straightening.

"Good," she announced finally. "Well then, Johnny, that gives you a bit of time to convince our girl out there to act more like a lady when Fleet's around."

Johnny nearly dropped the sandwich plate he was recovering from the floor.

"Does that mean she doesn't have to die? That we're going to keep her?" He held his breath, waiting for the answer.

Anna's voice sounded more positive than her words told when she replied, "Well, I didn't say that, exactly, but at least she's got some more time. Kenny's just got a call from the Japanese kennel." She shook her head as if to clear some stubborn cobwebs from between her ears. "There seems to be some confusion about exactly who owns Solitaire right now, so we can't do anything until that gets straightened out." Anna straightened up before shrugging her shoulders.

"The main thing is that this Asaki guy swears the dog's had all the proper shots, so she couldn't be mad. Hmmph! If she ain't mad, she must be real peeved about somethin', right Johnny?"

Her little joke went over like a lead balloon. Johnny was looking as though he had just been hit in the stomach with a sledgehammer.

"Johnny," she snapped to bring him back to attention. "Are you frettin' about that problem with the dog's paperwork? Don't. If I've learnt one thing from runnin' a puppy farm all these years, it's that paperwork's a very small part of ownership. We've got Solitaire, safe 'n' sound, in our kennel, and that's where she's gonna stay 'til this mess is cleared up." Anna's wink was meant to let Johnny know that, as far as she was concerned, the Akita bitch would never be handed back to the people who had mistreated her so cruelly.

"Anyways, ain't no sense dwellin' on somethin' you can't do much about – specially when you got a busy future to look forward to. Right, son?"

Johnny nodded, but he still didn't speak, so Anna rambled on in her most cheerful voice.

"We'll have to keep a careful eye on that girl for a while, you know that. We best keep her out of trouble until Fleet's temper calms some – but I feel real positive that Solitaire's gonna be a lot better from now on!"

Anna's beaming expression convinced Johnny that she was on his side and he finally returned her smile.

Jack seemed to take that as his cue to celebrate. He suddenly burst into full voice, yapping joyfully as he performed his showiest pirouette in front of Anna. Then he ran over and bounced against Johnny's knees several times until all three humans were laughing in appreciation of his antics.

"Well, lookee there! Seems our Jack is pleased with the news about Solitaire, as well!"

Anna was often struck by how she could read human understanding into the reactions of the excitable terrier to outside stimuli. Small wonder that she was beginning to hear animals talk now.

Jack stopped his rushing around as if Anna's mention of Solitaire had reminded him of something left undone. He trotted over to the wooden screen door, stuck his muzzle into the slot where it didn't quite meet the doorframe, gave a sharp upward push with his nose to release the sprung latch, and was gone.

The people left behind in the kitchen exchanged wondering glances until Anna stated flatly, "I guess it's time to go back to work."

CHAPTER 13

Solitaire wasn't surprised this time when she heard busy scuffling sounds and looked up to see dirt flying outside her run. Her expressive ears stretched forward in anticipation of company while she waited for the Aussie's moppish head with its perpetual wink to appear. Yet when the little dog's towhead finally popped up on her side of the fence, she deliberately modified her enthusiastic posture into one of greater dignity and detachment. Before any friendship could develop between them, the saucy terrier must learn to respect her position.

She remained where she had been, lying in the shade at the back of her run, but now she rotated her triangular ears slightly sideways and back, indicating stern displeasure, and raised her chin high above the level of the terrier's head. She wanted to be sure that Jack wouldn't be able to mistake her attitude of disdain as she peered down her broad nose at him.

Well, mouse, I see you still have not learned any manners. I am not at all amused by your habit of dropping in and out of my quarters whenever the notion strikes.

Jack twisted and pulled until his hind section was completely free of the earthen portal, then stacked all four legs squarely under his stocky body before testing that his tail was still attached and wiggling. Satisfied that all was in good working order, he indelicately – and unsuccessfully – used his rear paws to scrape the dirt he had worked loose back into the tunnel.

The gesture seemed more pompous than tidy to the Akita's mind, but she let it slide. With good health returning quickly, she was beginning to get bored of her solitary confines and was ready to welcome a small diversion, though she would rather Jack didn't know it. He was already too cocky by far.

But terriers aren't easily put off by haughty looks. Jack's belly was full from Johnny's lunch, it was a beautiful sunny afternoon for doing anything a dog might feel like doing, and he had come to visit his new friend.

Without hesitation, he pranced right up between Solitaire's massive front paws and reared to balance on his hind legs, stretching tall until he was able to lay a tiny tan forepaw against the dense black hair bordering her cheek.

Shocked into violent action by the terrier's presumption, Solitaire snapped her monstrous head around to face him, baring a ferocious array of sharp white teeth, but stopping just short of grabbing the tiny interloper. The smaller dog made no movement. He was stiff with dread at being so closely confronted with that awful maw.

Solitaire was immediately contrite. Her anger was still too close to the surface. It had risen so suddenly that she had almost loosed her temper against another canine, and that was contrary to the Teachings. She knew that, above all else, an Akita-Inu must retain her self-control if she desires to keep the dignity of the breed intact.

Slowly, Solitaire eased her clenched jaw muscles and raised her ears into a more amicable position, though she kept stern eye contact with the terrier. She was impressed that the little dog beside her had stood his ground, in spite of a slight tremble in the touch of his paw on her neck, and attempted to put him at ease.

Well. . . you can stop moving that ridiculous knob of a tail when you have to. I have never been sure if you were shaking it or if things were the other way around and it was shaking you!

Words of friendship were difficult for the Akita these days, and she knew she still sounded too harsh, but Jack seemed to accept her meager gesture with gratitude.

His tail began to quiver again tentatively as he slid quietly off her dark shoulder. A bit of wetness trickled down his belly and he shivered with relief that what could have happened, didn't.

Solitaire was sorry for causing the little fellow such discomfort and desired to make amends. She sniffed closely at Jack's muzzle, then drew her nose back in mock incredulity.

Ham! Your lunch was obviously better than mine, Tiny One. These humans must hold you in high esteem, indeed!

At that admission of his worth, Jack wriggled all over again, though not quite as excessively as before. It was obvious that he was still nervous about doing anything that might further irritate his prickly companion.

The excited baying of Anna's hounds broke the tension between the two dogs and alerted them to Johnny's rapid approach. Big and little, they watched curiously as the kennel boy raced down the path from the farmhouse and made a beeline for their run, arriving out of breath and falling against the steel fence in simulated exhaustion when he got there.

Such exuberance unnerved Solitaire, so that she pushed off the ground with her front feet until she had raised her body into a more attentive sitting position. She wasn't really frightened of Johnny, but if she needed to take any action, she was better prepared to do so from this posture. She wasn't surprised to see Jack run to the fence to welcome trouble, if there was any, the only way he knew how – head-on!

"Solitaire!" Johnny panted theatrically. "Guess what? Mr. Lorch just talked to a guy named Asaki, or something like that, from Japan. Do you remember him? He swears you've had all your shots, so there's no way you could have rabies. Of course, you still have to stay in quarantine until the time's up, just to be sure, but that won't be so bad with Jack and me to keep you company every day!" The boy's face was flushed with excitement as he called out his good news more to the world at large than to the two confused dogs staring at him through the wire.

Johnny hadn't realized it, but his pronunciation of the oriental name had been close enough to open a floodgate of memories for Solitaire. At first, the familiar sound had conjured a delightful vision of the small kennel in a mountain valley of northern Japan where she had been raised, but rushing in on the heels of that happy illusion came other murky, nightmarish images. Awful half-memories of cold and darkness filled with incredible longing threatened to sabotage the Akita's fragile peace of mind unless she was able to shut them out quickly. Her black eyes, that had been burning with interest only a moment before, turned to dull ash as she wrestled those inner demons for self-control.

Like Johnny, Jack was oblivious to the Akita's distress. He was openly enjoying the moment, barking happily and running around the kennel in dizzying circles for the boy's benefit.

His antics drew Solitaire's attention and made the furrows in her forehead deepen in frustration. She was sure that Johnny's words had meant nothing to the terrier, that his happy state of mind was simply a reaction to the boy's voice-sounds, nothing more. Jack's efforts to express himself were repugnant to her in that they were more in the nature of a mime; exaggerated gestures and body language. In her experience, animals that regularly reacted with such misplaced exuberance did so because they were unable to make their thoughts known on a higher plane. Jack obviously didn't have the talent or the fortitude to attain even the first Level of Listening, that of a 'communicator'.

As she watched the smaller dog cavort brainlessly, the unfairness of the whole situation struck Solitaire like a stone on her heart. How could that silly terrier be so blissfully ignorant of the cold realities of life when she was so miserable? The longer she watched his ridiculous antics, the more sullen the Akita's mood became, until she snarled contemptuously at the little dog.

So, is that what you were so excited about when you got here, Mouse? Did you really think that I would care what fate these insignificant humans may have decided for me? I have already prepared myself for Death's dark coming. It matters little to me now if He is early or late!

Jack sat down abruptly, facing Solitaire. His single eye widened questioningly and he cocked his hairy head in puzzlement.

Once again, Solitaire was appalled by the meanness in her spirit that kept making her lash out in anger at the little dog. And for what purpose? She had already decided that Jack was unable to understand her words, so her sarcasm was wasted on him, and her snarl had only served to frighten him again.

Their previous tension returned, neither dog knowing how to bridge the gap of their communication problem. Solitaire saw the look of panic that came into the terrier's eye just before he leaped to his feet, charged across the kennel, and darted down his hole; and she was saddened by it. Though she couldn't blame him for running off when she had shown such abysmal manners, deep inside, Solitaire felt a twinge of self-pity. She had thought Jack was beginning to care about her, but her haughty ways had put him off at last and now he had deserted her like everyone else in her sorry life had.

"I won't leave you, Solitaire."

Johnny was staring at her with such fierce determination that the lonely dog almost believed he had been 'listening' to her. She studied his face for an instant, but found no real understanding there. All she could see in the boy's expression was his intense desire to win her favor, and that was beginning to make her feel very uneasy. She rose and went into her doghouse.

***

Meanwhile, little Jack was causing a ruckus in the barn, running madly through the maze of dog kennels without stopping to touch noses with any of the inmates. This was not accepted etiquette and they were letting him know with a chorus of yaps, yowls, and a full-throated howl or two.

But Jack was on a mission! On he ran, past scolding Scotties, chiding Chow Chows and berating Beagles, until he finally arrived at the door to the grooming room. And it was closed. He checked to see whether it would budge with a nudge of his nose, but it had been firmly pulled to. He sneezed violently in frustration, causing his topknot of hair to fall forward over his good eye, and sat down to think.

In spite of the Akita bitch's baffling mood changes, the ever-optimistic Aussie felt as though he and she were beginning to enjoy a certain, albeit stiff, camaraderie. So when Solitaire had spoken of her own death as if that news was the reason for Johnny's visit, Jack had become very upset. But he was also puzzled by her remarks. The boy had sounded too happy to be delivering such bad news. And what about the gleeful excitement that Jack had sensed in the kitchen earlier? He had been positive that the humans there were enjoying a happy occasion. But the ending of a dog's life was never a good thing, no matter what Solitaire said about being prepared.

Jack had tried to mull the recent events over in his agile mind, but the only conclusion that seemed plausible was that his new friend was going to be killed because the humans had found out about her unique ability to communicate in their language. He had heard of such things happening, but had always thought that his people were more civilized. Except Fleet. Maybe this was how that human rat intended to punish Solitaire for biting him!

When the urgency of the situation had become clear to Jack, he had been wild with wanting to break his oath of silence and interrogate Solitaire because she obviously understood more of human speech than he did. But he had given his solemn word to Amber not to commune with the Akita until he was able to discuss her case with the Wise Ones.

His speedy departure from the quarantine run had come when he suddenly realized that if he waited until tonight to meet with The Owl and The Pussycat, Solitaire could be doomed!

While Jack sat outside the grooming room door, contemplating Solitaire's problem and what, if anything, he could do about it now that his route to the Wise Ones was blocked, the clamor from the dogs behind him changed in tone. Jack listened abstractedly to the difference until he came to realize that his fellow canines were letting him know they had faith in him. They were urging him on! No way could he let them down! Well, he thought determinedly, this Aussie still has a trick or two up his leggings!

He got to his feet and backed up a few inches, then a few more, calculating the distance to the door carefully. The kennel dogs quieted, curious of Jack's intention. Suddenly the little fellow lunged forward, back feet scrabbling on the cement floor in an effort to put the utmost power into his sprint. He drove his small body like a minuscule locomotive. The barking of his compatriots rose to a fever pitch as he approached the door. With a super-terrier effort, he leaped, twisted his agile body in midair, and pounded hard against the closed door with all four feet. As he bounced off, he twisted again and landed smoothly on those same four paws, then turned back to face the door expectantly.

He thought he had heard a click when he slammed against the door and was now gratified to see that it had, indeed, come ajar on the very first try and was swinging slowly inward. His audience went wild! But right now he had no time to bask in their praise. He had important business to take care of! They could give him their compliments later. He strode proudly through the door.

Once Jack had passed the entrance and was out of sight of the kennel dogs, he hesitated, no longer certain this was where he really wanted to be. Like most dogs, he hated the smell of the grooming room. He'd rather smell a road-killed skunk at close range than the sickly concoctions humans used to mask his own natural 'doggy bouquet'!

How did The Owl and The Pussycat stand it in here all the time? Well, the way he figured it, a dog could get used to anything if he was exposed long enough, and those two old dogs had been in this place since before he had been a twitch in his father's tail!

The story went that The Owl and The Pussycat had been named by Anna several years ago, on the occasion of their arrival at Welsely Farms. Even to the humans, their strange dual personality had been immediately obvious.

They were Shih Tzu Kou, Little Lion Dogs of China, a dog and a bitch; and how they came to be sold into Welsely Farms' care was an enigma that they never talked about, though others in the kennel population did.

According to rumor – much embellished over the years, Jack was sure – the Shih Tzu had arrived together in a single square wooden traveling crate that appeared tucked in between several larger metal pens in the back of an itinerant dealer's van. Fleet had been about to send the man on his way, as none of his stock seemed worthwhile, when Anna espied the strange kennel.

It was made totally of wood, lacquered in what must have at one time been brilliant crimson, though its color was dark with age and inconspicuous by then. Remnants of gold leaf decorations on the corners were worn too thin to discern what the artist had originally painted there. There were small windows set high up on both sides and these were barred with delicately chiseled wooden pegs, no barrier for any normal dog, but simply a reminder for one trained in proper manners. A third window was cut into the door on the front of the kennel and a yellowed ivory carrying handle was screwed onto the top. Anna had been captivated at once and tried to buy the charming container from the dealer.

"Sure, you can buy it, Ma'am," he had said, "but you have to take what's inside it, as well. I haven't been able to unload these two Chinkee dogs, and I'm ready to cut you a real good deal on them just to get them out of my van."

He hefted the small kennel easily and brought it to the rear of the van before opening it. The three people waited expectantly, but nothing came out the tiny door. Finally growing impatient, the dealer had reached in with one hand and pulled out a dirty gold and white gremlin of a dog, depositing him on the floor of the van.

Anna had recognized the dog as a Shih Tzu Kou, one of the three types of Foo dogs bred in the palaces of ancient Chinese Emperors. The dogs were supposed to resemble the mythical lions referred to in the Buddhist religion, but the Chinese had adopted that religion from India and there were no real lions in China at the time for them to copy. This gave the royal breeders the freedom to create dogs in the image of whatever they thought the sacred lions should look like.

The dog had sat quietly, blinking huge round eyes against the sudden light. He was very small for a Shih Tzu, under eight pounds, with a head that was much too large in proportion to his tiny body. His short legs might have been extremely desirable in the original 'sleeve dogs', but had seemed sadly deformed to Anna.

His short, sticky hair was mostly dull yellow in color with some tufts of black on the ends, and it stood out in all directions, almost like the feathers of a very disheveled barn owl. There were white markings on his chest, paws and tail tip. He had white on his muzzle as well, but his large black eyes had become infected and had been tearing for such a long time that his whole face was stained an ugly reddish brown.

The little dog's nose was so flat that he had difficulty breathing in the heat of the enclosed van. As a result, he was forced to open his wide mouth to pant as he gazed silently at first one, then another of the humans, moving his whole head to face each one in turn. To Anna, it seemed his expression was more bird-like than lionish and she had secretly named him 'Owl'.

By now, the dealer had dragged the other occupant of the kennel out into the sunlight. This female was larger than her partner, possibly ten or eleven pounds and more evenly proportioned, though she was just as dirty. A thick lion's mane of tawny red hair covered her body and she wore a dark mask, more in the style of a Pekingese than a Shih Tzu. When the bitch raised intelligent, almond-shaped eyes to examine her examiners, their color was not the breed's normal deep brown or black, but softly golden, like a jar of honey backlighted in a sunny window.

Anna had watched, entranced, as this Shih Tzu also studied each person slowly and carefully before turning back to focus on her mate; whereupon she walked over to him and nudged him affectionately under the ear in the way of an affable cat before lying down at his side.

Over Fleet's objections, Anna had agreed to purchase the two dogs. She had probably thought of her action as a harmless whim; the dealer hadn't asked much more than the value of the kennel for them and she was intrigued by their exotic appearance. Perhaps she had thought that breeding them to her modern-style Shih Tzu would bring out a more oriental quality in the resulting puppies. For whatever reason, The Owl and The Pussycat, as they were now known, were cleaned up and given a large cage in the grooming room, far from the hullabaloo of the main kennels.

"They came 'two to a box' and they'll stay together as long as they're here," was Anna's defense whenever Fleet protested the necessity of keeping two small dogs in one of the few larger cages.

She had given in when Fleet wanted to breed them, however. After all, nobody would deny her the necessity of having all the dogs in her kennels pay for themselves. She had never allowed them to breed with each other, though, for two reasons.

Firstly, Welsely Farms' market was for pets, and because there was so little dilution in their ancient Chinese blood, the pair's offspring would not be visually pleasing to the average American buyer who was looking for a cute, cuddly teddybear-type Shih Tzu, not these miniature gargoyles.

Secondly, she was never able to shake the feeling that it was not her right to claim the progeny of such a union.

Whether either of those ideas was instilled in her mind by the Wise Ones had always been a matter of some debate by the more enlightened dogs in the barn. All agreed that there was a mystical quality about the relationship between The Owl and The Pussycat that dogs don't normally feel, but few of them could believe that the old dogs were actually living legends, proof positive that the highest levels of 'The Teachings' were attainable in modern times. Jack had never doubted it.

After one final snort of disgust, One-eyed Jack drew a deep breath and entered the small oblong room. At least the window over the grooming table was open, providing a little fresh air. He padded past a skyscraper of towels on his left, one large floor-level kennel, and then another, before stopping at the third. The pen was empty, as were all the others on both sides of the crowded chamber. He thanked all the dogs in heaven for that! His business was too important to share with just any mutt who happened to be within listening distance.

From what had seemed to be an uninhabited cage on the second level, a cacophony of nasal snores fell down upon the terrier's super-sensitive ears, which he flattened in self-defense. Ooh! Those were definitely the asthmatic wheezes of a very short-nosed dog. Jack found it nearly unbelievable that the whole of that appalling din was being generated by just one animal – in his sleep!

But why couldn't he hear The Pussycat? Was The Owl still on his own? If so, Jack had second thoughts about disturbing the old dog. Wise he may be, but he did go on when The Pussycat wasn't there to guide his great mind along the right path toward solving the problem at hand.

Jack was about to slip back the way he had come when he remembered how crucial this meeting could be for his new mate outside. Resigned to do his duty, the terrier turned back and sat respectfully on the floor in front of the vacant lower cage, then held his tiny pointed muzzle in the air and gave a polite cough to inform The Owl of his presence.

Now Jack's fine hearing picked up other, softer sounds that were not quite obliterated by the ripping snores of the sleeping dog. He watched the top kennel expectantly and soon a dark shadow could be seen behind the front wires.

As she approached, The Pussycat blinked sleepily, her coppery eyes slitted against the afternoon sunlight that washed through the far window. She never slept well when she was separated from The Owl, so on this first day of their reunion, she had been practically comatose until Jack's coughing plea woke her.

She sat near the front of the cage, curling her tail around her front paws just like a feline might do and rubbed her cheek on the bars languorously before she looked down to the floor below where Jack sat patiently.

To the terrier's adoring mind, The Pussycat was not only wise and kind, but the most beautiful Shih Tzu he had ever seen. She carried herself like a noble Chinese lady, her plumed tail lying quietly on her flank like an exquisite fan. There was nothing sharp or conflicting about her. Her head and body were outlined in gentle curves, rather than hard angles like a bitch of his own breed might be. Her silky coat was a glorious harmony of softly blurred autumn colors, rusty red brightened by highlights of warm amber here or darkening to velvety chestnut brown there. He found her exotic golden eyes infinitely mesmerizing. Now those eyes dilated with pleasure until they resembled shiny copper pennies as she recognized her caller.

Jack! How very good to see you so soon after my return! You always know when I would most enjoy the pleasure of your company. The brood section is full of young, silly things at present. Do you know, there is not one 'communicator' among the lot? I had no one with whom to share the long hours in between.

She would never say the words, in deference to her longtime companion, but Jack knew that 'in between' meant the intervals in between breedings and the time she was returned home to The Owl's kennel. He respected her modesty in a place like this.

Please! You know I'm never allowed even a glimpse in that section, Pussycat! You tease me with descriptions of it! Jack shivered in mock distress, to The Pussycat's delight.

But Jack, I can see from the brightness of my window that it is still afternoon. Don't you normally have important duties to see to at this time?

Jack shrugged matter-of-factly.

Does a Dalmatian have spots? But I have news to tell you and Owl that is far more important than any of my daily tasks!

Now The Pussycat came wide awake. Her ears were elevated, framing her dark, pretty face in tawny fur and she waved her long tail with such vigor that its tip brushed back and forth across her pert nose.

Oh, do tell, Jack! How I long for fresh news to contemplate! No, wait until I wake Owl and you can tell us both together. Oh, I hope it's good!

The excitement that twinkled in her honey-colored eyes was Jack's reward for braving the unnatural cleanness of the grooming room. He winked his good eye and cocked his head playfully.

Is a Dinmont Dandie? It's better than good, Madame – it's important!

While Jack waited for the Wise Ones to reappear at the front of the kennel, he reflected on the important roles the two old dogs had played as spiritual guides and teachers for the barn's inmates since their arrival. He recalled the many lonely nights after his littermates had been shipped on and he was too old to stay with his mother anymore, when his only comfort was the voice he began to 'hear' in his head; the soft urgings of The Pussycat for him to reach out to her, and her ecstatic praise when he relayed his first coherent thoughts. Soon after that The Owl had taken over as his teacher, helping him to exercise his talent and instructing him on the different levels of 'listening', while The Pussycat's gentle mind went on to probe those of the other babies for signs of telepathic ability, always patient yet unrelenting.

Jack could only imagine what a disappointment he must have been to The Owl. Though he had become an adequate 'communicator', he was a little too active on the physical side for Owl's liking. That hairy pedagogue had lectured him for hours about redirecting his tremendous energy into contemplating the Teachings, so that he might one day rise to the status of 'Confidante', understanding the fullness of human speech as well as that of his fellow canines.

A petulant sniff brought Jack back to the present. He looked up to see both Shih Tzu watching him; one eagerly, but the other one with less enthusiasm than impatience.

Owl was ancient in terms of dog years and had lost much of his curiosity about the world around him, preferring his solitary meditations to the monotony of day-to-day living. He was perched with his furred forepaws clinging to the lower bar of the kennel door and his head tilted at a bird-like angle in order to see the messenger better.

Yes, yes, come pup, tell us what it is that you wish to impart.

Pussycat nuzzled her mate's ear in loving admonishment.

Patience, Adored. One-eyed Jack has come bearing news of great import. We should extend to him the courtesy of listening quietly.

Owl rolled his large dark eyes in exasperation, as if he didn't see any reason why, at his great age, he had to be courteous to anybody. The Pussycat waited until, with a slow shake, more like a ruffling of feathers, the old dog threw off such unproductive thoughts and settled himself more amicably to hear Jack's report, then she nodded to the terrier to begin.

Jack also made himself more comfortable. Telling his stories to Amber was simple pleasure, but relating the same tale to the Wise Ones would require total concentration and, most difficult for Jack, honest attention to detail.

He began by describing how he had noticed the new arrival and tunneled into her run to introduce himself. His saucy impersonation of the big dog's haughty attitude toward him was greatly appreciated by The Pussycat. Even the Owl's old eyes brightened with interest.

Akita Inu, heh? It's been a long time since I've come into contact with any of that ancient race. A very old breed of Japan, almost as old as the Foo dogs of China, and very dignified. However, the breed is more warlike, similar to the mastiffs of our memories.

Owl said little more during the ensuing discourse, but appeared to be carefully scrutinizing each fact as told by the terrier and judging them accordingly. The Pussycat 'oohed' and 'aahed' in all the right places, urging Jack to be as specific as possible and otherwise drawing the complete account as he remembered it out of the little dog. She used her heightened empath abilities to fill in the gaps that Jack hadn't thought he understood with knowledge she gleaned from his own telling of the events.

When Jack had finally told everything he had seen, heard, smelled or felt since the arrival of the Akita bitch, he was exhausted. The Owl and the Pussycat were thoughtful, not even communicating with each other for the time being. Jack figured they didn't have to; they must know each other's thoughts instinctively after so many years.

The Pussycat spoke first. Lately, she often took the lead when the issue required fast decision-making, Jack realized. It was only her reverential manner that made it seem as though she still deferred to The Owl on everything.

This is indeed important news, Jack. But we do not think you have to worry about the Bringer of Death coming for your friend anytime soon. We concur with you that the young human, Johnny, is of good heart and would not revel in an unfairness such as that.

However, you were wise to withhold your secret from this Akita-Inu. I believe that we have already met your friend, though she knows nothing of it. Owl and I have been listening to a strange voice in recent days and heard the misery in it, but whenever we tried to touch the owner of that voice, we found we were locked out. Her mind is very strong. By delicate probing in quiet moments, we were able to ease her spirit and give some small comfort to her. But Jack, I can tell you that Solitaire's mind is filled with a tempest of rage that threatens to destroy her!

If she is of noble breeding, as we suspect, then she has been raised with the Teachings, so there is probably little danger to you. But you must remember that even the most genteel Akita's sense of honor is that of the Samurai and it is possible that she may feel her sensitivities have been insulted if you approach her in your usual flamboyant fashion.

The Owl leaned forward and gave the terrier below him his sternest look.

And in her present mood, should that happen Jack, know that her punishment would be swift and deadly!

Jack cringed when he heard The Owl's admonition. His most recent experience with the beautiful Akita bitch had made him more apprehensive about her severe temperament, but he hadn't wanted to believe that she might actually be capable of killing him!

The Pussycat was solemn as she continued: *Permit me to review here what* you already know about the Teachings, Jack, so that you may better understand the gravity of this situation.

The Teachings guide the lives of all sensate beings, though each species chooses to organize them differently according to their own level of ability to understand them. I believe the humans refer to their version of the Teachings as the Ten Commandments. We think of them more simply as The Three Levels of Listening, because we dogs have never been concerned with the problems of worldly possessions and strive only for love and understanding among ourselves as well as between species.

All animals demonstrate their own wants and needs in an infinite variety of ways, of course, but few besides Man are able to appreciate the intricate patterns of true communication, whereby they can understand and, therefore, unselfishly assist their fellows in accomplishing what they desire. This is the reason we canines esteem humans above all else.

Even though some individuals may confuse us with their actions, we understand that Man's great mind is so complex that he still has problems tracing the cause of these deviations in his normally compassionate nature. We will always forgive any ill treatment by a single person, considering instead our love for the whole of Mankind.

Here, The Pussycat turned her dazzling eyes on Jack, filling him with the love she truly felt.

You and your little friend Amber were born with the ability to commune with others of your own species. Therefore, you are of the first Level of Listening. You are 'Communicators'.

Sorrowfully, less and less of our young are blessed with even this talent. This is the reason Owl and I spend the largest portion of our time trying to reach out to those puppies whelped here who show the greatest tendency to communicate. The gift must not be lost in our species as it has in so many others.

The second level is not inherited, but must be worked for: that of the 'Confidante'. At this level it is possible to understand the speech of humans and other animals, though there are not many species that have the ability to express themselves in an orderly fashion. It implies great trust. . .

Owl broke in here with a tired rebuke that Jack had heard many times before: *This level is within your grasp, Jack! You have but to apply yourself!*

Jack sighed. Would Owl never understand that it just isn't in the nature of a terrier to love all of his fellow creatures? To begin with, those barn cats would just laugh at him if he ever tried to commune with them! And the rats? Hah! That would be the day!

Thankfully, The Pussycat saved him from more of Owl's lecture by continuing her own discourse.

Thirdly, and finally Jack, is the level of 'competent', whereby the exceptional dog can not only listen, but can be listened to, by all of the other communicating species. It takes an enormous amount of contemplation on the Teachings and a great desire to truly understand our partners on this earth before we can aspire to this level. It is not a matter of wisdom, though that normally follows, but of righteousness, self-dignity, and love for all living things that brings one to this highest level. At this level, all Teachings of all the species are the same.

Owl ruffled his fur uncomfortably and exchanged meaningful looks with the Pussycat before stating in a tired manner: *What we find worrisome about your story, Jack, is that it seems one of our best, a full 'competent', is now denying the Teachings.*

CHAPTER 14

"What was it you wanted to see me about, Doc? Or was it just the smell of fresh coffee that brought you out at this time?" Ken teased amiably. He had been surprised enough to check his watch when he saw Doc's old Chrysler pull into the compound early this morning. Normally, if the vet showed up at all before ten, he was too bleary with alcoholic residue to accomplish much. But Ken's watch had been working fine. The time was only a little after eight now and here was Doc, sitting across the desk from him, looking as chipper as Ken had ever seen him.

"I wanted to get here early enough to talk with you before that pocket-phone of yours starts beep-booping again…and while the coffee is still fresh," Doc teased right back, ending the sentence by taking a short, comforting sip of his coffee. "Ah, that first taste at the start of the day is almost worth staying sober for."

Once again, he surprised Ken.

"I thought you didn't like coffee, Doc."

"I like coffee fine, when it's fresh. I just can't drink it like you do, after it's been reheated umpteen times throughout the day." The old man's mouth pulled tightly at the edges to show his empathy for Ken's tastebuds.

"Heck, Doc, sometimes, I don't even reheat it," Ken laughed. He blew on his steaming mug, tentatively put his lips to the edge, then decided against trying it. "I don't like it too hot."

Now it was Doc's turn to laugh. Both men put their cups down on the desk and sat back, comfortable in each other's company.

Doc was one of the few people around here that Ken could really relax around. The easygoing veterinarian knew his business and was there whenever Ken had a question, but he never tried to push his opinions on the management of Welsely's. That was good, because running a kennel this size meant taking a shortcut here and there that Ken didn't like to be reminded of.

Doc began the conversation.

"Ken, I spent last evening going over this new girl's medical records. As I've said before, there's no blood test for rabies so we just have to watch for any outward signs of the disease while she's in quarantine. I'll admit that when I first saw Solitaire, as Anna calls her, I shared your concern about rabies because she was exhibiting several of the early signs; she was pretty lethargic, couldn't raise her head, weak in the limbs. But the fact that she's improving daily negates any possibility of her having the disease. Besides, there's been no choking or salivating. And judging by the rather severe growls I've been hearing from her now and then, her throat muscles are certainly not suffering from any paralysis! Legally, of course, we still have to keep her in quarantine for the full ten days, but I'm really not worried about the prospect of rabies anymore."

Ken nodded his agreement, and Doc continued, "And I don't think the blood tests I took will prove positive for any other disease, either, unless you count verifying the drugs in her system. Basically, I haven't been able to come up with anything that answers *all* of our questions about her behavior. So I decided to do something I haven't allowed myself to do since I was a young man: I thought with my heart instead of my head. I let instinct guide me while I read through my notes again."

Ken smiled. He understood how every now and then a dog comes along and it appeals to something inside of you in a way that can't be readily explained. During his show career, he had felt the same way about a few dogs that had been brought to him for handling. Their outward appearances might not have been anything special, but something about them fairly begged to be given a chance. He had never been disappointed, either, because the same quality that had appealed to him seemed to attract the judges' attention as well. How often had he heard a judge explain the blue ribbon awarded to one of these dogs with a shrug of the shoulders and a resigned, 'He just *asked* for it'.

That's the attraction he had felt when he first looked at the photograph of the Akita bitch, too, and that was the reason he still felt she was important to his future plans. Now he was curious to hear how this crusty old vet was going to explain such charisma in a lowly dog.

"Ken, I agree with Fleet that Solitaire's problem is not physical, but psychological. Unlike him, however, I believe her current state of mind is a reaction to some recent bad experience, and not her normal temperament. I want to examine the bitch again when she can be handled closely." The old man took a deep breath and pursed his lips before he pronounced his diagnosis. "I think your Akita may be mixed up because she's just lost a litter of puppies."

Ken's expression was nothing short of incredulous.

"What? You mean she was pregnant and we weren't told about it? Do you think she miscarried? Is that what you're saying? How long ago?"

Doc lifted both hands in the air as if to fend off Ken's questions.

"I don't even know why I feel like I do. I don't know if it's just Johnny rubbing off on me or what, but that bitch out there really does seem depressed. It's unnatural. Almost spooky. And the only thing I can think of that would make any dog that unhappy would be if she lost her young ones.

"Unfortunately, there's no blood test that I can think of to prove pregnancy after all this time and she's too big and muscular to palpate her womb accurately, even if she'd let me. All we can go by is if her teats still show signs of milk, but I doubt they will. Starving a bitch will cut off her supply of milk very quickly. I'd still like to check her, though. Has she been behaving any better today?"

Ken shrugged, thoughtful when he replied, "I've told the boys to stay out of her run, except to feed her or clean up, but I think Johnny might be making some headway with her. He's been spending a lot of time hanging off that fence lately.

"You know, Doc, your theory might tie in with another mystery that's come up. I heard from the kennel in Japan yesterday."

"Oh?" Doc broke in. "Did they say why it took them so long to return your call?"

"Yes. They said they thought I was calling them by mistake. It was only after my second message that the kennel manager, a Mr. Asaki, returned my call to clarify the situation and to inform me that his kennel wouldn't accept any responsibility for Solitaire."

Doc's knitted brows were a sign of confusion. "He was that blunt?"

"Well, he was more courteous, but that was the gist of the conversation. Asaki insisted that neither he nor the owner of the kennel had any idea that the Akita had been shipped to the U.S. The last they knew of her was when she was sold about a month ago to a man named Leonard Trident. Yes, the same agent I bought her from. Asaki admitted that he arranged the sale, but denies knowing Trident was a dog agent or even that he was buying the bitch for resale."

"And you believed him?" Doc grunted incredulously.

At first, Ken hunched his shoulders, but then he sighed and shook his head 'no'.

"What about the Akita's papers?" Doc asked. "They must show the proper owners."

"They do," Ken agreed. "They are properly signed off by the kennel owner, Mr. Shibuya. But after I talked to Asaki, I checked the date of the signature. It was signed well over a month ago, before I had even heard of the dog. Trident just passed the papers along without ever registering the bitch in his name. It's done more often than you would think. We could fight that, I suppose, but on an international deal like this one, our attorney fees would be prohibitive. It looks like we're stuck with a sick Akita – or a dead one."

Doc didn't acknowledge that negative remark. Instead, he picked at a detail from one of Ken's earlier comments.

"You said they had sold her cheaply to the agent? How cheaply?"

Ken was ashamed to admit the exact dollar amount.

"Let's put it this way: I paid three times more for the bitch than they sold her to Trident for." He sucked on the inside of one cheek and wagged his head in frustration. "Man! I feel like a rank beginner! I can't believe I got taken like that!"

Doc seemed surprised.

"Why? Don't you think Solitaire's worth the money you paid for her?"

"Well, she would be if she had a better temperament..."

"Oh." Doc nodded, pretending he understood. "Well, that's probably why they sold her, then."

"Actually, no. Asaki was firm about that. I guess he handles most of the training at the kennel and insists they had never had a problem with her behavior before. Model kennel dog, apparently."

Doc looked bewildered again.

"Then we're back to the pregnancy hypothesis, which can't be proven and doesn't make much sense, anyway. Even if it was an accidental breeding, so what? They could have given the pups away – or culled the whole litter, if that's how they choose to handle things over there – and bred her fresh the next time."

"I agree. There must have been something else."

Doc worded his next question carefully.

"You know, Ken, I've lived in a glass house for too long to be comfortable throwing stones, but how do you feel about this agent, this Trident? Is he a dog-man? Or is he just in it for the bucks, as they say?"

Ken thought about that. Obviously, Trident had made an inordinate amount of money on the sale of the Akita. But did that make him a thief? Perhaps he had just been in the right position to take advantage of a great deal. But then, why hadn't he been up front with Ken right at the start? And why had the Akita arrived starving and drug-addled, not to mention in a vicious state of mind? It didn't make sense to Ken that even an unethical agent would starve an animal that he's hoping to make a lot of money on.

"I don't know, Doc," he admitted in a great exhalation of breath, "but I think there's something rotten in Amsterdam."

"Amsterdam? Holland? Not Japan?"

"I think that's where the Akita was when I bought her. I noticed 'The

Netherlands' – or however they say it in their language – printed in a few places on the shipping contract when I received it, but I figured they were references to the agent's permanent address, not the embarkation point of the dog. To tell you the truth, right at that moment I was much more interested in the bottom line of the contract, the amount of shipping fees. It sounds stupid, I know, but I can't read any of that foreign jargon, so I pretty much skipped over all of it until I got to the numbers with dollar signs in front of them – the amount I had to pay."

"Okay, let's talk about that. Who did you make the checks out to?" Doc thought he was onto something, but Ken dashed his hopes again.

"The shipping company, of course, and Trident. But that's not unusual. That's how an agent earns his commissions: he facilitates the transfer of both dog and dollars so that both parties end up happy. Normally, I would have expected the agent to take my check, clear it through his bank, then hold onto the money until the dog was delivered to me in good condition. At that point, he would take out his percentage and send the balance on to the seller."

"That sounds like a good system, but what recourse do you have when the agent is the seller and he's keeping the whole bundle for himself, even though he delivered an emotionally and physically-abused animal? I'm getting the feeling this Trident isn't the kind to make remunerations." Doc didn't mean to harass Ken, but it seemed like the manager could have been more cautious about the security of where his boss's – Anna's – money was going.

"Well, that's why agents are not supposed to deal in dogs on a personal basis unless they let their clients know in the beginning that they have a vested interest. Had I known Trident owned the dog at the time, I would have made different arrangements. But I didn't have a clue." Ken looked worn out. "I guess I'm just too trusting," he admitted.

Doc commiserated with Ken because he knew he had done his best. The young manager's biggest fault was the innocent nature that kept him from seeing the evil in others.

"He lied to you. There wasn't anything you could do," he offered.

Ken's slow-to-develop sense of outrage was finally beginning to build.

"You know, I wondered why that son-of-a-b sounded slimier than usual on the phone the last time we talked. I wish I had known then what I know now. I'd have given him a piece of my mind. Matter of fact, maybe I'll do that right now!" He pulled his phone out and began to search for Trident's long-distance number. "What the heck was Trident thinking, anyway?" he mumbled as he searched. "That he could send out a sick dog and let the peacefulness of a transatlantic flight improve her mood?"

Doc put a hand on Ken's arm before he could complete the call.

"Wait a minute, son. Let's not go off half-cocked, okay? Let's finish exploring all of the possibilities first, and then once we've done our own research, we can call in the authorities. There are laws in every country against doing business the way this Trident has. I can't believe someone as unscrupulous as he seems to be would be bothered by a phone call from an irate customer, but he'd have to listen if an agent of the local police force was to knock on his door.

"I think we should talk to the people in Japan again, too, to see if they'll back us up. This is an international incident now."

Ken wasn't sure if he wanted to go so far as to make formal charges against someone who lived half a world away, but Doc was adamant.

"I've seen a dog or two mistreated like that poor Akita out there," he stated, "and I've worked hard to ease their physical suffering, but I've never had the opportunity to go after the people who caused their pain before. I was always too busy doing my daily rounds. But I have time now, and this situation seems to me like one we can win! I'd like your permission to follow up on this Trident character and bring him to justice. Not just for Solitaire's sake, but for all of the animals abused by some sadist under the guise of making a profit."

Ken nodded dumbly, stunned by the strength of the veterinarian's convictions, but then his expression warmed and he offered his handshake to the courageous man. Doc grinned boyishly while he clasped Ken's hand in both of his.

When the moment had passed, Doc asked, "Do you have the shipping papers handy? Maybe I can help with them. I took a bit of German in school, and that's pretty close to Dutch, I've been told."

Ken said that he did and turned to the file cabinet to retrieve them while Doc drained his cup of coffee and poured two more. Both men were relieved to get away from the sentimental side of the issue and have something concrete to research.

They were gratified a little while later when Doc was able to make out that the listed owner of the dog as of the shipping date was a Japanese name. Neither one of them could pronounce it, but they compared the name with the kennel-name on the original advertisement that Ken had received to find they were identical. It was clear that Trident had been purposely hiding his ownership, or that the kennel was.

"Now can I call the bastard?" Ken looked at Doc with a malicious gleam in his eye.

"Why don't you hold off until we get all the test results in and I've examined the bitch again, Ken? Then we'll know more. The problem is that, if you were purposely duped by a dealer/kennel group that operates internationally, pressure from one lone kennel in Kansas may not bother them very much. They've probably been through it all before. We're going to have to be careful and work on a plan if we want to put these guys out of business for good.

"Why don't you try to get hold of that guy in Japan again? Better yet, I'll come in early tomorrow morning and place the call, myself. I've got a few questions I'd like to ask him, but I'd prefer to prepare some notes first. Though it sounds far-fetched, it's still possible that the kennel sold the dog to Trident in good faith and he was the one who purposely lied about it on the shipping documents. Still, I can't imagine how the kennel manager couldn't know Solitaire had recently delivered a litter."

Ken was eager for the satisfaction of telling Trident that he was onto his game. He was about to argue against the necessity of patience with Doc, but a polite knock on his office door stopped him. At his shout, the door opened and Fleet stuck his head in — and he was smiling genially!

"Good morning, Ken, Doc." He dipped his head at each of them, pleasantly. "I'd like to talk with you, Ken, when you have a minute. But don't let me bother you. I'll wait out on the porch until you're free."

The door closed, latching quietly. Ken and Doc exchanged quizzical glances.

"He wants something," Doc said simply. "Be careful."

They talked a while longer, and after a little soul-searching, Ken had to agree with Doc that the best plan of action would be no action at all right now. Ken was impressed with the old vet's objectivity about what was becoming a highly charged emotional issue. He had the feeling that once the truth was out things were going to get worse, so he took this opportunity to let Doc know how much he valued his advice. A much-inflated Doc left to do his rounds, promising to send Fleet in. Ken finished the last of his coffee in one swallow and waited.

When Fleet came back through the office door, he was still looking suspiciously contrite. He refused coffee, but took a seat in front of the desk. Ken noticed he wasn't slouching as he usually did.

"I'm sorry to bother you, but I did a lot of thinking last night. And a lot of drinking!" Fleet winced winningly as he held his good hand to his forehead.

Ken smiled in sympathy, as he knew he was expected to do, then waited for the other shoe to fall.

"I know I've been a real pain in the neck lately, and yesterday I was downright rude. I apologize. It's just this whole thing; my arm, the hospital — I hate hospitals. And I've been having nightmares lately." He added this last in a small voice, watching Ken's face to see if any pity registered there.

But Ken was too perplexed to feel sorry for his foreman. He just wanted to know what was going on. This was not the Fleet he had become accustomed to. If Fleet had a tail, he reflected, it would be between his legs right now.

"Anyway, I know I've got no right to ask favors after the way I've been

SOLITAIRE, A Dog Story

acting, but I just can't sit around all day and do nothing. I want to come back to work. Today."

When Ken's eyebrows raised in disbelief, Fleet sat forward and continued enthusiastically.

"I know I can't do all the physical stuff right yet, but I can still handle the managerial end. You don't have to bring in anybody new. You're already paying me, so let me help you out and keep the boys busy. I can handle the customer calls like I usually do."

Ken had the feeling that Fleet was looking for a reaction of some kind from him here, but he didn't know what it could be, so he kept his expression blank and waited to see what direction the foreman would take next.

Fleet seemed a little more comfortable when he continued, "Besides, my being here would leave you more time to work out the show schedule for this fall and get the specials up to snuff. I know how important that is to Welsely's future, and to you."

"I have been stretched a little thin by your absence, Fleet," Ken agreed wanly, "but the boys have been helping out a lot and we're managing okay." The truth of the matter was that the boys had been doing fine, and it didn't matter to him if Fleet took the next month off. It might even be the better idea until the Akita problem was settled. "You really need your rest right now."

Fleet shook his head forcefully to interrupt Lorch.

"I can't rest! I can't sleep! I keep having these awful nightmares about being attacked!"

The foreman looked so close to tears that Ken felt guilty for doubting his intentions. It must have been a terrifying ordeal for Fleet, and it would be a while before the shock of it would wear off. Maybe keeping busy would help the man to cope.

"Okay, Fleet. I understand. And we sure could use your help again. Welcome back!" Ken was honestly enthusiastic. Anything he could do to help Fleet get over his fears, he would do with pleasure. Except put Solitaire to sleep. He knew now that he couldn't do that.

"But what about the Akita, Fleet?" he asked carefully. "Can you handle being around her right now? Doc and I were just discussing it before you came in, and we're pretty optimistic that we won't have to destroy her. We think there might be a good explanation for her attack on you."

In his usual open manner, Ken was about to share with Fleet everything that he and Doc had discovered this morning, but something cold in Fleet's eyes when he mentioned the Akita made him stop. Ah! There was the old Fleet, buried inside this soft shell of contrition. Doc had warned him to be careful.

"You're making a big mistake, Ken. That bitch won't be around long before she bites someone else," Fleet said with only a trace of tightness in his jaws. "You'll see that she can't be trusted. And then you'll be asking me to kindly put a shot in her head. But I'm willing to wait."

His face drooped again in sadness as he added, "I just hope she doesn't hurt one of the boys or Ms. Welsely. That would just about kill that poor old woman."

Ken knew this last statement was purposely designed to make him feel guilty, but it didn't work this time. The boys and Anna were Solitaire's strongest backers, and he was rapidly gaining faith in their opinions. Doc's admission of support this morning had made it almost unanimous. Only Fleet was still unimpressed by the incredible dog, but Ken could hardly blame him.

"Look, Fleet, if you really want to come back to work, you're certainly welcome. But it's against my better judgment, at least until we get the Akita out of quarantine and back in the specials kennel, out of your way."

Fleet smiled. "It's all right. Really. I can handle it. Thank you, Ken." With that, he rose and strode out of the office.

But Johnny wouldn't believe that. He made up his mind right then that he would do anything he could to give the Akita the time she needed in order to heal herself. The first thing he would do was speak to Mr. Lorch.

CHAPTER 15

Johnny hitched a forty-pound bag of kibble onto his lean right shoulder, put his hand on his hip and walked without effort into the food preparation area of the barn. There, he slunk out from under the sack, letting it drop onto a pile of three of its mates. He had already opened several large cans of meat and the air in the small room was heavy with the delicious aroma of corned beef.

It wasn't corned beef in the cans, however, just a brand of dog food that had been made to smell like it. Johnny knew that from first-hand experience. When he was newly arrived at Welsely's, he had tasted the canned meat to see if it was as good as it smelled, but it had gagged him. "Dogs don't have a very sophisticated sense of taste," Doc had explained. "For the most part, as long as it smells good, they'll eat it." Since that day, Johnny had kept a sandwich handy in the small refrigerator for when he wanted a midmorning snack.

He emptied one of the sacks of kibble and several of the cans into a wheelbarrow, then rolled his short sleeves up over his shoulders and mixed it all together with his hands, adding a little water to help the ingredients combine more evenly. Abel appeared just as he was finished and took the barrow, replacing it with another empty one, and Johnny started all over again.

His arms deep in the gooey mass, Johnny had to avert his face to keep from sticking his nose in it as well; so he was in good position to notice when Fleet entered the barn. He swore a rather innocent curse. Life had been peaceful the past week without Fleet around. The boys knew their jobs and had done them better, Johnny thought, without being harangued by the foreman. Mr. Lorch hadn't had any complaints about their work, so Johnny didn't see why they needed Fleet around here, anyway. He spent most of his time on the phone or smoking his funny cigarettes out back of the barn – or ordering the kennel boys off on stupid errands. Although

Fleet did a lot of talking about efficiency and came up with some rather strange projects that he insisted would make the kennel run more profitably, it was Johnny's opinion that the foreman himself held the most unproductive position on the farm.

He finished mixing, wiped his hands and arms on a damp towel he kept close by, and took up the handles of the wheelbarrow, hurrying a bit so that he could get out of the small room without having to talk to Fleet. At the door, he turned right toward the small dog area, only nodding a quick greeting to Fleet before dashing on.

When they saw Johnny coming with his wheelbarrow mounded high with chow, the rows of small dogs went berserk. The best time of the day was here at last! Johnny went from one cage to the next, scooping some of the meal with his bare hand onto a folded piece of newspaper and slipping it underneath the bars to each individual dog. As he moved down the line, he talked to the dogs, calling some by pet names he had given them, but mostly talking to the group. He felt sorry that the poor animals in the barn seldom got petted and played with the way dogs liked; they seldom left their kennels at all except to get shots or to give birth. The least he could do was comfort them with his voice when he was nearby.

He was glad that Solitaire was going to live in the specials kennel after she was released from quarantine. The dogs there had a far better existence. They were groomed daily, had outside runs and were exercised regularly in the company of one of the kennel boys or Mr. Lorch. Johnny wished that considerate practice could be extended to the dogs in the barn as well, but Fleet wouldn't hear of it, saying they didn't have enough employees to waste their time 'coddling the stock'.

One by one, the dogs stopped barking as they tore into their breakfast, some of them eating the wet newspaper with equal gusto. Johnny could tell where Abel was on the other side of the barn by listening for the same phenomenon. He turned to head his empty wheelbarrow back to the prep room and laughed to see One-eyed Jack standing in the middle of it, licking up the bits remaining in the corners. Trust Jack to provide a little comic relief when Johnny really needed it.

"'Morning, Jack. Hasn't Abel given you any breakfast, yet? Come on, I'll see if there's anything left in the prep room." Johnny threaded his barrow back through the lines of kennels with Jack standing in the prow looking for all the world like a little sea captain navigating his ship homeward.

Fleet was still in the prep room when Johnny returned. He seemed to be looking for something, but Johnny didn't offer any assistance. Instead, he busied himself mixing up a special batch of food for Jack and the Akita outside. He was still giving Solitaire special feed until her appetite improved, and since Jack seemed to enjoy being treated special along with his ladyfriend, Johnny made enough for both.

While he portioned out the food into one gigantic steel dish and another less abundant container, he wondered why Fleet didn't just come out and ask him for whatever it was he needed. He also wondered if Mr. Lorch knew Fleet was in the barn. He thought the plan had been for Fleet to take a couple of weeks off. Well, he wasn't curious enough to open a conversation with the man. He poured a little of Doc's vitamin concoction over the mounded food in Solitaire's bowl and mixed it thoroughly, then left as soon as his preparations were finished, Jack bouncing gleefully along in his wake.

He hadn't realized that Fleet was not really looking for anything, but was surreptitiously watching him go through the motions of getting Solitaire's breakfast together. Now Fleet picked up the brown bottle and examined it carefully. He unscrewed the top and stuck it under his nose, then pulled it away quickly. It had an overpowering odor like cod liver oil, precisely what he needed to hide the sweet smell of the addition he was going to make.

Once out of the barn, Jack darted ahead of Johnny, straight to the quarantine run he was beginning to consider home. He popped through his entrance hole, quickly touched noses with Solitaire, then ran back to throw himself at the wire as Johnny approached. Again, he succeeded in making Johnny laugh.

"You can't fool me, Jack! I know you've been out of that run all morning, and now here you are acting just like all of the other prisoners, begging for your breakfast from behind the bars."

Johnny looked past Jack and was pleased to see Solitaire sitting quietly, but licking her chops in anticipation of breakfast. He opened the door to the run and stepped inside with the two bowls, cautious but unafraid.

"Good morning to you, Solitaire. It's good to see you up and about. Look what a delicious breakfast I've brought for you. No, Jack, the big one's for the lady."

He guided the terrier to the smaller dish, then went on talking as he stepped quietly outside the run and closed the door, staying to see that the Akita took all of her nourishment.

Jack was already finished his meal by the time Johnny sat down outside the fence and now he turned to see if Solitaire had anything left. She was still eating, so the terrier started toward her bowl. Suddenly, it seemed as if he had caught himself doing something stupid and he did a smart about-face, ending up at the water bowl instead.

If the little fellow's maneuvers puzzled Johnny, they did not go unnoticed by Solitaire, either. Though her muzzle was deep in the steel bowl, she watched Jack retreating and tried to feel good about him finally learning respect. But instead, his fearful reaction saddened her. The Teachings were very plain in holding that respect gained by fear was false for both parties. If she had been more patient, perhaps he would have grown to esteem her through faith and love, instead of concern for his own safety. Still, he had come back to her run this morning, so she would have a chance to rectify her errors.

She noticed that Jack was watching her carefully from the corner of his eye, and snuffled softly to get his attention. He seemed more than a little relieved when she waved her curled tail in a meaningful way and walked off to the corner of her run to relieve herself, leaving several mouthfuls of the tasty breakfast in the bottom of her dish.

Black nose quivering, Jack checked again that Solitaire meant for him to have it, then hurried over to see what she had left. The stainless steel bowl was so big that he had to put a front paw in to balance himself while he gobbled up the tidbits and the only part left visible was his fiercely wagging tail, pointing to the heavens.

Solitaire lay down and watched the Aussie from a small distance away, pleased that he seemed so willing to forgive her outbursts of temper. Jack had an adventurous soul and probably couldn't help his saucy manner, she reflected. Obviously respect meant different things to a terrier than it did to an Akita. She would try to be more patient with him.

Johnny watched the whole pantomime with a feeling of warm satisfaction, an emotion he wasn't that familiar with. He felt proud of his efforts to save Solitaire, though he realized he hadn't been the only one pulling for the beautiful dog and that her future was far from secure. Watching how she had purposely shared the last of her breakfast with Jack, he mused on whether that was her way of saying 'thank you' to the tiny dog. Would she ever say thank you to him?

An old school bell hanging on the outside of the barn jangled loudly, announcing a telephone call on the kennel extension.

"That's one good thing about Fleet's being here," Johnny told the dogs in the run. "I was getting awfully tired of answering the telephone to people who wouldn't talk to me." Solitaire's expression was as inquisitive as Jack's, so Johnny went on to explain.

"Seems like every time I answered that phone last week, the people didn't want to talk to anyone but Fleet. They sounded mad, too, and almost all of them hung up before I could explain why Fleet wasn't around. Then they'd call back up later and do the same thing again. And if they did talk to me, they were rude about it. It was starting to tick me off, I'll tell you. If it wasn't for that darned clangy bell, I would have stopped answering the telephone altogether."

Both dogs, their hunger satiated, were lying side by side in the sun, listening to Johnny's narrative. Johnny talked a lot when he was around dogs, less so when he was in the company of humans.

"I wonder what Fleet's doing that's making people so mad?" he pondered aloud.

Jack recognized that as a question and perked his ears as if waiting for the answer. Johnny liked it when the terrier did that and rewarded his cleverness with a broad smile.

A voice that seemed to come from inside the run said, "It's Fleet's distinctive personality that brings out the worst in people. I heard that the day Fleet was born, he made the doctor so mad, he hit him!"

Both Jack and Johnny jumped up too quickly from where they rested. Jack yapped nervously while Johnny bawled, "Aw, Doc! Where'd you come from? You scared me!" To cover his embarrassment, he joked, "For a minute there, I thought Jack was answering me back!"

"Oh, yes? Do you get much feedback from him, son?" Doc teased. "No? Well, it takes patience, I'm told. Dogs don't talk to just anybody."

Solitaire perked her ears to listen incredulously to Doc's chatter. Did the old man have any idea of how close he was to the truth?

But Doc didn't make any attempt to communicate with the dogs. In fact, he totally ignored Jack's gyrations and only gazed thoughtfully at the huge bitch before asking Johnny, "How's the girl behaving today? Do you think she might let me handle her?"

"Shall I get a lead?" Johnny was so eager to show Doc how well-behaved Solitaire was becoming that he didn't question the vet's reason for another examination.

A little later, Solitaire stood on lead, guarded but still, for the veterinarian to run his hands over her. Only when he felt along the underside of her body did she become tense and back away uncomfortably. Rather than force her to submit further, Doc grunted meaningfully to himself and told Johnny he could release her. He had found what he needed to know.

CHAPTER 16

Fleet kept himself busy the rest of the day in the barn's small infirmary, which doubled as his office, contacting any retailers who would have unknowingly received Kell's puppies instead of Welsely's during the last couple of weeks. Some of them had called during his absence and left their names when they spoke with Johnny, but he wanted to be sure nobody was angry enough to bypass him and talk with Lorch or the old lady, so he called them all. After apologizing, he made sure they all had his cell phone number to avoid this confusion in the future.

Ordinarily, a full day of answering complaints from irate customers would have put him in a foul temper, but today he was relaxed, dealing with each grievance in a calm, businesslike manner. When necessary, he soothed buyers' tempers with offers of large discounts on the purchase of future puppies, but he was careful never to promise actual dollar reimbursements. Earl always said that giving cash refunds to an unhappy customer made it far too easy for him to back out of their business arrangement; whereas giving credit involved the client ever more deeply with them because his rightful compensation was entirely contingent on future orders. Actually, Earl had put it more crudely as 'The more they cry, the more they'll buy.'

That concept suited Fleet to a 'T'. Not only did it serve to keep the cash money in his pocket right now, but on the day old lady Welsely ever turned him out, he would be taking half of her customers down the road with him.

While the indignant buyers' voices drilled in his ear, Fleet allowed his mind to wander. There sure didn't seem to be any major problems here.

He reflected happily on the cunning plan he had put into action this morning. To heck with Earl's stupid dogfight idea. He wouldn't have to wait that long for his revenge on Solitaire. If all went according to plan, by the time everyone showed up for work tomorrow morning that Akita bitch would only be a fond memory.

He realized he was getting worked up again and calmed himself with more pleasant thoughts. Maybe after the Akita thing was sorted out, he would take some time off as Lorch had suggested and go fishing or something equally lazy.

Late in the afternoon, Johnny came into the little infirmary to find Fleet looking very relaxed, feet up, listening to somebody else's complaints and not making any of his own. Johnny's curiosity was aroused. Was it possible that dog bite had taught Fleet some respect for others? He doubted it. Perhaps Fleet was taking some kind of medicine for the pain in his arm that was keeping him tranquil. If so, Johnny hoped he would keep taking it.

The kennel boy chided himself for such mean thoughts. After this last week of answering Fleet's phone himself, he ought to be a little more understanding of his foreman's problems. Some of those people really were as difficult to deal with as Fleet always claimed.

One of the few times anyone had actually delivered a complaint, it was from a man who had called wanting remuneration for medical bills on a Schipperke puppy that had arrived at his store sick with coccidiosis, a highly contagious intestinal infection. Johnny wasn't sure exactly what that disease was, but he knew for certain that they hadn't shipped any Schipperkes from Welsely's in the last six months at least. It wasn't one of the more popular breeds currently, so they only kept one bitch and she was pregnant now. When he had suggested as politely as possible that the customer review his invoices and call whatever other kennel was responsible, the man became indignant, insisting that he had the right kennel and if Fleet didn't get in touch with him within the week, he was going to cancel his account with Welsely's once and for all.

Worried in case he had done something wrong, Johnny had gone straight to his boss with that message. Mr. Lorch agreed that the man had to be mistaken, and since he had hung up without leaving the name of his outlet, not to fret about it. Mr. Lorch would talk to him if he called back. The man hadn't called back, so Johnny supposed that he had realized his error after all.

It was odd though, he reflected now, because two other people had called to complain about deliveries that he was pretty sure could not have come from Welsely Farms. At the time he had wanted to avoid any more outbursts, so he had just written down the messages for Fleet without further comment, but now he wondered how so many people could make such stupid mistakes.

Johnny nearly dropped the disinfectant he was reaching for as his mind suddenly clicked on the key. It was too improbable that *that* many of the dealers could all be making the same mistake. Something was going on behind the facade of Welsely Farms, and he was beginning to think that something was most likely connected with Fleet. The foreman's behavior had often seemed strange to Johnny, but he had never suspected it was brought about by anything other than a nasty flaw in his personality. Now he wondered if profit was behind Fleet's actions as well.

Memories of many puzzling incidents flooded Johnny's brain as he left the infirmary, anxious to get away from Fleet while he pondered his suspicions. With new clarity of mind he was coming to realize how each of those curious events was bound to the next by Fleet's eccentric ways of managing the barn.

There was the Cocker pup that had been returned to them in a Welsely Farms crate last month. The foreman had spirited the youngster away, crate and all, before Johnny could get a really good look, but he was sure that he had never seen that pup before – and he never saw it again. Where had it gone? Fleet's temper was not exactly conducive to anyone, especially a lowly kennel boy, asking him to explain his actions, so the mystery had remained unsolved.

And what about the day when Mr. Lorch had first arrived at Welsely's? He had called a meeting of the staff in the barn, away from Ms. Welsely's dominant person, to let his workers know what he expected of them and what they could expect of him. One of the things that he mentioned had troubled Johnny even then, but when he attempted to question the new boss on it, a black look from Fleet had warned him to keep his mouth closed and his ears open. He had put it aside while he listened to the rest of the new manager's prepared speech, but now the odd statement came back to him clearly. *Mr. Lorch had said that Welsely Farms' puppy mortality rate was far too high.* That just wasn't so, Johnny knew. Sure, they lost puppies from a litter now and then, as all big commercial kennels will, but he would guess a good 80% of their whelps grew up and were shipped out in good health.

Now Johnny wondered what had happened to all of those puppies that had 'died' on paper. It was part of Fleet's job to prepare the litter registrations for the pet stock and to keep records of live births, but it was Doc who usually turned in the veterinary reports. Was he somehow involved in this as well?

Johnny's resolve to investigate these and other mysterious episodes strengthened as he sorted through his recollections of recent events. He couldn't find a solid reason among them to go to Mr. Lorch right away, but he intended to keep a very watchful eye on Fleet from now on. No longer would he let these incidents slide by unexplained because, although the possibility of Ms. Welsely losing her money was a factor, he was even more concerned that there might be animals' lives at stake.

Abel's arrival interrupted his furious deliberations and the two boys began preparations for the final feeding of the day. Ms. Welsely was adamant that the kennel dogs' food should be portioned out evenly over the day, rather than given to them in one big meal. She said it not only improved the dogs' digestion, it improved their outlook because they had two things to look forward to each day, instead of only one. When Fleet had objected to the extra expense involved, she cut him short with: "Nonsense, we waste a lot of time and money around here, but keepin' our breedin' stock happy 'n' healthy ain't extravagant, it's just good business."

It rankled Johnny that Fleet, who was always trying to take shortcuts when it came to the care of the animals in order to save Ms. Welsely's money, was almost certainly stealing from the poor woman on the side.

Johnny was alone again, making up the two special bowls of food for the quarantine run when Fleet came by and hung himself on the doorframe.

"How's that Jap bitch doing, Johnny? You having any trouble with her?"

Johnny stiffened but didn't look up from his work.

"Nope," was all he said.

The boy's cool attitude ignited Fleet's temper, but he got it under control before Johnny could notice. He looked up to see the brown bottle was still on the shelf.

"Hey, kid, didn't you forget something?"

Johnny looked askance at Fleet, then followed the older man's gaze and understood.

"You mean Doc's vitamins," he stated flatly. "She only gets those once a day, in the morning." Why the sudden interest from Fleet, anyway? Surely he didn't care whether Solitaire took her medicine or not?

Fleet's mouth tensed, the only outward sign of his chagrin. No, it wouldn't work that way. The slight amount of rat poison he had added to the contents of the brown bottle had to be consumed in the late afternoon so that it would have the long night when no one was around to take effect. If the bitch took it tomorrow morning, there would be a good chance one of the boys would recognize the symptoms of poisoning and help her to expel it before it became deadly. The dosage hadn't been very strong to begin with because the Akita was still quite frail and Fleet figured the less evidence traceable to him, the better.

"Doc's too cautious sometimes," he almost croaked. "It seems to me if you put that tonic in her food twice a day, she'd recover twice as fast."

Johnny was looking guarded now, distrustful of Fleet's motives, so Fleet backed off, shrugging his shoulders disinterestedly.

"Hey, it's not for me, you know that. If it were up to me, I'd let the bitch die. But if she's going to stay here, anyway, I'd rather she got her health back as quick as possible so she can be moved into the specials kennel and out of my sight. It pisses me off every time I walk by those quarantine runs and have to look at her."

He left Johnny to think on that, hoping the boy's anxiety for the dog would make him act contrary to his better judgment.

It worked. Johnny had recognized the hidden threat in Fleet's words and now reached for the bottle. He wanted Solitaire out of Fleet's sight as much as the foreman did – or more. He didn't really think the extra dose of vitamins would help much, but surely it couldn't hurt. He shook a healthy dollop over Solitaire's meal.

One-eyed Jack came roaring in from one of the nearby wheat fields when he saw Johnny walking toward the quarantine runs. Anna always teased that the Aussie never walked when he could run, but now he was really pouring on the speed. Johnny thought that was good. The terrier needed to burn a few more calories if he was going to eat this well every day.

Jack circled Johnny twice to take in the delicious aroma of the prepared food then dashed off to his tunnel and slipped through before Solitaire even had time to raise her great head. Once inside, however, he skidded to an untimely stop, bewildered. Something had set his whiskers to tingling, a definite terrier sign of alarm. What was up?

He stood stock still trying to identify the reason for his discomfort until he was startled back to his senses by the gentle touch of Solitaire's nose on his back. She had come up behind him to wait by the door of the run as well. Her appetite was definitely on the gain and she was looking forward to dinner almost as eagerly as the little terrier was. Jack's tail had stopped along with everything else, but now it wagged a happy greeting as he shrugged off the tingling warning.

Johnny brought the two bowls in and set them down for the dogs. Jack sniffed the smaller one carefully but could not discern any sign of what might have bothered him before, so he downed it with his usual alacrity. Solitaire had not made a move toward her own heaping dish, yet; she was waiting in proper kennel manner for the boy to retreat first.

As Johnny was trotting off to finish his chores, he glanced back over his shoulder and chuckled to see the mismatched duo of scraggly little Australian Terrier and majestic Japanese Akita sharing the huge bowl of meal.

It was true that Jack's nose was in Solitaire's bowl, but he was not eating, only trying to get a good whiff of the contents. Was it the tin smell that was bothering him? Sometimes the canned dog meat did get pretty rank. No, he was sure that was okay. Doc's medicine, perhaps? But he was used to that scent by now and found it almost pleasant. What, then, had made his whiskers bristle again when he had approached Solitaire's bowl?

It took a few moments more for his sensitive nose to isolate the sickly sweet traces of an odor that sent shivers through his body. He had smelled that only once before, long ago.

One of the barn cats had brought in a sizeable rat to feed its litter. The rat wasn't struggling and that struck Jack as odd. Normally the cats liked to bring living prey to their young in order to teach the kittens how to kill. He had strolled over for a better look when he picked up an odd scent emanating from the dead rodent. Now, terriers such as he killed rats whenever they had the opportunity – that was why they were so highly valued by their humans – but they seldom eat the loathsome creatures. This particular rat, however, smelled downright delectable!

Jack had watched hungrily as the mother cat disappeared into an old crate that served as a den for her and her family, then he laid down by the opening on the off chance that an opportunity might arise for him to steal the carcass. He soon fell asleep waiting.

The next thing he knew, he was startled awake by rapid thumping on the side of the wooden crate. He jumped up, ready for danger, and was appalled to see the mother cat throw herself out of the small opening right in front of him and continue insanely beating her head and body about on the floor until the concrete was red with her blood. Her eyes were popping out of her skull and her short muzzle was scarlet as more of the sticky red liquid was projected with raging force from her heaving body.

Jack watched, fascinated, until the wretched animal finally found the only relief possible for such agony: in death. When the twitching stopped, he approached the carcass cautiously, then recoiled in disgust as he recognized the same sweet smell that had made the rat so appealing mixed strongly with the foul odor of the cat's bodily discharges.

There were no sounds coming from the crate behind him, and Jack turned to investigate. Though he didn't really want to know the fate of the kittens, he felt it was important to know what that new smell meant. All was still. He stuck his nose through the opening and took in the reek of blood and vomit – and sweet poison. Timidly, he entered and looked around in dismay at the tiny corpses. The kittens must have become ill first, after eating their small portions of the rat. Then, when the distressed mother cat had tried to lick her dying babies clean, she had ingested just enough of the poison to bring about her own lengthy convulsions.

That was Jack's first and only encounter with that sweet odor, but he swore that he would never forget it or the misery that it brought. A ratter must know the smell of rat poison!

Suddenly Jack's lips curled back and he leaped, snapping viciously at Solitaire's nose. The Akita's instincts to fight are strong and instantaneous. Solitaire didn't simply back away from her dish as Jack had expected, but instead grabbed the insulting terrier, spilling the food from her maw in order to catch him in mid-leap, and threw him to the ground. She was furious! Hackles raised, her immense body loomed over his frail one and he was sure his end had come. Only her great familiarity with the Teachings enabled Solitaire to hold off killing the terrier right then, but she snarled her frustration.

Now, mouse, you have gone too far! Do you dare to fight me for my food? Have I not treated you with generosity? Is this the way your kind repays friendship?

Jack tried to lie as still as possible so as not to rouse her ire further, but fearful trembling shook his tiny body as he whimpered breathlessly: *Please, Madame, don't eat that food! I stopped you to save your life! Please, just smell it carefully. You will notice that it has the odor of the 'Sweetness that Kills'. Someone is trying to murder you!*

With great effort, Solitaire began to calm her basest instincts. She backed off Jack carefully, but kept her hackles raised, a remnant of her anger that wouldn't go away entirely until it did. Keeping Jack in her sight, she stalked over to the spilled bowl and sniffed the food that lay around it. Sure enough, there was a different, slightly sweet odor, though it was not unpleasant and would not have put her off the meal if Jack had not intervened.

She swung her head back to the terrier, who was still lying on his back, not moving a muscle, and growled imperiously, though not unkindly.

Come here, mouse. Tell me of this 'Sweetness that Kills'. Who is trying to kill me? For what reason?

Still quaking, Jack crawled on his belly to the Akita's side. As he explained what he knew of rat poison, Solitaire's guard hairs slowly settled back flat on her back.

But if the 'Sweetness that Kills' is a disease of the rats, why do you suppose it is also in my dinner? Do the humans have control of it?

Jack had no quick answer for Solitaire's questions.

I hoped you might know that, Madame. You see, I'm only a 'communicator' and I don't fully understand the language of Man... Jack hated to admit any flaw in his persona, so he hastened to add, *... although I do fairly well, as you may have noticed. All I can tell you is that I've watched the boy, Johnny when he prepares our dinner and I'm sure he's never added the meat of a rat, so he must have added the sickness.*

This news just added to Solitaire's growing list of grievances against Mankind and she accepted the knowledge without any undue emotion. As she had thought, none of them were to be trusted, not even the boy. Now she turned her attention to a matter more important to her.

Why did you not tell me before, mouse, about your communication skills?

Jack had an answer for that one.

Without meaning any disrespect, Madame, but why haven't you asked? Mine is not the only open mind in this kennel, but not one of us have felt you trying to communicate. The Owl, who is so old and wise that he is able to listen to your thoughts even without your permission, was convinced that you had renounced the Teachings. Most of us were pretty frightened of what that could mean, so we have remained silent. Being as Owl knows I'm braver than most, he asked me to keep an eye on you until we knew for sure.

Solitaire thought about this. It was true, in her misery she had not made any effort to reach out to others. She had convinced herself that there were probably no minds worth communicating with in this strange country where there seemed to be such disrespect between species. A sin of pride. She knew she had a lot of work to do on improving her application of the Teachings to her own life – but she was no rogue!

And this 'Owl'... he was able to listen to my thoughts without me knowing of it? Surely his must be an extraordinary skill – without equal in my experience.

One-eyed Jack was relaxing now, enjoying being able to commune with this lady giant at last.

Oh, he has an equal, all right! His mate, The Pussycat, can listen to you just as easily, but she couldn't keep herself from asking questions all the time, so she had to stop.

She agrees with Owl that your mind is in terrible turmoil right now and it might be better to leave you to sort out your own thoughts, but she has never doubted your loyalty to the Teachings.

Solitaire's humility showed in her lowered ears and her black eyes glistened moistly.

She must be a kind bitch. I look forward to rewarding her faith one day.

I admit that I have not been keeping the Teachings very well in recent times. My heart is full of pain, and though it lessens daily, the ache still threatens to overpower all of my other feelings. I have not lost faith entirely, but my soul is in grave danger.

How can a 'competent' lose what they have strived to attain for their whole time here on Earth, you may ask? Hate! The need for vengeance! That man's image is burnt into my soul and I fear I will not regain my peace of mind until it is finally erased!

Now Jack's head bent to the side in curiosity.

What man are you speaking of, Lady? The boy, Johnny? Or is it a person in your past? But why does your past follow you here?

That seemed very un-doglike to Jack, to hold a grudge against a human, especially after they had gone from your life and couldn't hurt you anymore.

Solitaire looked both pained and confused, but she felt she owed the little dog some answers, so she replied.

Not the boy. If he is not to be trusted, it is simply because of his youthful ignorance. But the Teachings say that even humans can make mistakes, and I would sooner give the boy the benefit of the doubt.

It is the man known in my present as Fleet that troubles me. He had another name in my past. But no matter what he calls himself, I feel his cruelty like a blow to my heart whenever he appears. His sins against us are numerous, their category most heinous. One day I will make him pay for all the suffering he has introduced into this world.

Little Jack laid his ears down and shivered at the intensity of her emotions.

CHAPTER 17

Two weeks after Solitaire's arrival, Ken finally gave the go-ahead to move her into new quarters in the specials kennel. He, as much as anyone, had been relieved when the tenth day of rabies quarantine had come and gone without further incident. He had waited eagerly for the two-week canine disease restriction to pass as well so that she could be moved out of the quarantine run and away from the mean taunts Fleet threw in her direction every time he passed by. It was astonishing how aggravated Fleet's behavior had become. The man seemed intent on worrying Solitaire into another attack, possibly to prove his oft-repeated theory that she was born vicious and would never change. Ken could only agree with Johnny's remarks about how he thought adults were supposed to be more in control of their feelings.

That Solitaire returned Fleet's hatred was obvious but she, at least, seemed to be consciously trying to avoid another confrontation. Whenever she saw Fleet approaching, she would get up and meaningfully turn her back on him, lying back down with her chin on her paws and looking in any direction but his. The only signal of her continued aggression was the throaty growl that would not be stilled while he remained in the vicinity.

Apart from the fact that she would no longer touch her food if Johnny put Doc's delicious concoction of vitamins on it, she had behaved like a normal, healthy dog in every way during the last week. Between Johnny's special care and Jack's robust friendship, she had gone a long way toward regaining her former good looks and a semblance of her breed's normally beneficent disposition.

Though they couldn't keep Jack from his daily visits, all other rules of quarantine had been followed. Ken had worried that they were taking a chance breaking the 'no visitors' rule when it came to Jack, but Doc had sided with Anna when she protested that it was more important for

SOLITAIRE, A Dog Story

Solitaire's recovery to have a friend. Besides, Anna had pointed out that the little fellow seldom, if ever, visited the specials kennel anyway. He spent most of his time these days between Solitaire's run and the barn.

Doc had surprised Ken by volunteering to take over all communications with the kennel in Japan. That was fine by Ken. Doc seemed a lot more at ease dealing with foreigners than he was. Their heavily-accented English was difficult for him to understand; not only the words, but the meanings behind them. He was far happier doing what he did best, and right now he had his hands full preparing Welsely's string of specials for introduction into the national circuit of dog shows.

On the morning Solitaire was being moved to her new run, Ken came down to oversee the transition. Johnny had requested that Fleet be kept out of the area for this first outing, and Ken had agreed it would be a wise move. Fleet hadn't left without an argument, but Ken had maintained his stand for once and was now rewarded for his troubles with a glimpse of how relaxed and dignified Solitaire could be when she wasn't being tortured by the foreman's malicious presence. He was pleased to see that Johnny's patient efforts to befriend the despondent Akita had paid off. She left her home of two weeks without the slightest hesitation, walking obediently at heel beside Johnny, her lead slack between them.

Ken directed Johnny to take the Akita over to the exercise ring. She needed to stretch her muscles after her stay in quarantine and he would be glad of the opportunity to observe the beautiful animal a while longer. Head high, ears strongly forward, Solitaire's confident attitude as she walked around the ring on Johnny's lead could trick the watcher into thinking that she was the master and he only her minion, pacing himself to her powerful strides.

Ken's delight was obvious in the silly grin he wore. He hadn't been wrong about the Akita after all. She was a showman's dream; no matter that she seemed to have very strong personal preferences about who was going to show her. As long as they could keep Fleet away from her, he might be able to realize his own carefully laid plans and bring Welsely Farms and Kennels, Inc. into the glamorous world of big-time dog shows sooner than he had anticipated.

"She's got it, ain't she, Kenny?" Anna cooed as she slid into a seat beside him. "And she ain't afraid to flaunt it, either. What a hussy!"

Ken's grin widened, but he never took his eyes off the pair in the ring. He called out to Johnny to speed up a little so that the Akita could lengthen her stride, now slow down and stack her. On her handler's command, Solitaire stiffened into a proud statue of a dog, staring straight ahead, relaxing only the areas of her body that Johnny touched in order to adjust her position, then stiffening them again. Not that her stance needed correction – the Akita knew her business – but Ken wanted Johnny wanted to play with her, loosen her up, so that he could see what her reaction to the handling would be. After the boy had lifted all four paws, ran his hand up the back of her curled tail to induce her to raise it even higher, and set her chin at a slightly lower angle, he stood back and looked to Ken for approval.

"You're doing great, Johnny, and she's a real pro," Ken enthused. "It's obvious that she's been cooped up a long time, though. She's going to need a bit of roadwork to get rid of some of the slackness in her muscles."

He didn't mention that such weakness could also be the result of improper care while she was nursing a litter of puppies. Doc had suggested that they keep that information between the two of them until it could be verified.

"Come up to my office after you put her away, Johnny, and we'll go over what's needed. It'll take some effort, but she's in her prime and should bounce back quickly." Ken paused, still smiling, and glanced conspiratorially at Anna before continuing. "One more thing, Johnny. I've decided to look for a new kennel boy to take your place in the barn for the summer. I want you to help me out in the specials kennel full time from now on. You've shown you have a good hand with the dogs and they seem to like you. And, if it's okay with your folks, I'd like you to come along as my assistant when I head out for the local circuit next month."

Johnny's own muscles tightened when full comprehension of what his boss was saying hit him. This was the first time Mr. Lorch had said for certain that he would be taking an assistant with him to the regional shows. Johnny had felt sure that he would be the one who was chosen to go, but he hadn't wanted to count on it until he was officially invited. Now he let out a joyous whoop that startled Solitaire into staring at him, but she didn't move otherwise until he gave her the 'release' command. Even then, she just stood quietly, looking doubtful while Johnny ruffled her neck and hugged her broad head close to his shoulder.

Ken glanced at Anna to see if she appreciated Johnny's handling abilities as much as he did, but she wore a serious expression on her face.

"What's the matter, Anna?"

"Don't you think it's strange how Solitaire don't react when Johnny's all excited like that?" she asked. "If'n it was one of my hounds down there, it would have been jumpin' out of its skin with delight at havin' pleased its master. I ain't never seen a dog so – I don't know – aloof, before. Makes me wish she really could talk and tell us all about whatever secrets she's holdin' so close inside."

Ken turned back to watch the pair in the ring and realized how right Anna was. They still had a long way to go before Solitaire would be able to give enough of herself to be successful in front of a knowing judge. He hoped Doc's investigation would soon turn up some history to explain the bitch's frosty demeanor; maybe then they could work on conditioning the Akita's spirit as well as her physique. The two sides had to go hand-in-hand if she was to bring home the 'Best-in-Show' trophy.

Solitaire's new kennel was on the east end of the row of dog runs that backed up along the rear wall of the specials building. Ken made sure to put her in a run that was located as far as possible from the squalor that was the hound pack's enclosure. Now that she seemed to be putting her emotional problems behind her, he didn't want to take any more chances with the valuable bitch. The run was ideally situated to allow Solitaire the healthy benefits of Kansas's long, sunny mornings, yet she would be protected from the scorching rays of the afternoon sun by a leafy green cottonwood tree that spread its shade over the whole area later in the day.

Located as they were, these outside runs did not need doghouses. Instead, a small opening in the wall behind each one led to a cool and private kennel inside the specials building. Thin metal chains, hung closely together, dropped over the opening to make a fly-proof curtain that helped to keep the interior clean and cool while allowing the dogs to enter and leave at their own will. There were solid drop-down doors for the inside 'dormitories' in case it became necessary to keep the animal more confined, whether it be for the sake of cleanliness, health problems, or aggression.

As Johnny and Solitaire entered the specials building, the inhabitants lent their varied voices to the excited greeting that had begun outside with the baying of Anna's hounds. Shrill yips and yelps from the toy breeds combined with the frenzied barking of the spaniels and retrievers and the deep 'awoofs' of the larger working types into a symphony of sorts. Johnny laughed happily at the racket they were creating and called greetings to the dogs he knew as he walked past.

Padding alongside the boy, Solitaire seemed to be ignoring all the fuss as being beneath her dignity, but she was actually listening intently for any voice in the din that made sense, not just noise.

Johnny opened the door to a kennel inside the building for Solitaire to enter. There was an entry gate on the outside run as well, but it was better for her to get used to the new sights and smells while she was in the smaller enclosure. She would discover the doorway and venture out into the open run when she was ready.

Solitaire obediently walked through the small door into the new kennel and spun immediately to look askance at Johnny. She had enjoyed their short outing enough to feel frustration at being confined again so soon.

"Sorry, Solitaire," Johnny began, kneeling to be closer to her sad, dark face. He imagined he saw confusion in Solitaire's small eyes and the furrows on her brow seemed deeper than usual. "Poor girl, I know how hard it must be for you to be stuck in these cages all the time, but it's only for a little longer. I'm going to go and talk with Mr. Lorch right now to see what he wants me to do about getting you some real exercise. You just relax and make yourself at home for a while. I've got a hunch you and I will be doing all the running around we can handle real soon."

Solitaire still looked dubious, but Johnny's happy mind was already developing plans for getting his charge in shape.

"I know what we'll do, Solitaire. If it's okay with the boss, I'll bring my bike tomorrow morning and we can go out early, before it gets too hot, and run those big feet off of you. Would you like that, girl?"

He fancied he saw her features relax finally as, with a sigh, Solitaire turned from him to investigate her new surroundings. It didn't take long before she found the opening behind the fly-curtain and passed through it to find herself in the fresh air and sunshine of the outside run.

G'day, Mate! Well, they finally let you out of that display case, did they? I guessed this was where they were going to put you. I don't usually spend much time over this way. New building, so no rats yet. Hey, how do they expect I'm going to get in here? These new runs don't have many holes, do they?

Solitaire would have expressed her pleasure at seeing her old friend in these new surroundings, especially since he seemed in good spirits with a new puzzle to solve, but Jack didn't wait for her to finish her thought. Instead, he continued what he had been doing before she arrived. She was left to watch while he ran up and down outside the fencing, looking for a giveaway sag in the mesh, sniffing for softer earth, trying to find a way in. In the end he came up empty, but that small failure didn't sap his spirit.

No worries, m'Lady, I'll try inside. There's always a way, I say, sometimes you just have to look a little harder! And then he vanished.

Moments later, a fresh outburst from the show dogs inside the building told Solitaire that the Aussie was in there. She carefully nosed the fly-curtain aside and re-entered the dim sleeping area. There was Jack, nose to the ground, creeping around outside her cage like a frightened cockroach, checking every nook and cranny for a way to break into her kennel.

Solitaire dutifully examined the inside of her pen in an effort to help, but the well-bred Akita had never even thought of trying to escape from her kennels before and didn't have any idea of what she should be looking for.

This cage was constructed of slender steel bars instead of mesh like the outside runs. Through the bars on one side, she could see the nearby east wall of the building, which was lined with rows of hooks holding a wide array of dog-related tackle. On the front side of her cage was a tiny door that opened independently from the main one. Her water bowl was strung on a steel frame inside the smaller door. That would be to reduce the risk of a breakout during feeding, she surmised, proud that her mind was moving in the right direction. Plywood provided a secure wall on the third side, between her kennel and the next one in line. Solitaire had seen dogs fight over who 'owned' the common wall in some kennels, and though she had never had the problem, she appreciated the extra privacy that the wood provided. The fourth side of her cage backed up to the concrete block wall of the building and contained the opening she had just entered from her outside run. When she looked up, she saw a strong grate made of the same steel bars as the sides of the kennel.

It seemed hopeless, and Solitaire soon tired of looking for a way out. She decided to leave the problem of entry for the more experienced Aussie to solve, and lay down for a nap. As she drifted off, she absently wondered what strange circumstance could have taught Jack to regard breaking into and out of places as a personal challenge.

Got it! A head-clearing, nose-rattling snort of triumph wakened Solitaire a short while later. She looked up to see the dauntless Aussie standing on the other side of the bars next to her water bowl, obviously very excited.

Didn't you notice this little door, m'Lady? Of course you didn't, it's much too small for you to use and besides, you can't possibly open it from the inside, can you? Of course you didn't think anything of it. But they build these cages to keep dogs in, don't they? Never to keep a dog out, do they? Behold the expert, Madame!

Jack rose up on his hind legs to get closer to the door's steel latch. It wound around the framing bar, then bent inward to enclose a cage wire and back to the outside where, with a final twist, it snugged down over a horizontal bar to lock the door in place. All of Solitaire's immense strength would not have been enough to pull the wire latch inward, but One-eyed Jack simply gnawed on the outside end of the lock until he got a good hold and was able to turn it upward, freeing the door to spring back, wide open.

Solitaire was very impressed by her friend's clever feat. She tucked her chin in and got that strange slit-eyed, low-eared look that Jack was getting used to as a sign of extreme pleasure for an Akita. He avoided the water bowl and leaped lightly through the opening to land between her gigantic paws.

Solitaire lowered her muzzle to let him know how clever she thought he was, and was alarmed to smell a bit of fresh blood on Jack's mouth. He hurriedly licked it away, tossing his bushy head to show his lack of concern and assured her that he would get the hang of that latch soon, no worries. Just another one of life's little challenges. And a terrier never backs down from a challenge!

CHAPTER 18

Next morning, true to his word, Johnny wheeled into the dirt compound of Welsely Farms and Kennels just after dawn's yellow light had set the surrounding wheat fields aglow.

Though he had gotten up with the birds, he still hadn't had enough time to finish his home chores before he wanted to leave, and his father had met him on the porch, demanding an explanation. Johnny thought he could justify his omission by explaining how important Mr. Lorch said it was that he start Solitaire's roadwork today, but that only made his father angrier. An ugly scene had followed during which the elder Wales demanded that his son quit his job at Welsely's 'once and for all' and stay home to help his family with their own overly-large burden of work.

Desperate at the prospect of losing his job and his only opportunity to see more of the world than he could from the seat of a tractor, Johnny had tried to explain to his father how important his involvement with Welsely's – and the great Akita bitch – was to him.

"God made dogs to be slaves to Man," was his father's angry response. "It ain't the other way around. Yet you're telling me that you choose to leave your own family in a bind just so you can run off and serve a dumb animal?"

Disagreement had degraded to argument, and then his father's frustration had taken physical form when he backhanded Johnny, sending the boy sprawling against the veranda railings.

The sight of blood dribbling from his son's split lip seemed to quell the senior Wales's rage. When he reached to help Johnny get up, his apology was sincere.

"I'm sorry, boy, but I can't let you have your way in this. There ain't nobody else! Five generations of Wales's have worked this farm. Do you think you're the first one to rebel against this way of life? Hell, I know it's a hard life, but it's a good one." There was a great wistfulness in his eyes when he promised, "You'll come back to the land, son."

Johnny's feelings of shame and defiance had made him brush his father's helping hand away. He got up and walked off the porch without speaking, but when he picked up his bike to leave, his father had become furious again.

"You'll learn to love this farm, Johnny, even if I have to force you to, same as my pa done me!" he shouted.

Johnny had paused to return his father's glare. "You can hit me all you want, pa," he said quietly, "but you're never going to make me love this farm."

The two strong-willed characters had stared at each other a long while, each waiting for the other to back down. Neither did. When tiny droplets formed in the corner of his father's eyes and began to course down the worn leather of his cheeks, Johnny had looked away quickly and raced off down the driveway on his bike, blinded by his own emotional tears.

The ride between farms was long because Johnny couldn't cut across the fields as he usually did when he walked. He made good use of the distance, working the pedals of his bicycle hard until he arrived breathless but calmer in the kennelyard. He stopped off where a hose hung on the side of the house to wash away the blood from his mouth and the salt of dried tears from his eyes.

Sounds of morning, quiet coughing and the clinking of cooking utensils, drifted from the kitchen. Rather than refuse the invitation for coffee that he knew would come from Ms. Welsely, he dashed by the screen door and continued on his way to the specials building and Solitaire. He wasn't sure that his emotions were completely under control yet and didn't want to embarrass himself further in the company of people.

Solitaire was already outside in her run when Johnny entered the kennel room, but she poked her head back through the curtain when the other dogs barked their greetings to him.

"I guess you guys think you're going to get breakfast early, huh?" he joked, already feeling more comfortable surrounded by canines. "Jeez! If you're going to set up a racket like this every morning, I'd better plan on picking Solitaire up outside from now on. Quiet down, now. You'll have everybody running out here in a panic."

Unlike the poor animals in the barn who seldom saw the full light of day, Ken's specials got a great deal of attention between show training and grooming, and were well exercised. They settled down rapidly once they realized that Johnny was on a specific errand and that it did not include them. Only a wistful groan now and then reminded him of their eagerness for his company. He wished he could take them all out this morning and let them run free beside his bicycle as he pedaled down the long, straight country road.

"That'd be some sight, huh Solitaire?"

The Akita was fully inside now, waiting in her kennel like all of the other dogs to see what Johnny was going to do. It wasn't until he was quite near her cage that he noticed the small feeding door was open again.

"Darn! There must be something wrong with that door. I know I closed it properly after I fed you last night, but it's sprung open again. Well, let's go for our run first. I'll fix it when we get back."

He turned to the wall of tack where the assortment of dog equipment would do any pet shop proud. There was almost everything, from long, flat leather leads in many thicknesses that were used for obedience training; to short, rolled nylon 'tags' that were left attached to the collar of the bigger dogs when Ken was going to do some off-lead work. Ken believed that you never know when you might need to reach out and grab an errant dog and these made it easier to do so. There was also a great variety in size and color of 'all-in-one' rolled nylon show leads with adjustable collars for the conformation ring.

Complementing the leashes was a collection of collars; silver chain chokes, colorful rolled nylon slips, quality leathers, and some odd pieces of purely decorative value. A few couplers and extending leads rounded out the collection.

The only types of leashes missing were the most popular ones for the pet owner, those made of chain or flat nylon. Mr. Lorch said the first was no good for the dog and the second no good for the handler.

After considering all of his options, Johnny unhooked a six-foot leather lead, only three quarters of an inch wide, but well-stitched with a solid brass clasp on it.

"This'll do, girl. I don't like those heavy leads. Too hard to hold onto. And if you're going to break this one, you're probably going to pull me clean off my bike first, so what's the difference, huh?" He checked her expression, which seemed calm but interested, so he went on talking. "But you're going to be a lady today, I know. You still don't have the energy to cause me any real trouble. Mr. Lorch agrees with that. And by the time you do, you'll be trained. Or at least we'll know what to expect from you."

Johnny reached for one of the largest collars hanging on the wall.

"Mr. Lorch said one of these big-link chokes would be best. We don't want to rub any bald spots into your neck, do we? But we don't want you slipping out and running off, either."

Yesterday at their meeting, Ken had begun in earnest to teach Johnny the dog trade. He had pointed out the fact that, though the Akita's head was large, especially for a female, her neck was also incredibly thick and she could easily back out of a buckle collar. Also, in case Johnny needed to control her, chain was the best option. Nylon is just as strong, but a big-link chain was more comfortable and less likely to hurt the coat, to his way of thinking. Besides, often just hearing the rattle of the chain tightening up is enough of a correction for a sensitive dog, avoiding the need to 'choke' her as the name suggests.

Johnny squatted to open the low door of Solitaire's kennel and quickly slipped the collar over her flattish head. She accommodated him by lowering her ears and stood without pushing until he had snapped the lead in place, then started forward.

Suddenly, a small black and tan bullet shot out from between her paws and impacted on Johnny's chest. Taken by surprise, the boy nearly fell backward before he realized there was nothing to fear.

"Jack, you idiot! You scared me to death. What are you doing in there?" 'How did you get in there?' might have been a better question, but Johnny had already put two and two together and come to realize how the feed door had gotten open.

Jack was pleased to see Johnny, too! He had been sleeping late this morning, enjoying the comfort of Solitaire's new bed after a full night of guard duty. He had barked when the kennel boy came in, but so had everyone else and Johnny hadn't paid any attention to him. Well, he didn't need anything right then, so he hadn't seen any reason to leave his bed so early – not, that is, until he heard the click of a lead being attached to Solitaire's collar! Jack had come wide awake instantaneously. That meant that his friend was going out on an adventure and, of course, she would want him to accompany her!

"I'm going to have to talk with Ms. Welsely and Mr. Lorch about you, Jack," Johnny was still scolding. "When you open that door, Solitaire can't get to her water. But if we lock you out, you're just going to worry yourself ragged until you find another way in, aren't you little guy?"

That sounded about right to Jack and he wriggled under Johnny's hand to show his agreement.

Solitaire breathed a shallow snort. *The boy could have said he was going to tie your tail to your topknot, and as long as he said it in a kind tone of voice, you would have agreed, Jack! If you must be so demonstrative with humans, you really ought to learn how to communicate with them better!*

Solitaire's light scolding didn't upset Jack; he had heard the same complaint from old Owl for so long that it was like water off a Labrador's back by now.

In a lighter mood for Jack's cavorting, Johnny led Solitaire to where his bike waited up against the front wall. Jack hovered close by, but Johnny warned him off following them.

"Now look, Jack," he explained in a serious tone. "I know you like a run, but we're not playing today. This is work for Solitaire, and I don't want you slowing us up. You'd better stay here."

Jack did understand what 'stay here' meant, but chose to ignore that. He waited while Johnny took a strong hold on the leather lead and began walking his bicycle out of the compound, calling to Solitaire to follow, then he fell right into step behind them.

By the time the little group was past the farmhouse it was obvious that Solitaire had no fear of the turning bicycle wheels, so Johnny mounted up. Pedaling slowly at first, he watched the Akita carefully to make sure she knew what was expected of her and wouldn't bolt. He had faith that she wouldn't purposely harm him through willful disobedience; she had shown herself completely trustworthy on a lead. But he also respected her size and knew that she could easily upset his bike, doing a lot of damage to him in the process if something was to spook her.

He needn't have worried. Solitaire stayed on the left side of the bike, about three feet off on a loose lead, and trotted effortlessly. It was as Mr. Lorch had guessed; she was very experienced with this type of roadwork. Johnny recalled seeing a lot of news videos from Japan that showed the people riding bicycles everywhere. He guessed it was natural that their dogs would accompany them.

Jack was showing off, as usual. For a while, he ran beside Solitaire; then he sped up and dashed across in front of her and the bike, pretending he was chasing something interesting on the far side of the drive; then he fell behind just to show his mates how quickly he could catch up again.

When they reached the end of the driveway, Johnny again ordered Jack to 'go home'. The Aussie stayed behind the gate as the kennel boy shut and locked it, his expression immensely sorrowful. But as soon as he remounted, Jack bolted off to find one of his many trenches and popped out on the other side of the fence, in front of Johnny and Solitaire. Without altering her pace, Solitaire showed her appreciation of the terrier's wile with a judicious wave of her bushy tail as she passed. Johnny gave up.

Johnny's instructions were to keep the Akita at a steady trot for that first morning to see how she would handle it. He was impressed that, despite Jack's teasing and playful shenanigans, Solitaire never seemed inclined to break that pace. She behaved like a disciplined athlete, enjoying the run out in the fresh air but still concentrating on working her cage-atrophied muscles smoothly in order to build strength without stressing them.

Solitaire was enjoying herself for the first time in many weeks. It was wonderful to feel the early morning breeze flowing along her body, to work out the kinks in her powerful frame, and to enjoy the antics of her Australian friend as he zipped back and forth, exhilarated by her company. She was even feeling benevolent toward the youth riding on the bicycle beside her. He did seem to be trying hard to win her favor and this bit of freedom was a step in the right direction, as far as she was concerned.

Johnny noticed Solitaire shrug as if she was shaking a load off her shoulders, then pick up speed ever so slightly. If her trot had seemed effortless before, now the giant Akita seemed to be floating above the tarmac, she moved so lightly. He had the impression that she could go on long after his legs became tired of pedaling. He would have liked to test her, but Mr. Lorch had been firm about how long each day's roadwork should last. He called to get her attention while he slowed then turned back toward Welsely's.

On the return trip, Jack was not feeling quite as energetic. He had exhausted even his tremendous energy performing the zany antics of the first half of the run. Johnny began to feel sorry for him because the terrier's oversized sense of pride wouldn't let him lag and he was having to work very hard to keep up. His tongue lolled out the side of his mouth, long and flat as a Mexican tortilla, so that the maximum amount of surface area was available for evaporation. Johnny decided they had better stop for a rest before the little guy tripped on it. They were only half a mile from their gate now, so Solitaire had realized sufficient benefit from their run. Besides, Johnny really wasn't sure if the terrier could keep up the pace without hurting himself.

He stopped the bicycle and set it on the side of the road. Leash in hand, he called to the dogs to follow him into the wide ditch where they would get a small respite from the warming sun. Jack found the shade and immediately threw himself, belly down, onto the dark, cool earth. Solitaire seemed amused by this. She watched while Johnny made himself comfortable too, but did not lie down herself. It had been a long time since she'd been able to run in the open air and she didn't want to miss even a moment of this outing.

Like many show dogs, Solitaire had lived a life with few freedoms. She had never desired it to be any different; she knew no other way. Until recently, she had been content to live in a caring kennel surrounded by her friends, both human and canine. Even in the deepest throes of her anguish, though she wished to escape the cruelties of her life, it would never have occurred to her to attempt to break out of the physical bonds the humans placed on her. She was accustomed to being exercised one regular basis, however, and had begun to resent her confinement in the quarantine run. Like any athlete, she missed the unequaled sense of well-being that comes with strenuous physical activity.

This morning's exercise had certainly not tired her overmuch. It had merely stimulated her body and improved her outlook. She felt new interest in her surroundings and examined them with finely tuned senses of perception. Wet nose quivering, she took in the dusty smell of the fields, the hot tarmac, and the sweetly fragrant wildflowers that grew here and there along the sides of the ditch. She perked her thick, triangular ears forward to catch the rustle of a rabbit further up the trench. Her eyes, that for so long had resembled small bits of dull black charcoal, were shining with excitement and vitality as she gazed across the fields.

While Solitaire took in her surroundings, Johnny studied her and was pleased with what he saw. Her aura was one of perfect calm. Whatever had been tormenting her was forgotten for the moment. Her coat was regaining what Johnny thought of as the 'pelt' look peculiar to the Akita, where the heavy undercoat held the shiny guard hairs away from her skin at almost the same angle all over her body, giving a very smooth outline. It looked so deep and soft that he could not contain a sudden desire to feel its lushness.

He raised a cautious hand to stroke her deep flank and felt the Akita stiffen momentarily. But then she relaxed, accepting his advances politely if not enthusiastically. As he ran his hand along her flank and down her legs, he imagined he could feel a new, firmer tone to her muscles already.

He gazed at her a long time, smiling, until she finally surrendered to his adoration and turned her countenance full on him. Her eyes were slanted against the morning sunshine and now her lower jaw dropped to allow just the tip of her pink tongue to show between the rows of strong white teeth. Johnny was sure Solitaire was grinning at him!

Johnny was feeling much better for the morning's exercise as well. The uneventful ride had given him time to think his problems through calmly, with more understanding for his father's side of the predicament, but he still felt the need to talk with somebody about it and he didn't think the dogs would mind.

While Solitaire enjoyed what was turning out to be a lovely day, Johnny poured his heart out to her. He told her of his confused relationship with his father, his longing for freedom from the dullness of everyday life on a prairie farm, his loneliness.

Solitaire had squirmed uncomfortably when Johnny began his one-sided conversation, preferring to continue on with her run. She had turned her face from him, watching him distrustfully from the side of her eyes as he spoke of his bewilderment of life in general and of his father in particular. She wondered why he was confiding in her like this. What did the boy expect of her? Didn't he realize she had problems of her own?

But no matter how hard the heart of a canine, the misery of a lonely boy can warm and soften it. While Johnny confessed his small, private dreams to her, she came to realize how young and good and innocent the lad was and she found herself drawn inexorably closer to him. In the end she lay down quietly, her head on his feet in an action meant to give him comfort, and Johnny was moved almost to tears.

"Thanks, Solitaire," he choked back the lump in his throat, "I know there's not much you can do about my problems, but it feels good just having a friend to share them with. I wish I could help you in the same way ..." He stroked the soft backs of her ears, deep in gloomy contemplation, and suddenly it came to him what he had to do.

Though he would have worked his full day at the kennel and done this extra hour with Solitaire out of love alone, he knew he had to be realistic about the fact that his father needed his help, too. He would explain to Mr. Lorch that he would have to leave early on the days he took Solitaire out. Arriving at 7:30 like this morning, and shortening his lunch to a half hour, he could put in eight hours at the kennel and still leave about 3 p.m. That way he would have more time while it was light to help his family out on their farm. Perhaps he could ask his father to trade off some of his early chores for evening ones to give him extra time in the morning for Solitaire? Johnny thought there was a good chance that he would go along with that, as long as the work was still getting done.

And he was going to apologize to his father. That decision came harder than the first one because he didn't really think the affair this morning had been his fault. But if he didn't say he was sorry, the rift between father and son would only deepen until it became like the wide chasm that kept Johnny's dad so distant from his own father.

"You know, Solitaire, I hope I'm never as rigid as my pa is." The Akita was giving him her full attention, her expression somber and interested. "Whatever he says is the way it has to be. He never gives me credit for having an original thought."

Solitaire waited patiently for him to go on.

"I know what you're thinking," he confessed. "If I really mean that, I shouldn't be embarrassed to be the one to do the apologizing now. Right?"

Solitaire raised her ears to catch the wisdom in the boy's words.

The child is becoming a man!

Johnny was overwhelmed by an intense feeling of approval such as he had never felt before, and it was radiating from – from where? From Solitaire? Could it be?

He searched the Akita's features for a sign that she understood what was happening. Her eyes were dark and kind – and something more. Instinctively, Johnny knew that extra brightness in Solitaire's eyes was pride shining through. She was proud of his decision!

A whirring growl from the ditch beside them broke the charm of the moment. Solitaire was on her feet in an instant, searching the nearby fields for danger. She had already learned to trust Jack's ears and nose to be even more sensitive than her own.

The Aussie scrambled up the side of the ditch to get a better view of the approaching pickup. Johnny stood as well, but quickly ducked behind some low brush. He had recognized the man driving the truck out of the neighboring farm's road and he should have been ashamed of his reaction, but he stayed hidden, anyway, while he watched Fleet take a set of keys out of his pocket and unlock the gate. Johnny thought it was odd that Fleet didn't fumble with the lock or the handle. In fact, his movements were so smooth that Johnny had the impression he had let himself out of this gate many times before. That intrigued Johnny, particularly because that gate and the drive beyond it led to Kell's farm.

Johnny had never been to the farm next door. It was a place no one around the kennel talked about much because Ms. Welsely raised a fit whenever Earl Kell's name was mentioned. Rumor had it that Kell was white trash from back east – probably run out of the state back there – who was trying a hand at prairie farming. Judging by the shape of his fields, he wasn't trying too hard, either. He was mean, everyone knew that, and maybe a little stupid. Stupid enough to get Ms. Welsely mad at him, anyway. She would have nothing to do with the man she called 'part skunk, part snake, and all evil'.

Of course, that opinion could be biased by the fact that Earl Kell had chased her hounds off his property with a shotgun shortly after he had moved in. In retaliation, she had forbidden him to step foot inside her property line, under threat of having the pack sicc'd on him for real, and closed the farms' common access gate off. To this day, Anna ran her hounds on the eastern acreage so she could be sure they wouldn't 'catch some kind of ornery disease from that madman'.

Now here was her kennel foreman driving through Kell's place like he owned it. Johnny's mind sprinted back to his suspicions of a few days ago, and he wondered whether Fleet's familiarity with Kell tied in with them at all.

Just seeing Fleet get out of the truck was enough to send One-eyed Jack over the edge. His growls erupted into high-pitched barks of challenge and his tiny body tensed for action. Johnny started at the sudden outburst, then quickly reached up to grab the feisty terrier before he could rush the pickup and give away their presence. Luckily, Fleet either wasn't hearing or wasn't paying attention to Jack's angry yaps.

Probably because there was a dog in the truck barking as well, Johnny realized now. The sound was quite muffled, so he figured it must be in the travel kennel that was in the truck bed. What reason would there be for Fleet to have a kennel dog in his truck, Johnny wondered. Was it one of Welsely's animals that had gotten loose somehow and he was just retrieving it? But it was still awfully early for him to be out looking for runaway. Anyway, why would Fleet be in possession of keys to Kell's gate if he had just gone over to pick up a lost dog?

Solitaire! Johnny's mind snapped back to attention. He had dropped

Solitaire's lead in his hurry to catch Jack and now he panicked, realizing what could be about to happen. He whirled back to where the Akita was still standing, taut as a bow, but mercifully unmoving. The handle end of the leather lead was lying in the dirt and he quickly stepped on it. He knew that wouldn't stop the massive dog if she decided to charge, but it might give him an extra second to reach her with his hand. He blew a relieved breath when he held the lead and had her under control again.

Solitaire had made no move to attack. She was on the alert, but seemed more curious than aggressive. Johnny was having far more problems controlling Jack, who was still struggling and pushing with his tiny paws. His front claws raked Johnny's forearm while his back ones dug furiously at Johnny's torso, catching the boy's loose shirt and bundling it around the other side of his waist.

"Hold on. Hold on, little guy. Ouch! Calm down, now, and I'll let you go." Johnny's voice was apologetic. He wondered why One-eyed Jack had that kind of effect on him – on most people. Even Fleet was sometimes known to talk to the terrier as if he were human.

He knelt quickly to deposit the indignant terrier on the ground, but held onto his collar until the truck had driven off and there was no more danger of Jack giving them away.

Once on the ground, Jack was fairly spitting with rage at his ill treatment.

Put me down! Do you think I am a toy? Aussie's are ground dogs, not lapdogs! He paused in his yapping to shake his coat out so violently that his two front feet lifted off the ground. *And this Aussie knows that if that rat, Fleet, is coming out of that driveway, he's bringing more trouble for all of us! That property is where the mother-cat caught the poisoned rat, and that's probably where the 'Sweetness that Kills' in Solitaire's bowl came from. It must have been Fleet that put it there! I'm sure of it!*

Solitaire was following along with the terrier's reasoning, but showed no surprise at his conclusions. Listening to Johnny this afternoon, she was even more convinced that it was not in the boy's nature to do anything so underhanded. That only left Fleet and the other kennel boy suspect, but the stink of evil was on Fleet.

Hush, little friend, you are raving at the wrong human. We have a distance to go before we return to the kennel, so you should conserve your energy. After that, I am thinking that it may be time to call upon your friends' vast knowledge. When we get back to our kennel, please inform The Owl and The Pussycat that I am ready to commune with them.

CHAPTER 19

"Have you noticed all of these injections are out of date, Fleet?" Doc asked, his head buried in the infirmary refrigerator. "I can't find a one to shoot that pup with this morning."

"Uh, yeah, I know, Doc," Fleet replied distractedly. "Must have happened while I was out sick. I've already called the supply company and they're sending a couple of new batches. Should be here any day now. Don't worry. If you've finished his examination, have Abel put the pup away. I'll shoot him when the new stuff comes in."

Do wouldn't let the matter drop.

"Doesn't the salesman check that when he comes by? It's not good, in a kennel this size, to be out of the proper vaccines." He began sorting through his black bag to see if he had brought any.

"Nah, I don't like salesmen coming in trying to sell me something I don't need. I just order the stuff by phone. It's a lot easier."

Doc looked at Fleet over the rim of his eyeglasses, a little skeptical.

"I hope you're careful who you deal with. You could end up having a lot of problems. Do you get the vaccines in cold?"

Fleet had little patience for answering all of these questions. Did the man think he was born yesterday? Well, there was no sense in alienating the old vet, so he gave him the only answer that would satisfy him.

"Of course. I make sure of that."

Doc's search was successful. He raised a tiny bottle up to the light and inserted a clean needle into its cap. He pulled back on the syringe, then held his breath while the liquid was sucked out. It was an old habit of his and Fleet figured it must help to steady his hand. This was the second week Doc had arrived to do his rounds sober. Fleet wondered how much longer the vet was going to stay on the wagon. He liked him better when he was drinking; at least then he didn't ask so many questions.

"You ought to take those boxes out of the fridge so you or the boys don't use them by mistake. What do you do with the old stuff, then, if the salesman doesn't pick it up? You don't ship it back?"

"Once I get full credit for it, I throw it all away. They trust Welsely's by now, and like you say, the old stuff isn't any good to anybody." Fleet turned to leave the infirmary before Doc could think of something else to bother him about.

He emerged from the dark interior of the barn into the blazing midmorning sunlight. Ken and Anna were standing by the farmhouse, looking up the long driveway, so naturally Fleet turned to see what was holding their interest. It was Johnny, riding his bicycle up the driveway with the Akita bitch trotting alongside him and One-eyed Jack balanced between his crotch and the handlebars of the bike.

"Some people have more guts than brains," he muttered bad-naturedly. He couldn't imagine why Ken was allowing Johnny to take that wild animal out onto the road where she could easily get free and molest some stranger. They were going to be sorry someday. He turned back to his duties in disgust.

Johnny grinned when he saw his bosses, but didn't dare wave in case he unbalanced Jack. The terrier hadn't taken long to adjust to co-piloting the bike and seemed to relish the precariousness of his position. He extended himself far forward, putting his small weight directly over his forelegs so that he appeared to be the one steering the bicycle, and held his muzzle proudly into the breeze.

Solitaire's gait was almost jaunty, even after her long run. Her thickly furred tail curled high and tightly over her back, her ears reached forward with enthusiasm and she, too, held her muzzle up to catch all of the marvelous wind-born scents of the country.

Anna and Ken were thoroughly enjoying the show. They had always shared with each other the pleasure of watching a beautiful animal in perfect motion, though what was perfect was, in the end, a matter of opinion. Every breed has a certain gait all its own and every judge saw it differently. However, there were basics for each type of gait that must be correct in order for the dog to be shown successfully in the ring. As the Akita came on directly in front of them, they checked that she was trotting in a straight line, shoulder to hips. There could be no 'crabbing' as Ken called it, when an animal's back legs seem to be trying to outrun its front ones. Solitaire's forelegs were straight from broad shoulders to solid paws and these rose and fell in powerful rhythm, neither twisting nor flopping lazily.

"Now that looks like a dog with a purpose," Anna stated delightedly. She held that a canine member of the Working Group should always give the impression that it knows exactly where it is headed and the shortest way to get there.

Ken motioned Johnny to make a turn in front of the house and head away again so that they could see the Akita's hind movement, which was as strong and straight as the front. Mutually impressed, they slyly congratulated each other on what a fine eye they had for a dog.

As the bike slowed to a halt in front of them, Solitaire adjusted her pace then stood, panting lightly, while Johnny let Jack jump off, then dismounted himself.

"Well, Dogs' Paws!" Anna gasped in mock surprise. "What happened to Jack? He looks like somebody stepped on his tongue and squashed it all out of shape!"

They all laughed at the way Jack curled both sides of his swollen tongue up and inward, like cocktail ham rolls, before swallowing it back into his mouth and rushing to do his traditional jig in front of his mistress.

"I told him to go home a hundred times, Ms. Welsely," Johnny tried to explain, "but you know Jack. He just kept following us. I figured he'd tire quick and go back, but he stuck with us the whole way. Heck, with his crazy running around, he must have gone at least four times the distance Solitaire and I did! I finally took pity on him and let him ride the last bit. He took to it real easy, too!"

The three humans laughed again at the rumpled-looking terrier, which pleased Jack so much that he rose on his hind legs for another dance.

"You're gonna kill yourself one day, mister," Anna warned him. "It'll be a sad day, truly, but I'll hafta say, 'I told you so'. You can't just keep runnin' yourself out like you do all the time. You gotta rest sometimes, fella."

Jack wasn't sure if he was really being told off or not. He looked at Solitaire for guidance, but she didn't appear to be paying attention. Confused, he decided to lie down until he was sure. That brought on another round of laughter. Humans! Who could understand them? But he was too tired for their silly games right now. He stood up again and headed off at a slightly slower pace than usual to find a full water bucket and, maybe, some more sympathetic company.

As he crossed the sunny kennelyard, Doc was just leaving the barn. Jack liked the veterinarian. When he had lost his eye, it was Doc who had operated on him and helped to take away the searing pain. With each visit from the good doctor, the hurt had lessened until he soon felt as good as new. Jack repaid the vet's kindness by giving him a little special attention each time he saw him. Not anything like the circus he put on for Anna, but more than he showed for most other humans. He swerved to put himself in Doc's path.

"Hey, One-eyed Jack! How're you doin'?" Doc always greeted him in an accent closely resembling Anna's in an effort to put him at ease and show friendship. Jack appreciated Doc's efforts and now ran the short

SOLITAIRE, A Dog Story

distance to his feet. Like Anna, Doc never embarrassed Jack by picking him up. He didn't mind squatting down to the terrier's level in order to pet him.

"How's the eye, fella? No problems today? Goodness, you look like you could use some water." Doc looked around and spied an almost empty bucket under a tap on the wall of the barn. He dumped the warmish water and refilled it to the brim with cool water straight out of the ground. When he put it down, Jack jumped up on the side, letting his front paws dangle in the coolness, and drank his fill. That Doc sure knew what a going dog needed!

Jack stood down and licked the dripping ends of his moustache. He snorted his thanks to his friend then was off to do his own rounds. He was running very late this morning, thanks to Johnny! He nearly ran into Fleet's broad boots as he entered the barn and did a quick sidestep out of trouble. He didn't like the foreman much more than Solitaire did, but he did respect him!

"Abel!" Fleet yelled louder than was necessary, making Jack wince. "Bring that Yorkie litter in here and let's get going on these shots."

Shots? Time for a terrier to be going! And Jack disappeared into the dimness of the back of the barn.

Abel arrived with the pups, one stuck in his armpit and one in each hand. "They're here, Fleet. But hadn't we ought to wait for the new vaccine like Doc said?" He stood, still holding the struggling puppies, and waited uncomfortably while Fleet finished his preparations.

"Well, Doc ain't here now, is he?" Fleet finally replied. The sarcasm in his voice was meant to be a warning to Abel. "That old man is a royal pain, especially now he's off his liquor. He doesn't know what he's talking about; he's just complaining to hear himself speak."

Abel still looked doubtful, so Fleet reluctantly decided to explain in order to avoid future problems with him. He didn't need another 'Johnny' watching him behind his back all the time.

"These shots are fine, son. They've been kept in the refrigerator. It doesn't matter if they're a little old. I've used them a lot like that and haven't had any problems. That date's just the way manufacturers try to keep track of their stuff – it's not that important." He gave Abel a stern look to back up his words then grabbed one of the Yorkies from his hands. The puppy yelped in shock as the needle punctured his skin.

Abel looked as though he wanted to push the issue further, then shrugged it off and deposited the other two pups on the grooming table.

"That's it, Abel," Fleet said, picking up another puppy. "You're not getting paid to do the worrying. As far as I know, I am."

The day was a slow one in the barn in spite of the fact that they were short one kennel boy. Even Fleet had to acknowledge that the boys had done well while he was in the hospital. But then, he corrected himself, maybe that just showed that he had left everything in good running order and they had only had to continue his routine.

Whatever the reason for it, he was relieved that Ken hadn't found it necessary to spend too much time in the barn. That man knew too much. Johnny was smart, but his only kennel experience was here at Welsely's and all he knew he had learned under Fleet's tutelage. That had effectively blinded him to certain things. Ken, on the other hand, definitely had the experience to ferret out Fleet's little deals if he had a mind to. Thankfully, he didn't have the guts to do anything about it.

CHAPTER 20

After supper and the washing-up were done, Anna and Ken sat a long time on the wide veranda that stretched across the front of the farmhouse. Ken was finally enjoying a little respite from the stress of the last two weeks, and Anna was content to spend the long summer evening listening to him expound on his past successes in the show ring and his long-range plans for the new Akita on the national circuit. That was, of course, if she proved to have a more reliable temperament than it had at first seemed.

As usual, Anna was impressed with Ken's considerable knowledge of dogs, and show dogs in particular. It was good to see him excited about Solitaire again, too, now that the likelihood of her surviving this unhappy chapter in her life had improved greatly.

There were still a few problems to overcome before Ken's goal was fulfilled; he had been the first to point out that they hadn't heard the full story from Japan yet. But tonight, by unspoken agreement, the conversation between Ken and Anna retained a feeling of optimism as they discussed Welsely's future.

When the sun began to dip below the heads of the tall grasses in the distance, Ken declared himself tired and excused himself to complete a bit of paperwork before going to bed.

Anna watched the sun go down alone. As the bright orb sank, it seemed to melt like country butter, its warm golden color spreading slowly across the outlying fields. Then, just when the sun seemed ready to disappear altogether, its dying rays were picked up by some low clouds on the horizon and reflected back skyward in an encore of brilliance, lighting the world for a few moments longer. It was a wonder to Anna how, after the multitudes of evenings she had sat on the front porch of the old farmhouse alone and watched the prairie sunset, she could still be so deeply moved by its unearthly beauty.

In the twilight that followed, Anna left her seat on the veranda and went to the kitchen for the dish of leftovers she always kept for her hounds. Ken wouldn't allow his show dogs to be fed tidbits of human food, but the pack was hers to spoil all she wanted, and it went against her country logic to throw away perfectly good food when it gave the dogs so much pleasure.

She made her way along the graveled pathway toward the specials kennel and the hound run to the right of it. Before she was halfway there, she could hear the soft whining and snuffling of her pack as they lined up along the front of their run to greet her and collect their nightly morsels.

As she came closer, she crooned softly to them to keep them quiet. She often boasted to Ken that if anyone but she tried to steal into the area, her hounds would raise the whole county with their baying, as much a warning as the foghorns they sounded like, so he ought to be thankful that these guardians were here to watch over the fancy dogs in his specials building.

Anna fed the hounds and watched a moment as they worked out who was going to get what. She didn't worry about them fighting with each other over the food because hers was an old pack and their particular hierarchy had been worked out long ago. As usual, Lola, the matriarch of the brood, took her choice of the best pieces first, then fell back to let the more dominant mature males eat, and finally the youngsters. Here, there was a little squabbling, but the food was gone in instants and the ill feelings with it. Soon the entire pack was snoring again and Anna felt alone.

Without even making up her mind to do so, the old woman continued around to the rear of the building. The last remnants of the sun's light shone on the metalwork enclosing the back runs, making the collection stand out in the dusk like a shrine. Anna felt drawn to the end pen as if entranced. She wanted to go to the Akita, to spend some time with her, before turning in for the night.

She was a little surprised to see that Johnny was already there, as well as momentarily vexed to discover that she was not the only one her hounds would let pass. The boy didn't seem to notice her approach and remained where he was, sitting on the hard ground outside the kennel, his face pressed close to the smooth wire.

Inside the run, as far from the boy as she could get, lay the great Akita bitch, in a stately posture of repose. Her raised head faced Anna in acknowledgment of her presence, but no other movement showed whether or not she was pleased about it.

Anna hesitated, unsure now of her reason for being there. She felt uncomfortable, as if she had blundered in on something deeply personal. But the Akita's obsidian gaze drew her closer until Anna found herself resting against the wire fencing next to where Johnny sat.

The big dog raised her muzzle slightly to collect Anna's scent in nostrils and mouth, then her ears jerked forward in response to the woman's barely audible whisper, "*SOLITAIRE!*" She commanded her body to be still so that the humans would detect no anxiety in her outward posture, but she couldn't stop the excited tremor that raced through her insides.

Only moments ago, Johnny had arrived to sit, sobbing, outside her run. For the first time since her arrival, she had allowed compassion to overcome suspicion and had reached out to him with her mind. It was no more than a caress, meant to soothe the troubled youth; but it seemed the old mistress had felt it, too, for she had come to bask in the warmth of that light touch.

"Evenin', Solitaire," Anna greeted the dog again, a little louder this time so that Johnny might hear her as well. "Excuse me for interruptin', ma'am, but was this a private audience you was holdin' or can anybody join in?"

The Akita continued to stare at Anna keenly, ears forward and twitching, but was not forthcoming with any direct response. Anna laughed at herself when she realized she had been holding her breath, waiting for one.

"What a silly old she-goat I've become." She looked down to the boy sitting on the ground a little way from her. "But you know, Johnny, just between you and me, I still get the strangest feelin' around this dog – like we should be the ones listenin' to her and not the other way around."

When he heard his name spoken, Johnny seemed to realize for the first time that he had company. He broke free of his stupor and jumped up to find something for his boss to sit on, stammering an apology for his momentary lack of manners.

Anna touched him softly on the shoulder to calm the lad. She saw that he had been crying, his eyes still glittery in the low light. Another argument with his old man, she surmised. With the wisdom of age, she chose not to comment on his distress, instead lowering herself unsteadily to a seat on the proffered upturned feed bucket. After a few moments spent admiring the stars that were just beginning to appear in the night sky, she spoke again.

"Lovely evenin', ain't it? Still too early for turnin' in, so I thought I'd take a walk. And since I had a bit of cogitatin' to do, I thought I'd talk to Solitaire about it for a while. If you don't mind losin' the time, maybe you could help?"

Johnny watched her, waiting for her to continue. His look of concern, barely discernible in the growing darkness, made her feel a little self-conscious. She cleared her throat before beginning and was honored with the Akita's immediate attention. Blacker than the approaching night, Solitaire's eyes still managed to convey serious interest in whatever it was that Anna was about to say.

The regal dog's full attention on her made Anna feel nervous again. It was an odd sensation for her, being tongue-tied in front of a dog. Normally Anna had problems dealing with people, not animals. Animals had never let her down.

"You know, Johnny, that's the difference between dogs and people," she began thoughtfully. "When you talk with folk, you gotta be so careful of *how* you say things to 'em, as much as *what* you say to 'em. I ain't never been very good at expressin' myself in the proper manner. The Kansas prairie can teach you a whole lot, but communication skills ain't on the list.

Probably why it's so lonely for a lot of folks out here – they get used to wanderin' in and out of each other's' lives without ever really talkin' except about the price of corn or what's for dinner. Then one day when they have somethin' important to say, they just can't get it out."

Anna waited to see if Johnny wanted to add anything to the conversation, but the boy remained silent so she went on.

"Dogs, on the other hand, well, I always figured they could understand what you were getting' at, no matter how poorly you spoke. Whenever I've felt the loneliness, I've always been able to come out here and share my feelin's with my hounds. Even when my pa was still alive, and I couldn't make him understand the things a young girl worries about, I could always talk to my dogs. 'Course, they never gave me any good advice – nor bad neither, for that matter – but they listened and I felt they understood."

Johnny nodded his head emphatically to show that he was following Anna's train of thought, but he was unable to speak around the lump in his throat.

"You know what's been botherin' me about this girl, Johnny? Look how far away she's lyin', like she don't even want our friendship. There ain't a dog in the world that don't need people. Every dog needs a special person that they can bond with, someone to obey and be a companion to. 'Course, not all of 'em are lucky enough to find that special person right off, but I think that they're never really happy until they do."

"Like the kennel dogs," Johnny offered, finally trusting his voice not to crack. "They bark and jump around when anybody comes by, but they don't really care who it is. They're just bored.

"Did you ever notice their eyes, Ms. Welsely? Sometimes they look kind of blank. Like hopeless, you know? Abel says they're just stupid, but I think they just need a home of their own, and they know they don't have much chance of finding one in that barn. I'll bet if any of those dogs had a proper home with a family, they'd be totally different."

Ouch! That cut a little close to the bone, and Anna felt the pangs of guilt. She had always been aware that keeping canines in metal cages strictly for the purpose of profit was wrong, but what other choice did she have to make a living way out here? It was for that reason that she had always kept the kennel dogs at a distance, never allowing herself to get too close to them. One-eyed Jack was the nearest thing to a pet she had ever had. Even her hounds were more involved with members of their own pack than they were with her.

"Like Jack," Johnny continued, making Anna wince again. "He worships you, that's obvious enough. I used to think that he was livelier than the others because he was free to go wherever he pleased, but I've been noticing that he's the happiest when you come outside and he can be with you. He'd probably even stay in a cage if it was by your side all day long."

"Ha!" Anna sniffed, but she sat up a little straighter, tickled by that thought. "I wouldn't like to go so far as to say that, but you are gettin' my meanin', anyway."

Johnny leaned forward to press his face against the mesh of the Akita's enclosure.

"Do you really think that's what's wrong with Solitaire, Ms. Welsely?"

Anna was a little surprised at the conviction in her own voice when she replied, "I'd bet on it, son! That dog has a soul so full of loneliness it tears me up just to look at her. She's been searching for her true master for a long time, but a high-class animal like that wouldn't bond herself to just anyone. It would have to be a completely equal relationship, and not many humans have that much love to give."

"I could give Solitaire all the love she needs," Johnny whispered huskily, "if only she'd let me try."

Anna was glad for the darkness that hid her eyes, misty with sympathy for the teenager. She knew his need equaled that of the Akita, but she couldn't find the words to comfort him, so she sat in silence and wished, along with him, for true friendship to develop between the two desperate souls.

***

Do you remember the barking we heard when we saw Fleet this morning? Jack asked before he was all the way through the tiny entryway to Solitaire's kennel.

The Akita had come inside after her two human visitors left, but so far sleep had eluded her troubled mind. She made room for the terrier in her kennel while she assured him that she remembered the events of this morning quite well.

Well, I thought I knew the tones, so I had a look around the barn to see if anybody was missing. Nobody was, as far as I could see. But when I went by the stud section, I was hit full in the face by the wonderful aroma of a bitch in heat! Now, I enjoy such things as well as the next dog, but there aren't supposed to be any breeding bitches in that area. I figured I'd best investigate!

Well, I didn't have to go too far, mate. All of the dogs within four rows in all directions had their lusty noses pointed in the direction of the culprit's kennel. And there lay Moses, looking a bit abashed at the commotion he was causing, I don't mind saying.

Solitaire kept a dignified attitude in spite of the nature of Jack's news. This was a breeding kennel, after all.

I don't understand what you are proposing, Jack. Is this not in the normal routine for a place such as this? And who, or what, is a 'Moses'?

No, no, Madame! Well, it is normal in one way, of course. . . Jack was so eager to continue with his tale that he had been hopping up and down while Solitaire asked her questions. Now he stopped abruptly, as though he had suddenly remembered his manners. The Akita may be his friend, but she was still a female and probably didn't enjoy listening to such common talk. He dropped his ears and tail in quick apology, then concentrated on keeping all four feet on the floor while he answered her question in a more formal tone.

I am sorry, m'Lady! I keep forgetting that you haven't made the acquaintance of many of the kennel population. Jack couldn't hold this deliberate posture for long, though; his tail refused to stay still when he thought about Moses. *To tell you the truth, Madame, I've often wondered what Moses is, myself! All I know for sure is that he's kind of a rusty black color and is covered with long ringlet-kind of things. They hang everywhere, even over his face. I don't know how he can see like that. Obviously he sees well enough for what Fleet wants him to do, though!*

Jack's tail seemed intent on winding him up and he started jumping around merrily again while Solitaire tried to puzzle through what he was telling her. The creases between her eyes relaxed once she figured it out.

Ah! a Puli, no doubt. Moses is a Puli. The breed originated in Hungary, I believe. Quite obscure. I'm impressed to hear of one locally. But I still don't understand what the problem is.

Jack wagged his tiny head back and forth in exasperation.

The problem, m'Lady, is that the scent I smelled on Moses does not conform to that of any of the ladies around here. Fleet is up to his old tricks again!

Solitaire's brow furrowed again, so Jack threw his efforts at politeness aside and blurted out his discovery.

Fleet has been kidnapping dogs from here and taking them over there — the place he was coming out of when we saw him this morning — to provide service for their bitches. I'm sure of it, as sure as I know that a Rottweiler has teeth!

He used to do it all the time, but I think our mistress got suspicious and he had to stop. Our Anna does what she can to keep this kennel decent for us dogs and she wouldn't like to know that any of her studs had been used in a hell-hole like the one next door, you can be sure of that! Jack's tiny shoulders slumped. *Poor Moses, his days may be numbered. There is such a stink about that place that even I don't go willingly anymore. But I have been once or twice.*

The little fellow popped his one eye, then gave Solitaire such an exaggerated wink that her facade of dignity melted altogether.

Oh, Jack! You are such a scalawag! Is there nothing you haven't done — or wouldn't do, given the opportunity?

The Aussie feigned hurt feelings over Solitaire's teasing.

Madame, you do me a disservice! It wasn't my idea to go over there, but there aren't too many Australian Terriers like me around and Fleet kidnapped me the same as he did poor Moses! The first time, anyway. After the first time, I made my way over pretty regularly. Nobody seemed to mind, either. I was appreciated!

He drew himself up to his full fourteen inches and tossed the sandy hair out of his eye. But he deflated quickly as he continued his story.

That was a long time ago, before things got really bad over there. Things went downhill pretty quickly once those two started filling their kennels. They never understood that when you've got more population, you've got to work a lot harder to keep the place up. Or maybe they just didn't care. Whatever.

The little lass they had reserved for me died in her first whelping and they never replaced her, so I wasn't invited over anymore.

Solitaire felt the terrier was going inside himself to a place he seldom cared to visit. She laid her chin on the floor and waited patiently while he tried to arrange the telling of his memory.

I know I come off all cocky-like, like nothing can hurt me, but I wasn't always this tough. I liked that little sheila a lot, and she liked me. She wasn't a 'communicator' or anything, but we never had any trouble knowing what each other wanted. Anywise, I had been keeping company with her up until the whelps were due and was over there the night it happened. So was Fleet. He and his fat pal were in the house, drinking and talking crazy like usual.

It started just before midnight, the whelping. It was my first, as well as her's, and we were really excited. The Owl and The Pussycat stayed home, of course, but they were using me to listen in as well. I guess they were hoping for a promising youngster to educate, being as I had been such a disappointment to them.

After a couple of hours, I knew something was wrong. My lass was fretting something awful. I could smell blood, but there was no sign of any pups. I could tell that The Pussycat was worried, too. She said she knew that humans feel pain when they give birth, but she never had felt more than a twinge or two in her five go-rounds and it didn't seem right. She tried to use her talent to calm my sheila, and take the fear away for her, but after a while even her great mind couldn't hold back the terror. There was so much blood! And the spasms wouldn't stop!

"She's going to die, Jack!" the Pussycat told me. "There is nothing more that I can do. You must get help from the humans. Find Fleet quickly – before it is too late!"

Well, I was down off that cage and out of the kennel in a flash. I had been lending my courage to the poor wee thing, as well, and in turn had felt the depth of her pain. I was frightened, but I was sure that Fleet would help us, so I ran to the house like a devil was after me!

Oh, Solitaire, I tried! I jumped and clawed and howled like a werewolf outside that door, but the only attention I got was a boot thrown in my direction! Those two humans were so out of their minds on whatever it is they drink that they couldn't even get up to open the door. Even from the back porch, I could hear my wee lass screaming pitifully. They must have heard her, too, but they couldn't have cared less; they drowned out her cries with their own sodden laughter!

I could see I wasn't going to get any help from those boys, so I started back here to see if I could wake my mistress. Anna had never let me down before and she was the only hope I had left. But it was so far! Even as I ran, I knew I was going to be too late! Then the Owl caught my mind when I was about halfway home and bade me go no further. I was needed back at the side of my mate.

There was such finality in his message that it struck my heart cold!

By then, I was so exhausted and frightened that I just wanted to lie down where I was and wallow in my own misery. I didn't feel as if I could make it back to the kennel or face up to the devastation if I did; but old Owl wouldn't let me quit. It was his faith that kept me going, strengthening my spirit and calming my mind so that by the time I returned to my sheila's side, I was able to push away my own despair and concentrate only on easing her fears as she sank deeper and deeper into perpetual darkness.

She didn't go easy, either. The poor thing struggled to give birth even as she was drawing her last ragged breaths. But our pups were never born. They all died inside of her.

I stayed close by until she grew cold, then I dragged myself home to Anna.

Solitaire heaved a solemn sigh. She had empathized closely with Jack as he relived that dreadful memory. But there was something she had to know.

Yet with all the pain he caused you, you still do not hate the man known as Fleet? You never sought to punish him for his callousness?

The Aussie thought a minute, then answered truthfully.

I can't blame Fleet for the death of my family, m'Lady, if that's what you mean. The Teachings tell us that nature can be very cruel at times. We dogs have a strong instinct to strive, risking everything, to bring our young into the world. The males of our species may suffer loss of life or limb in order to prove themselves worthy of becoming the fathers of the next generation, but our females face even greater danger during the actual birthing process. Yet no matter what happens, we cannot deny nature or our instincts and so, in spite of the pain, life carries on.

I would have preferred that things had ended differently, but I accept what happened as part of the natural way of things. I hold no grudges against Fleet for his part in it.

Solitaire was unconvinced.

But this morning when you saw him, you became enraged. Explain that reaction, if you do not hate him.

Jack bristled.

Well, I'm not stupid, Madame. Just because I don't carry the bitterness of that night with me to this day does not mean that I can't understand what kind of creature we are dealing with, here. I guess that Fleet is what The Pussycat calls a 'necessary evil'. He feeds the kennel dogs and takes care of them, albeit in a cold, unfeeling way unique to himself, but the point is: he is a human and can do things that none of us can do, and we must revere him for that.

He's really not so bad if you just stay out of his way.

This last was added in an offhanded manner. Jack couldn't explain all of the intricacies of his emotions toward humans. He was only a dog, and not even a 'confidant'. Men were creatures of mysterious powers to him. Although he sometimes treated them in an irreverent manner, he knew like all dogs do, that when it came down to it, humans were the bosses in his world.

He hated to admit that he was all show to Solitaire. Her courageous battle with Fleet had been more than an outward show of independence. She had, if only for the instant, thrown off the yoke of obedience and conformity, and she was a hero in Jack's eyes. He tried to think of something to say to reinstate himself in her good graces.

I've known about Fleet for a long time. My friend, Amber, always says that I put up with him just because I enjoy having someone to pit my wits against. We have been antagonists for a long time, he and I, and the scales may dip this way or that, but they come out even in the long run. Especially since I have Anna on my side. Now there's a human being!

Solitaire thought that was a convenient switch in topics, but she welcomed the change. She had felt uncomfortably aroused, hearing that Jack's experiences with Fleet supported her opinion of him as an evil human being.

We seem to agree on many things, small Jack. I find this woman, Anna, to be particularly interesting. I have been pondering her role here. Tell me, what do you know of her?

Jack lowered his ears slightly as he lovingly contemplated the person he called his mistress. There was so much he could tell, but what in particular was Solitaire interested in knowing? Did she care to hear how kind and generous the lady had been to the kennel dogs back when she could get around better? How, back then, she had used her great wisdom to enrich the lives of all at Welsely Farms? How so many dogs owed their very lives to her gentle ministrations? Or, simply, how she always knew the proper way to treat a terrier to make him feel he was important to her without trying to make him into a silly lapdog like so many folks did?

I believe I can help you out here. Another voice simultaneously entered the minds of both Solitaire and Jack. When the Akita stiffened, Jack quickly calmed her by introducing The Owl.

Though she had been prepared to be impressed by The Owl's abilities, Solitaire found her heart was pounding with excitement in her deep chest. She could feel that here was a fantastically gifted mind.

The Owl modestly acknowledged her unspoken compliments. *I, too, am delighted to meet a 'competent' of your stature, Lady. Our little friend, One-eyed Jack, has boasted that my Pussycat and I have been monitoring your thoughts without your* consciously realizing it, and this is so to a point. However, we could never have entered your mind without your allowing it. I'm sure you didn't realize it, but even during those dark days when you were barely cognizant, your subconscious mind was reaching out in desperation for someone to help. We could not refuse you.

For a very long time we could not cipher what was real memory and what was nightmare. The two were intertwined in such hysterical convolution that we feared you were on the verge of madness! It was all we could do to soothe you and keep you from self-destruction until you were well enough to adjust to your loss. There was a loss, was there not?

A new, melodic, but obviously disapproving, voice made itself heard. *Owl! You promised you would not pry. Poor Solitaire will let us know if she wants to talk about those memories when she feels healed well enough to face them. Or she may choose not to. But that is her business, my love, not ours.*

The new voice was that of The Pussycat, Solitaire felt sure. These two were exactly as Jack had described them, and she already felt comfortable with them.

Welcome, Friends! And thank you for watching over me in my hour of need.

Never one to waste his own time on formalities, though he did drag on when others were waiting for answers, Owl broached the subject of Anna Welsely again.

I always knew Anna had the ability to 'listen' if she ever cared to. After all, she was the one who received the messages I transmitted when we first arrived here. Pussycat, do you remember?

Pussycat remembered.

But you are an exceptional 'competent' and it still took much effort to inject just a small amount of compassion into her heart at a time when we were in desperate need.

Quite right, my dear. Owl sounded almost jovial. *The humans must have thought I was in a state of catatonia, I was concentrating so hard to find a receptive mind among them. But you and I could not have lasted much longer in the heat of that van!*

Still, I thought Anna seemed to be getting a little clearer lately – though I've not been able to make the breakthrough that Solitaire, here, did on her first meeting. The years have surely given our mistress the insight necessary for 'listening', but I wonder what happened that she cares so much more now about this dog's well-being? It takes respect, too, you know. If one cannot be bothered to listen to the communicator, how can one hear the message?

The other three dogs agreed, and Pussycat added: *She's a good human, Anna, but she's worked so hard all her life that she just hasn't had the luxury of sitting back and reflecting on how she has used us – all of us – for her own ends.*

Jack couldn't contain his thoughts and broke into the conversation to stick up for his beloved Anna.

Of course she never really listened before! Have you ever tried to communicate with a pack of hounds? Hounds in a pack are all legs and tails, with only one brain! And that brain's too busy thinking up more mischief for all those bodies to get into, to make any attempt at communicating with an outsider, dog or human!

Solitaire felt a tinkle of laughter from The Pussycat and pulled her own lips back in appreciation of Jack's humor, but The Owl's voice did not sound amused.

There is no more reason that a hound can't become a 'competent' than there is that a smart Australian Terrier like you is not able to do so. It only takes a willingness to communicate and a little concentrated effort.

Solitaire grinned again as Jack squinted his one eye and laid his ears flat out to the sides, looking as if he had been physically squashed by Owl's mental rebuke.

Owl went on. *I do admit, however, that I see your point, young Jack. I also concur with you, my Pussycat. Anna has lived a very busy life and she has surrounded herself with canines that provide her financial gain and a little amusement rather than any real companionship. Perhaps now that there are these other people doing most of the physical work for her, she's taking the time to contemplate her past deeds and feels remorse. Perhaps she wants to make amends and feels that the unique plight of this bitch, Solitaire, gives her the opportunity to make a difference.*

Pussycat's warmth was genuine.

Well, my love, she did it for us.

Jack was confused.

I don't understand why you feel she made such a difference in your life. I, at least, am my own dog. Anna allows me my freedom, and I choose to stay by my mistress. But you two have no choice, locked in your cage as you are. You are prisoners here!

The Owl's voice took on a condescending tone.

One is never a prisoner if his mind is free, Jack. The Pussycat and I value our privacy and the peaceful state that allows us to meditate deeply on the Teachings. What would have happened to us in a private home where we would have to sit up and beg for our very dinner? Here, thanks to Anna, we are kept clean, well fed; most important, we are able to stay together.

But what of the indignity . . . , Jack began.

It is true, my poor Pussycat must suffer certain humiliations, Owl admitted.

Before he could finish, Pussycat spoke.

Oh, Owl! You shouldn't feel badly about that. If it allowed us to stay together in relative peace, I would sacrifice much more. Besides, I enjoy caring for the babies. You know that. And maybe this time our mistress will let me keep my litter long enough to see if one of them has the aptitude to become a 'communicator'. Do you suppose you could put that thought into Anna's mind, Solitaire?

A mental sigh from The Owl prefaced his surrender to The Pussycat's will.

You're feeling maternal already, my Pussycat? Yes, I am getting very old and you are nearing the age when you will no longer be allowed to breed. Perhaps it's time, and with Solitaire's help, we can try to sway the humans to our way of thinking on this.

Solitaire remained silent, nonplussed by Pussycat's suggestion. She wasn't sure what she should do about it. She had been able to hear human words all her life, but she had never really tried to communicate with them because she had never understood the workings of their minds. The boy, Johnny, was so typical of his race. His emotions swooped from joyfulness to abject depression, then soared to impossible hopefulness, seemingly without his being able to exert any control whatever over them. Actually, she reflected wryly, he was rather like the terrier with whom she currently shared her bed.

The woman was certainly interesting, though, Solitaire had to admit. But after so many years, she felt there was just too much to say to begin a dialogue now.

***

On the next farm, Fleet followed Earl down the rows of kennels stacked closely together, ten high against the wall on this side. Now and then, a small face with big frightened eyes peered at them from the interior of a dirty cage, but there was no barking, not even a whimper. Once the kennel at Kell's farm went dark for the night, a visit from the men who ran the place usually foretold disaster for some unfortunate pooch.

Tonight, the dogs were very much aware that a sad drama was being played out in their midst. They couldn't actually see what was going on in the bottom cage, but they didn't need to. The mixture of smells permeating the kennel room filled their sensitive noses with the scent of new life as well as the unhealthy reek of death. They were confused and upset – and very quiet.

"Now, where'd I put that bitch?" Earl was rumbling to himself. Fleet couldn't help him as he had little to do with the arrangement of the inmates here. "Ah! Here she is." Earl shone his flashlight into one of the lower cells, illuminating a sorrowful scene.

The mixed-breed bitch was a stray that had wandered onto the farm that morning looking for a safe place to give birth. She was not a pretty animal: average in size, with pale liver pigmentation bordering on albino. The pink skin on the top of her long narrow muzzle had somehow been scraped to the bone then healed over so many times that now it was just an unsightly lump of scar tissue. There was a strange deformation in the shape of her ragged body. Her long white fur was matted and thin, her hind legs covered in green, sticky afterbirth.

Three puppies lay by her side, one dead, two mewling weakly. She had no heat in her body to lend them any warmth. She had no milk in her teats to give them nourishment. She had no strength to clean them or to comfort them. She hadn't even walked on her own since her arrival and would probably have to be carried out when it came time for the shot that would end her wretched life.

Only her beautiful amber eyes, calm now that the labor had ceased, gave any hint that she might once have loved the human who had betrayed her to such a cruel fate.

Fleet turned away from that imploring gaze.

"Sonuvabitch, Earl! What are you going to do next? You know better than to bring strays onto the property. She could be carrying. . . " He stopped to examine her caustically. "Jesus! That heap of moldy fur could be carrying anything. She's so flea-bitten she makes me itch just to look at her. What on earth were you thinking about when you let her in here? You're putting our whole operation at risk."

"We're gonna need more sparrin' partners for Gatorbait – and these came free," was the sulky reply.

Earl's fixation with training his 'fighting' dog was beginning to wear Fleet thin. He talked about nothing else these days, and from the look of the kennel, he did nothing else, either.

Training? Fleet was being kind, calling those daily torture sessions 'training'.

Most people understood that at the core of any good training method there were two basic steps: clearly demonstrating a new routine in ways a dumb animal could appreciate and then practicing it as many times as it took to get it right. Fleet wouldn't argue against the importance of discipline in training and had never hesitated to use force to assert his will over a rebellious dog, but he still followed the primary rules. Watching Earl's methods, he felt his partner was doomed to failure because there was a lot more sadistic harassment involved in his training sessions than there was either of these tried and proven techniques.

But Earl wouldn't listen to Fleet's advice, insisting he had watched the Florida boys and knew exactly what he was doing. He maintained that it was only necessary to whet Gatorbait's natural bloodlust to make him a champion in the pit, and even spurned the idea of roadwork as superfluous.

"I'll make 'im so mean that he'll just kill whatever I put in front of 'im without havin' to chase it around none," he bragged.

This honing of Gatorbait's natural aggressiveness had to be done without the possibility of the dog getting hurt, Earl warned, because if that happened, it could scare him off fighting another animal altogether. Apparently, this protective attitude toward injury did not apply when it was Earl who was doing the hurting. But of course, that was discipline and altogether different.

Fleet had ignored this kind of backward logic until now. He had even held his tongue last week when Earl announced he'd found what he considered an ideal way to get rid of the excess population of cats around the farm: by using them to motivate his fighting dog. Earl had an intricate scheme planned, whereby he would trap the cats and put them into individual burlap bags that had holes cut out for their legs. The mouth of the bag would be bound tightly, giving the felines no room to maneuver. Thus blinded and incapacitated, they would offer little resistance when he grabbed each paw and snipped their long claws back so far they bled. When he was ready to train Gatorbait, he would tie one of the burlap sacks onto the long end of a pole that was mounted off-center on a stand with a universal fitting. Then he would stay safely behind the center and use leverage to control the up and down, forward and back movements of the baited end of the pole. The rest would be simple teasing.

The two men had imbibed heavily on the first evening that Earl intended to use the live bait, and Fleet had let himself be talked into participating. Once they were inside the mongrel's dark lair, however, he had a change of heart and instead stood meekly to the side while Earl rustled Gatorbait out of the pen by himself. The miserable beast was half-crazed with hunger and thirst, but Fleet knew that he wouldn't dare to attack his keeper after the beatings he had taken in the days before.

After he had securely fastened one end of Gatorbait's chain to a roof support, Earl began bobbing and weaving just out of the dog's reach, feigning rushes to get his attention. Gatorbait slumped miserably in a corner of the shed, trying to avoid direct eye contact with his tormenter, but Earl would not be resisted. He kept up his mocking dance until his challenge was finally met and Gaitorbait's angry yellow eyes locked onto his pale blue ones. As soon as he had the dog's full attention, Earl had raised his arms and jerked the upper part of his body spasmodically in an attempt to scare him. Then he lowered himself into a more threatening position, lifting his shoulders as if they were hackles and scowling with menace as he did so.

The ugly dog's lips had slowly quivered into a snarl and his muscles tensed to show his readiness to fight, but Fleet noticed that his hind feet had begun to back-paddle nervously on the wooden floor and his growl wasn't quite believable. Earl moved like an animal about the small space, staying low while he took exaggerated strides. On his way past the pole setup, he reached out to swing it so that the burlap bag on the end hovered tantalizingly close to Gatorbait's head in an effort to break the dog's gaze.

Fleet had been mesmerized by the beastly display. While he watched the hound's unblinking yellow eyes, he was struck with the notion that, if any dog could do it, Gatorbait might win this competition. He had been almost disappointed when, in the end, the dog was the first to look away, beaten by the sheer physical fact of his narrower head structure.

"Hah!" Earl had exclaimed triumphantly, straightening his posture. "He hates that, 'cause I always win a stare-down. Stupid dog! He knows by now he can't beat me. Don'tcha, son?" Earl relished his complete domination over the bound animal.

At that moment, the sack dangling above his head gave Gatorbait an alternative to focus his anger on, and he leaped for it. Earl had been ready for that and easily kept the bait hovering just out of the dog's reach as he jumped and snapped at it in a frenzy.

Fascinated as he was by the raw power of the hound's lunges, Fleet had been unprepared for the moment when Earl decided Gatorbait had worked hard enough and allowed him to snatch the bag. He had forgotten that there was a live cat inside; it had been too terrified to utter a sound all along, but now it screeched in agony as it was torn to shreds in a triumph of bloodletting.

The memory of what followed still made Fleet twitch uncomfortably. After being a witness to that disturbing ritual, he had decided that his buddy, Earl, was capable of just about anything.

"You'll never keep that bitch alive long enough to wean those pups," he muttered in an attempt to cover his old feelings of revulsion.

"I ain't worried about the bitch. I'll get rid of 'er in the mornin', if'n she makes it that long. I'm gonna put the whelps onto the beagle. She can handle a couple more. And when they're a little bigger, it's in the bag for them! Then Gatorbait and I will be able t'practice some more!" He giggled lustily at the thought.

Fleet was disgusted by his partner's abhorrent behavior. He thought of himself as a professional dog handler and although he trained hard, he felt he trained fair.

"I'll bet you used to love to tease the lions at the zoo when you were a kid, didn't you?" he asked sardonically. His derision was lost on Earl, however, who just laughed agreeably.

"Actually, the bears was my favorite. I always did love to hear 'em roar. Did I ever tell y'all 'bout that time at Sanders' Groves in Georgia? They used to keep this monster bear for their customers to see. ."

Fleet cut his partner off quickly. He didn't think he could bear to hear another of Earl's lurid tales right now.

"Earl, you've got to stop this stuff, now, before you make a real mess of things. You know how easily disease can spread in a kennel like this."

Earl's laughter fled in front of the roaring anger that turned his face purple and swollen.

"This here business is half mine, too! An' it seems to me like I got the dirty half! Y'all should try stayin' out here all day long takin' care of this place. I don't have no little kennel boys t'help me, neither.

"I don't do nothin' but pick up stinkin' dogshit all day long. I don't see nobody but you fer weeks at a time. I get so sick of listenin' to those critters bark, I could strangle the whole lot of 'em. And now y'all're jumpin' all over me just 'cause I'm tryin' t'have a little fun!"

"All right! All right! Enough whining!" Fleet couldn't take it when his own method of argument was used on him by someone else, and he backed down right away. "I'm not saying you have to stop; I'm not your mother. Just take it easy, Earl. And no more strays!"

Earl's lower lip was still sticking out and he sniffed petulantly, looking absurdly like an overgrown ten-year-old. But while his ire was quick to rouse, it dissipated just as fast.

"What I need is a real sparrin' partner for Gatorbait. He ain't goin' t'fight no cats in the ring. He needs to get used to the taste of dog-blood, ya know?" He rubbed his semi-bald head, thinking. "Fleet, why don't we ask around and see if'n any of the local fellers would like to put their dogs up? I got a pit dug already – we kin go anytime they like." He looked hopefully at his friend, eyebrows arched to form a tent over pleading pink-rimmed eyes.

Fleet realized Earl was in a desperate state, indeed. The loneliness of the prairie was proving too much for the 'home boy' and he missed his low-country buddies with whom he could share a few beers and some laughs. Fleet had to admit that he felt like that sometimes, himself. These prairie folk weren't the most open bunch of people he had ever met. But he had always been a loner and was used to it. Earl was as much a friend as he had ever had. A half-baked idea formed in his mind.

"Earl, I have been asking around for you, like I said I would, and there are some guys who are curious, but nobody in these parts knows much about fighting dogs. They sure like to gamble, though. I think they'd come if we took the first step and arranged something they could bet on."

"How're we gonna do that? We only got one decent dog. The ones I been breedin' are still too young to put up a good fight against ol' Gatorbait. Less'n yer gonna give me that Aye-kita bitch?" Earl was still hopeful.

"Don't I wish," Fleet said with baleful enthusiasm. "I haven't given up on getting that bitch, believe me, but it would just be asking for trouble, pulling anything while the boss is still doting so heavily on her. Her time will come. Meanwhile, things are going our way right now, so let's keep it cool for the time being."

Fleet's shrewd smile was a sign to Earl that his idea was taking on form now.

"Hey, suppose you get on the phone with a couple of your friends from back home – not the Florida group, but the guys from the Carolinas – and invite them to bring their dogs up here? From what you say, they'd probably be pleased as hell to let things quiet down a little back there and take a holiday where the police don't know them and the crowd's ripe for a good bet. We'll put on an 'exhibition match' to raise some local interest in the sport and introduce your Gatorbait to the pit."

The fat man smiled his gummy smile, his pale eyes pierced with malice.

"Those Florida boys don' like t'leave their swamps, anyways. But yer right about the Carolina bunch. They're always up for a party. And they'll learn these local fellers a thing or two about the rules of dog fightin'!"

The two men left, slapping each other's shoulders in happy camaraderie. They were laughing far too loudly to hear the tired groan of the stray bitch as she slipped off to her well-earned rest.

CHAPTER 21

There is sickness here, Jacques. I can smell it and it frightens me! Amber shuddered dreadfully before adding, in a low whimper: *The babies are crying...*

Jack circled slowly, nose-to-tail, on the narrow shelf outside the poodle's kennel, as was his habit when he was trying to think a problem through. He had bounced onto the high shelf only moments earlier, in a jolly temper until he came face to face with a very distraught Amber. She had been listening for his approach and was waiting for him, pressed against the side of her cage in eagerness for his touch, trembling uncontrollably. Her lower jaw was slack with fear, allowing the tip of her tongue to protrude between her front teeth where it quivered like a tiny pink fish out of water. Seeing his friend's normally soft brown eyes glaring darkly in contrast to the whites surrounding them shocked Jack so that he had rushed to Amber's side and leaned his tiny body against hers for comfort.

After a time, she had relaxed enough to confide in him, but he was confused. How could she hear the whimpering of puppies over the racket the other kennel dogs were making? The barn dogs were so bored and unhappy lately that they barked uncontrollably at the least little thing. The whole place was constantly in an uproar. But it was their only source of entertainment, after all, and he didn't blame them, poor sods.

Jack had noticed that most of the dogs he visited regularly were looking pretty ragged right now, but that was easily explained. Without Johnny in the barn to do frequent spot checks throughout the day to remove any solid waste, the cages were always dirty, so the occupants couldn't help but be the same. Old Moses was going to have to have his dreadlocks removed with the cow clippers, they were so glued together. Not for the first time, Jack was glad of Amber's special living quarters because she didn't have to deal with such things.

Can you not smell the sickness? Amber broke into his thoughts. Her brown eyes seemed to be asking him another question: *Why haven't you warned us?*

Jack squirmed uncomfortably. As the only dog who had the freedom to explore all corners of the Welsely property, it was his responsibility to keep the kennel dogs informed of what was going on in their small world. He had always been proud to be of service, yet somewhere along the line, he had missed an important detail.

He was ashamed to admit it to Amber, but after spending so much of his time in the clean, uncrowded luxury of the specials kennel with Solitaire and Johnny, he had begun lowering the volume on his nose, so to speak, whenever he came back to the barn. Had he let his friends down through his inattention?

Jack forced himself to stop circling and went to the far edge of the shelf, where he sat solidly down. He snorted loudly to clear his sinuses, then took a long, concentrated whiff of the stale air of the barn. And sneezed. The dirty-kennel smell in here was so overpowering that he was sure he wouldn't be able to detect a rat sitting three feet away from him! Things sure weren't the same as when Johnny worked in here! It seemed like the other boy just didn't seem to care enough about the dogs' well-being to do a good job; though in Abel's defense, Jack hadn't noticed Fleet pitching in to help him very much.

He glanced back to see Amber waiting expectantly for him to find the source of her fear, and drew himself up for another deep sniff.

Many different odors were easily discernable on the air, most of which could be called unhealthy. Jack thought he knew what was causing the worst of those smells. Every day, when he came in, he had to pick his way around the puddles of dirty water that were left behind after Abel hosed the kennels down in the morning. Those holes in the floor behind the cages, where the water was supposed to drain away, were choked up again. Maybe that's what was upsetting Amber. And for good cause. Once before in Jack's memory, the stench of the black muck that filled the drains had been a precursor of disease in the kennel. The humans had taken care of it that time, though some of the dogs may have been left a little the worse for wear, so he had faith that they would be able to do so again.

Jack's ability to think in the abstract was limited. He hated to leave his good friend while she was so upset, but it was time to do some serious investigating around the barn. Before he left, he pressed his furry cheek close to the bars in an effort to give the stressed poodle some comfort and was rewarded with a few warm laps of her tongue. He was slightly surprised to notice a stale odor on her breath, but he knew what fear tasted like on the tongue and reasoned there must be a smell to it, as well.

Please, Jacques, try to look in on The Owl and The Pussycat, as well. I know that you do not like to visit in that room, but I worry for The Owl. He is so old now, like a great-grandfather to so many of us, and he has been very subdued for the last few days. . .

At this news, Jack perked his ears.

The Owl? Subdued? I'm not sure that isn't for the best, my girl! But of course I will check on him, because it is unusual. Don't look so frightened, little one. Everything will be right as rain in no time. No worries!

With a wink of his bright eye, Jack turned and hopped down. All business now, he quickly scampered out of Amber's sight.

***

Doc had just pulled into the yard and was unloading his 'tool kit' from the trunk. He nearly backed into Abel, who had come up to stand behind his elbow, looking even more somber than usual.

"Can I see you for a bit before you get started on your regular stuff?"

"Why, sure, son." Doc was agreeable. He closed his trunk and followed Abel into the barn, where they proceeded through the rows of kennels and all the way to the rear of the building.

Doc couldn't remember the last time he had gone to the back of the barn. He seldom visited this section because it was where the adolescent dogs were kept. Since they were old enough to be finished their shots, but too young to be bred yet, they didn't usually require much vetting. On the occasion that one of the young dogs might need medicating, the kennel boys normally brought it forward to the infirmary for him to examine.

As he followed Abel, Doc looked to the right and left, noting how many of the cages needed a good cleaning. His surprise at the poor conditions in this corner turned to annoyance when he stepped into a large puddle of dirty water.

"When's the last time the drains back here were cleaned out, Abel?" he asked, testily. "This water's a darn good breeding ground for insects and bacteria and the like – and it smells putrid!"

Abel shrugged.

"Johnny did it a while ago, but I've been too busy since he left. It's always wet back here, anyways, from washin' the kennels down. And it always stinks."

Doc shook his head and made a mental note to talk to Fleet about this. Or maybe it was time to discuss the problem with Ken. He had made it a lifelong habit not to mess in other people's business, but now that he and Ken were working together on other things, he didn't think Welsely's manager would mind a word of advice. Ken didn't really understand the nature of a man like Fleet, and Doc felt he was giving the foreman altogether too much leeway in the barn. That could be a big mistake.

The problems Doc was seeing in the barn hadn't started suddenly.

SOLITAIRE, A Dog Story

They had mounted over several months, caused by such daily sins as hosing down the runs with plain water instead of disinfecting them properly; not picking up feces often enough in the exercise pens where the puppies played; and spraying for fleas and ticks once every two to three months instead of every two to three weeks. Recently, Doc had noticed Fleet stacking a few small wire cages on top of the larger kennels, then more on top of them as the inventory of puppies grew, until now there were virtual walls of dirty kennels in several sections of the barn.

As a result of this overcrowding, Doc was being kept busy treating eye and ear infections that were becoming rampant. In spite of his vaccinations, a few too many bouts of kennel cough were beginning to weaken the breeding stock. What was worse, coccidiosis had made its ugly debut among the puppies. A fairly common protozoan disease, coccidiosis spread quickly among animals living in conditions of filth. It lived in their intestinal tracts, waiting for them to weaken under the stress of shipment or another illness. Then it became aggressive, gnawing away at their insides until they weakened further and, often, died. Many times, the breeder didn't even know he had the problem in his kennel until the new owner of a sickened pup complained to him about it.

Doc was sure that Fleet had not let his bosses know that he had received such complaints. The only reason Doc knew was because Johnny had asked him about the disease a few weeks ago, saying a dealer had been grumbling about having an infected pup. After doing a few tests he was relieved to find it was not widespread, but had warned Fleet then that he must make sure the boys used disinfectant daily to clean the runs. Obviously, Fleet hadn't taken Doc's warning seriously because that standing water he had just walked into held no trace of disinfectant smell.

When Abel stopped, it was to indicate a lower cage where a litter of Yorkshire Terrier puppies was out of place among the older dogs' kennels. The babies were just about shipping age and should have been up and playing merrily. Instead, two out of three of them were sprawled on the floor of the cage, their eyes closed and their breathing shallow. Their fluffy black coats were sodden with filth from the kennels above them and now and then one would shake with ague. The third pup, a tiny female with huge golden orbs for eyes, sat huddled in the corner, shivering in fear of whatever had struck her brothers down.

"What's going on here, Abel?" Doc blurted irritably when he saw the mess. It was going on a month since he had taken an alcoholic drink and the mornings were rough enough without this. "These pups are filthy! Why aren't these kennels back here kept cleaner?"

As he spoke, he reached inside to remove the little female from the fetid tangle of her littermates, but when he lifted her, he saw that he was too late. Her belly and hindquarters were black with a mixture of blood and stool the consistency of river mud, and she stank much worse than the puddled water had. There was no mistaking that smell. Parvo! Doc lowered the puppy quickly and backed away, holding his breath to control the heaving of his stomach.

Parvo is the name of a particularly lethal virus that attacks the portion of the dog's digestive tract situated between the stomach and the small intestine. It continues from there to destroy the whole lower system of the animal. The dog loses all control of its bowel movements and the blood from the shredded intestines mixes with the fecal matter to give it its distinctively foul odor. It is nearly always fatal in young, unvaccinated puppies and could kill even older dogs if their inoculations hadn't taken well. Naturally, because of their smaller systems, it affects the toy breeds most disastrously.

Doc was suddenly angry. Angry as hell at knowing that the battle for these puppy's lives was over before he had even had a chance to help them. Damn Fleet for being such a secretive bastard!

"Fleet's been medicatin' 'em, Doc," Abel offered, in a lame effort to calm the old man's chagrin. "He said there wasn't no use panickin' everybody right away. Said it was probably just a isolated case. But it ain't. I found two more whelps sick this mornin'. I just thought somebody should know." The boy was biting his lower lip, frightened now. "I didn't know what else to do, Doc. I didn't want for Fleet t'get mad at me. I need this job. You won't tell him I showed you where they was, will ya?"

Doc's jawbones tensed and untensed as he picked up his bag.

"Show me the other sick pups, Abel. And don't worry about Fleet bothering you. He's going to have a lot of explaining to do, himself – to Anna!"

After Doc had examined the puppies, he told Abel to isolate all five of them and went into the infirmary to wash his hands. By then, Fleet was arriving for his day's work. Doc glared at the foreman, but didn't trust himself to say anything. Tight-lipped, he motioned Fleet to follow him to the farmhouse. The fact that Fleet did so without any argument was proof to Doc that he already knew how bad the situation was.

The two men went straight into Ken's office, where the coffee machine was just finishing its cycle. Ken looked up brightly, but his pleasant greeting remained unspoken when he saw the serious expressions on their faces. Doc asked him to call Anna into the office. Ken did so, then poured hot coffee into four mugs while they waited.

"Where would they get parvo from, Doc?" Ken was the first to ask after the veterinarian had disclosed his news. "We haven't had a shipment of dogs in for over a month now."

"Who knows?" Doc sighed. "It could have been carried in on the shoes of one of your delivery men from another infected kennel. Could be airborne, if any of your neighbors' dogs have contracted it. Could be your hounds, Anna, or even little Jack that brought it back to the barn. Have you had any strays around here lately?"

"No strays," Anna shook her head. "We're pretty securely fenced in. And my pack don't go off the property anymore. Neither does Jack, I don't think, although he can."

"Johnny takes him out when he does the roadwork with Solitaire," Ken volunteered, "but they stay on the road. I hear Jack's been riding the whole way on the handlebars, lately, anyway. I think that's pretty safe, isn't it?"

Doc nodded, but before he could clarify his opinion, Anna spoke again.

"But all the dogs've had their shots regular, ain't they? Except for the littlest 'uns, they oughta be safe. Right?" She looked to Doc for confirmation and was surprised to see that he was glaring at Fleet.

"Well, that depends," the vet replied, watching for Fleet's reaction, "on whether those out-of-date shots that I saw in the fridge a couple of weeks ago were really just an oversight or somebody's misguided attempt to save a few pennies."

Fleet was quick to lash out in his usual defensive manner.

"Now wait a minute. You're not blaming this on me! I do my best to keep the vaccines current, but sometimes the suppliers don't ship when they're supposed to. I have to use the old shots or none at all. Which is worse?"

Ken's normally mild features showed his complete surprise.

"Fleet, if you didn't have enough injections, you should have told me. I would have made sure you got them. There's always extra in the specials building. There's no reason to use old vaccines, for God's sake!"

"Aw, it doesn't happen that often," Fleet muttered, realizing too late that he may have already incriminated himself.

Doc had his suspicions about the vaccines and a few other things as well. Once this emergency was over, he would have that talk with Ken about getting to the bottom of Fleet's dealings. Right now, though, they would need everybody working together to pull through this with as few casualties as possible.

"The point is, parvo is a highly contagious disease. It could have come from anywhere, but it wouldn't have taken such a firm hold if the dogs in the barn were better looked after." Doc turned his still glowering countenance back on the foreman. "It's a mess in there, Fleet. I can't believe you've allowed things to get this bad. You're experienced in these things. You must have known parvovirus when you smelled it. Why, for the love of God, didn't you call me when I might have helped those poor animals?"

Fleet's whole posture was one of resignation.

"I had medication for it. I thought I could control it without any of our shippers knowing. They won't accept any of our packages if they find out about this and then what will we do with all those older pups? We're full to overflowing. We need to keep up shipments."

Anna had been silently pacing the floor behind the three men until now, but she lost control when she heard Fleet's statement.

"Keep up shipments? Good Lord! We can't send any of these animals anywhere 'til we get over this thing. If it's parvo, you know how contagious it is. After that, we'll be lucky if we have anythin' left to ship!"

Excitement flushed her lined face and burned in her eyes, causing Doc to regard her suspiciously until she calmed down enough to reassure him that her health was not at risk.

"You're lookin' at me all worried-like again, Doc. Don't. I ain't havin' no attack, except of 'disappointment in my management'. That includes you, too, Kenny. You're supposed to know what's goin' on around this place. I trusted you to take care of these things for me."

When Ken only hung his head, Anna looked as though she might slap him, but she gritted her teeth and stomped over to the east window instead. There, she stared off in the direction of the barn while she composed her emotional state.

Ken spoke in a hushed voice, never taking his eyes off his desk.

"I have no defense, Anna. You are absolutely correct. I should have been on top of the conditions in the barn. It's my fault that we're going to lose so many of our stock."

Doc felt sorry for Ken. His weakness in facing up to Fleet was going to cost him now; his honor was already a casualty, next would come his heart. Doc didn't figure Ken had ever experienced a parvo outbreak in those fancy show kennels he had worked at, so he probably had no idea of just how devastating the disease could be in a big breeding outfit like Welsely's. The immense weight of all those tiny lives that would be lost was going to remain on his conscience for a long time.

"We're all responsible," Doc stated flatly. "We're all experienced enough to know the signs of trouble, but somehow we've overlooked them. Now, what are we going to do to minimize the losses?" He was amazed at how calm he felt. The urgency of the situation helped him to forget his own needs, so that the jitters that had been in constant control of his body the last few weeks seemed to have disappeared.

"I hate to bring up the specials first," Ken started, his eyes begging forgiveness from everyone, "but we've got to cut them off completely from the rest of the animals. I'm not just playing favorites again; there's a big chunk of Welsely's money tied up in those dogs."

"Don't worry about your damn specials, Ken. They're probably quite safe." Doc didn't add that the reason they were not in danger was that Ken had personally supervised their injections, whereas the dogs in the barn had been deserted by him, left to become victims of Fleet's apathy. He didn't have to say the words. Both men dropped their glances, guilty of their separate crimes.

Fleet sat, shoulders hunched, with his elbows on his knees, and stared at the floor. He was too depressed to even defend himself. He had hoped against hope that he was wrong, and it wasn't parvo that was making the Welsely litters ill. He had taken all the precautions to prevent the spread of the disease since it had taken its first young victim over at Kell's eight days ago, but it seemed to no avail. Unlike the people at Welsely's, he could pinpoint the initial source of the virus there. The stray bitch Earl had brought into the kennel last week must have died from it. When she had croaked that first night, Earl just dug a hole out back and buried her and her whelps without bothering to tell Fleet or worrying about an autopsy. Now the virus was ripping through their kennel, killing three out of four puppies in less than a week.

Fleet had given Earl medication for those pups, but the big man whined that the stench made him too nauseated to take the time with the really sick ones. He felt it was more realistic to drown any pups that showed symptoms before they had a chance to spread the disease, if they didn't die on their own first. Fleet hated the fact that they were losing money on every little carcass they threw out, but in the end he didn't have much choice but to agree. He didn't have time to nurse Kell's pups, and he couldn't force Earl to do it. He couldn't force Earl to do anything his mind was set against.

Then a few of the adult dogs had begun passing odiferous diarrhea and even Earl realized that they must fight this disease if they wanted to save any of their breeding stock. But it was too late. On Thursday their kennels had been overflowing with marketable dogs; today was Monday and their inventory was halved, with half of those still alive deathly ill.

Fleet had hoped to send the healthy remnants of the litters out with Welsely pups before the news reached their dealers and they couldn't sell any of them. He had let Earl convince him that if a pup didn't get the disease when his littermates did, he must be immune and therefore shippable. He had known better, and now Anna had brought him back to reality on that matter in no uncertain terms. There would be no shipments from either kennel for at least another month. The loss of income was going to hurt. Not only that, he was tired of nursing puking dogs, most of which were going to die anyway.

And now it was going to start all over again here.

CHAPTER 22

Hmph! Well! A nice state of affairs this is! Jack lay in the sun in an outside run, tiny alongside the mountainous body of the Akita bitch, and he was fuming. Solitaire lay calm and as motionless as that mountain, anxious not to set the little terrier off again. He had just cooled down and seemed slightly more accepting of his fate. Without moving her head, the big dog slid serious eyes to the side of her head, the better to gage Jack's temperament; but the Aussie never shifted his own gaze from the side of the barn.

Solitaire had been delighted when Johnny opened her door and with a quick 'good boy', handed One-eyed Jack, her best friend, into her kennel. The terrier's tail was dripping water and his ears hung limply out to the side of his head, making Jack look like a drenched rag, but the Akita had wisely kept her observations to herself because she knew that only a cat gets madder than a terrier when it's wet! As soon as he felt the floor under him, Jack had whirled and tried to duck out the door before the boy closed it, but Johnny was ready for that maneuver and slammed it shut too quickly.

"Don't make any trouble, Jack! We've got all the trouble we can handle around here right now. You stay with Solitaire for a while, and behave yourself. Take care of him, Sol. Yours is the only kennel we have available that he can't get out of, but I sure don't envy you his company today!"

Solitaire's brow lifted and she had cocked her head to one side, questioningly. Why would Johnny say something like that?

Jack had waited until Johnny turned to go, then attacked the feed door with a mighty vengeance, trying to force his way out even though he knew that was impossible from the inside.

"That's enough, Jack!" Johnny yelled in a stern voice that Solitaire had never heard him use before. Every dog in the kennel winced. Clearly, he wasn't going to accept any more fuss from the terrier. What had Jack been up to? Solitaire had waited, almost sheepishly, for the dripping terrier to face her before inquiring as to what was going on.

Up to? Going on? Big trouble! That's what, m'lady! There's loads of trouble in that barn and I should be over there seeing to it, not trapped like a rat in this place!

Goodness, Solitaire had thought, more bad manners. Well, she had learned terriers could be like that. She was more puzzled than peeved when the tiny fellow 'elbowed' her aside and began a search for an escape route that ended after half an hour with absolutely no luck. Jack was almost dry by then, but still shivering with humiliation. He threw himself down on the warm concrete of the outside run and began his vigil of the barn.

Solitaire hadn't joined him outside right away; everybody had a right to privacy. But she had become concerned a few minutes later when her tiny friend continued to shake. Unsure whether Jack's ague was caused by anger or a low body temperature, she had padded out and cautiously positioned herself so that he could receive the comfort of her warm body if he wished. There would be time enough when he quieted to hear his story.

Never one to stay silent for long, Jack began, slowly, to relate the events of the morning. He told Solitaire about his visit to Amber that morning and the poodle's strange premonition of danger in the kennels. Afterwards, he told her, he had been nosing about the barn, gathering scents in the hopes of tracking down the cause of her distress, when Doc came in followed by Anna, the new boss, and Fleet. The kennel boy, Abel, had met them at the door and led them straight down to the back of the barn. Everyone was very serious. Of course, Jack had followed, figuring they might lead him to the source of the problem. Boy, was he right! And so was Amber! There was terrible illness back there, hidden from any who didn't know where to look.

Jack tried to describe the severity of what he saw; five young puppies infected with a black disease that filled the back corner of the kennels with the reek of death. His morbid description made Solitaire recoil in disgust.

Although he had been frightened by the smell alone, Jack had forced himself to stay while the humans examined the kennel's occupants. Two of the puppies were dead; he could tell from where he stood. The others were suffering greatly, and he grieved for them. The humans were also upset and angry. There were many cross words between his mistress and the men who did her bidding.

Suddenly, all eyes had looked down on the little terrier. He hadn't liked the feel of that, so he got ready to run! But as he was backing away, Abel had caught him and handed him over to Anna. His own beloved mistress had thrown him into the tub and soaked him thoroughly! After that, she had brought him here to Johnny, who bathed him again before imprisoning him!

Solitaire had been a good listener. No wonder poor Jack was in a spitting rage, with two baths in one day! And even though he was now in a place he had worked hard to be many times, she knew the locked door humiliated him.

The Akita made a conscious effort to bolster Jack's terrier pride by letting him know how grateful she was that he was here to inform her of the desperate nature of this emergency. She could still feel him trembling and knew the Aussie was seething mightily inside his tiny frame. Correctly, she surmised that a great part of his anger was tied up with concern for Amber. Solitaire felt her own bond with Jack strengthened because of her admiration for his brave spirit. She would help the little dog in any way possible, but what action could they take? Once the humans locked those metal doors, there was nothing any dog could do.

My friend, have you tried to reach Amber's thoughts? she asked solemnly.

Jack glanced over at Solitaire, misery in his dark eye.

Amber isn't that strong a 'communicator'. She wasn't born here and had no early training, so her talent was developed late. I have to be quite close to her before we can communicate. Even The Owl has trouble reaching her if her mind is on other things. Right now she is very fearful, so I doubt she'd be able to concentrate hard enough to commune with me.

Solitaire raised her head as though listening with her ears. When she turned back to Jack, she was very confident.

I have heard Amber, Jack. She is very worried and her thoughts are scattered, but she is well for now. It is true that she doesn't broadcast like The Owl or The Pussycat. She is very emotional, which always makes it difficult to communicate well. But tonight, when all is quiet, I will be able to speak with her and console her. She reached over to nudge Jack gently with her nose. *No worries, my little friend!*

True to her word, Solitaire attempted to contact Amber after the lights were turned off, but the Toy Poodle's thoughts were far too disjointed to make any real sense of them. Amber lacked the power to commune directly with Solitaire, and the shadowy images she was able to transmit were full of foreboding and intense loneliness, nothing suitable for Jack to know about. If Solitaire was to believe those images, half of the canine population in the barn was sick or dying, and that was just not conceivable to her. The Akita understood how fear could turn imagination into your enemy, so instead of reacting negatively to such stimuli, she concentrated on directing long, smooth waves of peaceful thought that calmed poor Amber's hysteria long enough to allow her to fall into a fitful sleep.

Though Solitaire tried to sound confident when she reported her contact to Jack, he guessed what was happening and became even more restless, gnawing on the cage bars as if he truly believed that they would give way under his minuscule molars.

The next few days drew out interminably for the lonely dogs. They seldom saw their human caretakers as they came and went – mostly went – in a hurry. The most amount of time Johnny spent with Jack and Solitaire was the first morning when they had watched curiously while he locked the dog that usually lived in the kennel next to theirs outside in his run. Then the boy had used a noisy tool to cut a round hole in the plywood divider between the inside pens.

"Ms. Welsely's worried that you two might get on each other's nerves, being locked up together like this," he had explained to Solitaire. "This hole's big enough for Jack to get into the next kennel if he wants, but not for you to follow."

Solitaire's understanding of Johnny's thought patterns was excellent by now, so she easily translated for Jack, but the news worried the Aussie all the more.

What's going on over in the barn, that they have to go to such lengths to keep me in here?

Every day, Jack pleaded with Solitaire to communicate with the kennel boy; *Ask him about Amber.* But Solitaire would not let her defenses down, even for Jack's peace of mind. Pragmatic as ever, she had a feeling that they would know soon enough what dangers were being faced over there.

Compounding on her concern for Amber was the fact that The Owl and The Pussycat hadn't made their presence known in several days. She knew they were out there somewhere because she could feel the imprint of their minds, but each time she tried to communicate with them, it was as if a door was shut against her. Were they using all of their mental energy to help the other dogs stay calm, as she was? Or had Amber been correct to worry about The Owl's health? Surely, if they were well, they would have had a moment out of all these days to confide in her?

She didn't let Jack know it, but she was beginning to share his frustration at not knowing what was going on. If her dignity wasn't so important to her, Solitaire might have begun to gnaw on the kennel bars, herself.

Then, on the third evening when Solitaire tried to reach out to Amber, she felt nothing but blackness. She was scarcely able to keep her panic at bay as she cast about for some clue as to why the poodle's mind-pattern was lost to her. Jack noticed her distress instantly and hurried to Solitaire's side, straining with all of his limited ability to hear what even the powerful Akita could not.

Where is she? What has happened to her? Amber! Answer me, little one! His thoughts boosted hers, but to no avail; there was no answer to their desperate pleas.

Jack could not concentrate for very long. He was a doer, not a thinker. He began running crazily up and down along the sides of the outdoor run, yapping shrilly, panic so obvious in his tone that all of the dogs in the area sat up and took notice. As usual, Anna's hounds were the first to join in with their own hysterical barking, and soon the whole of the specials building was inundated with a great swell of primal noise.

At first, Solitaire was alarmed and attempted to put a stop Jack's frenzied race. How did he expect her to concentrate with such a thunderous racket going on? But then something in the wild abandon of the dogs' chorus roused in her a strong awareness of her ancient heritage, bringing untamed emotions to the surface and demanding that they be set free.

The hounds' lusty baying could raise the dead, and the mournful howls of the herding breeds told of lonely nights filled with danger, but none of the sounds matched the Akita bitch's for pure savagery. With her deep, full-throated howl she seemed to be threatening the very night with dire consequences for visiting such suffering on her canine family.

Soon the lights in the farmhouse came on and Ken bolted out the back door, flashlight in hand. He raced to the specials kennel, wondering what kind of beast would cause the dogs there to react so aggressively. He threw the switch for the interior lights and kept his flashlight at the ready like a club as he scanned, nervously, for any intruder. But he couldn't see anything out of the ordinary except for a great number of purebred showdogs howling and yelping in collective lunacy. Still on edge, he hushed the inside dogs with a few well-chosen commands, then made his way out to the back runs, cursing Anna's hounds into silence as he passed by them. He was relieved to see that the big dogs in the runs behind the building were calmer now, though several were standing on their hind legs, leaning against the mesh and directing their barks at a disturbance in the end kennel.

Dread filled Ken's thoughts. Locking Jack in with the Akita had been against his better judgment, and now he was terrified that he was going to find a very unpleasant consequence for that action. He caught an inward breath and forced himself to walk forward.

Upon arriving at the end kennel, Ken was astounded to see the great Akita bitch sitting on her haunches in the center of the run, barking in measured cadence while a seemingly uninjured Jack whizzed around and around the outside edges. It looked to him like the Aussie had finally gone over the edge – and Solitaire was urging him on. At Ken's command, Solitaire was readily quieted, and they both watched sadly while Jack continued his laps and his insane yapping.

"Kenny? What's the matter with Jack?" Anna came up behind him fearfully, as if the little dog's craziness might be catching.

"I don't know, Anna," Ken shook his head in wonderment. "I found them like this."

Solitaire watched the old woman approach the wire and cling to it as she went down on one knee. Though she crooned soothingly to the terrier, Jack didn't break stride. In fact, he seemed not to notice his mistress was there.

"My Lord, whatever's wrong with him?" Anna asked. "Distemper, you think? Not rabies?" She didn't ask whether the Akita might have hurt him, because Solitaire was obviously as concerned as they were.

Ken stared, mesmerized by the little dog's antics.

"I doubt it. Maybe he's just gone stir-crazy. You said he's never been kept confined this long. If I wasn't watching it with my own eyes, I wouldn't believe it, though."

Anna struggled to rise and headed for the door of the run.

"We'd better get him out of there."

Before Ken could stop her, she had flung open the wire door and the terrier ran out. He stopped barking immediately and raced off, full speed, into the night. Anna and Ken looked at each other in bewilderment, then back into the run where the Akita bitch sat as before, except now her mouth was open wide in an unmistakable, panting grin.

"That little hoodlum conned us!" Ken exploded. "And Solitaire helped him! I was actually worried about the bugger!"

Anna shook with the first merriment she had felt in days.

"I told you Jack'd find a way out, if there was one. And I'll bet I know right where he's headed."

Moments later, a muted din from the barn confirmed that One-eyed Jack had arrived.

Jack had prepared himself for the worst when he entered the barn, but still the stench stopped him dead in his tracks for a split second. It really was awful! How could he have missed it before? No wonder his poor Amber had been so frightened!

He didn't hesitate for long, but raced past the stacked kennels on his way to the cubicle where Amber lived. The healthier dogs were excited to see him and yelped robust greetings, but he was afraid to stop in case the humans caught up with him. He rounded the corner and flew up the shelves, skidding to a stop on the top one. The feisty terrier refused to give in to disappointment when he found Amber's kennel empty. She couldn't be too far away! He wheeled and jumped back down, knowing where he must go.

His last time in the barn, he had discovered the sick animals were being kept in the rear section. Since Jack refused to believe that his friend was dead, he was certain he would find her back there! He ran on, courageously ignoring the danger signs that made his senses reel.

No! Stop! His nose warned him of the smell of death all around him.

Beware! His ears told him that the agony of the wailing babies could soon become his.

Protect yourself! On all sides, the cages were full of disheveled, pain-wracked victims of the disease. Only his heart's instinct defied all of the physical evidence and urged the tiny dog forward.

Amber needs you! Go to her!

He slid around the last stack of kennels and came to an abrupt stop before crashing into – another stack of kennels? That hadn't been here on his last visit. There must be a lot of dogs quarantined back here if the humans had built additional rows of cages to accommodate them.

Jack stood back to take in his surroundings and was thankful to see that his first conclusion was wrong. The kennels that had been piled high in this section were just more spread out, that was all. Now, instead of three rows, six cages tall, there were eight rows with only three cages on top of one another. Though it was probably a little more difficult for the people to get around in the narrower walkways, he could see how it was a lot better for the dogs that had to live here. Nobody liked living in a highrise – especially a filthy one.

The stench of the sick animals confined here was still almost overpowering to Jack. It was a smell you didn't get used to, and now it was blended with the strong odor of disinfectant into a disgusting compound that made the sensitive terrier wheeze in irritation. He was reminded of the smell in the infirmary, and at first that thought made him more frightened. Then he was struck with the realization of what it meant: *These animals are being looked after by Doc!* Suddenly, he was filled with faith that all of his friends would soon be well. After all, whenever the dogs had been sick in the past, they had been taken to the infirmary to get better, hadn't they? That weird perfumey smell must be part of the old human's magic! Jack had never liked Doc's medicine-smell before, but now he took comfort from it.

With renewed courage, he resumed his search for Amber and was almost feeling like his old self by the time he trotted around to the front of the cages. He stopped short again and stared at the sick animals kenneled there. They were a sorry-looking group, all right. None of them even had the strength to give a 'yip' when he suddenly appeared in front of them. Jack noticed that the cages were mostly filled with youngsters, the same as the first group he had seen stricken with the disease. He felt sorry for the babies, but also encouraged because that might mean that Amber was too old to be at risk. Then he heard a weak moan and his heart leaped into his throat.

She lay in a kennel about midway along the row, on the top. Only her tiny, beige muzzle showed through the bars. Excited, Jack ran to the kennel beneath the one that held Amber and jumped up on it, but he could see even less from there. Still balancing on his hind legs, he backed up as far across the aisle as he could and swayed there, barking frantically. There was no movement in the dark cage.

From where he stood, Jack could see a bladder filled with some kind of fluid with an attached tube hanging from her cage. He didn't know what that was for, exactly, but he had seen it on other cages in the past and it usually meant the dog inside was sleeping very deeply. Perhaps that was why Amber didn't answer him? Well, he would just have to wake her up! He was certain that she would feel much better knowing he was here!

Jack looked around for a way to get to the upper level of kennels. Several cases of canned dog food stacked against the far end of the line caught his eye and he raced off to investigate. While he was climbing up the pile, he heard noises from the barn entrance. He had been followed! Desperately, he climbed higher and faster. He had to rouse Amber before they caught him! She needed to know he was there!

The top of the stack of cases was level with the middle row of kennels. That meant that he would have to jump onto the wire top of the highest cage, no easy feat, especially in the dark. Jack's paws were almost as tiny as Amber's and they could easily slip through the wires, perhaps injuring him. He circled on the smooth surface of the cardboard case while he worried through the problem. The sound of approaching feet grew louder. He stopped circling and listened, then made his decision. What other choice was there for a terrier? Amber needed him, so he would jump.

He gathered himself for the leap, but before he could take off he was blinded by the beam of a flashlight. He hesitated, not knowing whether he should jump anyway or whether he should escape and try to reach Amber again later. Then, from the darkness behind the beam, he heard Anna's voice calling out to him.

"Jack, no! You'll hurt yourself!" She sounded scared, but then she continued more persuasively. "Stay there, little guy. I'll help you out."

Jack had always trusted his mistress in times of emergency; he couldn't bring himself to run from her now. The old woman approached cautiously and gathered him into her arms. To his surprise, he found they were both shaking with relief. He allowed himself to be held very closely for the tenderest of moments. It was the kind of moment when a dog and his human realize how much they depend on each other for so many things.

Anna understood and respected Jack's concern for the tiny apricot poodle, too.

"You sad little scruffball," she crooned. I know you're achin' to find out what's goin' on with Amber. I shoulda known we couldn't keep you outta here for long. Let's go see her, then."

The main barn lights flashed on.

Anna called, "I've got him, Ken. The little cuss was just where I thought he might be." She spoke lower for Jack's ears only, "I don't know how you knew about Amber, little fella, but it seems like whenever she needs you, you're there."

As she talked, she shuffled back down the row of kennels, stopped in front of the one where Amber was sleeping, and held the terrier up so that he could see his friend for himself.

Jack's heart nearly broke in two when he saw Amber's condition. It was worse than he could have expected. The poodle lay on her side, her breathing even, but very, very shallow. Her soft coat had been soiled many times by the fluid wastes of her body, and although it was fairly clean and dry now, it remained plastered against her fevered skin like tiny apricot waves. Without her fluffy curls, Amber's frail frame appeared too wasted to support life. One of her thin front legs was bare where all of the hair had been shaved from it and a hypodermic needle was firmly taped in place. The tube from the pouch Jack had seen was attached to the needle and a thick liquid oozed through it.

"I know she looks like a broken toy right now, but she's gonna be okay, little fella."

Anna was speaking in a soothing tone, but Jack was not convinced. Why didn't the humans wake Amber up? Why were they just letting her die? He knew she was cold because every now and then she shivered slightly. He pushed away from Anna's chest, struggling to get to the still figure in the cage.

"Now what do we do with him?" It was Ken, with Abel following behind. The boy was still rubbing sleep out of his eyes. He had been sacking out in the barn's infirmary since the onset of the plague and not getting much sleep.

"I'm takin' him into the house with me for tonight," Anna announced to everyone's surprise. "And I'm takin' Amber, too. Abel, make up a box with beddin' and get her ready to go, will you?"

"Yes, ma'am," Abel mouthed and looked around for a likely piece of cardboard.

"Has Jack ever slept in the house before, Anna?" Ken voiced his concern. "He may not be comfortable there, either, and then he'll keep you up all night. You've been working awfully hard these days, too, and you need your rest."

"I thought he was doin' a heck of a good job keepin' us up when he was outside in the kennel," the older woman retorted, logically. "Kenny, these poor little critters need our help right now. Even though Jack's okay physically, this whole situation has gotta be pretty darn confusin' for him. I think he could use a little extra attention. Besides, he's always had this thing for Amber, and he'll feel better if he can stay with her." She looked back at Amber's still body. "To tell the truth, I'll feel better watchin' over her, too. She looks kinda cold. . . the poor thing's so tiny to be this sick. . ."

Ken felt his throat constrict in sympathy. He had no more arguments, so when Abel arrived with the cozy-looking box, he gently transferred Amber and carried her out to the farmhouse.

CHAPTER 23

Be brave, little Jack! Your vigil will be long and difficult, but you will not be alone, for we will all be watching over our tiny sister. Amber is very far away from us right now, but she wants to come back. Have faith that she will recover and she will feel your love calling her home to us!

Solitaire was glad of Jack's closer proximity to Amber, knowing it would help the terrier to concentrate his efforts when he was called on. However, she felt that Amber was going to need more support tonight than Jack and she could give by themselves. It would take the will of all the sentient dogs in the kennel to hold the tiny poodle's flickering spirit when the time came, but two of the strongest minds on the grounds seemed to be missing.

It had been far too long since Solitaire had heard from The Owl and The Pussycat. Though she had been mightily curious about their absence, she had chosen not to add to Jack's worries by forcing the Wise Ones' attention. Now she couldn't wait any longer.

Solitaire held off until she felt Jack's mind begin the lazy spiral down to sleep, then she checked to make sure that Amber was still incognizant, and cleared her own thoughts in preparation for her undertaking. The farm was very quiet now, which would make her meditations easier. She lay in the moonlight of her run, eyes closed, ears slightly flattened to the sides. Her breathing became very deep and slow, and she could feel her power growing. She focused on the mind tracks of the elders in the barn. They must hear her this time!

Yes, Solitaire, I hear you! It was The Pussycat, and she sounded upset. *Please stop bellowing, Solitaire! Even the untrained babies can hear you and they are frightened. Truly you are a very talented bitch!*

Solitaire remained in her meditative state, though she altered her volume somewhat. She was not taking any chances on losing this contact.

Pussycat! So there you are! Haven't you heard me trying to contact you before? Where is The Owl? We must talk.

Though the Akita didn't like pushing her demands on equals, she was feeling very frustrated by the elders' recent silence and felt she was owed an explanation. When she heard Pussycat's teary reply, she was sorry for her impatience.

My Beloved has passed on, Solitaire. It was two days ago. . . He was one of the unlucky ones to acquire this black disease when it first made its appearance, and though he fought valiantly, it was too strong for his old body and it took his life.

While he was ill, he begged me to block my thoughts as he did his, so that the others would not feel his fear and his pain, and become disheartened. He was a great leader! Even through the worst of his ordeal, he broadcast only peaceful thoughts to the suffering puppies, but he would not open his great mind to receive even me in case someone else should get through.

After he died, I kept my mind barricaded against you and the others, Solitaire, because I was afraid. I am alone now, without my beloved Owl. It would only frighten the others if they knew that this plague has left me broken and hopeless. . .

It was a long time before Solitaire could reply. The Owl – dead! Every canine on Welsely Farms would feel grave sorrow at the old dog's passing. Most of them had been raised since puppyhood with The Owl's mind-voice as their only guidance in a world devoid of moral precepts. Without love or freedom, kennel dogs have only cold steel bars to shape their characters. The Pussycat, with her gentle ways, had taught the young dogs to love, but The Owl had taught them the self-discipline and strict adherence to the Teachings that could free their souls!

The Akita let her esteem for the honorable nature of the Shih Tzu Kou show through her sad condolences.

Poor, dear Pussycat. The Owl made a great sacrifice in choosing not to commune with you in his last days, for I know you were not only his mate, but his trusted confidante. But you are not alone now. You are well loved by all here, canines and humans alike. And even I can feel the presence of several undeveloped minds in your womb. Surely the promise of new life gives you some solace?

The Pussycat responded weakly.

It is all I have left to live for. . .

Solitaire was overcome with sympathy for the wretched Shih Tzu. She almost allowed herself to remember what it was like to lose someone you love more than life itself, but she caught herself before the grief took over and stood on her feet in order to physically shake off the emotion. There would be time for mourning later. She and The Pussycat must be strong if they were to save Amber's life.

I regret making your burden heavier with my demands, Pussycat, but those who remain here on earth require your assistance now. The tiny poodle, Amber, has been stricken by this dread sickness as well. I, with One-eyed Jack's support, have been working to hold her spirit, but tonight she has passed beyond our abilities to reach her. I don't know if it will be enough, but I implore you, Pussycat, to use your knowledge of her mind, and your exceptional power to join with us and call her back!

Immediately, the Akita was able to detect a strengthening of The Pussycat's mental aura. She was gratified to know that the prospect of serving another helped the compassionate Shih Tzu to turn her mind from her own sorrow.

Of course we will help, Solitaire! Amber has always been very dear to our hearts and we know her mind-track well.

The use of the 'we' pronoun did not go unnoticed by Solitaire. She didn't comment on it, accepting that The Pussycat still needed to think of herself as part of a couple. Or, perhaps with the immense strength of their intellects, it was possible that the Shih Tzu Kou were still able to communicate even though The Owl had gone on to a higher plane? Solitaire felt she still had many things to learn from The Pussycat and was glad to be joined with her in this noble cause!

***

Anna's bedside lamp was lit and an open paperback book lay on her chest. By the time she had gotten back to bed, she had been too tired to concentrate long enough to complete even one page of reading. She had just kept going over the same paragraph again and again, striving for comprehension, until she finally dozed off. Yet now she was wide awake, tingling with anticipation. Would it come again? She waited breathlessly for another mysterious summons, but there was only silence.

"Musta been a dream," the old woman sighed, disappointed, before rolling over to check on her roommates. To her surprise, One-eyed Jack was also awake and on the alert. He was standing directly beneath her bedroom window, staring out at the night sky with his big stand-up ears twitching like radar. <u>Some dream</u>, she thought, <u>when even the dog's disturbed by it.</u>

Aloud, she said, "What's the matter with you, Jack? Somebody walk over your grave?"

At the sound of his mistress' voice, the terrier glanced back quickly over his shoulder. He returned to listening at the window a moment longer, then relaxed his posture and padded over to the cardboard box where Amber lay sleeping next to Anna's larger bed. He, too, had been abruptly awakened by Solitaire's powerful summons of The Pussycat. But after the two bitches had exchanged their initial greetings, it seemed like they had tuned Jack, along with the rest of the kennel population, out of their conversation.

Upon reaching the poodle's box, he gently touched his grizzled nose to her shoulder. Amber felt much warmer now, thanks to the little blanket with which Anna had lined her bed. To a dog warmth is life, and Jack was satisfied.

An exotic wooden box behind Amber's bed caught his attention next. It held Anna's bedside lamp and some small knickknacks, but it seemed oddly out of place to him. It was covered all over with squiggly drawings of creatures like none Jack had ever seen, but that wasn't what had attracted him. Was it the slightly musty odor of old wood that emanated from it? Jack leaned closer, and puffed small, quick inhalations through his nose until he discerned the faintest residue of The Owl's scent and was jolted by the realization that he was looking at the ornamental crate in which The Owl and The Pussycat had arrived at Welsely Farms! He snorted incredulously. How could a flimsy cage like this one have kept any animal confined for long? He would have been out of there lickety-split, no worries!

Jack stepped carefully over Amber's legs in order to get closer to the source of the familiar scent. He gave the box a thorough going-over to detect if it held any tinges of The Pussycat, as well, but he found none. He hadn't had cause to think about it before, but it made sense that the odor of a sexually-mature male, as The Owl had been at the time, would probably outlast that of a young female. Here, in the alien surroundings of Anna's bedroom, the box seemed to Jack like a physical sign of The Owl's support, and it gave him comfort. He lay down in the narrow space between it and Amber, and quickly fell into an exhausted sleep.

Anna was tired as well, but she wasn't able to sleep again right away. Instead, she lay quietly and ruminated on the choices she had made in her life. She did that a lot these days. Was it just old age that made a person lie abed, rethinking every important decision she had ever made, instead of spending the nighttime hours sleeping soundly? Or was it guilt?

So long ago, when she was a young woman, she had told herself that she was going into dog breeding because she loved the animals, but in hindsight it seemed to her that all she had done was hurt her charges. She had purposely resisted feeling an emotional bond with any of the canines she had raised; how could she love one of a hundred dogs over the other ninety-nine? Even her hounds were only a means to an end. They gave her easy companionship, yet asked nothing in return. They were far more dependent on each other and on the pack as a whole than they would ever be on her.

She reflected on the fate of all of the puppies of so many breeds that had been born in her kennels in the last 30 years. What had become of them? Had they lived joyful, healthy lives? Or had they been cruelly mistreated, passed from hand to hand with no one to ever give them the love they required?

And what of the breeding stock currently living out their lives in their tiny cages in the barn? Where was the happiness in their dull existence? Was she doing them any favors by keeping them alive just so that they could perpetuate their species?

When she had been able to do the physical work herself, Anna had spent long hours out in the barn, playing with the puppies and grooming the older dogs. Even after she had hired Fleet to oversee the work in the kennel, she felt responsible for making sure that her animals were fairly treated. She had visited with them on a regular basis, bringing treats and toys, or just talking to them. She had pet names for each of them and called them by it every day. She understood how much dogs need human companionship; not just to keep them clean, but to give them love and personal attention. That was something Fleet would never comprehend.

Such was her worry toward the end, when even those short visits had become difficult for her, that she had hired in the new manager whom she hoped would take her place in caring for the deeper needs of the canine population at Welsely's. Kenny Lorch certainly loved dogs; she hadn't been wrong about that. He was knowledgeable as well as humane and she had felt confident that he would watch over all of the kennel dogs in the same way that she, herself, would. What she hadn't guessed at the time was how he reserved his love for those special pups with long and glorious pedigrees.

Anna's disappointment with Ken's management, or lack of it, made her feel very tired. She hadn't been able to sneak in her afternoon naps for the past few days, with all the problems in the kennel. She needed to rest, but how could she do that when so many small lives depended on her every day? It was obvious that she couldn't rely solely on her managers, yet she couldn't just close the kennels at Welsely Farms, either. Most of those dogs had been born and raised in a cage; retraining them to live in a family household would not be an easy task. Even if she was able to accomplish that, many of the breeding stock were getting older – and looked it after so many years of constant producing. Who would want them? If her efforts at providing them a good life while she was living had been less than successful, that only made her more determined not to abandon the kennel dogs after her death. She had to keep trying to guide Kenny in her way of thinking and hope that he caught on soon.

Too bad Johnny wasn't older, Anna reflected. He had the right feeling for the dogs. A manager needed that if he was to keep a large breeding kennel from becoming a puppy factory. Anna felt it was the little kindnesses, like making sure even the runt of the litter got his share of a meal, or taking the time to give verbal comfort to an ailing dog, that made life in a kennel bearable. She had watched Johnny spend his breaks, even his lunch hour, cruising the barn and playing with several of the inmates. The dogs loved him, too.

SOLITAIRE, A Dog Story

And then there was the thing with the Akita bitch. It was Doc's report of Johnny's impassioned defense of the new dog that had brought Anna down to the quarantine area to see what all the fuss was about. Without the boy's compassion, things might have ended up very differently for Solitaire.

The trouble was, even if Johnny was old enough to take over the management of Welsely's, he had too many strings binding him at home. Anna had known John Wales, Sr. and his family all their lives and knew he wouldn't let his son go easily. She knew, too, how protective farm families are of their only source of free labor - their children. There was no way that Johnny would even be able to get permission to go on the circuit with Kenny this summer. He was fated to remain bound to the Wales's land for the rest of his natural life. The poor lad would never be free to do what he wanted to do.

Anna's thoughts were abruptly suspended. There it was again! And this time she was fully awake. She concentrated on the odd babble of sounds that seemed to come from inside her head, barely noticing that Jack had leaped from Amber's bed to take a guardian's position next to it.

The sound had started very quietly but was quickly building in volume. Though Anna was positive words were being spoken, they were unintelligible to her, almost as if there was more than one messenger – more than a few – and they were all conversing on different planes. Anna was reminded of a woman she had heard speaking in 'tongues' many years ago on a rare visit to the local Evangelist church. A man sitting next to her, one of the senior members of the congregation, had tried to explain that she would never hear the message if she listened with her ears. To understand the true meaning, she had to listen with her heart. But the interpretation had escaped Anna then, as well.

"Maybe I'm gonna have to listen more careful this time," she said aloud, becoming more panicked as the tumult filled her head. "Maybe this time the message's for me!"

Jack turned to see if his mistress needed him and noticed that she had suddenly become rigid on the big bed. He was perplexed by the sense of deep anxiety that he gleaned from her posture. Anna had heard Solitaire's thoughts before – was she hearing them now? At their present volume, it would be hard for any 'communicator' not to hear them! But if his mistress was listening to the dogs' invocation for Amber's return, why did it frighten her? The Pussycat was simply joining thoughts with Solitaire to lead the rest of the sensate dogs in support of their smitten companion. They were beseeching Amber to answer their calls, to come back to this side of reality. Their mental voices exuded love and concern for the little poodle, nothing more.

Still, Jack sensed that the mental clamor was terrifying Anna, and he desperately wanted to help her. He was torn between his desire to be by

Amber's side when she awoke and his worry for his aging mistress' distress. Then Solitaire's mind-voice broke free of the rest for just a moment.

Stay where you are, little Jack! I, too, can feel the old woman's aggravation. I don't know how she is able to hear us, but we can't hold back our efforts in order to console her. Stay with Amber! She is very close now and will need you very soon. Call to her, Jack! Now!

One-eyed Jack was almost overcome by the mix of emotions that pulled him in two directions, but he did as Solitaire ordered. He laid his head back on his bony shoulders and crooned desperately, adding the persuasion of his physical voice to his mental one.

Anna sat bolt upright and stared, wide-eyed, at the spectacle. What on earth was happening here? She didn't feel physically sick, but she was certain that calamity threatened. Her head was reeling with the turmoil in her mind. Was this a stroke? Was this the sound of her brain suffocating? She lay back on her soft pillows and tried to calm her racing heart. So this was mortality...

No sooner had Anna stopped fighting and accepted what she thought was her fate, then she realized that her panic had been for nothing. The voices, softer again, seemed to have found what they searched for and were gently guiding it – her? – home. Anna felt flushed with relief, then that feeling was, itself, consumed by incredible joy. She remained where she was for a moment, luxuriating in the heady sensations... But she had to know!

She threw back her bedclothes with rare enthusiasm and crouched over Amber's box. As she expected, the Toy Poodle's fluffy head was raised and she was looking around dazedly, as if she was trying to assimilate the strange surroundings.

"Hello there, little Amber," Anna whispered, tears filling her eyes. "Welcome back – to your home and to your loving friends."

As if on cue, Jack bounced over the side of the box and began licking Amber's muzzle, excited and oh! so happy! After a few kisses, he jumped onto Anna's lap and stretched to reach her withered cheek as well, eager to share his excitement and joy with all!

Anna laughed as tears coursed freely down her face. She felt reborn, herself. She didn't know exactly what she had just experienced, or why she had been allowed to be privy to it, but she was ecstatic in knowing that canines have their own resources for setting things right when they need to!

CHAPTER 24

The barn was still dark when Johnny arrived, and very quiet. He stopped for a moment outside the door, reluctant to begin the morbid task he had ahead of him. Every morning for the last week, he had begun his duties at Welsely's by collecting the lifeless corpses from the make-do hospital section in the back of the barn, unhooking them from the useless intravenous drips, and slipping them as gently as he could into black plastic trash bags for later disposal. These early morning discoveries sickened him, yet he had taken the job on voluntarily. How could he face Ms. Welsely over a cup of morning coffee without being able to tell her which of the sick dogs had made it through the night and which hadn't? He also could not, in good conscience, leave the carcasses where they were, causing further distress to their wretched kennelmates.

Johnny drew a great gulp of fresh morning air into his lungs and pulled the heavy door open with a purpose he didn't feel. Once inside, he threw the main light switch, illuminating the stacks of stainless steel crates. There were no whines of greeting, no barks of recognition. Johnny stayed in the doorway until his eyes adjusted to the bright light, reflecting on how strange it was that if he entered the barn at any other time of the day or night, the dogs barked and raised a fuss. Yet these past few mornings when he arrived, he had felt as invisible as Death itself.

"Mornin', Abel. Time to rise and shine, boy!" Johnny called in false good humor when he came to the infirmary door. Inside, Abel was stretched out on a small army-type cot, his towhead thrown back, big mouth agape, pretending not to hear what he didn't want to. When Johnny flipped the room's light switch, he grabbed at the covers to pull them over his head, groaning like he was in pain. Johnny had no sympathy for Abel's drowsiness, and he shook the other boy ruthlessly until he hollered, "I'm awake! I'm awake!"

The whole crew at Welsely's was exhausted after spending the last couple of weeks in an all-out effort to contain the parvo epidemic in the barn. Johnny most of all. He had not been willing to ask his father about lightening his load of chores at home again; he was determined never to ask his father for any favors ever again. Nor did he feel comfortable enough to confide in him just how desperate the situation was at Welsely's. What good would it do, anyway? His father had already shown how little he cared about Johnny's interests.

After making sure Abel was on the rise, Johnny forced himself to go into the kennel area of the barn to inspect the damage the previous night had wrought. The dogs seemed to prefer not to watch while he performed this new and disgusting ritual. As he hurried past their silent cages, Johnny wished that he could explain to the animals that he was here to help them, that this plague was not his doing.

He made himself check each occupant of every cage. Many of the dogs were sleeping, but their casually still forms didn't fool him; he knew well the stiff, unnatural posture of the dead. To his huge relief, every one of the dogs in the area seemed to be breathing comfortably. Had they finally beaten this rotten disease? He gathered his breath and checked the cages again; afraid to believe the nightmare was ending.

He found an empty kennel in the top row and tried to recall who had occupied it. Oh, yes, he remembered, it was Amber, the Toy Poodle. Johnny let his breath escape in a long sigh. He was not surprised. When the poodle had shown the first signs of having contracted the parvovirus infection, no one had given her much of a chance for life. At her most robust, Amber was nothing but skin and bones; she had too little strength to call on to fight the contagion. Still, they all had struggled to save her life and now Johnny felt the emptiness of failure in his gut. He wished he could cry, but he felt too darned tired to make the effort.

Instead, he set his mouth into a firm line and started back to the infirmary where Abel was shuffling into his clothes. He was beginning to understand why Mr. Lorch, after his many years in dogs, drank so much coffee. Right now, he felt a strong desire for a steaming, black mugful. Abel met him at the big door and the two boys headed off in silence toward the lights of the farmhouse kitchen.

Johnny's despondent mood quickly turned to surprise when he stepped through the screen door of the kitchen to be welcomed by an overly exuberant, and obviously healthy, One-eyed Jack.

"Hey! What's Jack doing in here, Ms. Welsely?" he asked. "He didn't break out of Solitaire's run, did he?"

As soon as the words left his mouth, he felt an uncomfortable cold chill on the back of his neck. What had happened last night? Was Solitaire okay? He stared at Anna, not able to form the final question.

Anna finished taking the coffee mugs down from an overhead cabinet before she responded.

"Don't worry, young'un, that big gal's just fine. She ain't sick or anythin', if that's what you're thinkin'. Didn't Abel tell you about all the excitement around here last night? No, I guess not. He doesn't look like he's even woke up, yet."

Anna poured two cups of java for the boys and placed them on the wooden table in front of them. Abel immediately began spooning huge amounts of sugar into his.

"Woke up?" he muttered grumpily. "I don't feel like I ever got to sleep. Damned dogs. I need a day off. . ."

After his short fright, Johnny felt wide awake.

"What happened last night, Ms. Welsely? I saw that Amber is gone from her kennel...Is she...?"

In answer to his half-formed question, Anna nodded at a cardboard box sitting in the corner of the kitchen. Johnny raised an eyebrow when he saw the thick cord hanging over the side of the box and plugged into a nearby wall outlet. A heating pad? There wasn't any sign of the usual I-V system that they hung up by a very sick dog, so this one must be healthy, or at least recuperating. He tiptoed over to see who was inside the makeshift bed, hoping it was the missing poodle. Jack ran before him and hooked his tiny pointed chin over the cardboard side possessively, checked its occupant, then watched with a saucy sparkle in his eye as Johnny approached.

Amber was awake, and weakly raised her head while her other end quivered delicately to welcome the kennel boy. Johnny turned a huge grin toward Anna before kneeling on the floor beside Jack.

"Well, there you are, little girl! And you look like you're going to be just fine. Jack, stop licking her before you drown the poor thing!"

Amber didn't seem to mind Jack's attention. She leaned her cheek into the terrier's ministrations and closed her eyes contentedly. When Jack finally slacked off, Johnny was able to stroke Amber's tiny head. He marveled at how gigantic his hands looked in comparison to the minuscule bitch and wondered at what strength of spirit she must have, to have survived the ravages of a disease that had killed so many of the larger kennel dogs.

Behind Johnny, Anna was spinning a high-spirited tale of 'her' little Jack's cunning and how the terrier had probably saved Amber's life. Johnny thought Jack looked content with himself, indeed, as he listened to her happy chatter. Like most dogs, he seemed to enjoy conversations that included his name a lot.

Ken entered the kitchen from the dark hallway just as Anna was saying, "...I think I better keep the poor wee thing in the house with me for a while. Leastwise, 'til the parvo's gone for good. She's too tiny to breed, anyways. I've always known that. I guess Fleet figured she'd grow some more, but I don't believe she's gonna get any bigger than she is right now. I ain't never had a housedog before, but this one's kinda special, right Jack?"

"What are you talking yourself into, now, Anna?" Ken asked lightly, taking in the congenial atmosphere in the room and adding to it. He had slept like a log last night after their little adventure and had woken up feeling more refreshed than he had in days.

He stooped to pet the two little dogs on his way to the mug of coffee that Anna was pouring for him, and commented on how the pair seemed to belong there already. Ken had always enjoyed the company of house pets and his action was meant to show everyone that his earlier comment was in jest. He continued his verbal teasing, though, saying that he thought Anna was getting too frail to be chasing her pack of hounds all over the county and he would be relieved to see her exchange them for a nice little lapdog like Amber. Then maybe she'd let him tear down that awful pen.

He reached for his mug of coffee, but Anna purposely held it just beyond his arm's length.

"Careful talkin' to me like an old lady, Kenny! I might just keep those hounds in their place out of pure stubbornness!"

Ken smiled apologetically and Anna turned the steaming cup over to him with a good-natured wink.

Instead of going straight through to his office, Ken pulled a chair up to the old wooden table.

"How's it looking in the barn this morning, boys?" he asked almost offhandedly. Seeing how well Amber was doing, he thought he knew what the answer would be. In his experience, when a deadly disease spared one sufferer in a kennel, its strength was gone. Welsely Farms might lose one or two more puppies, but their hard work had paid off and most probably the rest of the dogs would recover.

Johnny was pleased to reply.

"Real good, Mr. Lorch. I thought Amber, here, was our only casualty during the night, but that sure doesn't seem to be the case."

Abel leaned back in his chair and closed his eyes, then allowed his mouth to erupt into a wide yawn.

"Great," he said, shaking his head to clear the cobwebs. "Then I can get back to my own bed and a decent night's sleep."

"You looked like you were sleeping pretty well this morning, Abe," Johnny kidded him.

The others laughed along with him. It felt good to be making easy conversation again, and they all stayed longer than they should have around the kitchen table. Doc's horn blasting from the barn reminded them of their separate duties.

SOLITAIRE, A Dog Story

"Abel, go on down and open up for Doc," Ken ordered. "I'll be down shortly. Tell Fleet not to expect Johnny first thing, either."

Johnny was instantly curious. There was still a lot of work to be done in the barn and he felt guilty leaving it for Abel. Fleet wouldn't be happy if he had to chip in with any extra kennel work, either.

Abel got up to saunter out the door, looking unconcerned about the day's workload ahead of him. He always worked at the same speed and with the same effort anyway. If less work got done because there was only one kennel boy, so be it. It wasn't his problem.

Anna called after him to send Doc up after his rounds to take a look at Amber and he nodded his head in acknowledgment without turning around.

"That young'un was born tired," Anna stated to no one in particular as she began clearing the coffee cups.

Ken got up from the table and carefully replaced his chair in its position. He thanked Anna for the coffee and nodded for Johnny to follow him to his office.

It was still dark in the hallway, but some of the early light had made its way into Ken's office, enabling him to walk straight over to the coffee machine in the far corner without switching a light on. He pushed the machine's 'On' button and stood for a moment, staring at it, until it started making the gurgling noises that meant a fresh pot of brew was on the way. Thus assured, Ken walked back behind his desk and turned his desk lamp on.

Johnny, standing just inside the door, watched him in fascination. Ken's coffee habit was a joke between the two kennel boys. Abel was sure he took the machine to bed with him, but here, Johnny smiled to himself, was proof that he did not.

"Come in. Come in and sit down, Johnny," Ken called, not noticing the boy's preoccupation with his morning ritual. "I think we need to have a talk, and since I'm not sure how busy I'm going to be today, now seems like as good a time as any."

Johnny brought a chair from beside the window and settled himself across the desk from his boss.

"First off, Johnny, I want to tell you that I'm very pleased with your response to the emergency situation we've been handling all this week. I know how difficult it's been, coming in early and working late – and not having a lot of success to show for it. It's pretty depressing when any highly contagious disease strikes in a kennel, but parvo has got to be the worst. It runs right through a dog, and there's not much we can do to stop it. This strain seems to have been particularly virulent, but it looks as though we've got things in hand now.

"Now we need to talk about next month. Do you know yet whether you'll be able to go to Topeka?"

Johnny looked down at the desktop, and began to wag his head from side to side, showing his building disgust. How could Mr. Lorch put aside the memory of all those dogs who had died so horribly? For himself, he knew he would dream about the slew of unvaccinated puppies who hadn't had a chance against the disease for a long time yet. Unlike Abel and Fleet, Johnny had not been so repulsed by the foul odor emanating from the sick animals that he could not show compassion for them. He had stayed close to them in their misery, doing what he could to ease their fear and suffering. He felt responsible for their lives, and it had hurt him deeply to see each one of them die.

The part that hurt him the most was the number of vaccinated adult dogs that had caught the disease. They had well-developed personalities and were friends in his life that he would miss. The old Shih Tzu, Owl, had faded away in his hands, even as he was administering medication. He had been led to believe that inoculations protected the dogs from such loathsome diseases, and he didn't understand what had gone wrong.

"What happened, Mr. Lorch?" he blurted, taking advantage of his boss's talkative mood to get some answers. He leaned forward aggressively on the desk. "I thought we gave shots against parvo here. Why did so many of our dogs die?"

Johnny's abrupt questioning surprised Ken, whose intent had only been to compliment the boy on his conscientious attitude before going on to discuss his plans for the summer circuit, but he cleared his throat and tried to answer him.

"I don't know how much Doc has told you about parvo, Johnny. I suppose you've seen enough of the symptoms, at any rate, to know what kind of a disease it is – and how rampantly contagious. Even if all of our dogs and puppies had good, up-to-date vaccinations, a certain percentage of them still might have succumbed to the parvo." Now came the hard part. Ken squirmed in his seat like a schoolboy until, with a final intake of breath, he was able to force the words out. "But the main reason we lost so many dogs was that, through no real negligence on anyone's part, our supply of vaccines was bad..."

Johnny stared at his boss.

"I thought Fleet was in charge out in the barn," he said shortly. "Wouldn't that make it his responsibility to check on the vaccines?"

Ken showed his annoyance at the kennel boy's brusqueness, but he didn't shirk the question.

"I haven't ignored the fact that the reason we were so hard hit was due to an error in judgment by Fleet." He exhaled loudly to show his exasperation. "I've already decided to let Fleet go."

That was more like what Johnny wanted to hear!

"When?"

"I'll give him his notice soon. I've wanted to do it for a long time, if you want to know the truth. But there have been so many extenuating circumstances...the injury he suffered in the attack being an important one. I knew that if I let Fleet go after that, I'd have to have a mighty good reason to give him."

"I can give you five."

Johnny was almost belligerent now and Ken reacted by becoming impatient, as well.

"Well, your five reasons are just your word against his, Johnny. Except for this latest thing with the vaccines, I'd have to say he's done a fine job."

Latest thing? Fine job? Johnny was indignant.

"Fleet murdered our dogs! How can you just forgive and forget something like that?"

"Johnny, as you get older you'll understand that we all make mistakes. I'm sure Fleet didn't get up in the morning and say, 'Let me see. What can I do to knock off a few innocent puppies today?' I have to believe that Fleet made a mistake, nothing more."

After opening and closing his mouth several times, Johnny decided he had nothing more to say. He was beginning to feel like a darned goldfish. He stormed out of the room, down the hallway and out the back door. Though he heard Ken call after him, he didn't stop moving until he reached the specials building.

While he was keying the lock, he heard the kitchen's screen door slam behind him.

"Oh God," he groaned, "Please let him just leave me alone for a while."

He worked faster at the lock, but before he could pull the kennel door open, he was hit in the back of his legs by One-eyed Jack, hell-bent to catch him and determined not to be left out.

Johnny's frown flip-flopped into a smile, as it usually did when the Aussie was around.

"Darn you, Jack! I should have known it was you coming out that kitchen door. At least you never disappoint me – you're always a nuisance!"

Jack wriggled all over with pleasure at what he perceived was a compliment and darted into the dark interior ahead of the boy.

Solitaire showed her delight at seeing her two friends coming through the doorway by barking as excitedly as the rest of the dogs, throwing dignity to the wind. She, along with the other specials, had sorely missed Johnny's attention since he had been helping out in the barn. Ken had been good to them, keeping them spotlessly clean and fed, but the dogs knew instinctively that it was the young kennel boy who really cared about them, and he had their loyalty.

Jack rushed to Solitaire's cage first thing and they nosed each other through the bars, their nether ends wagging joyously. Comparing the sedate jiggling movement of Solitaire's tightly curled tail to that of Jack's knob scribing erratic circles in the air, Johnny had another chuckle.

"Good morning, girl." He had the door open and was on his knees ruffling Solitaire's dense fur affectionately.

The Akita lowered her ears and 'smiled' contentedly until the static electricity from Johnny's rubbing built up in her coat, and she had to shake her whole body to get rid of the ticklish feeling. Johnny raised his arms to shield his face, laughing again in mock distress, until Solitaire turned to look full into his eyes. He stopped laughing then, though his smile remained. Slowly, she moved her head closer and licked his nose with a great deal of tenderness — and not a little timidity. Johnny beamed, feeling like a special honor had been bestowed upon him. It didn't matter anymore that the people around here upset him as much as his father did at home; he could put up with that. He knew he could never willingly quit his job at Welsely Farms if it meant leaving Solitaire behind.

"I guess wishing to own you is so far gone from reality that I could be committed for it," he whispered against Solitaire's dark mane, "but I do. I wish we could both take off from here and go. . . where?" The reality of the situation hit him like a rock. "Where could we go, Solitaire? I couldn't even afford to feed you, let alone take care of everything else we would need."

He gave the big dog another hug and rose to his feet. Solitaire wasn't allowed out for roadwork because Ken worried about spreading the disease to neighboring farms, but it was still early enough to take her for a little exercise in the training ring. He left her kennel door open while he found a lead and collar.

Solitaire stood where she was, halfway out of the cage, and waited expectantly. She would not bolt for the door as the more ignorant kennel dogs might do, Johnny knew. Like Johnny, she had accepted her life here. She had nowhere else to go, either.

Jack ignored the interplay between Johnny and Solitaire, bypassing them to go directly through the Akita's kennel and into her outside run. There, he determinedly marked several key areas, guaranteeing her protection from any stray males that might happen through while he was away. That done, he kicked and dug with his back paws as if to affirm his scent warnings with a rude display of contempt. After one final snort he ran back through the opening, just in time to accompany his pals to the training ring.

Once in the ring, Johnny began to put Solitaire through her paces: first walking, then trotting slowly. Jack seemed to enjoy the trotting part and ran in circles around them, barking, until Johnny decided he'd had enough.

"Sorry, Jack, but this isn't for your benefit. You get enough exercise with all your running around this place." With those words, Johnny

SOLITAIRE, A Dog Story

deposited the Aussie outside the wooden gate and slammed it shut in his surprised little face.

Jack could probably have found a way back in there if he really tried, but it hadn't been that much fun, anyway. All Johnny and Solitaire were doing was running around in big circles; they weren't going anywhere at all. He was a busy terrier who had better things to do with his time, so with a shake of his head that traveled down his long body and ended in a tight snap of his tail, he was off toward the barn.

Back in the training ring, Johnny started working Solitaire again, watching with a critical eye as her muscles stretched into the longer movements, rippling with untapped power. He had learned from Mr. Lorch that the working breeds needed a lot less exercise than the other groups did to maintain their strong bodies, but even knowing that, Johnny was impressed that the Akita didn't seem to have lost any muscle mass as a result of her recent period of inactivity.

They gaited quickly, making several rounds of the arena until Johnny had to stop. He was puffing so hard that he couldn't speak, and could only praise Solitaire's performance with a congratulatory touch of his hands. Solitaire was eager for more exercise, but stood quietly by his side while he caught his wind.

Suddenly, she stiffened. The gate opened slowly and Ken walked in, looking a little sheepish, Johnny thought.

"She's looking good, son. I'm glad to see you're working her again," Ken said.

"Yessir, Mr. Lorch. Solitaire's fine." Johnny smiled affably to let his boss know that he was feeling more relaxed after the exercise. "I'm the one who's suffering. Without my bike, it's pretty tough to keep up with her."

"Yeah, I've been thinking about that problem. We've got a lot of big dogs here, and not enough boys on bikes." They both chuckled, trying to get comfortable with each other again. "I've never liked those electric treadmills, though. The dogs must get as bored with that as we do. But it's obvious we need to do something."

"What about a pool?" Johnny suggested. He had read about some kennels using them in one of Ken's magazines. Besides the fact that it was a great source of exercise for the dogs, he wouldn't mind being able to take a dip in it after work when the hotter weather came.

"That's a possibility. We're lucky enough that we have the room for one, and we could build it ourselves."

Ken seemed to want to say something else, so Johnny remained silent, stroking the short, velvety fuzz on Solitaire's crown.

"Johnny, I know it's hard to accept the way I do some things around here, but I really do have the best interests of Anna and the dogs in mind."

"Then get rid of Fleet," was Johnny's immediate reply. He reddened a little, embarrassed by his own impertinence, but he didn't back down when Ken gave him a long, sideways look.

It was Ken who finally surrendered.

"Look, I'm planning to talk to Fleet later this morning, but it's only going to be a warning. I can't let him go just yet. You know how shorthanded we are around here; if we lose another pair of hands, we'll be in big trouble. We need Fleet to keep working until we can find his replacement." He paused in order to emphasize his next statement. "I expect you to get along with him until then."

Johnny couldn't argue the fact that they were shorthanded in the kennels right now. He hung his head, his silence signifying reluctant assent.

Ken laid a hand across his apprentice's shoulders.

"Besides, son," he reminded him cheerfully, "we'll need an experienced man here when you and I head out on the show circuit. Topeka is coming up in a few weeks!"

The corners of Johnny's mouth twisted downward and his eyebrows drew together as, once again, anger molded his expression. When he raised his face to Ken's, his eyes were flashing warnings that made the older man pull his hand away in surprise.

"Mr. Lorch, even you can't be that blind! There's no way I'm going to be able to go out on the circuit with you this year. This year or any year! You know the problems I've had with my father. He's never going to let me go! Period! So why don't we just forget about it, okay?" Against his will, Johnny's eyes threatened to run with tears of fury and self-pity.

Ken was immediately contrite.

"I'm sorry, Johnny. I guess I have known all along that there wasn't much hope your father was going to let you go. Anna warned me that I was being selfish, instigating the problem the way I have, but I really hoped it would turn out."

Johnny nodded his acceptance without speaking, wishing they didn't have to talk about it, anymore.

Ken seemed to understand that. He coughed self-consciously before changing the subject back to safer kennel matters.

"Anyway, Doc's offered to help us out around here a bit more until we can find some new people. We really need more kennel help. I've been remiss in hiring, but I didn't realize how scarce manpower was going to be when the farms are working. I'll place some more ads in the classifieds this week.

"Oh, and I've decided to take over the ordering for the barn from now on, medical supplies as well as food. That's going to hurt Fleet's feelings, but he just doesn't seem to have a head for detail. He's let a lot of stuff get by him, so I've decided to take it completely out of his control."

Johnny thought that was an excellent idea and told Ken so. Often, the food in the barn was so far out-of-date that he worried about feeding it to the dogs. He had often wondered how that could happen with the huge amount of dog food they went through every day.

Ken wasn't finished.

"I fully intend to let Fleet go, Johnny, but filling his shoes may take a while. That's one of the reasons I've put up with so much from him – I'm not really as blind as you think I am. When I first came to Welsely's I had already put the word out that I might be looking for a new foreman, but nobody with any proper credentials in the industry wanted to come out here and work on a breeding farm like this one."

"You mean a 'puppy mill'," Johnny stated flatly.

"Yes, right now Welsely's is a puppy mill. But I'm going to change that, Johnny! I've got plans to make this place into one of the top quality-breeding kennels in the country. We've got the know-how, the talent, and with Anna's continued good will, the money to do it.

"I try to think of this plague we've just endured as a major culling of our stock, that's all. We didn't lose any of our good animals."

What a lousy thing to say! Johnny swore softly under his breath, causing Solitaire to raise her head to look questioningly at him. He stroked her worried brow and the velvety backs of her ears, and the anger went from him as suddenly as it had come. He wanted to hate Ken for being so indifferent about their losses, but how could he when he knew that he, himself, would willingly let every other dog in the barn die if it meant saving Solitaire's life.

CHAPTER 25

Fleet threw open the door to Kell's main kennel building and was overwhelmed by the poisonous stench of sick and dying dogs. His first shocked gasp pulled the putrid air into his nose and throat, where it gagged him and made his stomach heave violently. Shaken, he fell back to the outside of the building and leaned against the rough wood wall, eyes closed, gulping fresh air until his body calmed. His physical reaction to the disgusting smell of parvo was made stronger by his despair of ever getting away from it.

Eventually, when he felt the danger of his losing bodily control was past, Fleet straightened up to slam and lock the kennel door, as if wood and iron alone could keep the fetid air inside. Then he turned to face Earl.

"Sonuvabitch! I thought you said you cleaned up in there, man! I told you to use disinfectant this time, not just the hose. Are you trying to kill off the rest of our stock?"

Earl's chubby face drooped in a hangdog expression of despair. His pale blue eyes, resting in their puffy bags, begged openly for pity. The parvo had been raging through Kell's kennels for over three weeks now, and even for a man of Earl's rough temperament, the carnage had been disturbing. He didn't want to argue anymore; all he wanted to do right now was sit at his kitchen table and drink beer until the hard realities of his life softened and faded away. As a matter of fact, that was exactly what he had been doing when Fleet found him a few minutes ago.

"I did clean as best I could," he pouted. "The damn critters jest keep makin' messes all over the place 'til I can't keep up." Earl could see that his whining only irritated Fleet more, but he was too unhappy to care.

"Anyways, how d'you think I feel goin' in there ever' day? I ain't got no little helper-boys t'make my life easier, y'know."

Fleet would have liked to remind Earl that it was his own stupidity that had started this whole catastrophe in the first place. By taking in that mangy stray bitch just to have something live to throw at Gatorbait, he had made his own miserable bed. But Fleet knew that such a comment would only ignite the dry tinder of Earl's paranoia and then nothing would get accomplished, so he tried a more sympathetic approach.

"Believe me, Earl, I'd have helped you out if I could. But remember that I warned you when this thing started that I couldn't risk going back and forth while the dogs were infected. That would have spread the parvo both ways like wildfire and we would have been caught out for sure. Then you'd have had those government inspectors you like so much all over you like bumps on a gator."

Fleet's use of one of his buddy's favorite phrases worked to sap some of Earl's hostility. Now he introduced a third person into the conversation, hoping to steer the remnants of Earl's animosity in a new direction, away from him.

"I had my work cut out for me over there, too, you know. That fool veterinarian must have thought he was God or something, for chrissakes. He wouldn't let up doctoring any of the sick ones until they had turned cold and stiff. Christ! He had us running around like idiots trying to save whelps that weren't worth the money spent on their medicine. Pretty poor business practice, if you ask me."

Earl sniffed in agreement. He silently congratulated himself that one of the first things he had done when he realized that the parvo had become epidemic was to go around with his kennel bucket, drowning all the newborn whelps. The way he figured it, they had no chance of fighting the disease so they could only spread it. Nor had he bothered wasting medication on any of the older breeding stock; dollar-wise, he didn't think they were worth it.

Fleet seemed to be following his friend's thoughts when he asked carefully, "Got a final toll, Earl?" Then, when Earl pretended he hadn't heard, "How many dead?"

"How'm I supposed t'know how many're dead?" Earl mumbled peevishly. "I can't keep track of ever' dead pup around here."

Fleet glanced sharply in Earl's direction. Was that guilt he heard in his partner's voice? If so, he had a feeling he wasn't going to like what came next. But he needed to know. He also needed to stay calm; he knew from experience that Earl could be dangerous if he felt cornered. Slowly and deliberately, Fleet reached into his back pocket and withdrew his billfold. Pressed inside one of its compartments was a neatly-rolled joint, which he took out and stuck between his taut lips. He ignited the end, and while he savored the sweetish smoke in his lungs, he pondered how to re-phrase his question so that he could get the information he needed from his partner without riling him.

"Well then, buddy," he started companionably, though tenseness edged his voice, "how many dogs do you think we have left inside? You ought to be able to count that far." He began another long toke.

Earl muttered a number that stunned Fleet so that he choked and almost let the joint fall from his lips. Kell's had lost over two thirds of their canine population during the last three weeks! Welsely's kennel had been hit just as hard by the disease initially, yet they had ended up losing only a couple of dozen of their youngest and weakest animals. With shaky fingers, Fleet straightened his cigarette and inhaled deeply, trying to keep a lid on his simmering temper. It would be easy to lash out at Earl right now, to blame his laziness for the greater percentage of their loss, but Fleet knew that would only lead to a violent argument. Besides, the fat idiot couldn't help the way he was.

Fleet had discovered early on that when there was a fast buck to be made, Earl was the ideal partner to have; he was energetic and totally lacking in moral civility. The trouble was, the moron couldn't see ahead of his pig-nose in a longer-running scheme. Once Earl got bored of a scam, or if it developed a glitch, he was the first rat to abandon the proverbial ship.

Fleet had been on the phone plenty the past week, doing more coddling than he cared to in an effort to keep Earl on the job, on the farm – in the damn state, for chrissakes! Earl was in favor of pulling up stakes and high-tailing-it back to the Carolinas where his drinking buddies would help him forget all about Kansas and dogs and the whole stinking mess that was Kell's kennel, but Fleet wasn't ready to write off his investment here yet. Threat and counter-threat had heated up the phone connections between the two farms until, in the end, Fleet had taken a chance and come over to talk face-to-face with his partner.

Now that he knew the loss Kell's had taken, Fleet wasn't so sure he was doing the right thing in convincing Earl to stay. Perhaps he should have let him go home when he wanted to; the kennel population might have fared better on its own than it had under Earl's tender care – it sure couldn't have done any worse!

Fleet's expression was heavy with disgust as he turned away from his partner and made for the house.

"Let's go get a beer," he said, "and figure out what we're going to do next."

Once inside the house, away from the stink of the kennels and with a cold can of beer in his hand, Earl seemed to recover some of his self-esteem. He took his usual chair at the kitchen table and began to babble nonsensically in his childish joy at having company.

Fleet sat across from him in silence, his beer can between his hands and his head bent as if in prayer. He marveled that even now, with most of their cages lying empty, Earl didn't seem able to comprehend the relationship between the 'worthless whelps' he had let die – or hastened to their deaths – and the high-priced merchandise that was the partners' profit. As usual, it was going to be up to Fleet to find a way out of this mess, but right now he didn't see how he was going to do it.

Things had gone from bad to worse for him over at Welsely's, too. Somewhere along the line, he had lost control of the barn. Doc had taken it over while the plague was on them, and had never left. Now he and Ken were tearing the barn apart and rearranging the whole kennel without even consulting Fleet. They were going about the work boldly, too, as if they were taunting him, and he was forced to hold his tongue while his cleverly-constructed tangle of kennels was dismantled. That had been a big disappointment to Fleet; he often used the clutter of the barn as a shield behind which he could spirit a stud dog away to Kell's for a day or two.

The disorderly way the kennels were kept had also made it a simple matter for Fleet to pretend to cull a litter of pups, then smuggle any 'sickly' runts over to Kell's for shipment at full price under their own label. But now Doc had tagged each individual cage with pertinent information concerning the dog(s) it held, and required the kennel boys to physically check each occupant twice a day when they doled out their meals.

The reorganization hadn't stopped with the kennel area, either. Ken had requested that Fleet help Doc go through the paperwork files in the infirmary next. Fortunately, when the parvo had first struck, the idea of Doc spending so much time in the infirmary had made Fleet uneasy, so he had taken advantage of the initial chaos to smuggle any incriminating files out of harm's way. Two weeks ago, he had dropped them off for safe storage in Earl's office, if that's what you could call the messy hole under the stairs.

Fleet sighed miserably. He may have avoided being caught out for now, but if he didn't have full control of the health records for the pet stock, he wouldn't be able to 'kill off' stolen Welsely pups on paper anymore, then secretly transfer them to Kell's breeding facility. Someone was bound to notice the discrepancies pretty quickly.

The worst blow of all, though, had come just this morning when Ken had informed Fleet that he would be doing all of the ordering of food and medicine from now on. That was going to cut into the partners' profits big-time, and without the monstrous gains they had been pulling down to date, there would be no incentive for he and Earl to stay in Kansas any longer. All in all, business was looking pretty rotten for the partners. The great well of free breeding stock and kennel supplies from Welsely's had dried up for them.

"Aw, Fleet, cheer up, buddy," Earl pleaded. He didn't like being around unhappy people.

Fleet focused tired eyes on his partner's less-than-attractive features.

"What's left to be happy about? We don't have any stock, and without stock, we haven't got a business."

"Who cares? I'm more'n half-tired o' dog shit, anyways. Let's jest move on down the road, why don't we? Huh?" His face brightened. "We could leave t'night!"

Fleet didn't have any doubt that Earl would happily do just that; leave in the night without any feelings of remorse for the fate of the helpless animals they would abandon to a slow death locked in their cages.

"What about Gatorbait?" he asked, morbidly teasing to see how far his friend was willing to go.

"We could take 'im with..." Earl began, but Fleet cut him off quickly.

"No way! You're not getting me in the same truck as that monster!"

Fleet's obvious chagrin tickled Earl, who began to gurgle happily.

"Y'all ain't ascared o' one leedle doggie, are ya?"

"Not as long as he's locked underneath that roof grate you made for him, I'm not. But I don't think there's a man in two counties who would want to be around the day you let him out."

Earl enjoyed hearing how frightening his fighting dog was and wanted to extend the conversation.

"Ya know, Fleet, ol' Gatorbait is got to be the meanest thing around here. It'd be a real sin not t'wait around a couple more weeks for the boys t'git here 'n try 'im out."

Fleet rolled his eyes and slumped in his chair again. He regretted ever agreeing to invite Earl's 'swamp-buds' for a free-for-all. He hadn't expected it to be arranged so quickly, but things must be too hot for the boys back home judging from their eagerness to come out west.

Earl seemed not to notice Fleet's distress.

"They'll be here soon enuff, I reckon. They're travelin' real light 'cause I told 'em I got enough of my own youngsters round here t' fill in the roster."

Fleet was surprised.

"You've still got that much stock?"

"Well, some of 'em are a little weak, but they'll put up a fight, I reckon, if'n we put 'em in a pit with some mutt who's as ornery as they are!" Earl grinned as if he was letting Fleet in on a wonderful secret. "I been bringin' 'em up right and they was pretty strong afore the sick, so most of 'em made it through alright."

Fleet silently cursed any God that would allow those monstrosities Earl had been breeding on the side to live through the parvo while their valuable purebred stock had fallen like flies. He shook his head in amazement, but Earl took the gesture as disagreement and was immediately defensive.

"Any one of 'em would beat that Aye-kita y'all keep braggin' about in the pit!" he boasted. Even he didn't believe that, but he had his pride to protect.

"You don't know what you're talking about," Fleet muttered. He covered his anger by feigning boredom with the whole conversation.

"Oh yeah! I know more'n you think!" Earl shouted, his mercurial temper rising.

Fleet knew he'd done it now. He unconsciously raised his shoulders as if they would take the brunt of the angry storm he knew was brewing, but he wasn't worried enough to let go of his beer can.

"Y'all think I don't know what's goin' on around here, don'tcha?" Earl's snarled. "Well, I know we're broke, that's what! And we ain't got enough food fer all those dogs to last the month, I know that! We need to do somethin' to make a whole lot o' money purty damn quick, and y'all don't have any better ideas, so why don't y'all jest shut your uppity mouth fer a change, and let me get on with puttin' on this dogfight!"

Fleet's smoldering expression was meant to warn Earl that he was treading on dangerous ground, but Earl was too fired up to take heed.

"Y'all say things ain't goin' too well over t'Welsely's. Well, I've got news for y'all, Mr. Foreman: you're bein' run out o' that place on a pole, but you're so stupid, you ain't even caught on, yet!"

That revelation stunned Fleet. He stared down at the table so that Earl wouldn't see the confusion in his eyes and claim victory.

"Lorch isn't that devious," was all he could think of to say.

"Oh no? Didn't y'all say that he 'n the vet've been pal-in' around together a whole lot, lately? And now they're givin' ya conniption fits in the barn, right? Even a home-boy like me kin add two and two t'gether!"

Paranoia set in quickly once Fleet accepted Earl's reasoning. The changes being made at Welsely's did seem to be specifically designed to humiliate him and force him out. But when had he lost control of the situation there? Even though the horrible plague that had ravaged Welsely's kennels could be said to be the direct result of his mistake, he had felt secure in his position because Ken seemed to feel more guilty for his own shortcomings in the situation than angry because of Fleet's. Doc was the one who seemed to hold a grudge. It could be that Earl was right about the old man being behind Ken's new aggressiveness.

But Doc wasn't the only one who blamed Fleet for the parvo epidemic. Anna had been distant and cold to him recently, too. And the kid, Johnny. That one didn't even try to hide his hostility these days.

It occurred to Fleet that everything had gone bad for him since that first day when the Japanese bitch had attacked him. Instead of having sympathy for his wounds, everyone at Welsely's seemed to have become infected with the Akita's animosity toward him. How he would love to get rid of that animal! With that thought in mind, an old idea began to take on new appeal for Fleet, and for the first time that evening, he smiled.

"All right, Earl. I'll go along on this dogfight scheme of yours." He gave Earl a sly look. "Maybe I'll even add to the fun. How much more do you think people would pay to see that Akita bitch fight?"

Earl didn't answer specifically, but his scowl turned around until he grinned from ear to ear.

"Now yer talkin', buddy! You 'n me, we could make some real good money if'n we was t'bring a ringer like that one into the pit! We could even fool the back-home boys into bettin' against her – and they bet big! They think their dogs're the toughest things in the country, and well they may be, but they ain't met that devil from Japan!"

Fleet chose not to remind Earl about his earlier boast. When the cards were down, they were still partners and should always try to back each other up.

"We're going to have to plan this carefully, though, if we don't want to end up in jail. It's one thing to hold pit fights, but it's something else again to steal an expensive showdog to use in them. Besides, it's not going to be easy to kidnap a bitch her size and temperament," Fleet said.

Earl was overjoyed that he and Fleet were friends again and wanted to be helpful.

"I got me one o' them shock sticks fer trainin' Gatorbait," he offered. "If'n y'all know how to use one o' them, it's easy to control any size animal."

Fleet nodded thoughtfully.

"That'll help, but we may need more than that. She's going to fight us and we don't want to hurt her so bad that she's no good in the pit. Maybe I can figure out a way to slip her a mild tranquilizer earlier in the day."

"Haw! Y'all told me she won't let you anywheres near 'er. I don't think she's gonna eat no pills outta your hand.... But I got a idea. I seen the boys use dart sticks t'break up fights between their dogs. The sticks're about three foot long an' got a weeney little tranquilizer dart in th'end. Don't put the dogs out long, only so much time as it takes t'put 'em away. One o' them might work on 'er!" He seemed pleased with himself as he waited for Fleet's response.

Fleet smiled slowly, his eyes closing dreamily as if he was picturing the fallen Akita at his mercy.

"Yeah, that might do it real well. Think they'll mind if we borrow one?"

Earl rocked back on the kitchen chair until the rear legs groaned in protest and folded his hands comfortably over his belly.

"I'll get it, okay. The boys're sportin' fellas, an' they'll welcome a little new competition. They're such good sports, I was thinkin' mebbe we should let 'em run the fights the first night. Let 'em get comf'table with the local crowd, an' all – an' more careless with the money they think they're gonna win. Then we'll bring in yor Aye-kita bitch on Sat'day night an' pit 'er against the toughest o' the winners. Believe you 'n me, when the boys see that purty showdog come in the pit against their experienced fighters, they're gonna bet large – very large!"

Fleet allowed himself a quick chuckle before becoming serious again.

"We also have to think of what we're going to do with the bitch afterwards."

Earl seemed surprised.

"Why? If'n she loses, nobody's gonna give a damn. An' if'n she wins, the boys'll pay us big bucks for 'er, don't worry!"

"No!" It was Fleet's turn to be vehement. He leaned across the table to make sure Earl was listening to him. "If we steal that dog outright, old lady Welsely will know it was me and put the cops on our trail for sure. We have to leave her here when we go and hope the police blame your buddies for her injuries."

"Look, pal-y," Earl began, looking straight into Fleet's eyes to make sure he was being understood. "Win or lose, that bitch's gonna take a bad beatin'. She ain't gonna be no purty showdog after a fight with Gatorbait. If'n y'all leave 'er here in that condition, you think th' old lady's gonna take it any kindlier?"

Fleet knew Earl was right. But as much as he wanted revenge on the Akita, he was more interested in making a clean getaway. He was about to call the whole idea off when Earl sat up straight and slapped his mountainous thigh.

"I got it! When we're done playin' with the bitch, win or lose, we take her out on the highway in front o' Welsely's gate and run over 'er with the pickup a few times! Throw 'er in the ditch, an' they'll jest figger she escaped by herself and got hit by a car, that's all. They wouldn't even think t'trace her 'accident' back t'here until we're outta state!"

Fleet stared, unbelieving, into Earl's crazy blue eyes for a full second.

"You are a sick sonuvabitch!" he expostulated before he could help himself.

Earl looked genuinely hurt.

"What? I'm jest thinkin' it'd cover up the fight marks. And y'all've been goin' on 'bout wantin' revenge. The dog'll be half-dead anyways, by that time. We'll jest be helpin' her along is all." He lowered his head self-consciously and fiddled with something in his lap.

Fleet wondered what he had gotten himself into and whether his partner was turning into a maniac. Maybe when he and Earl moved off down the road, they should go in different directions. Trouble was, right now they were still dependent on each other for a grubstake, so he calmed himself down and made the effort to hold things together for just a while longer.

"Okay, Earl. Look, we'll worry about that part later. We'll probably just lock her up with the rest of the stock when we take off."

When Earl looked up shyly, his eyes watery and red-rimmed, Fleet went a step further to smooth the situation over.

"You're right, buddy. We're going to turn a quick profit on these dogfights, and then we'll be able to set ourselves up somewhere else – anywhere you want, as long as it doesn't smell like dog shit!"

He thought for a minute that Earl was going to hug him, but instead the big man wiped his nose on the back of his hand and got up for two more beers from the fridge so that they could cement their agreement.

CHAPTER 26

It didn't take long for Welsely Farms and Kennels to come back, stronger than ever, after the plague. The barn, cleaned and rearranged, with two new multiple-dog exercise pens out back and a monstrous fan that kept the air circulating inside, was a far more comfortable place for those whose lives began and ended there. Some of the heartier breeds from the specials kennel were transferred to the barn and any pregnant bitches from there were brought back to live in a special section that was set up for them in the new building. It was a circular pattern of distribution that made Anna very happy because now she could be sure that the dogs in both buildings would be treated in a like manner.

One after the other, the bitches that had been transferred gave birth to healthy, squiggly little bundles of fur that mewled and struggled, grasping onto life even as they fastened hungry mouths on their mother's teats. The specials kennel sounded like a maternity ward and the bitches living there that were not in whelp came into early season because of their instinctive longing to proliferate their species.

The sparkle that had left The Pussycat's coppery eyes with the death of her beloved Owl returned to glow warmly with a new kind of light whenever she admired her family. There were four girl pups and a boy suckling by her side. Sleek as tiny seals, their shiny coats varied in shade from dark gold to reddish-brown. Three of the pups had distinctive patterns of white across their shoulders, on the tips of their tails and on their legs. When they raised wrinkled noses from their mother's belly, they showed off nicely marked faces with small white topknots and muzzles joined by a white blaze between their eyes. The other two, both female, were of the darkest mahogany with black faces like their mother.

To The Pussycat, the most beautiful of them all was the boy. Though smaller than his sisters, he was the most demanding at her teat. His coat was the richest gold, his white shawl the widest and more luxurious, his boots the most symmetrical and his head, even with its milk-face profile, showed great size and promised to be the most handsomely marked. In appearance, he could have been the son of her Owl and The Pussycat drew comfort from her belief that her lost companion had been reborn in this most wonderful pup.

Anna visited the kennels each morning to watch the process of regeneration. It was as old as time, this pattern of wild renewal after depletion, and it filled her with hope. And each morning, a little stronger and more vivacious, Amber followed her mistress on her rounds.

After visiting with all of the new mothers in the specials building, Anna and Amber made a habit of going around the back to see Solitaire. Anna always got a kick out of watching the two absurdly dissimilar bitches make their polite greetings.

Next, Anna would continue on around the building to the hound run by herself. Amber never, ever followed her there, preferring to wait by Solitaire's enclosure. That was a wonder to Anna because she didn't think that Amber could have any recollection of the pack's attack on her – she had been unconscious the whole time, hadn't she? Still, no matter how she cajoled the tiny poodle, Amber would not approach that side on her own, and if carried, she trembled with such obvious terror that Anna felt sorry for her and let her go.

Jack, on the other hand, seldom missed an opportunity to flaunt his freedom in front of the hounds, and as soon as he heard them greeting Anna, would come bounding from wherever he might have been and cut between her and their run. His enmity was returned by the old matriarch of the pack, Lola, who showed her loathing by going for the terrier every time he came close to the wire. The Aussie danced just out of reach of Lola's snapping jaws, but he wouldn't leave. If Anna tried to shoo Jack away at these times, the hounds seemed to take that as permission for them to chase the terrier as well, and they were all too willing. Anna didn't like the way this relationship was heading, but she wasn't quite sure how to stop it. She decided to trust Jack's proven intelligence and rely on him to stay out of their way when the pack ran free, for run they must! One day soon, she would leave Amber safely in the house and take them out on a long hunt.

Solitaire and Johnny were becoming a close twosome. They worked together every day once Ken gave them the go-ahead to resume their roadwork. They also spent long hours in the practice ring, making sure the Akita knew what the boy was asking for with every light twitch of the lead. She learned to trot proudly and surely forward, not trying to outguess Johnny, but relying wholly on him to guide her in any change of motion or direction. Under Ken's watchful gaze, the pair found and practiced

Solitaire's showiest gait until they moved with graceful perfection as a team. Often, Johnny became tired or bored but he kept going by reminding himself of another sage bit of Anna's advice: "To be top dog in the show ring, not only you gotta have it, you gotta show you have it. And that means practice."

Ken was still not resigned to leaving his apprentice home when the circuit began. He had tried taking Solitaire's lead now and then, but he wasn't able to make her perform like Johnny did. The way it looked now, if Johnny didn't go, there was no sense dragging Solitaire along, either.

The rest of Ken's string of showdogs were ready for the circuit, including the newest member of their ranks. He had delighted Anna the morning he told her that Maud, one of Lola's get from her final litter, should be moved inside and groomed for the show ring. He had put the hound with Abel in the practice ring and it had made for another good pairing; the lad and the dog moved with the same loping gait and were just as lazy as each other when at rest.

Yes, Ken Lorch was a contented man at last. He surprised himself with his acceptance of his role as mentor. He really enjoyed helping the boys learn their trade and found that he was just as able to bring out the best in a dog from a distance as on the end of the lead. He was also proud of the changes he had wrought in the barn that he no longer thought of as Fleet's territory. After all, he had a dozen specials housed in there now and they needed his expert attention every day.

Fleet was being surprisingly compliant through all of this. Ken, true to his non-combative nature, took that as a blessing and did not question why. He just assumed that Fleet felt guilty after botching the vaccines order, and he tried to make the healing process easier for his foreman by never mentioning it again.

Doc was always warning him to watch out for some kind of backlash from Fleet, but Ken couldn't see the danger. Though he had cut back the foreman's duties considerably right after the epidemic, Ken felt he had explained his reasons carefully enough so that Fleet's sense of worth took minimal damage. As a matter of fact, he thought that Fleet seemed happier in his current position than he had been when he bore more responsibility.

Ken reflected on Doc's attitude now, as he made his way back to the farmhouse from the barn. The vet seemed suspicious of everybody recently. The morning after their talk, Doc had telephoned Mr. Asaki, the kennel manager in Japan, but he had told Ken that he wasn't happy with their conversation. He thought the man was being purposely evasive and he insisted on calling back again to speak with the owner of the kennel. It took him two such calls before he finally got through to Mr. Shibuya.

To Ken's surprise, the two had struck up a warm relationship. Lately, if Ken came into his office very early in the morning, he might find Doc seated behind his desk, involved in a very long-distance telephone conversation with Mr. Shibuya. When Ken became curious enough, he asked Doc what he had learned so far.

"Between my new friend, Mr. Shibuya, and I, we have found out that Trident has a long and colorful history with the police in several European countries. He has been charged with several counts of fraud and one of drug-trafficking, but has never served time because the charges are fairly minor and he just leaves whatever country he was doing business in and goes home to Holland before they can catch him. One of his clients in England even tried to pin him with animal cruelty, but wasn't able to prove it, so the guy walked again. Trident's a pretty slippery fish; that's why we need to construct a finer net to catch him. It's also why I'm working so closely with Mr. Shibuya."

Ken was impressed at how much information Doc had already uncovered, and he wanted to help.

"How about contacting Interpol?"

"I already have, with good results. They have Trident on record for smuggling animals across international borders and are very interested in putting him out of business for good if we can give them anything concrete to go on. I've sent them copies of the shipping contracts, as has Mr. Shibuya, and wrote a professional report on the Akita's state of health when she got here. I'd like you to sign that."

Ken readily nodded his agreement and Doc continued.

"So far, Interpol has traced down the physical address in Amsterdam where Solitaire was supposed to have started from, but they said it turned out to be fake; the folks who lived there didn't know anything about Trident and there was no kennel on the property. They know his house – or rather apartment – address, but his landlord told them Trident's been out of the country for the last three weeks or so. Nobody seems to know where. I imagine he's on a buying spree for new stock."

"Has Shibuya let you know why he sold the Akita to Trident so cheaply?" Ken wanted to know.

"No, he hasn't volunteered that information, and it's pretty tricky getting anything out of him if he doesn't want to talk about it. The inscrutable Oriental thing, you know. He only said that she turned out to be a disappointment to him and that he had allowed his manager to arrange the deal. Apparently, Trident was at his kennel at the time of the sale, so he must have known if there was a problem when he bought her."

As was his habit when he had a problem to weigh, Ken considered the myriad possibilities in Doc's statement, then slowly dismissed them, one by one, based on his experience with the interesting bitch.

But Doc wasn't finished yet.

"I really don't think Shibuya meant to cheat anyone. In fact, he seemed genuinely surprised to find out that Solitaire is in the U.S. Unlike Asaki, who seemed to want to close the book on the whole Akita story, Shibuya offered right away to compensate us for all the trouble we've had with her. I got the impression that money is not a problem for him. He made it very clear that he doesn't want the dog back, though. Strange.

"I asked him whether he believed Asaki could have been in cahoots with Trident on this deal, and he said 'no' at first. But after we talked a while, he admitted that he had been experiencing problems of a personal nature with his manager. He didn't expand on those, but I didn't think his personal problems were any of my business, anyway. Still, I must have made him wonder because he agreed to question his man again, using the information we've uncovered so far to unnerve him. Maybe if Asaki's rattled enough, he'll confess to whatever he knows about Trident."

Ken certainly hoped so; he hated real-life mysteries and would be happy when he could put all of this behind him.

CHAPTER 27

It was Friday afternoon, and the last week had been a tough one for Fleet. He had spent most of his days wandering around Welsely's kennels, mumbling to himself and doing nothing worthwhile. It had been difficult to put on a happy expression whenever Ken came by, but he had made the effort and somehow managed to convince his immediate boss that he was relieved to be able to share his burden of responsibilities.

As he browsed restlessly through the pet kennels in the barn, taking mental note of ages, sexes and breeds, frustration welled in him. Welsely's had the puppies his retailers were clamoring for, yet Ken still wasn't shipping any stock. How long was he going to wait? Those pups looked healthy enough. Why was he stalling?

Fleet stopped pacing when he came to a blank wall at the end of one of the rows, then turned on his heel and stomped back to the front of the building. He passed through the open door and immediately turned left to go on around the back of the barn. He needed a cigarette, but one of Doc's new rules forbade smoking in the kennels. Fleet knew he wasn't being paranoid when he took that rule personally because he was the only one on the farm that smoked. His hatred for the vet was growing along with his frustration, and he couldn't wait for the day he could clear out of this place.

Behind the barn, he lit a cigarette and took a puff before he leaned back against the sun-warmed wall and willed himself to relax. He had to stop worrying about Welsely's kennel problems now. Let the old lady and the rest of her crew drown in their own stupidity. He wouldn't be there to help anymore because he and Earl were closing up shop right after the last dogfight on Saturday night and disappearing from these parts forever.

The only regret Fleet would leave Welsely's with would be that he hadn't been able to figure out some way to kidnap Ken's prize bitch for the fights. He and Earl had gone through a dozen scenarios, but had eventually come to the realistic conclusion that it was impossible for any intruder to sneak past Anna's ever-watchful hound pack and into a building full of barking dogs to grab a monstrous Akita bitch who would love nothing more than to eat the interloper's face. Fleet was disappointed about not being able to punish Solitaire for everything that had gone wrong for him since the cursed day she arrived, but giving up his hopes of making a pocketful of money on her hurt even more.

In the beginning, he had turned a cynical ear to Earl's forecasts of immense profits from the fights. He had his share of vices, but gambling wasn't one of them and he found it difficult to believe that people would throw that much good money into a dirt pit after their favorite fighting dog. His attitude had changed quickly, however, once the boys from the Carolinas started to arrive. It was clear that those fellows would not have packed up their dogs and crates and risked crossing three state lines to get to a two-nighter in Kansas unless they knew there was some decent money to be made here.

Earl's house had been full of beer-guzzling, loud-laughing swamp characters all week. Ever since his buddies had arrived, Earl hadn't sobered up long enough even to train his precious Gatorbait. Yesterday, Fleet had asked him about that and he had replied that there was "enough hell-raisin' goin' on out there to keep 'im on his toes." That was true. The South Carolina boys' dogs were even rowdier than they were.

Fleet had been careful when he spread the word around the nearby towns about the pit-fighting trials to be held tonight. He hoped he had been careful enough. At the time he had allowed Earl to talk him into this deal, he'd never actually seen two dogs in mortal combat and hadn't realized how gruesome such a contest could be. After a week of richly descriptive storytelling by their guests, however, he was getting uneasy. How the local men were going to react to such a grisly sport was difficult to gauge, and he didn't want any trouble this late in the game.

One of the most experienced of the southerners, a runty old man named Billy, had tried to console Fleet with tales of guys being so impressed with their first fight that they put down money on his winning dog's future whelps right then and there so they could have their own fighting dog. As a result of his dog's prowess in the pit, breeding had become a good moneymaker for him.

"Y'know, Billy," another man interrupted, "I never could figger how one beat-up ol' dog could stud the number of pups you've sold as his. 'Specially after he got his balls mangled in that fight over to Tullis last year. I didn't figger he'd ever function proper after that, yet you keep on sellin' his pups to this day."

Old Billy visibly sagged at this suggestion of wrongdoing from one of his good buddies.

"Well, son," he started slowly, "that's what's so nice about havin' a really tough dog like 'Jake'. Nobody's ever had the nerve to check his balls that close." He smirked mischievously, eyes bright with mirth. The rest of the party had laughed riotously along with his joke. It was always 'Buyer Beware!' when you bought a dog from this group.

Another of the men, who seemed better-spoken than the rest, tried to convince Fleet that pit-fighting was instantly addictive as a spectator sport, and once the locals saw one good fight, they'd be sure to come back for more the next night.

"When you're there, man, you don't mind the blood and guts. You're too caught up in the beauty of the survival of the fittest. The top dog's the only one who should live, which means the other one naturally deserves to die. Hell, after a few rounds, you don't even mind losing your betting money, as long as the fight was good enough."

In spite of their eagerness, Fleet was still unsure. But these were not inexperienced men, and when they were finished teasing their new pal, they let him in on their normal m.o. for working a virgin crowd.

"We brought us a coupla 'dud' dogs along. You wouldn't know it to look at 'em – they act tough enough – but they're all used up. They ain't got the cajones anymore to stick it out in the pit with the new dogs. We put 'em in for the first fight. They dance around and growl, mebbe rip each other up a bit, but they won't clench. The crowd starts getting hungry for a little more action. The dogs keep threatenin' each other, but they're too scared of getting' hurt to go for it. Soon the crowd gets bored. They start screamin' for blood.

"We pull the old dogs out and put a coupla Earl, here's, untried youngsters in. Normally, the young'uns don't get into it right away – less'n it's one of Billy's 'naturals', that is..." This was greeted with appreciative guffaws. "Anyway, the youngun's take a little proddin' and by now the crowd's wild enough to egg 'em on. They really get into it and by the time the first kill of the match is made, those boys'r ready for it. After that, they only want more blood and better dogs. The bets start pourin' in. The meaner the show, the more we make. And we always save the best for last. Believe me, those boys'll be so spent and happy by the end of the night, we won't have any problems with 'em."

Fleet asked, "But what if some sore loser decides to go to the sheriff?"

The group from South Carolina exchanged solemn looks and a few flexed hairy forearms in menacing gestures. Earl laughed from deep in his belly, shaking like Jell-O on a plate.

"Would you turn these fellas in over some measly dog's life?"

Fleet had no more arguments.

The site of Earl's pit had proved to be ideally located for the fights, far from the homes of his closest neighbors, in a dense thicket of brush and tall grasses surrounded by wheat fields. However, the Carolina boys didn't feel the pit was deep enough for the spectators' safety, so they had spent the last day building a wall around it out of odds and ends of wire, corrugated tin and wood debris. They had worked like a happy group of Santa's more malicious elves in anticipation of making a lot of money very quickly.

It was the thought of all that cash coming into the Carolina boys' hands first, before he got his take, that was jangling Fleet's nerves. Night after night, he had listened while they drank beer and made sly jokes about cheating other newcomers to their sport, until he had felt the panic rising in him. For what was he, if not a newcomer, when it came to fighting dogs?

Throughout the last couple of weeks Fleet had built so heavily on his conviction that Earl's buddies were completely devious that now, with only a few hours left to go, he was desperate. He had to know what they were up to. A raging thirst suddenly came over him, which made up his mind. Abel could finish up in the barn. Right now, he just wanted to get back to Kell's farm the quickest way possible.

He looked around surreptitiously, but there didn't seem to be anyone about, so he headed away from the barn in a direct route toward an overgrown corner of the yard. Not since the new manager's appearance had Fleet taken the chance on using this back route between the farms. He knew it was risky; he could easily be spotted on this bright afternoon, but he was frustrated to the point of not caring.

***

Johnny was outside, hosing down the run next to Solitaire's. He was working in his t-shirt sleeves, having removed his outer work shirt so that he wouldn't get it wet. The afternoon was warmer than usual and he was beginning to feel sleepy, when he was startled to attention by the Akita's growl. He darted a quick look about to see from which direction Fleet was approaching, for the foreman's presence was the only thing that never failed to upset the easygoing character that Solitaire had relaxed into. When he didn't see anyone coming along the normal pathways, he turned back to the Akita to determine the nature of her problem. She was staring at something off in the distance, behind the barn; her square head raised, ears tilted in a posture of listening.

Johnny squinted his eyes to follow her gaze, thinking that perhaps one of the barn dogs had gotten loose and was making a run for it. At first, he didn't see anything at all, but then he noticed the tiny figure of a man making his way through the back section of Welsely's property. He was a fair distance away, but Johnny could tell by the man's stride that it wasn't a stranger. It was Fleet.

Watching him from this distance, Johnny supposed that Fleet could be chasing a small runaway. However, he didn't seem to be searching in the grass so much as watching the horizon. To Johnny, it looked a lot more like he was involved in some new mischief and was afraid of being spotted. The boy's curiosity was piqued, but not so much as his sense of foreboding.

"That Fleet's a menace. Where do you suppose he's off to?" he asked Solitaire, strolling over to the mesh wall between them. She acknowledged his words with a flop of her tail without taking her eyes off the man in the distance.

Boy and dog watched as Fleet paused for an instant at the bottom of the field, then vanished. Solitaire glanced back over her shoulder at the kennel boy as if to confirm whether he had seen the same thing. Johnny waited a few seconds, trying to pick out Fleet's figure again. Where had he disappeared to? In an effort to expand his range of vision, Johnny climbed partway up the chain wall of the enclosure and was rewarded with the sight of Fleet hurrying into the shelter of a handy stand of gray-green trees in the next field.

This was the second time he had seen Welsely's foreman on the wrong side of the boundary fence. The first time, he hadn't done anything to follow up on his suspicions, but in light of recent events, Johnny didn't trust anything that Fleet did.

The trouble was, he didn't know exactly what he should do about it. Though he couldn't believe Welsely's foreman was up to any good while he was on Kell's farm, he couldn't imagine what kind of trouble he could be getting into, either. Should he go to Mr. Lorch with his limited facts and probably get a lecture on minding his own business as a reward? Should he go to Doc?

Johnny had recently found a new ally in the old vet. Doc had never been overly fond of Fleet, though as long as he only saw him through an alcoholic stupor, he would never have passed judgment on him. These days, however, Doc backed down to no man. Sober since just before the onset of the parvo, he had worked alongside the crew at Welsely's and struggled harder than any of them to save even the weakest victims. Johnny had the impression that Doc felt their losses as intensely as he did.

Afterward, when Mr. Lorch had asked for his input, Doc had thrown himself into the renovation of the barn with almost fanatical vigor. The kennel boys joked about the vet's 'crusade' to set Welsely Farms and Kennels, Inc. on the road to salvation, but they were privately impressed.

Johnny had almost cheered when Doc wanted to inspect the breeding records that Fleet kept in the barn. He was sure that there must be all kinds of discrepancies in those papers that would give Mr. Lorch more than enough evidence to ask outright for the foreman's resignation. Fleet had

SOLITAIRE, A Dog Story

squirmed and twisted as usual, trying to get out of handing the files over, and almost had Mr. Lorch convinced of the fruitlessness of such a search. But Doc was insistent, so Mr. Lorch had no choice but to straighten his spine and order Fleet to assist Doc with whatever he needed.

The results of that search had been disappointing, however. Days of careful examination of the paperwork by Doc had brought no major misdeals to light, and Fleet was still here. But that didn't signify innocence to Johnny, only cleverness. He felt positive that Doc was on the right track and he was eager to help him out. Perhaps if he followed the foreman now, he would find out something that would give Doc the key he needed to unlock the puzzle that was Fleet.

Solitaire seemed as restless as Johnny was. Like most dogs, she was wary of abnormal movements, and she instinctively distrusted people and animals outside of their usual situations. Every now and then she groaned impatiently and changed her position, though she remained alert to the smallest movement in the field.

"We need more evidence, Solitaire," the boy declared matter-of-factly, confident that the Akita had followed his thoughts and knew exactly what he was talking about. "I'm going to see what he's up to."

The decision made, he coiled his hose inside the dog run and prepared to exit through the rear gate. Solitaire had jumped to her feet when she heard the resolve in the kennel boy's statement and now stood by her door, waiting for him to open it.

"No, girl. You're not going. How in the world would I hide anything as big as you on a secret spy mission?" he joked. He stuck the palm of his hand on the mesh in front of her wet nose to let her know she was to stay, then struck out for the barn.

He hadn't gotten far when Solitaire began to raise a tremendous fuss behind him. He turned to see her standing up against the side of her run, stretched to her full height with her paws nearing the top of the six-foot cyclone fencing. The Akita's deep bark was not a plea; it was more of a demand to be taken along.

Johnny was undecided. If he left Solitaire here, she would surely alert everybody, including Fleet, to his departure. But he couldn't take the Akita where he was going; though he didn't fear for his own safety, he knew there was always danger for Solitaire where Fleet was involved. He started back toward her, intending to plead for her cooperation.

Solitaire's protest was already being acknowledged. Ever alert to his friend's needs, One-eyed Jack had heard the Akita's barking and was on his way from the barn. He dashed past Johnny to bound against the mesh directly in front of Solitaire and hang there, intent on ascertaining what her problem could be. She stopped barking immediately, though she stayed on her hind legs. Her expression became comical as she peered down between her front legs at the tiny terrier far below her. In that position, the heavy layer of skin around her neck fell forward over her head, wreathing her face with furrows of dark, glossy fur and giving the impression that the only reason those creases didn't completely cover Solitaire's face was that they were held back by her stiffly pointed ears.

"Well, there," Johnny laughed, "now that you have some company, I'll be going."

Solitaire pushed off the wire, lowering herself gracefully until she was nose to nose with Jack. The concern she transmitted to the terrier was so strong that he remained at attention, standing against the mesh, until he heard her wishes.

Jack! You must not let the boy follow Fleet on his own. There is trouble in everything that devil turns his hand to. I cannot stop Johnny from in here, so you must go along to watch over him. Hurry to catch up!

Jack knew an important order when he heard one! He whirled away from Solitaire's fence and dashed after Johnny, catching up with him halfway to the barn. In his hurry to do as Solitaire asked, he hadn't taken the time to question where he and the boy were headed, but he guessed he would find out soon enough.

Johnny didn't acknowledge Jack's presence, but continued toward the yard behind the barn. Once there, he could see signs of Fleet's passing and followed the broken stalks of weeds until he came to a small gate located in the northeast corner of the back fence. Though he had never noticed the gate before because of the dense foliage that had grown up around it, he was not surprised. The previous tenants on Kell's acreage had been happy to let Anna run her hounds after the vermin on their property, he knew, and she had probably used this entrance quite a bit back then.

Jack stuck his head through the wide wooden slats of the gate and scented the air to ascertain how long ago Fleet had passed. He could easily have pulled his shoulders through as well and charged into the next field, but he didn't like to give too many secrets away, so he waited politely until the gate was opened.

Guiding Jack out of the way with his toe, Johnny unhinged the ancient gate. It startled them both with a belligerent creak before falling back slackly to let them through.

"I guess there must be a trick to opening that," Johnny apologized lamely to his companion, then the two of them struck off for the trees as quickly as Fleet had done.

Jack soon lost any nervousness and gave himself over to the enjoyment of a new adventure. He coursed through the long grasses, tail up and nose down, in search of vermin tracks. Johnny had to exert himself to keep up but soon he, too, felt the exhilaration of an unplanned outing. They traversed the first field and encountered another fence. This time, instead of bothering to search for a gate, the boy jumped over it while the Aussie went right through the wires. Halfway across this meadow, which was also untilled, a rambling farmhouse surrounded by several scattered sheds came into view.

Johnny had to do a quick sidestep to avoid stepping on his diminutive companion when the Aussie stopped dead in his tracks to listen. He was accorded a disdainful look for his clumsiness and had to wait circumspectly for the terrier to go on.

Jack maintained his position, pointed muzzle lifted high into the air and nostrils vibrating as he breathed in the wind-born stench of a kennel. There could be no other reason for the smells of canines and filth that mingled together on the breeze. Dogs, even multitudes of dogs, do not choose to live together in such corruption unless they are trapped there behind bars. With a solid wheeze, Jack expelled the stink from his nostrils, then leaped forward, eager to resume their expedition.

They hadn't gone much further when he stopped again, the ringing bays of what seemed to be numerous dogs filtering through to his ears. A strange hunting pack! They were still a long way off, but Jack stiffened with dread as he tried to pinpoint the direction from which the dogs would come.

Moments later, Johnny heard the hounds' baying. His first thought was that Ms. Welsely had her pack out, but one look at the bristling Aussie beside him told him differently.

Jack tried to use his own particular body language to convince the boy that now might be a good time to head off in the direction of home and safety because this adventure was beginning to turn sour for him.

But Johnny was oblivious to the terrier's anxiety, mesmerized as he was by the pack's progress through the tall grasses. He felt a shiver of excitement as he watched the dogs coursing across the open field. A time or two, he had accompanied Ms. Welsely when she sent her pack out and had been fascinated by the methods used by the frail woman to control the beasts. One short whistle or two could change their direction; a terse shout, if they were close enough (and there was no prey in sight), brought them home.

Ms. Welsely had explained to Johnny that her jurisdiction of the hounds when they were running began and ended with Lola. The old matriarch was the brains of the pack, having been on many hunts, and she knew firsthand both the excitement of the kill and the punishment for disobedience. The other dogs followed her lead and she followed Anna's commands – mostly, but not always. After one particularly disappointing day, Ms. Welsely had confided to Johnny, "There ain't a full-blooded hound worth his kibble that'll give up a chase easy, and you can't force 'em off every time or you'll break 'em. You got to allow a hound his independence. Unfortunately, that means he's gonna disobey you now and again."

Johnny wondered which dog was the head of this pack. Probably it was that big gray out in front, as the rest seemed to be running loosely together at his heels. Perhaps it was because they were an untidy mixture of breeds, but Johnny thought that the group didn't have the smooth cohesion of Anna's pack when they were on the scent. He looked about to see the whereabouts of their handler, but there didn't seem to be any humans around at all. Nobody was guiding the hunt. Ms. Welsely would never allow her pack to run without her because they could be a danger to themselves and to any stray farm animals once they were 'runnin' hot'.

Johnny looked about to check that Jack was okay, and was surprised to see the normally feisty terrier hunched between his legs, trembling with abject terror. Sympathizing with the little dog's discomfort, he reached down to raise him to a safer perch, and for once Jack didn't protest being handled.

Johnny had almost forgotten about Jack's frightening run-in with Anna's pack, but now he realized how precarious their position was, out in the open field with nowhere to escape should the hounds turn. He didn't know how well-trained this pack was; they could be vicious with strangers. He was measuring the wisdom of turning back through the field against taking temporary cover in one of the farm buildings, when a group of men emerged from one of the larger sheds on the property. He was so relieved to see humans that he didn't care if Fleet was among them. The foreman might have some tough questions, but so did Johnny. Rather than call out and risk the unwanted attention of the hounds, Johnny walked slowly in the direction of the weathered shack.

A sudden collective roar from the pack startled Jack into jumping nervously against Johnny's chest. The hounds had run down their prey and were eagerly tearing it to pieces. From this distance, Johnny couldn't see much of the victim except for small patches of it that were being thrown in the air and snatched at by the dozen or so maddened dogs. He had expected their prey to be a fox, which could easily outdistance the hounds in these open fields, and was surprised to hear the chase ending so soon.

While he watched, the pile of dogs seemed to rise from the ground and shake. From the center of them emerged a shape he recognized as a dog – one of their own! The big gray animal he had thought was their leader had actually been their quarry! He felt sickened by the remorseless exhilaration with which the victors tore at the body of their fallen comrade, and turned his eyes away.

A gruff cheer went up from the group of men near the building when they heard the noise of the ferocious battle. One of them shouted, "Hank, you better git yore ass in gear and collect that brute 'fore they eat 'im up all together!" He needn't have bothered because Hank was already running down the field, club in hand, yelling futilely at the dogs to 'Off'. He seemed to be the only one concerned with the fate of the downed dog, which led Johnny to believe it must have been his. The men left behind hollered cruel taunts about Hank's dog not being so fast, after all, and cackled gleefully at their own humor.

What kind of people held such contests with their own dogs? Johnny held Jack closer to him and shrank down into the tall grasses. Against such people, their only hope lay in concealment.

When it seemed they had run out of jeers and catcalls, the group of strangers sauntered over to where Hank was trying to keep the pack from closing in again on his bleeding mongrel. They had heavy chains with them, and one by one, the snarling dogs were pulled off and subdued, none too gently. It occurred to Johnny that there was little difference in barbarity between man and beast with this crowd.

He braced himself to make a run for it if they headed back his way – except he still didn't know where he would run to. He could feel Jack's heart beating wildly against his chest as they both waited tensely for the excited baying that would announce that the hounds had circled back and picked up their trail. However, the dogs stayed quiet and soon the men's voices began to fade, as well.

In unison, terrier and boy drew relieved breaths. Johnny raised himself to see that the men were keeping on in the direction the hounds had been headed. They were spread far out across the field so that their dogs couldn't scrap with one another and conversation was limited to curses and complaints. Johnny was surprised to see Hank walking slowly behind the others with his gray dog leashed and trailing him. He would have sworn that dog had been killed, so vicious was the fighting, yet there it was – limping and bloodied, for sure, but still able to go on. He whistled softly in astonished admiration for the strength of the brute.

Jack took that as his signal for release and began to struggle against the strong hold Johnny had on him. Scenting no new malignancy in the air, he took the time to shake the feel of Johnny's hands out of his coat then turned with a questioning look in his one bright eye. What next? Would they return home now? Or continue with their outing? Either way, he would accompany Johnny, as he had promised Solitaire.

Now that the danger was past, Johnny relaxed too. Where moments before he was in dread fear for his life and that of his dog, now his boyish sense of adventure was back. After all, he reasoned, the strangers had left now, so he was free to do some snooping around in peace.

"What do you say, fella?" he unknowingly turned Jack's interrogations back on him. "Are you game to go on?"

The Aussie rolled his good eye and cocked his head to listen carefully for signs of the men's return. When he heard nothing threatening, he relaxed and wiggled his short tail in what Johnny took as complete agreement, so they set off once more for the nearest of the outbuildings of Kell's farm.

Johnny kept a careful eye on Jack, watching for any more negative reactions as they drew closer to the old shed. He wasn't sure if there were any people left behind, and the tiny dog had already proven that his senses were infinitely sharper than Johnny's own.

Since the easternmost wall of the structure was totally without windows, Johnny decided that would be the safest approach. Cautiously, he made his way toward the front of the building, lingering over each movement in an attempt to be as quiet as possible so that he wouldn't alert anyone to his presence.

Jack wasn't sure why Johnny was moving so slowly, but he sensed his tension and skulked stealthily behind, in comical imitation of the boy.

When they reached the corner, Johnny turned to hiss at Jack to 'stay back'. Jack was so dismayed that he sat down with a bump! They must be on a very important mission, judging from Johnny's puzzling behavior.

Cautiously, Johnny spied around the corner. The front side of the garage, for that's what it was, was made up of one big wooden door with peeling paint and rusty hinges. Embedded in the large door was a smaller one that allowed the entry of people only. Though its size suggested that this building had been used to store farm equipment, as far as Johnny could see every piece of equipment on this farm was sitting out in the yard, rusting into nothingness. He judged the garage as being unimportant to his mission and looked around for someplace more interesting to explore.

Situated here and there about the compound were a dozen or so small wooden shacks, probably built at different times for various types of storage. They all appeared to be empty now, or at least Johnny hoped so because they looked too decrepit to provide shelter for anything.

"The best thing that could happen to this place would be a tornado blowing through and taking the whole thing away." he confided to Jack in hushed tones. "It looks deserted."

Warily, Jack rounded the corner. With his first glance, he took in the messy rubble heaps pushed against the sides of the various structures, the piles of rusting steel everywhere, the grayness of old paint and decaying wood. Nothing had changed since the last time he was here.

If the terrier relied as heavily on his sense of sight as Johnny did, he might have agreed that the place was deserted. But his sensitive nose was being blasted with smells, most of them offensive but some quite interesting. He licked the air to 'taste' the myriad scents, and listened to quiet rustlings inside the sheds, all of which meant that there certainly was life here.

But if Johnny was not blessed with the dog's acute physical senses, he was gifted with a power of deductive reasoning that made up for it.

"That low building over there, Jack," he pointed directly across the yard at what might once have been a stable. "It's as rundown as the rest of the place, but look! It has new wood boarding up the windows."

Johnny turned to explain his theory to the Aussie who, in turn, studied the boy's expression keenly.

"That looks like Fleet's work to me," Johnny concluded, his voice serious with accusation.

The grave sound of Johnny's discourse was not lost on Jack, especially when he mentioned the name 'Fleet'. The little dog sneezed in distaste before looking away to study the barricaded barn. He was not afraid of encountering the foreman here – he had seen him here many times before – but he was sensitive to the danger that Solitaire felt was awaiting Johnny. This was a bad place, he knew from past experience. If Fleet was here, that made it worse. Perhaps they should leave now?

He turned to see that Johnny was halfway back along the side of the garage already, so he had to hurry to catch up with him. Stealthily, the two crept on from shed to shed until they reached the broad side of the old barn.

They were stealing toward the front door, walking as carefully as if they were threading their way through a minefield, when Johnny finally heard the muffled sounds that came from within. He paused, mid-stride, picturing another pack of ravenous beasts inside, ready to tear him and Jack up as soon as he opened the door. But only sharp yaps from a couple of young puppies at play broke the silence, followed by a series of disinterested barks from some bored dog that was just testing the air. It sounded peaceful enough to Johnny, much like Welsely's barn on a lazy afternoon. Then the realization hit him. A kennel? He hadn't heard anything about Earl Kell running a kennel over here. He mulled the idea over in his mind, feeling almost a proprietary interest. After all, this was something within his area of understanding.

Johnny slouched against the wall and pondered the stunning possibilities of his discovery.

Now here was a neat reason for Fleet's clandestine visits to Kell's. The puppies that seemed to appear and disappear from Welsely's: they must have come from over here. The weird delivery complaints: those were sick puppies shipped from this place, not Welsely's. And the 'dead' animals that Johnny had never seen die? Fleet must have been stealing them, then lying about it in the paperwork. But did that mean Doc was a suspect, as well?

Johnny didn't want to believe that the vet was in cahoots with Fleet, but what other deduction was there? Doc may have only been pretending that there was nothing wrong when he examined the breeding papers for the barn stock; his conclusions had surprised and disappointed a few people besides Johnny.

His ruminations were interrupted when he noticed that Jack was puffing up in order to answer some idle challenge from a dog inside. Johnny quickly shushed the terrier before the growl could clear his throat, then rose to his feet. More than ever, he wanted to know what was going on here – and how it affected Doc.

There was still no sign of humanity around the farm. Johnny felt fairly confident that, alone, he could sneak into the barn by the unhinged side door, but he was worried about what he should do with Jack. It was a given that the dogs on the inside were going to do some barking when he entered, but if he allowed a strange terrier into their midst, they were sure to raise the roof with indignation! And that would clearly announce his presence to anyone who might be left in the house. He had to take a chance on leaving Jack out here to fend for himself – the Aussie had always proven to be very good at that, anyway. Johnny waited until the restless terrier's attention was caught by some new thing across the barnyard, then opened the door.

It was very dark in the building, the only light being what he was letting in the door. It smelled a lot worse than the barn at Welsely's ever had. Part of the reason was that there wasn't any air circulation, since all of the windows were boarded up and there was no sign of fans. At least he could be sure there weren't any other human beings inside; no one could have stood the smell with the door closed! He heard some scuffling and a few nervous whines, but it didn't seem like the alarm was going to be raised. These kennel dogs had suspiciously little interest in the comings and goings of their caretakers, Johnny thought.

He ran a hand up both sides of the door, looking for a light switch. Finding nothing, he was about to extend his search, when the tiny silver bell at the end of a light pull reflected a dot of sunlight and caught his eye. He stepped forward into the kennel, at the same time pulling the string.

"Oh, Jeez. . . ," escaped his lips before he remembered to keep silent. He looked about him at dozens of towers of filthy cages with their wretched occupants. Revulsion filled his mouth with a bitter taste. He tried to back away from the nearest cages, but came up hard against another column that weaved tremulously above his head. The pitiful creatures inside the upper cages scrambled to hold their positions, yet none of them cried out. He spun about to keep it from falling, only to come face to face with the sorrowful visage of a weeping cocker spaniel.

For weeping she was, her sad eyes oozing a sickly green mucous that covered her muzzle and stained it a dark, smelly red. Her dull gold coat had grown out and felted into one continuous mat, except around her hindquarters where she was so scarred from her own vicious chewing that hair would no longer grow there. The skin there showed as a thick, ugly, gray patch, its texture more fitting for the hide of an elephant than that of a dog. Johnny knew the cocker was in abject misery, living with a chronic itch that would never leave her until she chewed herself through to the bone. On top of everything else, he could see that she was very pregnant. And yet, though the sad bitch stayed huddled miserably in the rear of the cage, she showed the inherent personality traits of her breed by timidly waggling her pudgy knob of a tail in the faint hope that Johnny would prove to be a friend.

At that moment, Johnny felt a great loathing for his race. He was embarrassed and humiliated that his own kind could so cruelly treat a species that only desired to be allowed to serve them. His pain rose in him until he couldn't draw a straight breath, and he found himself inhaling in ragged puffs. Stumbling to the door, he threw it open and collapsed against the outside wall. It was several moments before he was able to catch his breath again, and by then his disgust had changed to storming, self-righteous fury.

Thankfully, Jack had made himself scarce and was out of harm's way, so Johnny moved by himself toward the back door of the farmhouse with long, determined strides, and took the veranda steps two by two. There was only a screen door, but he pounded on it as heavily as he could without breaking it. No one answered on whom he could vent his rage, so he was left to fume impotently on the porch until he heard Jack's angry barks and turned to locate him.

The Aussie was digging furiously at the foundation of one of the wooden sheds, making Johnny think he was after a rat or some such thing. You couldn't keep that terrier down if there were vermin about! He called Jack off and watched as the little dog stalked away, stiff-legged with indignation.

A few of the kennel dogs that had joined in halfheartedly when they heard Jack's excited barks were still making noise. Johnny listened incredulously. Not all of the barking was coming from the direction of the barn! He took off at a run for the nearest shed.

When he got to it, he peered through the rotting slats of the hut's wall. As he feared, there were dogs being kept in these horrible, dirty shacks, as well! His anger mounting, Johnny cast about for something with which to pry the padlock off the first shed's door. The wood was so rotten that he didn't think it would be too difficult. He picked up a piece of metal rebar that was lying along the side of the shed and returned to the door. However, he quickly changed his mind about forcing a way in after he put his face close to the crack again to check on the number of animals being housed there, and almost had his nose bitten off. Obviously, the dogs in these sheds were not in secure cages – and they weren't friendly. Johnny didn't blame the brute for attacking him; it was probably maddened by the same deplorable conditions suffered by the dogs in the barn, but it made him realize that he would need help before he tried to free any of them.

Johnny felt positive that Fleet was involved in this operation, but how could he prove it? If he called in the authorities right now, there was no doubt they would arrest Earl Kell, as the owner of the farm, for animal abuse. But without proof, there was a good chance that Fleet would be able to talk his way out of any charges the county might bring against him, the same as he talked his way around Mr. Lorch and Ms. Welsely all the time.

Johnny was still mulling over his options when he spied Jack across the farmyard. The terrier appeared to have forgotten his anger and was his normal jaunty self again, investigating a clump of tall weeds that covered the house's foundation. Watching the little fellow's carefree enjoyment of the sunny afternoon made Johnny even more determined to free the pitiful dogs he had found here. More importantly, he wanted to bring all of the people who had caused their misery to justice. He headed back to the house, determined to find something that would incriminate Fleet.

This time, knowing nobody was at home, Johnny circled the outside looking for an open window or some other method of clandestine entry. The house was not very secure, he discovered, with almost every window raised to let the afternoon breezes blow through. It occurred to him that, if the windows were wide open, the doors of the house were probably not locked, either. He went back to the rear of the house and felt almost sheepish when the screen door's latch clicked open easily in his hand.

The door opened directly into the farmhouse kitchen, which was almost as filthy as the kennels had been. Johnny's initial impression was that the house had been ransacked, but the mountains of dirty dishes on the counters and the piles of empty beer cans in the corners of the kitchen showed him that this mess was still in the making; it was being created purposely by the inhabitants, probably the same group of men he had seen working their dogs in the field.

He made himself ignore the mess in the kitchen and searched for some room where records on the dogs being bred here might be kept. One quick circuit of both floors was enough to ascertain that there was no particular room set up as an office. Then he began opening doors to see if he could find some kind of storage space. He tried the kitchen pantry, which was almost empty, and a downstairs bathroom that hadn't been functioning properly for a long time. The third door he looked into was the one he wanted. A small storage room under the stairs was full to bursting with boxes of books, files, and loose papers.

Looking through all of them would have been impossible in the short time he had, but Johnny deduced that if Kell filed his paperwork as lackadaisically as he kept the rest of the house, the most recent information would be in the front few boxes. Last in, first out, he figured.

Johnny crouched down and pulled out a cardboard box that was sitting in front of the rest. His deductive reasoning was immediately rewarded when he found that the box contained a stack of manila folders marked with familiar labeling. Fleet must have removed these folders from Welsely's infirmary office and brought them over here before Doc had a chance to go through them.

The next box down, one advertising a leading brand of canned dog food on its sides, drew his attention because they used that type of food regularly at Welsely's. Moments later, he was able to congratulate himself again. The bookkeeping records, if you could call them that, for Kell's kennels were an untidy affair, with disorganized files overflowing with crumpled receipts and loose invoices. Johnny's pulse quickened when he examined some of those invoices and found they were simply copies of bills that had been paid by Welsely's, and overwritten in red to show what portion of the supplies had been sent along to the next kennel: Kell's.

Johnny braced himself against the wall to study this wealth of evidence. He thumbed his way through several files containing forged litter registrations, dual invoices, and false shipping papers with Welsely Farms and Kennels, Inc. listed as the shipper. He marveled that Fleet had been crazy enough to keep such incriminating files in his infirmary office all along. It was proof of how confident the foreman had been that Ms. Welsely would never replace him.

Johnny folded a few of these faked documents together with one of the invoices from Welsely's and put them in his jeans pocket to keep as evidence, but his curiosity still wasn't completely satisfied. He was about to reach for another box when he heard the heavy scraping sounds of several pairs of boots on the front veranda and knew he had overstayed his visit. Hurriedly, he threw the boxes back into the small room and closed the door. There wasn't time to close the boxes properly, but Johnny wasn't worried about the owners noticing such a small indiscretion in all of that clutter.

He bolted for the nearest window, thankful that it, like all the rest, was wide open, and crawled out onto the wide porch as quietly as he could. There he stood with his back pressed flat against the wall until he discerned that the group was making its way through to the back of the house; then he headed in the opposite direction.

Johnny had never before heard such strong accents as these strangers had. Obviously, they were not from around here! Maybe he should wait around to see if he could figure out why the strange group was here in the middle of the Kansas prairies? He made his way back around to the kitchen window closest to where the men were arguing.

They seemed to be having a loud disagreement about which of their dogs would go into the ring first tonight. In his ignorance, Johnny thought the men were planning to exhibit some dogs in a show like Mr. Lorch did, but their arguments about the cruel rules of their game soon made him realize that they were talking about another sport entirely. He was stunned, unable to contemplate exactly what it all meant.

A strong hand closed around the back of his neck. He gave out an involuntary shout of surprise, then rose obediently with the pressure of that hand.

Johnny knew he wouldn't be able to fight this man physically, so he forced himself to relax and took a noncombatant, yet still defiant, posture. After all, this was America and these men were in the wrong, not he. He didn't think they would dare do anything to hurt him.

The man pulled Johnny around and searched his eyes intently while Johnny, in his turn, took in the man's rough features and felt fear for the first time. The man's eyes were of a blue so pale that they seemed almost colorless next to his red, sunburned skin. Johnny tried to back away from the fleshy, sweating countenance before him, but he was being held too firmly.

Once the man realized he had caught a young teenager who was obviously scared as hell of him, he relaxed a little, though he still held fast to Johnny's neck.

"What're you up to, boy?" he asked gruffly. "What're you doin', sneakin' 'round out here?"

Johnny spoke out quickly, with all the courage he could summon, hoping to intimidate with his self-righteousness.

"I came looking for Fleet," he answered, cringing only slightly in case Fleet should happen to be in the house with the others. "I work on the farm over there – Welsely's – and I thought I saw Fleet come this way earlier..."

The man looked at him with mean little pig-eyes, seemingly unable to judge if he was telling the truth or not.

"I'm just looking for Fleet," Johnny repeated hastily, using the familiar name as a shield against whatever this horrible man had in mind. "Do you know where he is? I've got a message for him." He volunteered the false excuse in order to explain his presence at Kell's farm in a manner that he hoped would lead the man's suspicions away from his snooping. He didn't want him to get curious enough to search his pockets and find the evidence to prove that he'd been inside the farmhouse.

Earl scowled, confused by this new state of affairs. Nobody was supposed to know that Fleet came over here, but maybe this kid had a legitimate reason for trying to find him. He raised his chin and squinted down his nose at the boy.

"How'd y'all know he was over thisaway?" he asked.

"I just happened to see him leaving Welsely's," Johnny replied nonchalantly while trying to shrug out of the big man's grip. "Hey, listen,

I'm not looking for any trouble, mister. I just thought I'd do Fleet a favor, but if he's not here, I'll be going."

Suddenly, the man grinned at him, a big, ugly, open-toothed grin that Johnny did not feel was meant to be friendly.

"Fleet's gone into town fer a bit, son, but he'll be back right soon. Prob'ly better if'n y'all was to wait inside fer 'im. What'd y'all say yor name was?"

As he talked, he forced Johnny forward, hand still on the back of his neck, along the veranda toward the back of the house. They turned the corner and found themselves confronted by One-eyed Jack, standing stiff-legged with challenge in the middle of the porch.

Baffled, Earl stopped to stare at the shaggy little dog, obviously trying to figure out where he came from or if he was one of the kennel dogs that had gotten loose.

Jack returned his stare, as belligerent as any Rottweiler, his scant mane prickled out like a fully-loaded pin cushion.

Their absurd standoff was broken when Johnny seized the opportunity to kick sideways at Earl's shin bone and duck out from under his hand. Shouting in pain, Earl still had the presence of mind to grab the boy again before he got clean away. The confused moment was Jack's cue to jump into the fray, and he did so with great aplomb. He wove in and out between the big man's legs, jumping up to bite the calf of whichever one he shifted his weight to so that Earl couldn't stay balanced long enough to give him a kick. His teeth couldn't do much damage through Earl's denims, but he unbalanced him enough to provide Johnny with another opportunity for escape.

Jack ran and circled and jumped and fought ferociously, using all of his speed and cunning. Johnny helped by squirming around until he could use his right hand to punch Earl in his beer-filled gut, causing the man to bellow again, though more in surprise than pain. His shout set off a whole chorus of laughter. All three combatants froze and turned slowly to face their audience.

"Grab that mutt!" Earl shouted, with little of the slow-witted 'good old boy' left in his manner.

"Jack! Run!" Johnny ordered before Earl's large hand slapped him tightly around the lower half of his face, effectively shutting off any more sounds from his mouth.

Still laughing uproariously, the other six men closed in on Jack, calling "Here, liddle doggie", and holding their arms wide in what was supposed to be a welcoming gesture.

Jack stood quite still, looking from one gnarled set of hands to another. The instinct to flee was strong in him, but he wasn't sure if he should leave Johnny. The men moved closer, their half circle drawing around to entrap the beastie. Jack rotated his head from side to side, taking in their actions as he slowly reversed. Now his back was up against the rail! Reinforcements would be good right now! Then, with sudden clarity, he knew what he must do! After a last, apologetic glance at Johnny, Jack did the smart thing – the terrier thing! Faced by insurmountable odds, with no help on the way, he ducked out! The group of men was left empty-handed, astonished by the speed with which the terrier pulled his wiry body through the porch railing and hit the ground running from the yard.

"Ah, let 'im be," one of them said to disguise his disappointment before turning his attention back to Earl and his captive. "Who we got here, Earl?"

This was the first time Johnny heard his captor's name and he felt tremendous relief. When he had looked into the man's ugly face, he had been frightened that he had stumbled upon a gang of murderous drifters who would think nothing of killing a local kid. But if this was Earl Kell, he had roots here and would probably be more cautious about hurting a neighbor. However, when Johnny really thought about it, he realized that more cautious didn't necessarily mean less dangerous for him.

Earl's face broke into that gummy grin again. He had finally put two and two together, and his face was lit with appreciation for his own intellect.

"I know who y'all are. Yer that kid Fleet's always cussin' about, Johnny Wales. Haw! I shoulda knowed it'd be y'all causin' so much trouble. I thought that mutt looked familiar-like, too. Well now, ain't Fleet goin' t'be happy t'see y'all here!"

A saner voice rose above the rest.

"No, Fleet ain't going to be happy to see the boy, you jerk."

Earl's mouth shut with a thump.

"Now, Bobby, you ain't got no call t'talk t'me thataway."

"Well, you are a jerk if you're thinking of telling Fleet about the kid. He's already as nervous as an old horse in a slaughterhouse about the fight tonight. If we give him any excuse, he's going to bolt. We've already discussed that. And if he knows this boy's been here, he'll call the whole thing off for sure and then we'll be out a lot of our own time and effort."

The other men grumbled agreement, which left Earl to rethink his strategy. It didn't take him long; Earl was a simple man who only knew a few ways to do things.

"I don't guess we can kill 'im. . . ," he started, then looked up to see if that was what the boys were getting at. When they wagged their heads morosely, he fished about in his mind for another solution.

"I got it! We jest won't tell Fleet the boy's here! We'll gag 'im an' put 'im out in Gatorbait's shed 'til the weekend's done. No one'd dare look fer 'im there 'til after we're long gone." He turned sparkling, pink-rimmed eyes to Bobby, the man who had spoken before, for approval. Bobby nodded and the gaiety returned to the party as they ushered the unfortunate lad in their midst to his temporary quarters.

CHAPTER 28

Jack sprinted through the fallow fields as if Satan's own hunting pack was on his trail. Not once, but twice he burst through the thick undergrowth to flush shocked rabbits from their afternoon tea, yet he paid no heed. He had to warn Solitaire about Johnny's predicament! He was much too far away to communicate mentally, even with a strong mind like the Akita's, though she surely could reach him if only his thoughts weren't whirling around like he had a Tasmanian Devil inside his head.

Jack's loyal terrier heart verged on breaking when he thought of how he had failed both Solitaire and Johnny. Solitaire's faith in him to keep control of the situation had been undeserved; he had let his guard down when he went nosing off after yet another interesting smell. The place was full of them and the Aussie hadn't been able to contain his insatiable curiosity. Now look where it had gotten him. And poor Johnny! The memory of the roguish-looking humans surrounding the kennel boy on that porch spurred the Aussie on to another burst of speed. He had worries aplenty about the damage those types might do!

***

Back at Welsely's, Solitaire lay in her kennel, stunned by the series of visions she had drawn from One-eyed Jack's mind.

Not long after Johnny and Jack had left the kennel by the back way, Ken had arrived to check on the dogs and administer any medications that were necessary before the specials building was closed for the night.

Solitaire had gone inside to watch him at his labors, but she soon grew bored and decided to check on how her friends' explorations were going. She had lain in her kennel as though she was sleeping, but in reality she was experiencing the world through the odd angle of the diminutive terrier's one good eye. She had closed her eyes to allow the full sensation of Jack's delightful experiences to wash over her, and had felt the Aussie's pleasure as he and Johnny cavorted across the open fields in complete freedom. How she would have loved to join them!

Her mane had bristled with protective anger when Jack heard the strange hounds and her paws had twitched futilely in her eagerness to protect him. She had startled Ken by growling out loud, drawing a glance that seemed to reassure him that the Akita was only dreaming.

Solitaire's sigh was as heavy with relief as those of Johnny and Jack when the strange men had left the area with their pack of dogs. She had felt sorry for Jack and nearly reached to mentally soothe the little dog's anxiety, but his fear had left him as soon as the pack moved off, so her support wasn't needed.

When the two adventurers had entered the yard at Kell's, Solitaire had caught the same scent of filth as the terrier had and her body trembled with yearning to warn her friends away from such a sinister place. She had become impatient with Jack when he wandered away on his own investigations, losing Johnny from the picture altogether, but since there was nothing dangerous stirring the terrier's senses, she relaxed and even dozed for a while, herself.

Jack's sudden discovery of the unfriendly personality in the shed had startled Solitaire out of her sleep. She had bolted upright in her kennel, letting out an explosive 'woof' that made Ken jump half out of his skin, as well. He had been tending the Labrador across the way, and turned to scold Solitaire for being spooked by a silly nightmare.

Solitaire lowered her ears, looking sheepish, until Ken turned away. She lay back down to concentrate, but by the time she was able to focus on Jack again, the little terrier was wandering away from the farm compound, curiosity leading him on as usual, and there was still no sign of Johnny. Solitaire was becoming concerned about the boy's whereabouts and would have reminded Jack of his duty, but he suddenly whirled by himself and scampered back to the house.

Solitaire whined miserably, not knowing what was happening with Johnny.

Ken shot her another puzzled glance.

"What's the matter with you this afternoon, girl?" he asked in a kind voice meant to calm the Akita. "You're missing Johnny, eh? Well, don't worry. His father probably needed some extra help and called him home early. We both have to be patient about that. He'll be back first thing tomorrow morning, don't worry."

Although Ken's remark was well-intentioned, Solitaire knew he didn't have the slightest idea of what was going on. She made an effort to control her physical reactions more carefully, however, as the next quick tumble of events played in the theater of her mind.

She could see Johnny, followed closely by a mean-looking stranger. There were cryptic shouts – when was that Jack going to learn to comprehend human speech? – and then everything was in an uproar. The bits and pieces Solitaire was able to retrieve from Jack's confused intellect were anything but comforting; flashes of boots and legs, howls of pain (thankfully not Jack's nor Johnny's!), and then dirty hands with fat-knuckled fingers seemed to be reaching for the terrier from all directions.

Run, Jack! Don't let the evil ones catch you, whatever you do! She had been so sure of his imminent peril that she couldn't keep herself from giving the Aussie a mental 'nudge' in the right direction. The speed with which the images passed while the little animal cut through the shrubbery, beating a hot retreat home, had made her so dizzy that she was forced to break away from his thoughts.

Ken was just finishing up as Solitaire bolted through her curtain to await Jack's arrival in her outdoor run. Long moments passed before she saw the minuscule dust cloud that rose from the heels of One-eyed Jack as he sped back down the path from the barn.

Before he got halfway to her run, she clamped onto his fractious mind.

No, Jack! Do not come to me. I cannot help the boy while I remain within these steel walls. Time is of the essence. You must make the humans understand our need. Run to Anna, Jack! She understands more than anyone here. Try! Try hard to make Anna understand!

Without slowing, Jack adjusted his course for the farmhouse.

In the front of the specials building, Ken had just turned his own steps toward the house and his office when the terrier stampeded into him. Startled, he jumped aside, then gazed in bewilderment as Jack scuttled up the path ahead of him.

"What the heck is going on around here?" he asked superfluously, expressing his own confusion even though he knew there was no possibility of getting an explanation from Jack.

Solitaire was about to remind Jack that he might need Ken's help to get inside the farmhouse, when The Pussycat's soft touch diverted her attention. The wise bitch's mental tones, that had always been so clear and strong while The Owl was with her, were daily becoming fuzzier, making communication much more difficult. Every one of her litter of five puppies was talented, and dealing with them on her own was wearing her out.

Solitaire was reluctant to sever her hold on Jack's consciousness, but it was necessary in order to concentrate on The Pussycat's message.

In answer to Solitaire's polite inquiries as to the babies' health, The Pussycat groaned.

Thank goodness they must sleep a lot right now! I will certainly need your assistance, and Amber's too, to educate them when the time comes. Jack could help, as well, but I'm not sure if I should entrust their impressionable minds to that scalawag! What is the 'terrible terrier' up to, anyway? Just now, I thought I overheard some agitation in your communications with him.

The Pussycat was not as receptive as she once was, but since she was kenneled only a few yards away from Solitaire's run, it was impossible for her not to overhear some of the Akita's communications.

Solitaire apologized for involving the Shih Tzu; she hated to put any more problems in The Pussycat's already heaping dish.

I'm sorry if we have distressed you, Pussycat. It's nothing Jack has done. It's the young kennel boy, Johnny, who is in peril! She explained what had happened, making sure she was broadcasting slowly and clearly.

The Pussycat listened carefully in her deeply empathetic way so that, in the end, she had heard more in Solitaire's story than the Akita meant to tell. With every image she was given, she could feel how Solitaire's devotion to the young kennel boy had grown. She wondered if the aristocratic Japanese bitch, with her aloof manner and studied indifference toward all humans, even realized this. If not, perhaps it was time to make it clear. The Pussycat was not normally so intrusive, but Akitas could be stubborn and this might be Solitaire's last chance to return to the ways of the Teachings.

The Shih Tzu began her probing in a gentle manner.

Is there nothing more you can do to help Johnny, Solitaire? I fear that Jack will have a difficult time knowing if he has been understood as he doesn't really 'listen' to human speech. Have you given thought to communicating with our mistress, yourself?

The Pussycat's faith in her talent should have pleased Solitaire, but instead the Akita's brow-creases deepened with irritation.

As I told you when we first met, I have no desire to explore that part of the human mind. Human thought-processes are so convoluted. I admit that at one time I, too, wondered if it was true that the old woman heard my thoughts. But since that first day, her understanding has seemed more intuitive than literal. I cannot say that there is any special gift involved in her desire to understand us, save that of compassion.

Even in the face of Solitaire's testiness, The Pussycat was persistent.

And what of the night when we searched for Amber? You knew Anna was there. You felt her presence. And she certainly felt yours.

Solitaire recalled her feelings during that occasion. What was it that The Pussycat wanted to hear from her?

Yes, I admit that I felt a new presence. And I thought it was human. But there were so many others filled with so much emotion. . . I'm sure I could not remember Anna's touch well enough to establish an immediate dialogue with her, and we need help now!

When The Pussycat did not respond, Solitaire was forced to continue lamely.

Besides, even if it is possible that the old woman has some comprehension, she doubts herself. She makes jokes about the voices she hears, thinking it a disease of age instead of the wonderful gift it is.

The Pussycat snatched this opportunity to scold her large friend.

Solitaire, our mistress is not the only one to belittle a gift. You possess a marvelous talent, unheard of in this country where there is so little compassion between species, yet you do not use it for the common good. Instead, you dwell in your unhappy past, maintaining a facade of arrogance to keep any human who could love you at a safe distance.

Solitaire was shocked and wounded by The Pussycat's unexpected reprimand. She felt she had been sorely misjudged. What did The Pussycat know of her past and the pain that was so difficult to bear that she had wiped it from her memory, leaving only hatred to cling to? Solitaire could barely conceal her indignation, but the Shih Tzu continued relentlessly.

While my beloved Owl was still with me, we had many discussions about your 'competency', Solitaire. When you first arrived, we worried because you were so angry and seemed full of hatred for humankind. That is not the way of the Teachings.

We were encouraged, however, when your dignity saved you from the insanity of wreaking vengeance on the innocent. Thus, you were befriended by Jack and by the boy, Johnny. We felt their intercession would give you the time you needed to reason more calmly; to apply your substantial wisdom to evaluating your position and deciding on a positive course of action.

Secretly, we hoped you would confide in Anna, who had already shown her willingness to listen, and thereby heal yourself. But although she has remained open to you, you made no advances. We were puzzled. It is the canine way to seek out the company of humans, yet you showed no sign of needing or wanting the attentions of that worthy lady.

Solitaire interrupted to defend her actions.

I hold our mistress in as great esteem as you do, Pussycat. When I first looked upon her face and heard her voice calling to me, I felt a deep longing to be with her. But I also felt her infirmity. When my mind touched hers the first time by accident, it almost overwhelmed the poor woman. It has been fear of hurting her that kept me from trying to renew the connection ever since.

It may be that our mistress has the talent to form half of a 'competent' pair one day, and possibly little Amber will aspire to become the other half, for they are becoming close. But it takes time to develop the necessary rapport for full communication, as you know. To be frank, I do not know if either of those two ladies' frail bodies will be able to struggle on that long. . . If I were to force communication on Anna now, without proper preparation, who knows what the strain would do to her?

Here was the opening The Pussycat had been aiming for.

Then what about the kennel boy, Johnny? He is young and strong and deserving of your consideration. He has taken many risks for you – for all of us. But it is you he loves. Solitaire, let your old feelings go and focus on living now. You must take a chance and trust the boy. Maybe then, you will recover the love of mankind your faith requires.

Solitaire protested this awkward turn in the conversation.

But Johnny is not much more than a pup, with a mind full of turmoil. He has a good nature, but he struggles constantly with his own problems of self-purpose. What could he possibly offer to me in a relationship?

The Pussycat's mind touch was beginning to fade. Her five little ones had woken up and were fussing for her immediate attention. Before she gave herself over to ministering to their needs, The Pussycat focused her thoughts to impress one last, stern message on Solitaire's mind.

Owl once confided to me that he believed the only thing keeping you from fulfilling your status as a 'competent' was your Samurai pride. He worried that your need for bloody revenge would always overpower any feelings of love that tried to surface; that in your fight to maintain your dignity, you would forget how to humble yourself to a beloved master, placing his safety and concerns over your own self-conscious pride.

Johnny is a lonely young man-child, going through changes in his life that he doesn't understand. Now is when he desperately needs the kind of unquestioning love and companionship that a dog gives her master freely. The benefit to you? When you are able to devote your life unselfishly to your master, there will be no more room in your heart for hatred.

Solitaire seemed about to dismiss Pussycat's lecture as unimportant, but the little dog would not let up.

Your rage is controlled now, Solitaire, but I can feel how it simmers just beneath the surface of your emotions. Unless you banish that evil from your soul altogether, it may surface at a time when you have need of the strength of love.

With the truth so evident before her, Solitaire began to feel panic rise. Once, she had been so sure of her place in the world. Feeling benevolent love for everyone when her life had been balanced had been easy, and she had risen to the status of 'competent' with little effort. But then her existence had been tragically disrupted by horrendous events that had left her careening out of control. How could she do as The Pussycat asked, and form the bond Johnny needed when she wasn't sure which direction her life – or Johnny's – was going to take?

The question is simple, Solitaire: Can you love Johnny as your master? If the answer is 'yes', you will find a way to save him – and, in doing so, yourself!

Solitaire clung to The Pussycat's final question, wrapping her wild thoughts around it like an anchor to stop them spinning in her head. Did she love Johnny? She cared about Johnny enough to want him to come back to her unharmed, but did she love the boy? She hadn't thought it possible to love a human being again after the hurt they had caused her, yet she couldn't deny that she felt more content in Johnny's presence. She looked forward to his arrival in the kennels every morning and was happy even when he wasn't beside her, just knowing he was close by, somewhere on the farm. But she felt the same way about One-eyed Jack and he certainly was *not* her master.

No, if she was to be honest with herself, she had to conclude that she did not really love Johnny in that way. She was only being loyal to a boy who had shown her kindness and supported her when others would not.

Having come to that conclusion, the big dog was disconsolate. What kind of a canine was she, that she did not feel the need to give her love to her true master? She was hard and icy inside, like the rugged peaks of her ancestral home in the Akita province of Japan. Had she always been that way? Solitaire turned her thoughts inward in candid self-examination....

Her first memories were happy ones of playing by her mother's side. Her dam was an extraordinarily beautiful bitch, gentle and doting of her young. Solitaire's puppy impressions were of an immense protector whom none would dare confront, one who kept her family warm and safe from the outside world. Inside the world of the whelping box, however, it was an entirely different story. The mother Akita seldom interfered as Solitaire and her siblings began early to fight for their share of her attentions.

Solitaire remembered those baby-wars with her brothers and sisters. Why they fought, no one ever thought to question. Perhaps it was the way sister's earflaps bobbled over the front of her forehead when she pranced, or the peculiar way brother's tail corkscrewed when he was ready to pounce that made the young Solitaire want to jump on them and trounce them both. Perhaps it was revenge for the wicked way her siblings would pull on the fuzzy 'Cossack hat' of fur that formed between her own ears whenever she was concentrating. Or perhaps it was just Nature's way of preparing them for life in a bigger world. But no matter the reason, all of the puppies battled tirelessly until the day came to separate them from each other, and from their mother.

Ah! The loneliness of that first night alone in a strange new bed! Solitaire remembered how she had tried to be brave. She hadn't wanted to cry. But the forlorn whimpers of her littermates far off in their own dark kennels melted her resolve so that soon she was yowling hysterically for the company of her former enemies. Just when she had believed that her misery would consume her, Solitaire felt the light impression of her mother's mind on her own. Happily, she opened herself to the familiar touch and was surprised to feel other compassionate caresses emanating from all corners of the huge kennel in an attempt to comfort her. As a tiny puppy, she was made to know the first lesson of the Teachings: a receptive mind was all that she needed in order to draw on the strength of others in her own time of need. This mutual support is the basis of the canine family.

Over the next few months, most of Solitaire's brothers and sisters had been taken away from the home kennel, never to be seen again. The pups that remained were taught diligently by their mother and other wise kennel dogs in the elementary rules of the Teachings so that, wherever they went, they would find support and fellowship. After that first night alone,

Solitaire had embraced the Teachings with all her heart, and had excelled in them until her mental prowess matched the physical power that was developing on its own in her body.

Solitaire recalled being aware from an early age that the human caretakers at the kennel considered her special. When her handlers took her out to teach her the ways of the show ring, the 'Owner of All Dogs', the one they reverently called Shibuya, was often present. She should have felt honored by his attention, but even at that age Solitaire was arrogant. Was it not true that she was the embodiment of generations of breeding of the best Akita stock in the land? Did not her lineage shine with the names of the great stars of the ring? Though the wise dogs of the kennel warned her of the consequences, Solitaire's pride grew as her body matured.

It became obvious that Solitaire had inherited the great size of her illustrious father instead of the more delicate build of her exquisite mother, and some in the kennels began to talk of this as a bad thing. Chief among these was the First Assistant, a small man known as Asaki, who often teased the growing pup, saying she should be sold into the city police force where her great size would be of benefit, instead of an embarrassment. Solitaire, a 'Confidante' who had already mastered the rudiments of the Second Level of Listening and so knew the venom in his words, had covered her hurt with a mask of dignity.

The fact of her largeness seemed unimportant to the Owner when he beheld his favorite, however. During her training exercises, when her balanced gait showed her powerful body off to its best advantage, Shibuya bragged incessantly about her perfection. One day, he made it known that he desired to exhibit Solitaire before other humans, judges whose opinions he valued. The First Assistant had become very indignant and argued that Shibuya would lose much face by putting an incorrect animal in the show ring. But his outburst only annoyed the Owner, who then insisted that Solitaire be entered in the very next exhibition.

The judges were as impressed with Solitaire's quality as the Owner had hoped. She had strutted so proudly before them that they made little comment on her unfeminine size, overlooking that fault in light of her excellence in all other areas.

Solitaire remembered the sweet feeling of vindication she knew when the First Assistant had paled at the sight of her first major trophy. It hadn't even bothered her when he complained that the only reason she had won it was because the judges were becoming too influenced by the crude Americans (a term Solitaire had never heard until then) and that they had lost sight of the Japanese Standard for Akita Inu. She did get upset when he said that soon they would be exhibiting *longhaired* Akitas at the shows. That remark was uncalled for.

Everyone knew this was a great insult. The unfortunate Akita Inu who is born with a long coat is ostracized in Japan, as it is the world over. Although all Akitas are known to carry the gene that can result in the creation of long-haired offspring, a true longhair cannot be shown with such a fault and is seldom allowed to breed. Never, in Solitaire's line, had there been a longhaired puppy.

Shibuya also became incensed when he heard rumors of his manager's remarks. He confronted Asaki while he was working in the kennels and dressed him down before all of the lesser caretakers. The First Assistant was forced to apologize for his error in judgment while the others looked away, embarrassed by his public humiliation.

By now, Solitaire had reached maturity and a mating had been arranged between Solitaire and the half-brother of her father. 'Sanjiro' was a splendid animal, regal in bearing and as handsome as Solitaire was beautiful. This was an important factor because, like her wolf ancestors, no Akita bitch would ever accept the attentions of an obviously less dominant male. Such instinct guarantees she will bear only the progeny of the strongest, insuring the success of the species.

Solitaire sighed as she remembered how, in the week prior to the onset of her heat, she and Sanjiro had frolicked as puppies together. Loyalty being another important factor for an auspicious mating in the Akita breed, the Owner had wisely allowed the young bitch to form an emotional bond with her future mate before they both came under the stress of physical need. Solitaire had felt an immediate affection for the big stud dog's courtly manner and resolved she would have no other.

Her first encounter with man's treacherous nature had come soon thereafter. One of the First Assistant's duties was to keep track of the date when Solitaire would be the most fertile and schedule the initial mating for that day. However, his bitterness still consumed him. He purposely lied to the Owner about the date, all the while planning an altogether different breeding to take place the night before.

Solitaire recalled the events of that night vividly. She had woken in the dark hours, aware that someone had entered the kennel building. The other dogs hadn't barked, but she felt their minds were as alert as her own. Soon she heard the mincing footsteps of the First Assistant, accompanied by the heavy padding of a large dog. She had sat up, curious but unafraid when Asaki stopped in front of her run. At his side was one of the guard dogs, a big rangy Akita of lowly birth who had a long coat of reddish-yellow hair. Solitaire had become suspicious only when the First Assistant unlatched the door to her run and dragged the cowering dog after him through the opening.

The male Akita had good reason to be fearful, as Solitaire proved by instantly turning on him with bared teeth, intent on driving the ignoble stranger out of her kennel. There was nothing the hapless dog could have done in that situation. He was securely leashed, so he couldn't run and there was nowhere to hide. To turn on a female of his kind, even to protect himself, went against his strongest instincts. The only action left to him was to cower low, his ears flat against his head, and prepare to take the beating he was sure would come.

But the First Assistant was cleverer than to allow any injury to occur to either dog before they had accomplished the deed he was planning. He quickly stepped between them and wrapped a stout rope around Solitaire's neck before she could follow through on her threat of violence. Twisting neatly, he had forced the large bitch off-balance until her head was between his knees. At first Solitaire was only confused by this violation of her dignity, but when she heard the First Assistant urging the intruder to sniff her hindquarters and even to mount her without waiting for her acceptance, she became furious.

Her upbringing had been too genteel to prepare her for such an assault, however. Raised to respect the sanctity of human flesh, she had not bitten the legs of the man that held her. Instead, she bucked wildly, twisting and backing against the tight rope until she was so strangled that she could only cough hoarse threats at the despicable cur behind her.

The male dog had held back, nervous of approaching Solitaire, although he certainly would have liked to. Moments after he had entered the bitch's run, his nose had told him that her time to breed was upon her. He would have been willing to wait, since there were no other suitors around; with patience, her invitation to breed might have come. But the First Assistant was not so longsuffering. He roughly pulled Solitaire's bushy tail to one side and held it there while calling rude encouragement to the willing but wary male.

Once he realized that the bitch was not able to turn on him, the dog had become bolder. He whined and pawed at Solitaire's hindquarters, and finally reared to clasp her body tightly between his front legs. Feeling his tremendous weight on her back, Solitaire had tucked, desperate to protect her vulnerable areas. But moments later, when the pressure against her yielded, she had known the battle was lost. She was not able to stop her loins from spasming, instinctively drawing forth his seed. With her panting attacker still lying atop her, she had keened in the savage fashion of her wolf forbears, her shame at the dishonorable coupling sharpening her physical pain.

The next day, the Owner had insisted on being present for what he believed was Solitaire's first breeding. If he was surprised that, in spite of her inexperience, Solitaire was eager and willingly submitted to the more practiced Sanjiro's advances, he hadn't shown it. Once the tie had been completed, Shibuya was content that all was going according to his plans. He could not have guessed with what spite his minion had plotted to foil those plans.

Solitaire sadly recalled her feelings of despair when her litter was whelped and two of the brood showed signs of becoming long-haired like their real father. Her aristocratic blood had turned cold when she first saw them, yet her mother's heart could not turn the two away. She had taken them to suck along with the others and learned to love them just the same.

The Owner of All Dogs had been inconsolable, however. Never had the Akitas of his line begat a single long-haired pup. Still, there was no reason that he would suspect foul play. He was aware that the gene that stimulates the Akita's hair to lengthen and grow luxurious is a recessive one that often skips generations to pop up in the most unlikely breeders. Sanjiro had proven himself by siring many litters in the past without any longhairs; therefore Solitaire was blamed as the carrier of the offending gene.

The First Assistant had taken quick advantage of the Owner's distress, advising him to sell the disgraceful bitch and her litter as quickly as possible. Too humiliated to be stubborn, the Owner had betrayed Solitaire into the hands of her adversary.

In her kennel at Welsely's, Solitaire rose and shook herself, as if that would rid her of the sensation of worrisome excitement that was building. She circled once before lying down again, then forced herself to relax to allow new mental images to run on in a steady stream. These images appeared less as faded recollections than as painfully sharp visions, and her first reaction was to suppress them again, but if she was ever to overcome her current problems, she must be brave enough to face her past.

Since the night of her forced breeding, Solitaire had become more apprehensive about the motives of men, so when the stranger arrived at the kennel wearing hard-soled shoes that made a discordant clacking noise as he approached, her nerves had tingled with ugly premonition.

The strange man stood in front of Solitaire's kennel, coldly examining her through the wires while he exchanged words with the First Assistant. She was amazed at his appearance; he was not of the Oriental race that she was accustomed to. He stood head and shoulders above Solitaire's caretakers. The man's face was pale as the winter sun, though it was not so rounded, and his eyes were blue like the sky. He had a mane of longish yellow hair that was pulled away from his face to hang down the center of his back. The man had an oddly sweet odor to him, unlike anything she had ever smelled before, and that had made her uncomfortable even then.

"You've done well, Mr. Asaki," he said. "This bitch will fill my order well, once I get her back in shape."

Solitaire remembered experiencing some difficulty in understanding the man's words, but she had felt this encounter was important and had strained to catch the reason for it.

"I told you that little trick would work," the tall man chuckled mirthlessly. "I've pulled the same thing a few times when I had a client for a dog that was not for sale. It doesn't matter whether the animal is male or female, either. A bad litter from what an owner thinks was a good mating will sour anyone on their prospective breeding stock.

"I can't believe you used that ugly guard dog of yours, though. That was a real stroke of genius. Quicker that way, too. No way the pups could have looked anything but bad right at birth – even with a beauty like this one for their mother."

Solitaire's heart began to pound as the gist of the conversation became clear to her. So this man had been behind the unspeakable acts of the First Assistant! Who could this person be, she wondered, that she had never seen him before, yet he held such power over her life?

"You'll have to get rid of the pups right away," he went on matter-of-factly. "I'm certainly not interested in them and I don't want my buyers to know about them. Do away with them today and start getting the bitch back in shape for shipment as soon as possible." The man licked his thick lips as he stood admiring his purchase. "As a matter of fact, bring her out here now, Asaki."

Solitaire was perplexed by the man's odd terminology. What did he mean by 'do away with them'? She wasn't sure, but instinctively covered her little ones with her body to hide them from the man's icy gaze.

The First Assistant obediently picked up a kennel lead and entered Solitaire's run.

Though Solitaire felt only disgust for the First Assistant, she relied on him for her very sustenance, so did not physically object to him entering her family den. She would have preferred not to leave her pups with this stranger hanging about, but didn't fight the lead once it was in place around her neck. She rose and followed obediently out the door.

"You had better lock her in a kennel on the other side while I do this," the stranger advised. Confusion touched his features, but the First Assistant moved Solitaire off and locked her in a wire cage.

Solitaire waited patiently in the small cage for another caretaker to come and take her back to her run – and her puppies. She had no premonition of danger, other than her tingling uneasiness in the strange human's presence. Why would she have? Except for the unfortunate night of her first breeding, no human had ever tried to hurt her. There was nothing in her sheltered past that could have prepared her for the coming nightmare.

A shrill yelp brought Solitaire to her feet instantly with her thick, triangular ears perked in the exact direction of the sound. One of her babies was being handled unkindly! Though there were no more cries, she kept her mind focused on the undeveloped thought patterns of her puppies as she paced in nervous circles. She felt that her whole litter was uncomfortable and unhappy, but had no idea why this should be so.

Now there were several loud shrieks, more indignant than frightened, but still painful to a mother's ears. Solitaire's apprehension turned to desperation and she gnawed on the wires of the cage in a futile attempt to break out. The metallic taste of blood from her own badly torn gums fueled her panic and added to her fear for her young.

Suddenly, the tall stranger appeared just inside her range of vision. In each of his big hands, caught by the furry scruff of its neck, was a screaming puppy. Solitaire had to line her body up against the front grate of the kennel and push her face into the wire in order to see them and there she watched, helpless, while her little ones dangled in his cruel grip.

"Asaki!" the man called peremptorily and waited while the First Assistant caught up to him. "Open that door."

The First Assistant's eyes grew wide. "Mr. Trident, no!" he stuttered. "You can't do that. . ."

The man he had called Trident looked into the face of his Japanese cohort and laughed at the weakness he saw there.

"Don't worry, Mr. Asaki. It will all be over in a little while. They won't last long in there. Brrr!" He shivered humorously, then became stern again. "Come along, now, and help me get this thing done. I don't want to put this deal at risk. If we get rid of these whelps right now, there won't be any mistakes."

The First Assistant looked about nervously. Then, seeing that they were alone except for the dogs, he opened the freezer door. He stood as in a trance while Trident walked inside the box. Immediately upon their release, the puppies' ky-yiing ceased, though their plaintive whimpers attested to their continued unhappiness until the First Assistant closed the sound-proof door.

Confusion rattled Solitaire's usually tranquil mind. Why had the men left her babies in the food-box? She had never thought about the freezer as a bad place before, rather as a place of plenty, but dogs were never kept in there.

Trident reappeared with another two squealing babies. Solitaire stiffened in anger that anyone would treat her children so harshly. But what could she do about it from this cage? She watched him walk through the door again and come out empty-handed. The fourth time he returned, he only carried one puppy, the last of seven.

Solitaire remembered now how she had whined with need when the man headed toward her cage. He held the puppy, one of the longhairs, cradled in his arms and was stroking it in loving fashion as he knelt in front of her.

"You see, girl, this is all your fault," he whispered greasily. "If you hadn't been such a shameless hussy, I wouldn't be here and your children

SOLITAIRE, A Dog Story

wouldn't have to die."

Then he left her to watch hungrily as he dropped the last baby in the box with the others. When all of the pups were inside, he locked the freezer and removed the key, which he then handed to the First Assistant.

It had all happened very quickly. Then the two men had walked out of the building leaving Solitaire to try to figure out what had occurred. With the trust of a canine, she could not believe that the humans had harmed her children, yet she knew that the time for them to be taken from her was very far away. She had been separated from her litter only briefly and already her teats were rounding with rich milk for their next meal. She moaned anxiously and began to pace her small cage again.

Only when she reached out to touch her pups' minds again did she understand the horror of the deed that had been done. An overwhelming sense of terror paralyzed her mind. Her babies were becoming cold and frightened in that black, empty place. They were crying out for their mother to help them! Though they had found each other in the dark and scrambled into a heap, their pathetic warmth was leaving them quickly in the frigid surroundings. They needed her and she was failing them. Her babies were dying!

The truth blasted through to Solitaire's conscious mind and she leapt to her feet in stunned disbelief. But she was no longer in Japan; she was far from there, in her own comfortable run at Welsely's.

My children! she keened, a long drawn-out wail for the young ones lost to her.

The other dogs in the specials kennel seemed to understand that hers was a private sorrow and, for once, they didn't join in. They crouched silently inside their individual cages, fearful of the Akita's pain.

The Pussycat was not frightened, only saddened by Solitaire's keening. For the first time, Solitaire had been able to recall the events that had happened immediately before the clouds of confusion overcame her. She had remembered the cruel acts that had stirred her hatred to such insane proportions that she had to be drugged in order to go on living. She finally understood why she felt the need for vengeance, and why she could not let go of the intolerable pain that tortured her soul and kept her from loving anyone, human or canine. But The Pussycat also knew that now that Solitaire had boldly faced her past, she could begin to heal.

Eventually, the ache inside Solitaire subsided. She understood why her friend, The Pussycat, had pushed her to question her own motives for remaining indifferent to humankind; if she was to fulfill her destiny as a 'competent', she must forgive the injuries done to her. Her unfortunate children had long ago found serenity in the long sleep of death, and now she must find some peace within herself. That peace could depend on Johnny's safety.

Solitaire looked around her kennel with a new desire to escape that sharpened her reasoning. She had watched One-eyed Jack enough times to have faith that there was always a way out, if you just looked hard enough for it.

The metal of the kennel walls would never bend to the strength in her jaws, Solitaire was sure, nor would the concrete floor part under any amount of frantic clawing. But the privacy panel between this kennel and the next one was made of a more compliant material. Her attention focused on the small hole that Johnny had sawed into the plywood for Jack. It was only slightly bigger than a rat's hole, but by crouching down on her forelegs, she could press her furry cheeks against it and peer through. As she had hoped, the door to the kennel next to hers, the one that had been left empty for Jack's benefit during the parvo epidemic, was still ajar.

Solitaire quickly formulated a plan of attack. Johnny had been careful to cut the opening smoothly, except where the saw marks crossed each other on the upper corners. That didn't give her teeth much to grab onto. She experimented at pulling on the corners of the hole with her front paws and was rewarded when a thin layer of wood splintered away. Exulted by that small victory, she continued digging until the hole was slightly enlarged, its edges ragged. It was necessary for her to lie down in order to clench the uneven side between her strong jaws, then use the opposing strengths of her neck and shoulder muscles to wrench more of the plywood loose. Bit by bit, the hole was widened until she could put her head through, then her neck. When she was able to push against the panel with the full might of her shoulders, it yielded with a sharp crack. She backed up and shook the splinters from her coat. Her first escape had been accomplished!

The other kennel dogs went wild with excitement at a runaway, but Solitaire hushed them with a thought. Only the hounds outside the building continued to bark, Lola being uncowed by Solitaire's superior mind.

Solitaire knew where she had to go, having a perfect map in her memories, even though it was from the much lower viewpoint of the Australian Terrier. She barely stopped to sniff behind the barn. Johnny's trail was clear to her.

CHAPTER 29

One-eyed Jack raced up to the back screen door of the farmhouse, but was disappointed to find that there was nobody in the kitchen to let him inside. He barked frantically to let his mistress know he was here, but there wasn't any movement inside. Anna often disappeared in the late afternoon, and Jack recalled Amber telling him that they usually went upstairs to take a short sleep then. Deciding that was the case, he barked even louder and more shrilly so that they would be able to hear him from the bedroom. He was so involved in that noisy activity that he didn't hear Ken stomping up behind him on the porch.

"Jack!" – he seemed angry – "Quiet!" The terrier winced. That was a command that he understood from experience meant 'stop barking right now or you're going to get thrown in a kennel out back where you won't be found for a week!' He stopped yapping, but he couldn't help whining in an effort to convey his sense of urgency to the frowning man.

When he heard Jack's plea, it had almost seemed as though Ken understood. His expression softened and he unlatched the door. But when a hopeful Jack tried to scamper past him and through the door, Ken scooped him up and carried him down the hall to this office, instead. After he closed the door, he deposited the struggling bundle on the oval rug.

Jack's pride was severely wounded. He tried every trick he knew to make Ken open the office door, but the human sat behind his desk and steadfastly ignored Jack's efforts. The reality of the situation threatened to overwhelm the terrier; how did he think he was going to convince anybody to follow him in order to save Johnny when he couldn't even make Ken understand that he needed to get out of this room?

A sudden explosion of barking by Anna's hounds gave Jack the break he needed. Ken leaped to the window, but couldn't see what was aggravating the beasts.

"Now what?" he muttered, on the way to the door. As soon as he cracked it, Jack scurried out and raced up the stairs toward Anna's bedroom.

For a moment, Ken seemed undecided as to whether he should chase Jack or find out what all the racket was about in the specials building. In the end, he bounded up the stairs after the Aussie and caught up with him before he could scratch too loudly on the bedroom door. From her spot on the bed, Amber yapped in protest of all the excitement going on outside her mistress' door.

Anna's sleepy voice called, "What is it? Is that you, Kenny?"

Ken gave Jack a dirty look as he held him securely in his arms. "Now look what you've done, you little monster!" He pushed the bedroom door open and poked his head in.

Anna lay in her big bed, blankets pulled up to her chin, while Amber kept watch at her feet.

"I'm sorry if we disturbed you, Anna. I don't know what's going on with the dogs today; they've all been really barky and foolish since earlier this afternoon. I'm sure there's nothing wrong, but I'll check. You finish your nap."

Anna mumbled something about 'somethin' in the air', turned over onto her side, and immediately began to drift back into sleep.

When Jack realized that he wasn't going to be allowed to go to his mistress, he struggled wildly, but couldn't loosen Ken's firm hold on him.

Amber! You must wake Anna! Try to let her know that Johnny and Solitaire are in trouble!

Before the stunned poodle could acknowledge Jack's pleas, Ken backed out the door and closed it softly. He tiptoed down the stairs, scolding Jack all the way for being a nuisance. He walked down the hall to the back door, opened the screen, and threw the troublesome terrier out onto the porch.

"Now. If you're as smart as Anna thinks you are, you will stop pestering everybody and get lost for the rest of the afternoon!"

Jack held his ground, reluctant to give up his quest, until Ken shouted, "Git!" Then he whirled and leaped down the steps, his mind made up for him. Obviously, he wasn't going to get anywhere with someone whose attitude was so unfriendly!

He went directly to the hounds' pen to investigate why they had been raising such a fuss, but by the time he got there, they were laying about as if nothing had happened. Jack was feeling so peevish that he didn't even have the heart to tease the stupid beasts. Scowling to himself, he trotted around the back of the building. Solitaire would want to hear about his ill treatment at the hands of that bad-natured manager. The Akita wasn't in her outside run, so he continued on around the building until he came back to the front, and slipped inside the door.

When he got to Solitaire's kennel, he couldn't believe his good eye. What could have possessed the Akita to tear up their shared bed like that? Had she really gone mad? Or had it been necessary for Solitaire to use extreme measures to escape from the cage? Yes! A sense of pride came over Jack when he realized that Solitaire had escaped on her own. It could only have been because of his past guidance that she had been able to grasp the whole idea of escape; the Akita's deliberate way of thinking had been much enhanced by his teaching her the premise by which a terrier lives: where there's a will, there's always a way!

By the time he finished examining the torn plywood barrier and the gaping door of the next kennel, Jack was as impressed by his friend's bestial strength as with her astute mind. An animal as powerful as the Akita probably wouldn't need his help to rescue Johnny. Still, he reasoned, two minds are always better than one, and sometimes a small body could go places and find out things that a larger one could not. Convinced he was still needed, Jack cast about, sniffing the nearby area for signs of Solitaire's passing. Outside the door, he deciphered in which direction she was headed and found himself racing back across the fields he had already traversed twice that day.

Solitaire was concealed in a large thatch of wild corn just outside the barnyard, surveying the enemy terrain. From Jack's mental pictures, she easily recognized the house and the low barn. To her right was the outbuilding with the big door that Johnny and Jack had explored first. The door was open now and several men were lounging around in the shade, drinking beer to ease the heat of the late afternoon. Solitaire was downwind from them, memorizing their individual odors so that she would not be taken by surprise later. This was a difficult task due to the stench that washed over her from the rest of the place.

She was lying so quietly in the long grass that Jack had to rely on his active sense of smell to locate his friend. When he did, he approached cautiously, announcing his presence in her mind before showing himself. The Pussycat's warning about letting her be didn't frighten him too much, but he had already learned his lesson about the dangers of trespassing when the Akita's thoughts were focused elsewhere!

Come forward, little Jack. Do not be frightened. I welcome your assistance; who knows better than you how to free an unwilling hostage?

Solitaire was, indeed, glad to have Jack join her. In her haste, she hadn't considered that she might need the terrier's vast experience in breaking into anything without a lock on it. She watched from the corner of her eye as the little fellow crawled on his belly into the clearing she had made with her body, but refrained from welcoming him in the usual way, with a wave of her tail, because even that slight movement might draw the eyes of the men.

Instead, when Jack got close enough, she leaned over to sniff his tiny muzzle. This was tantamount to handing over the leadership of their endeavor and the Aussie accepted with comical dignity, squirming ahead to take his position by Solitaire's monstrous forepaw.

Jack didn't like the fact that the men weren't involved in doing anything right now. With nothing to occupy their minds, the least error on his part would bring them running – and their vicious pack of dogs as well. He sighed resolutely. Well, there was nothing for it – since he had no idea where they were holding Johnny, he had to take his chances on moving in closer to ferret out the boy. He conveyed his plan to Solitaire, who was more than a little disappointed to be left behind, though she had to admit that her bulk made her a far better guardian than a scout.

Jack, on the other hand, was so tiny that he barely parted the thick grasses on his way through the field. Within moments, Solitaire lost sight of him altogether and had to rely on his mental echoes to follow his movements until he resurfaced behind the garage, running the short stretch from the cover of the grass to that of the building. Solitaire understood that he was retracing his footsteps from his earlier visit with Johnny, checking everything out on his way to the farmhouse. Jack came into view again as he darted across the ground in front of the veranda. He was headed toward the steps, on his way to searching the main house. Solitaire stifled a gasp at the Aussie's temerity!

Suddenly, Jack slid to a dusty stop at the bottom of the stairs. He stood rigid a moment, testing the air, then dropped his nose to the ground and headed off in a completely different direction.

What have you found? Solitaire broke her mental silence, impatient to know if Jack was still on Johnny's trail, or whether he had found something more interesting to take his attention.

The boy is here, m'lady, no worries. Make your way toward the far shed, the one set back behind the others. That seems to be where they took him. Use all of your caution, Solitaire. These small buildings scattered around are occupied by some very unfriendly types. Noisy, too!

In spite of her excitement, Solitaire kept her movements slow and measured as she backed away from the sight of the men. Once clear, she galloped in a great loop far out into the field, then turned back toward the farmyard and emerged from the grass slightly behind the shack that Jack had indicated to her. He was already there, combing the area around it for some way to enter.

Soon he found a split in the boards big enough for a rat to get through. Since he needed slightly more room than that, he began to dig. Solitaire approached, desiring to help, but the terrier snapped her a withering look that said she had no idea of what was required, and went on paddling the dirt away from the opening. Humbled, Solitaire sat down with her back to him, once more taking up her position as sentinel.

Inside the shack, Johnny had been sitting on the dirty floor for what seemed like hours, but was probably no more than thirty minutes. His long legs were cramped from being spread-eagled out in front of him, his arms and torso were tied to a post behind his back, and he was having a difficult time breathing around the cruel gag in his mouth. When he heard scratching sounds coming from somewhere behind him, he tried to turn his head to discern what kind of burrowing animal was out at this time of the day, but his shoulders were bound so tightly to the upright support that he wasn't able to move. He began to perspire, thinking the beast that he was sharing this prison with might be trying to get out.

Earl and the others had brought him to this shack, the farthest one from the house, and had unlocked the door before shoving him ahead of them into the darkness. Temporarily blinded, Johnny had tripped over an old burlap sack lying on the floor and fallen into the wooden panels of a stall at the back of the building. There, a monstrous brute had leaped up to meet him, roaring with madness and snapping yellowed fangs inches from his face. Johnny had screamed like a girl before he could stop himself and threw himself backwards so hurriedly that the Carolina boys had nearly peed themselves laughing.

The dog in the cage had never stopped raging while he was being tied up, until even Kell had become concerned. He had said something about not wanting the dog – he called it 'Gatorbait' – to tire itself out before the show tonight, then Johnny could hear the sounds of a heavy grate being lowered. Gatorbait had been quiet ever since, but Johnny could still hear its awful breathing.

More scurrying sounds directly behind him made Johnny freeze so that, for the second time this afternoon, One-eyed Jack had to use his nose to find a friend.

Johnny whimpered with relief as the little dog jumped all over him in ecstatic greeting. He felt sure that the terrier had returned with human help this time and he eagerly strained to hear the sounds of his rescuers.

Jack could readily see why Johnny wasn't talking to him, what with that dirty rag across his mouth, but he didn't know why the boy didn't just get up and walk out of this smelly place. He recalled his surprise the first time a rat hadn't run away at the sight of him, but that had been because it had been clumsy enough to catch a hind leg in a trap. Well, first thing, he would sniff around Johnny's feet to be sure they weren't stuck in some kind of snare.

When that proved not to be the case, Jack circled around behind the kennel boy to see if he was on a leash. Jack had been little more than a pup when he had gained first-hand experience with being tied up – and chewing through the cord to free himself. That had been before the kennel boys started to use chains to hold him in one place. Thank goodness Anna had put a stop to that practice! A dog in a cage is a prisoner, but a dog on a chain is a pitiful thing, defenseless against the mean desires of any passerby, be it insect or canine or human.

He began to inspect Johnny's bonds. They were thick, but at least they weren't metal chain, so he could try to chew through them. Wait! Jack stiffened with sudden dread when he walked behind Johnny and heard the nasal sounds of a live animal coming from the darkness at the back of the shed. The breathing seemed forced and held the hint of a piping growl. For the slimmest of moments, Jack wished that he had let Solitaire dig her way in first – a big Akita like her was much better equipped to handle this kind of situation – but he soon collected his nerve. It was up to him to find out what danger this new animal represented for himself and Johnny so, straining to see in the gloom, he tiptoed closer to the iron grate behind which the beast lived.

Jack could see the shadowy outline of a canine in the enclosure, but he couldn't figure out why it was just lying there. He was convinced that if the thing intended to attack him, it would have done so by now, so he allowed his terrier curiosity to take control as he approached closer than his intellect warned he should. If it wasn't for his keen vigilance, Jack might have walked right into the maw of the beast. A quick tightening of muscles was his only clue that the creature was about to attack, but that was enough to send him skittering back out of the way, in time to avoid Gatorbait's swift and deadly rush.

Solitaire, waiting just outside Jack's rat-hole, was startled by the bellicose snarls coming from within.

Jack! What manner of beast is that? Are you safe? And the boy? She couldn't discern any clear shape in the dark field of the terrier's vision, and the smells from inside the shed were too confused for her to draw any conclusions of her own.

No worries, madam! The boy and I are fine. Thankfully, someone has been thoughtful enough to lock that one up behind strong bars. It is some sort of large hound, I believe, but even more ferocious and stupid than most!

The consternation hidden behind Jack's brave assurances fueled Solitaire's anxiety about Johnny's safety. Impatience drove her to push her head through the small hole in the wall and try to force her shoulders through as she had in her pen, but the wood wouldn't give. Earlier this afternoon she had been successful by tearing at the wood around a small hole, so now she went to work on this one with high expectations. Unlike the clean plywood of her kennel, this wood was old and rotten. With every pull of her paws she knocked off large, jagged pieces. Inside, Jack became agitated by her actions and began barking and dancing around the hole, urging her on to greater efforts.

Now Johnny became really frightened. He couldn't see what was bothering Jack, but those snuffling noises had to be coming from a very large dog. He worried that one of the savage dogs he had seen earlier had gotten loose and was after Jack. Brave and courageous as the terrier might be, he was no match against one of them. Then Johnny heard a frustrated whine that filtered in from the other side of the hole.

It sounded like Solitaire, but how could she have gotten here? It was impossible that she could have escaped her secure kennel. Slowly it dawned on him that if Solitaire was here, she must have been brought by someone from Welsely's who was looking for him! He wanted to call out to let his rescuers know where to find him, but that wasn't possible around his choking gage. He groaned in his frustration.

That sound was enough for Solitaire. Her heart leaped with joy upon hearing Johnny's voice. Even more determined, she tried to drive her body through the opening, pushing hard from behind. She could smell the rank animal caged inside and worry made her reckless. She pulled out and began digging furiously at the wood again with teeth and claws. The ripping sound of the wood breaking filled her ears and Jack's wild encouragement so excited her that she disregarded the racket rising from the next shed. She was even too intent on getting to Johnny to register alarm at the heavy thuds of several running feet approaching. Once she was with Johnny, they would face all comers together! Just a little more and she would be through. She pulled her head out of the hole for the last time – and briefly noted that she was surrounded before she fell crashing to the ground.

Jack stood stock still. Through the hole, he could see a circle of legs forming around his friend's limp body. A stout club rested against the thigh of one. He prodded Solitaire's unconscious mind, but there was no response, and for one panic-stricken moment, he feared she must be dead. An anger such as he had never felt rose in his little chest and he rushed fearlessly out among the horde of boots, snarling his rage.

The surprised men began hopping about, involuntarily lifting their feet in a kind of dance to avoid being bitten. Earl was the first to compose himself enough to aim a vicious kick at the terrier's head, but Jack was too fast. He easily skipped out of the way, then whirled to catch a pantleg before Earl could lower his foot again. While the angry man jerked his leg back and forth, Jack held on tightly. He didn't really know what he was doing; only that he must give Solitaire the time she needed to get to her feet – if she was still alive.

Unable to shake the stubborn terrier loose, Earl picked up his club and tried to bash him with it. Jack chose that moment to let go and the fat man struck himself a resounding blow to the shin. The Carolina boys were reduced to tears as they watched the ridiculous antics of their host hobbling around the yard, bent at the waist, trying again and again to pound the quicker, mouse-like Jack into the ground.

The sounds of the struggle outside the shed frightened Johnny into action. He thrashed and chewed hysterically until he was able to work his gag loose, then with his mouth bleeding and saliva running down his chin, he screamed for Jack, for Solitaire, for anyone to hear him.

The laughing men sobered up quickly when they heard the boy's shouts.

"Somebody better shut that kid up," old Billy muttered. He didn't like all this action outside of the pit. "Fleet'll be here any minute and we don't want that kid screamin' his lungs out."

The others agreed.

"Earl! Leave off hittin' on that fool thing and open up this door," one called.

Earl heaved his club at Jack in one last effort to injure him, then turned, cursing because he had missed again.

When the door was opened, allowing the light of day to enter the shack, Johnny was able to bring his panic under control.

"What happened to my dog?" he spouted, aware that he sounded more brazen than he felt. "She'd better not be hurt! That dog's worth a lot of money, you know! You'll be in big trouble if she's dead!"

Earl was in a black mood. He was about to take it out on the helpless boy by cuffing his ear, but something stopped him in mid-motion.

"What'd y'all say, boy? Somethin' 'bout that wuthless mutt out yonder?"

"She isn't worthless! She's a very valuable show dog, and you'll be sorry if you've hurt her!" Johnny wasn't sure how far his bravado would get him, but he had to take the chance to help Solitaire survive.

A slow grin crept up Earl's ugly features, though it never reached his eyes.

"That's that Aye-kita dog, ain't it?" he asked, slyly. "The one Fleet's so scared of. Haw! It sure don't seem so tough t'me!"

The men stood about in silence, confused by Earl's change in mood as he talked almost politely with Johnny.

"Don't worry y'self, boy, she's jest learnt a few manners is all. She'll be right as rain in no time." Turning to let his buddies in on the joke, Earl winked at them and gushed, "I sure hope so, anyways. If'n she comes to by then, we got us a brand new contender for the last fight t'nite!"

One of the others groaned.

"That bitch doesn't have the heart to stick it out in the pit. Look what happened to her after just one little smack to her head – she's knocked silly. She's big enough to put on a show against one of our dogs, that's for sure, but she don't seem that fast or that tough. I wouldn't bet on her lasting five minutes against Jake. . ."

"No!" Earl erupted, his flabby features taut and contorted in anger. "Not Jake! She's gonna fight Gatorbait! I been waitin' fer this dog and I ain't goin' t'let 'er fight nobody else! She's mine! I caught 'er and she's mine!"

Johnny was astonished by Earl's childish outbreak. He wondered how he could possibly bargain for his freedom with such a turbulent character. Looking around at the other men, he found no champions. No one seemed inclined to go up against Earl, if only because they respected his natural ferocity.

When none of the men argued further, Earl calmed himself.

"'Sides, y'all heard Fleet tell how she got the best of him. That there Aye-kita," – he pointed with his thumb in the general direction of the comatose dog – "she's real smart. And she's got enuff experience to put on a good show for the fellas. I think Gatorbait'll chew her up into liddle pieces, too, but who cares? I think ol' Fleet'll enjoy the show, anyways; he hates this bitch that much."

Solitaire lay where she had fallen, conscious now, but deeply confused. She didn't like the sound of the strange voices coming from near Johnny's location and felt she should be defending the boy, but she couldn't raise her head for some reason. She would just lie here a little longer until she got her bearings...

Jack had other ideas. He hadn't run far when the oafish human had thrown that stick at him and now he reappeared out of nowhere, having felt Solitaire's conscious mind awakening. Ignoring his own safety, he pounced on the huge Akita, pulling at her ears, her tail, even her paws. His tiny nips made Solitaire twitch uncomfortably, but she didn't have the strength to fight him off. Finally, Jack sat down and whined.

Solitaire! M'lady, please! You have to wake up! Those nasties will be back any moment and I'd rather we weren't here. Get up, Solitaire! This last was communicated with the intensity of a command, strong enough to cause Solitaire to open her eyes.

Johnny? was the only thought she could form.

The lad's okay for now, but we've got to get more help. You have to make the effort to communicate with our mistress, Solitaire. She can do things! We need Anna to help Johnny now. Please get up!

Jack sprang away from Solitaire's side just as the men rounded the corner of the shed. He melted into a little spot of shade at the side of the building, but stayed to watch their intentions.

"Well, y'all better get *your* dog into a cage, then, b'fore she comes to all th' way," old Billy was saying. "I don't know if she kin fight like Fleet sez, but I believe I'd play it safe and not take any chances. That's one helluva rip he's got in his arm."

Earl sent one of the boys off for a containment kennel before swaggering over to gloat above the downed dog, immensely pleased with his own cleverness. As he approached, Solitaire grunted a dull warning. It was a weak effort, as she still could not lift her head, but Earl kicked her for it anyway.

Incensed by such cruelty, Jack blasted out of his hiding place, yapping all the way in an effort to turn Earl's attention from Solitaire. This time, however, he was not lucky enough to take his old adversary unawares. Earl waited for the terrier to come within biting range of his pant leg, then feigned a step back and kicked out with his left boot. Unbalanced as he was, he didn't have much strength behind the blow, but his steel toe caught Jack in the ribs hard enough to drive the air from his lungs in a sharp yelp of surprise. The tiny body rolled several times, then lay crumpled in the dirt.

Dizzy with pain, Solitaire reared her massive head up and heaved her tortured body to her feet. She tried to lunge at Earl, but her vision was blurred and she ended by falling at his feet, mortified by her feebleness. He pivoted on his right leg, wild-eyed when he thought the great dog was on him, then gleeful as he saw her stagger and fall.

"Well, glad t'see y'all are feelin' better," he smirked. "That's good, on account of y'all've got a date tonight. He's a real nice fella an' you wouldn't want to disappoint him."

***

Fleet was being persecuted and it hurt. Those Carolina boys had outmaneuvered and outnumbered him at every turning, using his own words against him and making him feel like an outsider. Now that his swamp-buds were here, even Earl seemed to think it a great game to make Fleet feel like shit.

He had risked discovery by taking the back route from Welsely's this afternoon, only to be sidetracked as soon as he got to Kell's and sent off on a stupid errand to town. They had seen him off with snide reminders that it had been his idea to keep the boys' presence a secret so that the local authorities didn't get curious. How could they hold that against him, for chrissakes? The boys didn't exactly blend in with the local farm folk, after all.

In retaliation for his stratagem, they had been making him do all of the running for the supplies they were going to need tonight – mainly beer. Well, Earl's old van was full of kegs of the stuff to add to the cases he had brought earlier in the week.

His nerves were so taut that they were threatening to catapult him over the edge. He was as anxious as the boys were to get this show on the road, though for very different reasons. Earl and his buddies were looking forward to the pit fights with an emotion akin to lust. Fleet just wanted the money to get out of Kansas and back to eastern civilization – and anonymity.

He slowed the van when he reached the farmhouse and pulled around the back to unload by the kitchen entrance. Someone's face disappeared from a curtained window just as he turned the corner. He cursed, embarrassed and angered by what he saw as yet another childish act of harassment.

Before he came to a full stop, a stream of men poured out of the back door of the house. Their welcome seemed particularly jovial, which made Fleet even more tense. Earl offered him one of the cold cans of brew he was holding, then thumped him on the back like an old chum as he filled him in on how well the preparations were going along. Bobby suggested that the kegs should go straight over by the ring, and even offered to take them. Fleet was mystified by this change in attitude, but before he could say anything, Bobby and two of the others jumped into the van and drove off.

Fleet turned his attention back to Earl, who was still running off at the mouth in his best 'alibi' fashion. The remaining men seemed to be crowding them, smirking at a joke that Fleet was not privy to. Something major had happened during his absence, Fleet was positive, but he knew he would have to be patient until the boys decided to tell him what it was. He took a big swallow of beer and followed the party back up the stairs to the kitchen.

"Fleet, ol' buddy," Kell announced after the first beer had wet his insides, "me 'n the boys've got a great surprise for you!"

Fleet's smirk was only obvious in the straightening of his lips. He had known that if he didn't rise to Earl's taunts they would soon tire of teasing him and let him in on their game, but he was amazed they had given in so quickly. Whatever had happened, they sure were eager to tell him about it. He said nothing, waiting for Earl to make the next move.

"I can't tell y'all about it, Fleet. Ya gotta come over to the pit an' see for y'self."

The other boys murmured agreement and began jostling their chairs. Fleet sat a moment longer, trying to work out whether he was being made the butt of another of their ridiculous jokes. In the end, he decided that it was probably only another dog; that seemed to be all these guys ever got really excited about. Well, he wasn't going to find out sitting here. His chair scraped noisily as he slid it back and stood up.

Everybody but Earl fell back to let him go through the door first. In a gesture of camaraderie that was truly worrisome, Earl slapped his arm around Fleet's shoulder. They started down the steps together, with Earl gushing about how pleased Fleet was going to be. He never stopped babbling while they crossed the yard, but Fleet was aware that he was being purposely steered by that 'friendly' arm, around the outlying sheds and toward the hidden fighting pit in the distant field.

CHAPTER 30

Solitaire raised her head slowly, careful not to aggravate the pounding there, and looked around. She was in a metal crate in the back of a strange van. The side and back doors were flung open, allowing the low evening sun to flood the inside with heat and light. All that Solitaire could see out the side door of the van was a conglomeration of tin and wood debris in the middle of a thicket of bushes and tall grasses. Groaning, she pulled herself to an upright position, but even with her head pressed against the mesh on the top of the crate she could not see over the grass. She whimpered, hot and thirsty, and worried that things had gone very wrong.

An answer to her whine came from inside the pile of debris, and it came in the form of a hostile snarl. A few other dogs barked with equal enmity from locations nearby. Solitaire couldn't see where they were or whether they were crated or loose, though she deduced they must be caged or they would have followed up their insults with a physical attack. Tentatively, she reached out to communicate with them, but recoiled as if she had been burned. Theirs were brutish minds, full of roiled images of blood and pain. The only clear emotion among them seemed to be a generalized hatred for all living things.

She looked around for Johnny. Was the boy here as well? She peered into the front seats of the van, but there were no passengers. She listened, but heard nothing aside from the wind in the bushes and some far-off yapping that made her think she was still on Kell's property. The mucous lining in her nose was too dry and her tongue too swollen with thirst to get much information from scenting the air and she sat back in disappointment.

Solitaire was guiltily aware that her own recklessness had led to her being caught in this distressing situation. The rescuer was now in need of rescuing. In her concern for the boy, she had been neglectful of her own safety. Thus had the fat man been able to sneak up behind her, and eventually, to hurt little Jack. The memory of One-eyed Jack being struck down while he tried to protect her made her fur bristle. It was a lesson she wouldn't soon forget.

The sun was getting lower over the western fields. Solitaire's innate sense of timing told her that about two hours had passed since she had been caught off-guard by the men who were holding Johnny. Anything could have happened to him by now, she admitted to herself, and it would all be her fault.

Why hadn't she trusted the boy enough to communicate with him earlier? Right from the first, she had known he was a good lad who would never hurt her nor betray her confidences. If she had but opened the pathways between them, she would be able to commune with him now and at least be certain whether he was alive or dead. She knew now that it was her old enemy, pride, which had kept them apart. She had pretended that she didn't care enough to explore the pathways of Johnny's mind and now she had no chance of finding them. But she could find Jack's – if he was conscious yet after that brutal kick.

Before she could collect her thoughts to try, the sound of male voices rising from across the field stole her attention. The voice that was more boisterous than the rest, she recognized as belonging to the man who had attacked her and Jack. Her lips raised of their own volition into a quivering snarl. She would not be taken by surprise again.

It seemed a long time before the men came into view. While they approached from behind the tall grasses, Solitaire concentrated on Earl's tones in order to cipher his intentions. His words were so jumbled from his southern dialect as to be incomprehensible to her. But it wasn't just the language that came out of his mouth that she didn't understand, it was his whole muddled way of thinking that was foreign to her.

The men appeared just behind the van, where the dirt road entered the thicket. Solitaire was prepared for their arrival, but the sight of the hated Fleet in their midst took her completely off-guard. Her muzzle parted – not in a snarl, but in surprise. But why was she surprised? She should have expected that man-devil would be behind all of these dirty deeds.

Fleet stopped in his tracks when he recognized the occupant of the kennel and he, too, stared open-mouthed for a beat of his heart.

Solitaire recovered first, her expression changing from one of shock to the one she normally wore in Fleet's presence: extreme malevolence. Her snarl, so profound that it distorted her features into those of some hideous gargoyle, caused Fleet to half-raise his arm protectively. This seemed to amuse Earl, who guffawed loudly.

"Don't worry y'self, boy," he crowed. "That crate's locked good – she can't get at y'all."

Fleet lowered his arm before throwing Kell a murderous glance for embarrassing him.

"How in hell did you get her away from Welsely's?" he asked.

Earl was all innocence when he answered, "She jest came wanderin' in here, didn't she, boys?"

The boys made various murmurs of agreement, but added nothing to Earl's story. They were still uneasy about how Fleet was going to take this.

"Anyways, we was sittin' in the garidge havin' a beer a coupla hours ago when this 'un shows up out front 'n I says, 'That looks like the Aye-kita bitch what bit Fleet. Let's ketch 'er an' see what Fleet wants t'do with 'er. He might want t'use 'er fer the fights t'night, since he don't have no dog t' enter. Far as I can see, this 'un owes him big-time for all the trouble she's caused.'

"Was I right, Fleet? She owes you big-time and this is yor chance t' collect. Put 'er in the pit t'night with Gatorbait, and y'all stand t'make some real good money on her."

Fleet's mind churned while Earl blabbered on. He stared at the Akita bitch snarling in her cage and self-consciously rubbed his right biceps, still feeling the pain deep within the tendon of his arm. He had almost given up on any hope of revenge as being too risky. But now here was the bitch, caged, nasty as ever, and at his mercy. It seemed to him like destiny.

"Are you sure nobody saw her come over here?" he asked Earl.

"Well, I ain't sure if anybody saw 'er leave, but nobody spotted 'er here – me an' the boys, we caught 'er pretty quick. And nobody's been 'round lookin' fer 'er," he lied.

Fleet wondered how they had managed to catch the devilish creature, but put off asking for that story until later. For now, he reveled in his mastery over the bitch. He was eager to see this animal punished for injuring his arm, that was for damn sure. If it was up to him, he would shoot the Akita between the eyes right now and bury that godawful big body of hers right here in the middle of nowhere.

Still, Kell's idea of making a profit on the Akita's suffering was very appealing, too. And he could still shoot her later, at his own convenience; she was the one who had gotten loose and trespassed on his and Earl's property, and around here, that was a capital crime for any dog.

Fleet's cautious nature came to the fore as he thought of some things that should be taken care of to make sure that no one traced the bitch over here. He turned to his partner to explain.

"Good work, buddy." he congratulated Earl. "And you're right, I do deserve a little payback from this bitch. We probably wouldn't even be talking about leaving here, if it wasn't for her.

"I'm going back to finish up over at Welsely's so nobody gets suspicious. I'll make sure the gate's closed and there aren't any tracks to lead anybody this way. If you say she came around here late in the afternoon, its possible no one even knows she's missing yet. The kid that takes care of her goes home pretty early.

"Chances are, they won't even start looking for her until tomorrow, but maybe I can think of something to send them off the wrong way if they do. They're so stupid over there, they still trust me."

That caused a round of laughter from the boys, led by Earl's raucous brays. Everyone was relieved to see Fleet in a better mood. Now they could all enjoy the fights equally. The boys did like to have a good time.

Fleet stared long and hard at the captive Akita again before turning to go.

"Make sure you don't take that bitch out of the crate until I get back, Earl. She's a tricky one and I don't want to lose her now!"

***

Jack had only had the wind knocked out of him, but even that was a jolting experience and it had taken some time for him to recover. Thankfully, Kell's intentions of doing greater harm to the terrier were waylaid by Solitaire's courageous, if feeble, attack so that Jack had been able to drag himself out of the way before anyone remembered to stomp on his head.

For the last couple of hours, he had lain in the shelter of a stack of rusting metal bars that were probably intended for bolstering the sagging perimeter fence one day. They smelled rank, but he suffered in silence. Even a rambunctious terrier like him can learn when it's wiser to lay low and wait for the dark. But what then? How was he going to get help for his friends?

This afternoon, his best efforts to get through to Anna had been foiled by Ken's protective measures, and he had been shooed off as a nuisance for his trouble. But maybe Amber had been more successful; he would check with her.

The sun was getting very low now and Jack was feeling rested. He dragged his sore body out from his hiding place and looked around, wary of whoever or whatever might be waiting for him. Seeing no movement at all around the yard, he walked stiffly over to the hole Solitaire had made in the wall of Johnny's shack and listened carefully before he entered. It was very quiet inside. The monstrous dog he had encountered earlier had been led out of the shed in chains some time ago.

He found Johnny still sitting on the floor. The boy looked uncomfortable, but his head had fallen to one side in a manner that Jack understood to mean he was sleeping. Jack didn't disturb him, but waited and listened long enough to be convinced that Johnny's sleep was peaceful, then started the long trip home.

His progress across the fields was rather slower than it had been earlier that day. He was exhausted and his ribs hurt with every step. By the time he squirmed through the back gate of Welsely's, the sun had set. He was surprised to find everything closed up and peaceful. Even Anna's hounds were quiet except for the buzzing of their snores. Hadn't anyone missed them?

On his way back home, he had come up with the idea of asking for The Pussycat's help. She might be able to reach Solitaire, which he had not been able to do all afternoon, and verify her health, at least. But he was disgruntled to find that the specials building was locked up and dark for the night. He called with his mind-voice to no avail. These days, Pussycat wouldn't be able to hear his weak voice from this far away unless she was concentrating, a tough thing for the busy mother dog to do.

He thought about barking outside the doors to get The Pussycat's attention, but then he would also wake the pack and then all hell would break loose, confusing the issue all the more. With a sigh, Jack turned and limped toward the back porch light shining from the farmhouse.

As he approached the door, Amber's dear profile stood outlined in the bottom of the screen. Well, at least someone missed him. His step lightened, and he bounced up the steps to her.

Jacques! I have been so worried! I was so sorry for you this afternoon, but there was nothing I could do.... Amber's large brown eyes oozed sympathy for the maligned Aussie.

Anna must have seen the poodle's tail wagging, because she called out, "Who's there? Is that someone for me or for you, Amber?"

The old woman's relief was plainly written on her face when she saw the Aussie standing outside the door. She hadn't slept well after he left, and noticed that Amber seemed worried, too. The poodle had stared at her for long moments, an anxious expression crowding her lovely face, but Anna wasn't able to figure out what it was she wanted. When Ken first told her how adamant the terrier had been about waking her, she had been mildly curious, but as the afternoon wore into evening, she began to feel guilty for turning Jack away when he obviously needed something from her. Like Amber, she had been on edge, waiting for him to make an appearance.

"Come in. Come in, little guy," she called to him as she tripped the latch. "Where've you been all afternoon? I guess you missed your dinner, didn't you? And now you're probably ravenous, right?"

Jack was pleased to know that his absence had been noticed, after all. And he was hungry. He just might eat a little of the tasty leftovers Anna had saved for him, in order to gather strength while he thought about what he would do next.

Amber and he sat side by side while their mistress prepared a big bowl of scraps. The poodle wanted to know everything that had gone on, and when he was finished telling her, she sat quietly beside him while he ate.

After Jack finished eating, he rubbed his moustache clean on the kitchen rug, complacent for the moment.

Amber communicated what she had been thinking about.

Jacques, I have been trying to decide on our next course of action. It has been very peaceful here all evening. I do not believe that anyone is even aware that Solitaire is missing from her kennel. Nor do they realize that Johnny is in danger. The dogs in the specials building must have been fed by somebody else because they have not complained nor called attention to themselves in any unusual manner, and you said the big doors are locked, so all seems usual.

Anna has been inside all day – I could feel that her bones are aching more than usual today – and I have endeavored to give her a little of my warmth. The boss is occupied in his office, unaware of any problems outside, I am sure.

Jacques, if we can't alert the humans to Johnny and Solitaire's absence, I'm afraid that our friends may be lost!

Jack concurred.

But how are we supposed to do that? We've both tried our best to communicate with Anna already, and nothing's happened.

Well, One-eyed Jacques! Amber scolded. *I never thought I would hear you give up on something before it was accomplished to the very best of your ability! We're not 'competents', not by a long way, but we are house pets and that gives us an edge; we live with the humans. If we stay alert tonight, if we watch and listen for an opportunity to express our concern, we may still be able to get their attention.*

Jack wasn't sure how that could work, but he felt better having a plan, and he was very proud of Amber for not allowing him to give up.

While the two tiny friends were working out the logistics of their scheme, a car pulled into the driveway. There was the sound of feet pounding up the front steps and then someone was banging on the door. Both dogs ran for the door, barking eagerly to welcome a friend or see an intruder off.

They passed Ken coming out of his office, a look of bewilderment on his face because people seldom came to the front door of a farmhouse. He waited for Anna to catch up, then they both followed the dogs to see who it was.

"I'm sorry to bother you folks," the strange man apologized, then relaxed as he saw a face he knew. "Evenin', Ms. Welsely. You're lookin' well."

"Why, John Wales! I haven't seen you in years! What brings you out all this way? Neighborly visit? Nothin' the matter with Johnny, I hope?"

Both Jack and Amber picked up the formal politeness in Anna's voice and judged that she didn't think much of this person. They stood stiffly, shoulder-to-shoulder in front of her feet in case she should need their help.

The man smiled weakly at Anna, then glanced over at Ken.

"Oh, forgive my manners," it was Anna's turn to apologize. "This here's my manager, Kenny Lorch. Kenny, this's Johnny's pa."

The men exchanged quick courtesies and Ken invited the man in. He came as far as the hallway before blurting out the reason for this visit.

"Johnny ain't been home today. His ma's worried. Is he here?"

"Why, no, I don't believe so." Ken and Anna looked askance at each other. When was the last time they had seen the boy? Come to think of it, neither one remembered seeing him at all this afternoon. Ken offered the senior Wales a seat in the living room and went to call Abel. Perhaps the other kennel boy knew where he was.

Anna excused herself to go to the kitchen and make some tea. As she left the room, she noticed Jack was sniffing the man's jeans. His curiosity raised an odd thought in her mind. Could that have been Jack's problem this afternoon? Had something happened to Johnny? Without stopping in the kitchen to put on the kettle, she went right out the back door and down to the specials kennel.

The hounds heard her coming, and roused themselves to greet her with short, quiet yips and thumping tails. She shushed them before hurrying around the back to Solitaire's run. She didn't see the Akita, but she did notice Johnny's work shirt dangling from the top of the chain link fence. The boy would have worn that home at the end of a normal day.

Anna's mouth went dry, but she didn't let herself panic yet. She called softly for Solitaire to come out of her kennel. As she waited for a response, she realized that she was listening with more than her ears. It was silly, she knew, but there was a blank spot in her mind where she had gotten used to the imprint of the Akita. Anna no longer had any doubt that both the boy and the dog were missing, and possibly in trouble.

She took down the shirt and hurried to the front of the specials building to let herself in. The sleepy dogs she passed blinked as their eyes adapted to the sudden bright lights. One of them, the Shih Tzu, whined so unhappily that Anna had to stop to console her. As she was petting the little dog, she looked beyond her to the untidy pile of debris in Solitaire's kennel, evidence of the Akita's forceful escape.

"Don't worry, little Pussycat," she crooned, trying not to let her own discomfort show. "We'll find her, and Johnny too."

The Pussycat laid her cheek against Anna's arm while the woman stroked her softly tousled head and continued to wonder aloud, "Who closed up in here this afternoon, anyway, and didn't notice that one of the dogs was missing? That Abel's as lazy as Ludlum's dog, but he knows what would happen if he ignored a mess like that! Did Solitaire escape first and Johnny close up to go after her? That'd be in character for the boy, but I don't know. . . Why would Solitaire up and run off with no reason?"

The Pussycat suddenly pulled away from Anna's hand, and fixed her mistress with a meaningful gaze.

"What're you tryin' to tell me, huh?" Anna asked, feeling a bit self-conscious. "You know who did it, don't you? And it wasn't either of those two, was it? Well, that leaves Fleet..."

The Pussycat's soft paws gripped Anna's wrist and she pulled tensely at the weathered skin, all the while staring worriedly into the old woman's eyes. Anna stared back, stunned by the feeling that she knew exactly what the little dog was thinking. She almost fought the sensation, but realized there was nothing to be afraid of, and possibly a lot to be gained from it.

"You're tellin' me Fleet had a hand in this, eh? Well, girlie, I have to admit that makes more sense. I ain't seen that scoundrel all afternoon, either. He's been awful quiet lately; I shoulda known he was up to no good – that man don't give up 'til he gets his way. He better not have hurt either one of those young'uns, or I'll have his head!"

Anna's bluster quickly gave way to fear as she realized what she had just said. She didn't put it past Fleet to harm the dog if he thought she had wronged him, but was he reckless enough to hurt Johnny? She hoped not, but couldn't quiet her feelings of urgency, as she rushed back to the farmhouse. By the time she arrived back in the living room, the two men were deep in serious conversation.

"I guess I've been pretty hard on him lately," John Wales Sr. was saying. "There's just so much work to do on a farm and he ain't interested in how it gets done. If he don't learn now, while I can teach him, who's gonna take care of the place when I'm too old?"

"Are you sure Johnny wants to spend his life on the farm?" Ken asked gently, but rather pointedly, Anna thought.

"'Course he does. Or, at least, he will once he grows out of this stubborn age. He used to love to drive the tractor. He was always followin' me around the fields, since he was a little sod. But since he's been workin' here, he's got different ideas. . . I never wanted him to take a job off the farm. I knew it'd cause trouble. Now he'd rather defy his own father than quit."

Ken thought he understood the man's disappointment, though he still considered he was making too much out of the normal teenage need for independence.

"Mr. Wales, I've had some long talks with Johnny since I've been here. He's my best hand with the dogs and I'd love to have him spend more time here. But he feels his responsibilities to you and the farm more than you know. I think he's been worried about whether he can please you without losing his respect for himself in the process.

"He's only a boy - and you're a young man, yet. There's enough time for him to learn the things he needs to know about farming later. I think you're driving him away with your demands. Ease up a little. Let him get his feet under him before you harness him to a plow."

In spite of her anxiety, Anna stood back a little from the doorway and listened, impressed with Kenny's grasp of the root of the problem. Recalling that he had been raised in a small town in the Midwest, too, she wondered if his advice came from experience. She guessed the scenario Johnny and his pa were playing out these days had been played out many times before, in many parts of the world. Hopefully, this man-to-man talk would make some sense to her stubborn neighbor. Right now, though, they had to find Johnny.

"Solitaire's not in her kennel."

Ken jumped up as if a spring had come loose in his chair.

"Solitaire is missing, too? Well, it's my guess that where we find one, we'll find two." He turned back to Wales, who was also standing. The man turned pale and asked if that was the new dog that Johnny had told him about.

"Yessir. Those two are thick as thieves. Johnny's the only one who can handle that dog – and she could be a danger if she's loose without him."

Wales was ashamed to have to ask.

"D'you think he stole the dog and ran off with her?"

Anna's response was firm.

"No. She definitely broke out of her kennel. You should see the mess, Kenny. I don't think Solitaire would have done that unless she had a pretty good reason. But I ain't positive when she did it or who went after who. Frankly, I'm worried about the boy. His bike's still out back, and I found this hanging on Solitaire's outside run. Fleet. . ." Anna didn't know how she was going to explain her insights about the foreman.

She was saved from that embarrassment by Jack's sudden intervention. When the terrier saw Johnny's work shirt in Anna's hand, he began leaping and barking hysterically. This was his opportunity! Amber's plan had worked!

I know where they are! Follow me and I'll take you to them! Follow me!

In his excitement, Jack ran halfway down the hall to the back door, then back again. Once more, he yapped at the three surprised faces and dashed off down the hall. This time, he went sliding out the screen door before he could stop himself. Unable to get back in, he stood on the porch and yowled for the humans to follow him.

"He must've got Johnny's scent off this shirt," Anna concluded.

"That's just how he was acting this afternoon," said Ken.

Anna straightened her shoulders.

"Well, that's enough to convince me that somethin' has happened to Johnny. My mind's been riled since I woke up this afternoon, maybe that's why; I just had a feelin' that somethin' was wrong.

"Come on. If we're gonna find the boy tonight, we'd better get a move on."

Ken looked dubious and Wales looked downright baffled.

"If Johnny's anywheres in the next three counties, my hounds will be able to track him down." Anna explained impatiently. She was becoming irritated with Jack's ear-splitting barks and the men's slowness. She turned and stomped out of the room ahead of them, saying, "I'll get the pack ready while you two're makin' up your minds."

CHAPTER 31

A night hunt is just about the most exhilarating thing a hound can think of doing! Anna's pack voiced their pleasure and excitement as they did everything else – in a great, booming chorus of bays, the drawn-out barking typical of the hound breeds. To Anna, the sound was invigorating, and she found her own pulse racing as her dogs' fever heightened.

They were given the scent of Johnny's workshirt, left behind when he departed the kennel in the heat of the afternoon. One by one, they dutifully sniffed it according to their training, but they didn't really need to. They had observed, enviously as always, the comings and goings of this afternoon. If they couldn't see directly the route that first Johnny and Jack, then Solitaire had taken, they had benefited from their superior hearing and old Lola's knowledge of the secret gate behind the barn and the glorious open fields beyond it.

They didn't need One-eyed Jack's needling, either. The Aussie ran among them when they were first let out of their run, barking crisp orders like a pint-sized drill sergeant. But when he tried to bully the old matriarch, Lola, into leaving before all of the young dogs were through taking the scent of their quarry, he was issued an unexpected challenge.

Lola's eyes glinted eerily, like rubies in the dark, as she leaned her head low to mutter a profound warning in Jack's face.

Watch yourself tonight, One-Eye! We of the Pack have taken your abuse time and time again and do not love you for it. Beware, little dog, that you do not humiliate us further, for it is a dark night and the delirium of the hunt will soon be upon us all. I cannot vouch for your safety – nor would I care to! Remember that we do not do this thing to help you or your lofty friend, the Akita. We do it for the boy-master – and for our own lusty pleasures!

Jack was shocked to hear the old bitch's words. He had never given the hound pack enough credit to believe that they might have 'communicators' among them. They were a group unto themselves at Welsely's, never bothering to include the 'city breeds' in their deliberations. It was because of this outcast status, which they had brought upon themselves, that Jack had teased them. Now, he felt shame for his numerous callous remarks in the past and phrased an elaborate apology.

Please, madame, forgive me! I meant no harm. It has always been worry for my friends that drives me to such a frenzy of intolerance, for I do not understand the ways of the Pack. If you will only lend your superior skills to our task tonight, I promise that in future I will treat you and your family with the respect you deserve.

Lola still glared at him, but her ears rose and fell forward slightly, into a more relaxed position, giving Jack the courage to add: *If you prefer it, I can lead you quickly to the place where the boy is being held. No strain on you and you'll still get all the credit But I was too weak to follow where the strangers took the Akita, and she may be in worse trouble than Johnny. Please, madam, you must look for Solitaire as well! Without your exceptional powers of tracking, these humans will never find her in time!*

Lola snorted to clear her sensitive nostrils for the trail, insolently spraying the Aussie with the residue. Jack's neck fur ruffled and he tensed up at the vulgarity, but just as he was about to fly in the hound's face, he remembered how much Solitaire's safety might depend on the pack's willing help, and that meant Lola must agree. As he walked, still stiff-legged, away from Lola, she added the final insult to his injury.

We do not need your offer to lead us, rodent-killer! Our noses will take us more swiftly to the boy than if we were to wait for your short legs to make the run. I repeat my warning to you: Stay out of our way!

Jack was thoroughly humiliated, though he couldn't blame the Pack for treating him as cruelly as he had treated them in the past; one apology could not make up for so many negative instances. In spite of Lola's rudeness, he vowed to keep his promise to her. If the Pack used their talents to locate Solitaire tonight, he would be a friend to them for the rest of his life. It would be tough, for they were an earthy bunch, but a terrier's word is his bond!

Noting the obvious friction between Jack and the pack leader, Ken spoke to Anna about leaving the Aussie behind, but she would have none of it.

"He's as worried about that boy as we are, I'm sure of it, and I think we may have an easier time of findin' Johnny if he comes along." She darted a glance at Jack, who was sitting, cowed for the time being, behind the humans' legs. "I'll take the little devil with me in the pickup. Though I hope not, we may need transportation once we find those two, and I ain't really up to a run in the fields in the dark, anyway. Just keep these headlamps lit so I can see which way you're goin' and I'll follow along on the road."

Wales strode down the dark path from the house, carrying two strap-on head lanterns and a long bundle under his arm.

"Do you know how to use a shotgun, Ken?" he asked, beginning to load cartridges into one of the rifles. "I always keep these in my truck in case of varmints, and we may just come up on some tonight."

Ken was aghast at the possibilities that short question implied. He had been off the farm for far too long to remember how useful a shotgun could be to those making a living off the land. When he backed away from the weapon, mumbling the old adage about those things causing more problems than they solve, Anna stood forward and took a firm hold on the loaded shotgun.

"I can use it, John. No need to start trainin' Kenny, here, tonight. Besides, if he ain't used to runnin' with one of these, he'd probably shoot his own foot in the dark. I'll bring it with me in the truck."

Wales seemed utterly confused by a man who didn't know how to shoot, but he shrugged it off and loaded the second shotgun for himself.

Before climbing into the truck, Anna gave the word for the hounds to 'Git on out!' and they leaped forward as one. Ken had never been on a run with the pack before. Seeing how fast they moved out, he was panicked about being able to keep up.

"Shouldn't we have harnesses on them or something?" he asked, too late he knew.

"Don't worry, Kenny," Anna explained. "My dogs are used to workin' off-lead. The old girl, Lola, will let you know where the pack is so you can follow 'em."

The senior Wales had spent enough hours of his boyhood following the hound packs on hunting expeditions to offer Ken a little of his own wisdom.

"When they're excited like this, they get off fast, but most times they overrun the trail and have to circle back to pick it up again. We'll be able to catch up to 'em while they're at it. Once they've settled down to the track, they'll be more careful, and a lot slower."

While they waited for the dogs to pick up the scent, the men strapped their headlamps in place and adjusted the beams. Wales told Ken that Anna Welsely's hounds were reputed to be the best in the county, maybe the state, and he watched them with respect as they worked the start of the trail.

Everyone was surprised at the turn the hounds took. They had expected to be led out to the roadway, but the pack veered off behind the barn.

"I don't like the looks of that," Anna complained, leaning out the window of the pickup. "That man, Earl Kell, don't like himself, for gosh sakes; he certainly ain't gonna take kindly to us lot crossin' over his property! I better git on around the road way and warn him about my pack comin' through so's he don't do anythin' stupid."

She threw the gearshift into reverse so hard that Jack's head disappeared quite suddenly from the passenger's window. He popped back up right away and a lively breeze blew through his topknot as the truck backed quickly out of the kennel yard. Ken was astounded by Anna's dexterity. As long as he'd been there, the mistress of Welsely Farms had never even given a hint that she could still drive.

Lola was the first to the gate at the bottom of the yard, but not by much. Johnny's scent was strong here and the whole pack began milling about, ears sweeping the ground to help fill their capacious olfactory glands with it.

As the men approached, the hounds' whines became more insistent. They definitely wanted to be let into the neighboring fields. For a brief moment, Ken considered returning them to their kennel and going it alone rather than take the chance of Anna's loved pets running into Kell's shotgun. But Johnny's life might depend on them finding him quickly. He pulled the gate open.

The lean hounds raced over the rough ground, vying with each other to be the first – behind Lola, that was. They didn't lower their muzzles to sniff the trail again. Their sensory organs were so highly developed through training and hereditary that the path before them seemed almost to glow with the scent of their quarry. They ran at breakneck speed, yet every new smell they crossed was automatically registered and categorized. This was where the arrogant Akita bitch had passed several hours ago. And these were the footprints of the vermin-chaser, going and coming, both times. The hounds were also aware of Fleet's passage through the field, though they disregarded that as unimportant to this hunt.

Halfway across the first field, Ken was already winded, and Wales offered to stop for him. In the light of his headlamp, Ken could see that Wales' face shone with exertion, too. He shook his head and struggled forward.

"Don't worry about me. I'll come along at my own pace. Those idiot hounds have to slow down soon!"

Wales seemed relieved that he wouldn't have to wait.

"Okay, I'll keep going." "Can you follow? Just listen for Lola's bawlin'. There! That's it, now. Do you notice the difference? Anna says not to trust the others 'cause they might get off on the trail of a fox or somethin' and we could end up in the next county. But Lola's the steady one; she won't leave the scent she's been given."

Ken reflected that Wales was enjoying himself more than he should under these circumstances. But then Ken, of all people, was well aware of how uplifting a properly trained and conditioned animal could be. In front of them, there were half a dozen such animals carrying out their master's bidding in perfect symmetry. Ken had often handled different breeds of pack hounds in the show ring, where their solo performances were less than riveting. Now, as he watched Anna's pack running, he realized why. This multitudinous form was their natural way of being: all of these dogs working together created one entity.

Though Wales had reckoned they would, the hounds did not stop to circle back on the trail. They continued on through the night, broadcasting clear directions for the slower humans to follow, until they came to a group of buildings. Lola pulled up at the edge of the strange compound, suddenly unsure of herself. It wasn't only her training to avoid inhabited areas that made her balk at entering this property; it was also the unusual smell of a great number of foreign dogs. The rest of the pack formed up behind her, sharing her concern, until Wales arrived with Ken panting on his heels.

Wales stood in the long grass with the dogs and studied the farm's buildings with sad eyes.

"I know the man who used to own this property. He'd like to die if he saw it in such ruin," was all he said, but Ken knew he was thinking that his revered acreage could end up the same way without the interest of the new generation – his son, Johnny.

What are you guys waiting for? The boy is here! Come on, I'll show you!

Lola squinted into the light spread by a tall yard lamp to identify the yapper and was disgusted when she realized that One-eyed Jack had somehow beaten the pack here. The infuriating Aussie was barking his head off as he scampered in from the other side of the compound. Anna emerged from the shadows on the side of the farmhouse.

"Don't seem to be anyone at home," she shouted, "but the gate ain't in the best condition, so I jimmied it a bit and drove on in. Anyways, Jack insisted on showing me around, so I found the yard lights. Lord, would you look at this place!" She seemed as disturbed by the condition of the farm as Wales had been.

"Why won't the hounds go in, Anna?" Ken asked when he had caught his breath.

"Don't worry about those darn hounds!" Anna said. "They're trained to stay away from the neighbors' dwellin's – good trainin' out here – but they ain't leavin', either. They followed a strong trail to this place. Right now, they're just mighty frustrated 'cause they can't finish it. I say we listen to Jack and do some explorin'."

Jack began to bark again, and hunkered down on his elbows with his tail in the air – a surefire way to beckon anyone!

"I agree that Jack seems to think this is the way to go, but I'm not so sure that he even knows what we're looking for," Ken complained.

"Well, he's pretty damned insistent for a dog that doesn't know where he's going!" Wales pointed out, starting forward into the light of the farmyard.

As soon as he was sure the humans would follow, Jack jumped up and ran down the uneven line of sheds until he disappeared in their shadows.

The people followed as quickly as they could, but by the time they rounded the corner of the second-to-last shed, there was no sign of the terrier. They looked about, throwing light from their headlamps in all directions, but all that did was make moving shadows out of the dark buildings.

"That little monster could vanish behind a blade of grass," Ken groaned in frustration. He whistled quietly and was badly startled when Jack popped out of nowhere to bounce against his shin. Cursing, he put a hand out to capture the lively Aussie before he could disappear again, but Jack avoided him by scurrying back into a ragged hole torn in the side of the shed.

Johnny's father examined the tumbledown shed and was disappointed to see that the door in front was padlocked. He walked around it to see if there was a window they could force, but the walls were solid.

"Well, that hole Jack went into looks almost big enough for me to enter," Ken offered. He had to summon his courage to explore the hole; he had never liked tight spaces much. While the others watched, he adjusted his headlamp and got down on his hands to have a look. He wrinkled his nose, exhaling sharply when he was blasted with the rank odor of a wild animal's den.

"Good Lord, what lives in here?" he whispered.

"What is it?" Anna asked.

"I don't know, but it stinks worse than a polecat!" Ken's heart raced when he heard a movement that wasn't Jack coming from the inside of the shack and he jerked back out of the hole with unseemly alacrity.

Wales held his rifle at the ready for whatever disturbed thing might come out of the opening after him, but nothing did.

Reticent about sticking his head into the hole for another look around, Ken took the lamp from his forehead to use it as a handheld light and flashed the beam from a little farther away. The first things he saw reflected in it were Jack's silvery forepaws, which were dancing about like impatient wraiths in the blackness. Whatever was in there didn't seem to be bothering the cocky terrier, so he dared to go closer. He held his breath against the stinking air and slowly waved the light around until it caught another movement.

"It's Johnny!" Ken shouted, triumphantly.

Johnny had fallen into a deep, exhausted sleep, from where he had treated Jack's efforts to revive him like a bad dream. He had no desire to regain consciousness in his current uncomfortable situation; while he slept, he felt neither pain nor fear. But though he shrugged the concerned terrier off in irritation, Jack refused to go away, and slowly Johnny was forced to come to his senses. When he opened his eyes, the glow from the light shining through the hole behind him was enough to snap him completely out of his stupor. He tried to scream, but his throat was parched and the gag hurt his bruised lips. The only sound that came out was a pitiful whimper. Frantic that he might not be discovered, Johnny had struggled against his bonds, turning his body far enough around to be able to kick his feet in Ken's flashlight beam.

The senior Wales had heard his son's faint cry and was already running around to the building's padlocked door, Anna close behind him. He slid his rifle barrel between the solid arms of the padlock and heaved mightily, but the lock held. He glanced at Anna, as if in apology for his actions, then turned the shotgun around and swung its butt against the panel where the lock was attached. His first blow went right through the old wood. By now, Ken had joined them and together, they finished the job by kicking the doorframe loose. Both men hurried inside to free the boy, who was sobbing with fatigue and relief. They worked as quickly as they could on Johnny's bonds, then Wales grabbed his son up and carried him from the squalid shed.

One-eyed Jack bounced and bounced to express his happiness at their happiness! Anna and Ken stood back while father and son exchanged bearhugs and emotional tears.

Out in the fresh air, Johnny recovered quickly from his fright. Once his tears had dried and he could trust his voice again, he asked about Solitaire.

"She was here, too," he croaked, his throat raw. "Have you found her yet?"

Ken stuck out his lower lip and shook his head 'no'.

"We figured she'd be with you, son."

Everyone looked disappointed.

"She was here, Mr. Lorch. She was with Jack, trying to rescue me. She dug that hole in the wall, but those guys caught her. They hit her pretty hard," Johnny faltered, the memory painful, "but I don't think she's dead. I heard them saying they were taking her to 'the pit', wherever that is. They were joking about Fleet being happy about that."

"So, Fleet is at the bottom of this," Anna drawled. "I figured as much."

"That Fleet," Wales interjected. "Isn't he the one talkin' up a dogfight around town?"

"A dogfight!?!" Ken's professional honor was insulted by the mere mention of the word. "I can't believe Fleet would have anything to do with a dogfight. He's a pain in the neck, but he wouldn't stoop that low. He likes dogs."

In the dark, Johnny rolled his eyes. "No, Mr. Lorch, Fleet doesn't like dogs," he stated, firmly. "He likes to make money off them, that's all. Look. I've got proof of what I'm saying!" He thrust his hands into his pockets and pulled out some crumpled squares of paper, then unfolded them with trembling fingers as he explained to the adults what they were and where he had found such incriminating evidence.

Anna cocked her head to listen.

"You say there's dogs in these sheds? Why don't they bark? We've sure made enough of a ruckus out here tonight."

"I don't know, ma'am," Johnny admitted. "There were lots of them. They were in pretty bad shape, though. Maybe they're too sick to bark, or too scared."

Anna was mystified by kennel dogs that didn't bark. However, there would be plenty of time later to search out those unfortunate victims of Fleet's aspirations. And there had better not be any of Welsely's stock traceable to this hell-hole! She swore an oath to find out for herself at the earliest opportunity.

"I'm sure that's the name I heard," Wales reiterated when his son finished his explanation. "I didn't pay it any mind when a guy in town told me about it, but if it is the same man, your dog's in a hell of a lot of trouble right now."

Suddenly, Lola's particular bawl cut through the night air like a banshee's scream. Her old nose had been put out of joint when Jack beat her to the scene of Johnny's rescue; that was one more insult to her pack's pride from that rat-bag. But the terrier had admitted at the start that he already knew where Johnny lay hidden, so it couldn't be counted as a fair contest, really, could it? The real challenge was going to be who was able to find the Akita bitch first.

Lola had known she was breaking training when she surreptitiously crept into the compound, but how was she to figure out the riddle of the Akita's disappearance if she didn't get close? She put her snout to the ground and snuffled the area where Solitaire had lain, then moved in ever-widening circles to pick up the path she had traveled. A few minutes later, Lola was able to trace the bitch's path backwards, but it seemed like she had come so far, then just disappeared into the atmosphere.

Hmmm. The ancient hound would need to call on all of her experience to figure out this enigma, but she was determined to find her quarry.

She stuck her nose close to the hole in the side of the shed and inhaled deeply. Yes, the Akita bitch's smell was strong here, as was the rat-chaser's. But there was a third dog's essence here, as well. Its scent was overlaid with the same malodorous stew as the inside of the building the Akita had been trying to enter. It had walked outside, though not through the hole, at about the same time as Solitaire's disappearance. Lola followed his tracks (for now she could smell his sex as well) over the top of the Akita's last lying-place, then along some fresh tire ruts that headed outwards from the compound. From there, she had made a huge leap in logic for a hound: this vehicle was linked to the Akita bitch's sudden disappearance. When Lola gave victorious tongue, the pack surrounded her, and as one, they sprinted away into the darkness.

"That's my girl," Anna gloated. "She's onto another track. Probably Solitaire's, though it could be a 'coon just as easy. Let's go find out!"

Ken was as excited as the rest, but he urged caution.

"Anna, you can't go running off after those hounds. And Johnny's hurt. Why don't you two bring up the pickup? You ought to be able to find some service roads close enough to follow our headlamps."

Anna was miffed. This was as much action as she'd seen in many years and she hated to miss any of it, but she finally agreed that Ken was right.

"Did you bring your cell? Give it to me and I'll get hold of the sheriff on the way in case we need a little more help this time."

Johnny didn't intend to give up so easily.

"I'm not really hurt," he begged his father and Mr. Lorch, "just scared. But I want to help Solitaire."

Wales' fear for his son's safety had hardened into a need for justice and he admired Johnny's fortitude.

"Is that other shotgun still in the truck or did you bring it with you, Anna? Give it to Johnny. He knows how to use it. We may need to persuade these guys to give the dog up, if what my son says is true."

Ken had another thought.

"Anna, see if the sheriff can get hold of Doc, too." He saw the glint of panic in Johnny's eyes, and explained. "Not necessarily for Solitaire, son. But, if there's a dogfight going on somewhere out there, some poor animal's bound to need a vet.

"And even if there isn't, we'll need a vet to substantiate our charges of animal cruelty on this Kell fellow."

Johnny seemed relieved by that explanation, even happy, as the three men started after the hounds.

Jack ran ahead of the people, arriving at the lighted perimeter of the yard just as the last of the hounds left it. He would have loved to chase after the bigger dogs, but instead he waited circumspectly for the humans to catch up. Lola's warning had not fallen on deaf ears; he was far too sensible to take the chance on being mistaken for a rabbit in those dark fields.

CHAPTER 32

One by one and two by two, the more curious men of the town had drifted in, until now the pit's corrugated steel walls were circled three deep by the crowd. Other men had pulled their trucks up to illuminate the arena with their headlights and were using them as movable bleachers. Icy kegs of beer were cracked hours ago so that by the time of the first fight the local yokels would be 'feelin' no pain'. And that was just fine with the Carolina boys, who were grinning like hyenas on the sidelines in anticipation of making a killing on enthusiastic, but poorly-judged side bets.

Solitaire was frightened by the unnatural aggression of the animals held in cages all around her. Except physically, they bore little resemblance to any canines she had known. They paced like caged wildcats, raving and tearing at each other through the bars whenever they happened to come face to face with their neighbors. Though their metal crates were separated by a safe distance so that no injuries resulted from these clashes, the dogs' constant bickering devastated Solitaire's nerves.

Now and then, one of the southern boys would come by to whip the dogs into even greater frenzy for the enjoyment of the local fellows. He would shout foolish names like "Bone-Crusher" or "Strangler" or "Gatorbait" as he ran heavy sticks up and down the bars of individual cages, aggravating an already noisy situation as the dogs rose to the bait time and again. But none of the boys could get a rise out of the Akita, no matter how much they teased. She stayed hunched over like a great bear in the rear of her cage, barely able to conceal her fear of the human lunatics as well as the canine ones.

So frustrated were the bullies by her lack of reaction that they complained to Fleet.

"That bitch ain't got nothin' in 'er"

"She's a dud!"

"Y'oughta put her out as blood for one of the younger dogs, and not waste Gatorbait on her."

But Fleet wasn't disturbed.

"She'll fight," he said, "and when she does, you better have put your money on her."

Earl took this as a proper challenge to his dog.

"Y'all 're gonna hafta wake 'er up, first!" he tossed back at Fleet. "At this rate, Gatorbait'll have her by the jug'lar 'fore she even opens her eyes!"

The delighted laughter that ensued embarrassed Fleet. The plan was for Earl to tout his own dog, in order to get the odds up, while they placed their money on the Akita, but Fleet thought his partner was taking his role much too seriously. Angrily, he picked up a club and headed for Solitaire's kennel.

He never got close enough to rap the bars as the boys had done. Solitaire was relieved to see a recognizable foe at last and launched herself toward him, her black face distorted by overt hatred. Fleet coolly reversed his club, turning the small end toward the charging dog, and jammed it hard into her breastbone. She dropped to the floor, grunting heavily with pain, but rolled back to her feet swiftly enough to grab the hurtful object in Fleet's hand before he could withdraw it from the cage. He held his end tightly with two hands, laughing along with the others at the Akita's mad tug-of-war.

Solitaire felt the cruel taunts in their laughter like barbs on her skin. She would get even with this hated man for humiliating her. Berserk with anger, Solitaire ripped at the wooden club, splintering it into matchsticks in her frustration. The Akita wasn't just tearing up the piece of wood in impotent anger; she was letting Fleet know what would happen to him should she ever get her freedom.

This display of fury had the desired effect on Fleet, who suddenly dropped his end of the stick as if it was burning his hands. A mental picture had come, unbidden, into his mind. In it, the big dog was towering over him, pinning him to the ground and ravishing him with the same gusto she was using on his discarded club.

To cover his trepidation, Fleet faced the crowd and asked, "Any of you still believe this bitch doesn't have any fight in her?"

"Yeah, she'll fight," Earl agreed. "If'n we put y'all in the pit with 'er, anyways! But will she fight another dog? There's the rub!"

There was a murmur of agreement, then all eyes turned on Fleet, who smiled tightly.

"Then your dog'll eat her," he shrugged, exuding a calm indifference he did not feel. "Either way, I win."

The boys showed their approval of his callous attitude with a rousing chorus of 'Attaboy's'.

Earl slugged back his beer in one long swig and bellowed, "All right, boys. Let's bring out the dogs!"

Glowering in frustration, Solitaire retired to the back of her cell to await her next opportunity to punish Fleet. She knew it was coming; it must come, or she would never be totally free of her anger.

The locals crowded around the pit, excited yet apprehensive about the bloody spectacle they had come to witness. From opposite sides of the ring, two rangy men led two equally threadbare dogs in on rusty chains and loosed them before stepping hurriedly out of the way. The minute the dogs saw each other across the ring, their tired features erupted in fierce-looking snarls. They circled each other slowly, stiff-legged, each trying to scare the other into backing down, and building up his own courage at the same time. Eager shouts of 'Git' im!' and 'Eat 'im up!' failed to start them, and soon the drunken crowd got more belligerent than the dogs they were watching. One man threw an empty beer can at the nearest dog, which caused him to jump, looking away from his opponent for an instant. In the split second that he was distracted, the other cur flew at him, hitting him on the shoulder and knocking him down in the dirt. The first dog's legs flailed desperately as he tried to right himself before the other could clamp strong jaws on his jugular. But the other dog had acted offensively only to defend himself, and now he returned to bristling and strutting along the far wall. His show of intimidation worked. The first dog seemed to lose his nerve entirely and could only cower pathetically on the spot.

As Earl's cronies had predicted, the local men were disappointed. They booed and hissed until the frightened animals were removed from the pit. Goddammit! They had fortified themselves with booze in anticipation of a gory show and now they wanted to see some blood!

Earl nodded to old Billy, who accompanied him to the kennel area. They dragged a couple of mixed breed dogs out of their crates. The animals were so young that they might have played together if they hadn't been driven to the edge of sanity by their cruel treatment at the hands of Earl and the boys. Now they saw each other only as something on which to vent their rage. They barely waited until the men left the pit before they closed, savagely ripping at each other's coat and spreading a satisfying amount of blood about the ring. But they didn't have the experience to deliver any killing bites. When enough blood had been spilled, and before the contest got boring for the spectators, the exhausted pups were pulled apart and taken from the ring. They had learned a few lessons and would be stronger competitors in their next fights. So had the crowd. They screamed for more and better dogs.

It was time for the purebred Pit Bulls. The boys only kept a few of these awesome dogs because they were costly to fight on a regular basis. Pit Bulldogs were born knowing how to kill. Every time they were entered into the ring, one of the combatants was fated to end up dead. The Pit Bull Terrier's method of fighting involved little unnecessary bloodletting; he did not rip and tear as most canines did. There was little bluster in his manner. He simply bided his time until he could catch his opponent close to the throat. Once he saw his opening and he clamped onto the other dog, nothing could shake him loose. The Pit Bull's immensely strong jaws and shoulders, combined with his low center of gravity made him the perfect fighter in the pit. Against any other breed, he could not lose. Against another Pit Bull, the one who got his deadly purchase first was the victor. Often the death scene was long and drawn out, with the other animal dying slowly of asphyxiation. Sometimes it was mercifully quick, when the jugular vein was ripped wide open.

This contest between two Pit Bulls would have ended in the first way. Bobby's brindle dog was the favorite going in, and he proved to be the fastest. The men watched, fascinated, for several minutes while Billy's white and pink dog's struggles grew weaker and his breath came in shallow whistles. But before his breathing stopped altogether, the dog was mercifully spared. In an odd moment of compassion, old Billy called 'Uncle!' and hopped into the pit to separate the two animals. It took Billy, Bobby, and another man with a spark-stick to pry the brindle's jaws loose enough to drag the limp white body away from him. Both dogs were spattered with blood, but the brindle wore his proudly. His whippy tail wagged gleefully as he received congratulatory pats from his master.

Fleet stared incredulously at the wildly animated mob surrounding him. The Carolina boys were happily walking among them, covering bets and paying out winnings between the fights. Even though Fleet calculated that the boys were doing most of the winning, knowing their dogs as well as they did, the locals didn't seem disappointed in the least. Fleet found it hard to believe that these men were the same dullards he had to cajole into coming out to give the dog fights a try.

When Earl shouted, "Are you ready for a good fight now?" the excited crowd voiced their eagerness. The boys were right. You didn't have to come from the swamps to enjoy this bloodsport.

"Fleet, I'll give y'all a hand takin' yor bitch outta her crate," Billy volunteered. "We got to do this careful-like. We wouldn't want t'hurt the liddle thang, would we?"

For a change, Fleet was able to appreciate the black humor in the old boy's reminder. He enjoyed a laugh as he picked up two of the heavy dog chains.

"I'll try to be real gentle with her," he promised.

Solitaire was still lying, miserable and confused, in the back of her cage. This time, when she saw Fleet approaching, she didn't waste her energy on another futile attack on the bars. But she didn't cower away from him, either. Instead, she stood to her full size, relying on her commanding presence to keep the man at bay. Aside from taunting her as the others did, what harm could he cause her in here?

Fleet's expression was cold and black as a winter night when he stared into the Akita's eyes, and Solitaire understood his malicious intent. Yet her gaze remained locked on his, unintimidated, and she further emphasized her willingness to do battle with a deep, inviting growl.

"Not me this time, my lovely," Fleet crooned, a loose smile hung on his lips. "But you'll get your chance to prove if there's any real fight beneath that swagger."

He began playing with the chain in his hands, loosening and drawing in the loop end of it until Solitaire realized that he was going to call her out. As much as she hated being held in this cage, she didn't think her odds were any better on the outside of the bars while this bunch was around. She eyed Fleet suspiciously as he bent to open the door and proffered the expanded oval of chain. Did he think she would just walk into it? She backed off a few steps until her haunches rubbed up against the rear wall of the cage. Now he would have to come in to get her. A throaty rumble was meant to warn the foolish man of the consequences should he attempt to do that.

Solitaire's right ear flicked as her attention was momentarily distracted by a man's giggling coming from very close behind her. Then a searing, burning spasm of pain reached through her hip, raced through her long body and clasped onto her heart, making it throb wildly in protest. Terror-stricken, she bolted straight into the waiting loop of chain. Fleet yanked the circle tight around her neck and jumped out of the way with a shout of triumph. Before the severely agitated bitch could recover her composure, another man threw his chain around her neck and she was held captive from two directions. She could neither jump at her captors, nor lick her own wound.

"You boys sure know how to handle a dog," Fleet applauded, mimicking the southern boys' manner. "Yessir, you sure do!"

Old Billy's grin went from ear to ear as he stood up from behind the metal cage, brandishing an electric prod.

"Been known to rustle a cow or two, too, ain't we boys? That oughta make her mad enough t'fight, now."

In this comradely mood, the men escorted Solitaire to the pit entrance. She had no choice but to follow where they took her. She couldn't turn right or left, and if she fell behind, she received a painful kick from another chuckling man behind her.

The crowd parted like water when they saw the huge animal being led by two sturdy chains. "What is it?" they all wanted to know. "Is that some kind of wolf? Is it as mean as it looks?"

"Bet your money on it, gentlemen!" Bobby was doing his hawking routine for the coming fight. The Carolina boys were working the same game as Fleet and Earl were, but from a different angle. They, also, had pooled their resources in order to better control the odds for this last match. The Akita bitch had the look of a real fighter and the size to go with it. In the pit, she would make Gatorbait look positively puny. Naturally, the ignorant locals would think their bets were safe with her. The boys would watch the odds stack up in her favor, then cover the bets just before the dogs were let loose. It wouldn't take long for the crowd to realize the difference between a trained fighting animal and an oversized lapdog, but by then Bobby would have their money in his hands.

The doors behind Solitaire closed and she found herself in a narrow chute. The men holding her lead chains dropped their ends, which she immediately tore from around her neck. Ignoring the pain she still felt in her right haunch, she looked about for a way out of the dark hole. Corrugated tin walled in both ends of the tunnel and the crude grating laid across the top of the ditch dashed her hopes of escape. She could only wait patiently for whatever mischief these perplexing strangers had arranged for her.

Several of the spectators leaned out over the top of the chute, their faces looking oddly distorted as they stared down at her. Some of them had drunk enough courage to taunt the wolfish dog, but most just seemed interested in examining her. She could see money changing hands across the gap over her head. Now there was cheering as more people arrived on the opposite side of the pit, and most of her audience left.

Solitaire listened to a loud voice announcing the next fight was between an 'All-American', whom he called 'Gatorbait', and a Japanese wolf-dog. Was that her? While she was contemplating the meaning of that announcement, the wide piece of tin across the front of her chute was thrown back, giving her a glimpse of a small blood-spattered arena. Cautiously, she started toward the center of it, hoping to find some escape from this nightmare. She jerked spasmodically when the metal gate clanged back into place behind her. Such lack of composure in a fighting dog seemed to invoke a great deal of hilarity in the men ogling her from around the outside of the pit.

Solitaire, disdaining to look up at their laughing faces, did a quick survey of the pit. The straight metal walls enclosing it convinced her that she was still trapped. Mystified as to what she was expected to do all alone in here, she sat squarely on her behind to think, then, with a twinge of pain, rolled more carefully onto her left haunch.

Now that she was here, in the center of all the clamor and surrounded by the smell of freshly spilled blood, the place where the next act in her life was about to be played out, Solitaire was not frightened. She was prepared to face whatever lay ahead, just as long as there would be an end to this nightmare. The Akita's outward appearance seemed so tranquil that one drunkard, already a know-it-all after witnessing three fights, called out, "You guys had better get the other dog in there before she falls asleep!"

Another tin shield opened across from Solitaire and the crowd hushed expectantly as a tall, grayish-blue dog emerged to meander into the center of the fighting pit. The transformation of Gatorbait from canine companion animal to grotesque killing machine was complete. Earl had shortened his ears and stitched them himself, but they looked as though they had been bitten off. His flat, ugly head was a roadmap of cuts and scrapes from training fights. His body was lean and sinewy, with more tendon than muscle. He smelled like a skunk in heat.

The dog's odd, side-winding gait reminded Solitaire of the little grass-snakes she had seen at Welsely's and she wondered if he had been born like that or if he had suffered some injury.

Gatorbait's glazed stare, as he looked about his surroundings, lacked any real interest – until it locked on Solitaire. The creepy sensation she experienced when his yellow eyes found hers made the Akita's skin crawl so that her hackles rose on their own, without conscious effort on her part. Gatorbait immediately accepted what he perceived to be her challenge and swung around to face his adversary, his long, pink tongue flicking out to lick the end of his muzzle in lewd enthusiasm for the bloodbath to come.

Solitaire's revulsion at the sight of such a creature caused her to rise warily to her feet, never taking her eyes off him. She did not want to engage this demon in battle; if there was a way out of this, she would have taken it. But Earl's friends had made sure that there would be no escape from this pit for either dog, except in spirit form.

Solitaire wondered whether she should try to commune with this brute, but when she recalled the tortured souls of the other pit dogs, she decided not to risk it. For a male canine to threaten injury on a female in combat probably meant that his instincts had been so suppressed by his training that there could be no communication between them, anyway.

And what about her instincts? Yes, she was the daughter and granddaughter of warriors, but could she rely on her fighting instincts to carry the day when she had virtually no experience other than playful sparring? The dog before her was going to try to kill her, she knew. She had never killed before. And yet, as she composed herself for the coming battle, she realized that the thought of doing so did not sicken her. The Akita's savagery was not buried as deeply within her psyche as it was in most breeds. It lay just beneath the civilized surface of her personality, and was easily provoked.

Made bulky by the extra thickness of her standing hackles, the Akita bitch's gait seemed to roll as comfortably as a grizzly bear's as she began the ancient rituals of the challenge. Men who had placed their bets on her shouted encouragement when it looked as though she was going to be the aggressor in this fight after all. Seconds later, they were astounded to see her rolling in the dirt.

Gatorbait had learned from his training sessions with Earl that the time to attack was when your opponent least expected it; there was no time for manners in the pit. Unfortunately, he had been fooled by the impression of extra mass given by the Akita's thick coat. Though he had knocked her off her feet with his surprise charge, he had not delivered any injurious blows. So astonished was he to have his jaws clamp shut on nothing but fur that Gatorbait missed his opportunity to press his attack on the downed bitch. By the time he finally turned around Solitaire was standing again, braced for his next rush.

This time when he came at her, the more powerful bitch easily took the jolt on her shoulder, then leaped straight into the air, which unbalanced her attacker and sent him sprawling. Though she landed directly behind him, in the instant it took her to whirl around Gatorbait was already on his feet again. He understood what his fate would be should he remain down for long.

The clouded blue hound stood a moment, confused and peevish. Most of his training fights had been rigged so that he would never lose, yet this opponent easily thwarted his attacks. In a sudden fit of bad temper, he charged like a bull directly at Solitaire. She watched him coming, offered her shoulder again, then delicately stepped aside at the last moment so that Gatorbait ran right past her, skidding to a stop just before he hit the wall.

Earl was apoplectic with rage that the Akita bitch should make his trained fighting dog look so bad. His obscenities were making even his buddies choke with embarrassment. They believed the poor man was about ready to tear his hair out, if he had any.

Fleet plainly was enjoying his buddy's pain. Those good old boys had teased him long enough and now it appeared that he was about to get some retribution. If Solitaire won this bout, his pride would be patched and his pockets would be full of the southern men's dollars. Plus, he would have the extreme pleasure of being able to shoot the damned bitch afterwards. So pleased was he, he could barely keep from laughing out loud with the rest of the crowd.

Solitaire watched Gatorbait's pale eyes carefully. Though she could tell he was still seething when he rose from the dirt, he hadn't run at her a third time. She didn't think the mongrel would give up this easily, so he must be planning alternative moves – moves she felt confident she could outmaneuver. She knew she was winning this fight and the exhilaration of power was on her. Up until now, she had not pressed her advantage, but her blood was becoming heated and she found herself looking forward to thrashing this creature, if only to demonstrate the Akita Inu's ability to do so.

Come, you hideous monster. Pit yourself against the get of generations of warriors and learn your place.

Solitaire paraded back and forth in front of Gatorbait, offering him first one shoulder, then the other. Her tail was bunched into a tense knot and her clenched paws threw up pebbles and bits of dirt as she scraped them menacingly over the ground. Her ears were forward, alert to any movement on the dog's part, yet no snarl lifted her features.

Bobby thought this looked wrong.

"That bitch don't understand the rules of this game," he murmured, more to himself than to anyone around him. "She ain't attacking. She's just baiting him, like it's a game or something."

"She's in for a surprise, I think," Billy mumbled.

Gatorbait stood on the other side of the pit with his head low, glaring at Solitaire out the tops of his yellow eyes and calculating his position. He didn't like to be mocked, but he was used to it enough to know that if he did nothing, the heckler was sure to get overconfident and make a slip.

The crowd was beginning to get impatient again. Over the course of the evening, they had been built up to a pitch of excitement and now this lack of action in the pit was letting them down. Earl didn't hear their complaints, however. He was concentrating as hard as his dog was. What was Gatorbait looking for, anyway? What did he see that Earl didn't?

The next time Solitaire changed direction, showing Gatorbait her right hindquarter, he dug his claws into the earth and catapulted his rangy body full at her. Solitaire had been waiting for such a move. Confidently, she set her mighty shoulder against the mongrel's rushing charge. Gatorbait closed rapidly. Suddenly, he jogged wildly to the left, plowing into Solitaire's right hip, instead of her shoulder. He had noticed a slight limp where the Akita's haunch was still weak from the electrical shock she had received. Perhaps there was pain there? This charge would tell him.

Solitaire went down, surprised herself by the scorching pain in her hindquarters. Gatorbait could have gone for her throat right away, but he knew it was too early. The bitch was still very powerful. Instead, he showed sinister cunning by choosing to build on the weakness he had discovered. The fur on the Akita's haunch was as thick as anywhere else, but he had leverage going for him now that she was down. His frighteningly powerful jaws tore a huge gash across her thigh before he jumped away.

Solitaire's reaction to her pain was typical of her breed – instantaneous and deliberate. She flip-flopped her heavy body to protect her bloody leg at the same time as her head snaked back to grab her enemy in a death grip. But he was gone. She jumped to her feet to chase after him, her savagery aroused by the pain he had caused her.

Gatorbait had not expected such a speedy recovery. He had no time to run. When the infuriated Akita reared on her hind legs, ready to pounce on him, he had no choice but to rise to his hind legs as well and meet her in a face to face clash. Though their muzzles were equally high, her weight was too much for him and he was rolled backwards. She followed him down and lay so low and close upon him that he couldn't get any purchase to throw her off. His long legs could only claw ineffectually at the air around her body.

Gatorbait felt her smothering weight against his chest as they fought the close duel. His only chance now was to guard his throat from her slashing jaws. Panicked, he thrashed his head from side to side, teeth gnashing, trying to catch a vulnerable spot on her face. Solitaire made her eyes into slits and locked teeth with her victim in the same way as she had fenced with her siblings, almost playing with him. She was secure in the knowledge that her body's natural armor of fat and fur would protect her eyes, face and neck. The stringy, short-haired hound beneath her would be the all-out loser in this contest. His bared throat was hers for the taking whenever she pleased.

The crowd howled for blood! Solitaire knew the ultimate thrill that came with victory. Primal rhythms beat in her ears, urging her to take her kill until, with a last snap at Gatorbait's face to warn him to stay down, she broke the spell and leaped off him.

I was foolish for not giving you enough credit, shy one. You are a worthy opponent. Yet I have no wish to kill you and cannot understand why you should want to harm me. Let us both call this contest ended and go our own way in honor.

When someone pounded his shoulder, an anguished Earl peered out from between his clasped fingers. He couldn't believe what he was seeing. He had figured once the Akita took Gatorbait down, that was the end of his dog. Now, seeing there was a chance, he began screaming for Gatorbait to get up, somehow making himself heard over the tumult of the rest of the crowd.

Gatorbait opened his eyes, surprised that the Akita's bite hadn't killed him. He rolled quickly to his feet, afraid that his opponent might change her mind, then put some distance between them so that he could think this puzzle through. But before he could run too far, Kell's maniacal shrieks reached his ears, reminding him of his lot in life. Gatorbait's training, mean as it was, had instilled in him the need to kill above all else. Now the hatred poured back in on him, erasing his fear. He could not abandon the fight while there was another living thing to punish. Especially since he had learned what he needed to know in order to finish this in his favor.

He turned again to confront Solitaire, reassessing his opponent. She was bigger and much heavier than he, which made him the faster dog. And now her speed was further reduced by her injuries. He would continue worrying her hindquarters until she became exhausted. Then, and only then, would he risk getting close enough to tear out her throbbing jugular. Something akin to pleasure, but more sadistic in nature, rekindled the fire in his yellow eyes.

Solitaire had calmed the madness in her own breast. She was concentrating on regaining her powers of clear thinking when she caught the fevered gleam in the gray dog's eyes. How could he have any fight left in him after being beaten so soundly? It was only through her mercy that the cur was still breathing, yet there he was, challenging her to engage him in conflict once again. She snarled contemptuously in answer to his dare, promising to teach him the lesson her warrior blood had been calling for all along.

Gatorbait began circling, forcing Solitaire to do the same. Now and then, he lowered his head to fake a charge on her back legs. Always, she met him with snapping teeth. But to do so, she had to whirl on her haunches and every time she put too much weight on her right hip, it sent a current of pain down her leg. The poorly placed electric prod had done the real harm earlier, damaging the nerves in her hip, and Gatorbait's slashing had added insult to her injury by tearing the supporting muscle. Now her tired hindquarters threatened to collapse beneath her.

When his opponent's reactions seemed to have slowed enough, Gatorbait risked a closer feint and had the stub of his right ear torn open for his impatience. Most dogs' earflaps are very sensitive to pain and his were still aching from Earl's surgery, so Solitaire was rewarded with his awful screech – just before he jumped for her throat.

His hold on her neck was not a good one; again his teeth ground against nothing but nerveless skin and fur. The thick dewlap under Solitaire's chin stretched to allow her to turn inside her own skin, even while Gatorbait held on, and she was able to use her fangs to tear into the back of her enemy's neck and shoulders, slashing his flesh into crimson strips. Finally, after she mangled his other ear, he gave up his hold and jumped clear.

Gatorbait was streaming blood from his ears, head and front quarters, but they were only surface cuts. Solitaire looked as clean as when she entered the pit except for the deep red mark where Gatorbait had torn her back leg, yet they both knew that wound was the critical one.

The crowd was overjoyed to see some blood spilled at last. Oblivious to the fact that they might be losing their bets, they were slapping Earl's back and congratulating him on his dog's cunning.

"Ya see, Fleet?" Earl bubbled happily. "That's what trainin'll do fer a dog. Makes 'im think smarter, knowin' the consequences if he don't. Yor bitch don't have a chance agin 'im now he's had 'er throat. He'll be right back at it!"

Solitaire was panting from exertion and pain. The heavy muscle and thick fur that had been her advantage thus far was becoming a handicap for the Akita. She was slowing down too much, allowing Gatorbait too many opportunities for attack. Her best chance was to finish her opponent quickly, before her wounded hip gave out entirely.

Gatorbait wasn't about to let his opponent catch her breath in such a close battle. He feinted and snapped with renewed energy, inviting her to attack him. The more she lunged, the more pressure would be put on that back leg.

Solitaire would not accommodate him. She waited patiently, only swinging her head to defend herself, as he grew braver, coming in closer and closer to that crippled hind leg.

The time was right. Gatorbait did not retreat from his pass. His mouth was open as he propelled himself straight at the Akita, determined to take her down.

With a mighty effort, Solitaire reared as though to let the dog through, then came crashing down on top of him, her wide jaws gripping the whole back of his neck. She leaned into her grip, turning her head to off-balance her prey, and raised a hefty front paw over his back to push him over. As Gatorbait fell, Solitaire kept readjusting her hold until she felt the throbbing of his life-vein between her teeth. One rip and this enemy would be no more. The crowd hushed, waiting to witness the grisly end to this magnificently-fought duel.

Solitaire's mind was in chaos. Her violent hatred for Fleet and unrelenting quest for vengeance had turned her so far from the Teachings that she was about to – wanted to – murder one of her canine brothers. She could no longer see out of her eyes, nor hear beyond the rushing in her ears. The inward call of her barbarous ancestors, the same ones who had bequeathed to her the fighting prowess she had used tonight to save her own life, whispered urgently for her to take her enemy's. At the same time, her lifelong acceptance of the Teachings made her hesitate.

But she was Akita Inu, and her blood was samurai! Ancient breed memories passed through her mind's eye; memories of running down the timid elk in its wild mountain pastures and marching off to bloody war alongside determined Japanese soldiers.

But she was also Akita Inu, noble guardian of man and his vassals. Other memories of sitting guard over mixed herds of fluffy sheep and agile goats, and spending quiet hours watching over the master's children washed over her.

Solitaire's fierce hold on Gatorbait's throat lessened imperceptibly, but then suddenly she was being swept away again to the age-old hunt. She could hear the full-throated baying of her pack-mates, eager to bring down their prey!

Wait! Solitaire released her adversary's neck to raise her head and listen. She wasn't hallucinating now. The sound of a hunting pack in full tongue was real. She picked out Lola's cry leading the Welsely hounds forward!

All at once, the mob above the pit was split by a rolling movement as the closely-packed men tried to make room for something they respected. Their shouts were no longer jubilant, but hysterical as they backed and tripped over each other in their attempts to get out of the way.

Beneath Solitaire, Gatorbait was struggling to rise. A cursory glance told her that there was no more fight in the mongrel, so she allowed him to crawl out from between her legs, and watched while he slunk to the far edge of the pit. There he remained, peering fearfully from the shadows at the panic above him.

Anna's pack had come upon the men in the open field. Here, there were no boundaries marked by human structures to restrain them, and Lola led them straight into the center of the gathering. The wildly excited hounds were incensed by the sights, the noise, and especially the smells of the bloody conflicts that had taken place in the pit this night. They raced through the crowd, knocking grown men to the side in their exuberance. The men scattered like chickens in front of them and raced for their trucks, eager to escape the violence.

As Solitaire watched, a particularly rounded man was pushed by his mates into the corrugated tin wall of the pit. It gave way beneath his weight and fell in toward Solitaire, landing at her feet. She stared, shocked, at the man who had ridden it down. When he looked up to see the ferocious wolf-dog towering above him, the petrified man began screaming for his buddies to help him. Solitaire cocked her head, puzzled by his reaction, but the poor man took the concerned wrinkles that appeared in her forehead to mean deadly intention. He rolled to his knees, crawling for his life toward the pit wall. Rocks and dirt were kicked loose as he tried unsuccessfully to scale the incline until at last a friend on the higher level hauled him up over the side, and they both took off for the open fields.

Solitaire looked back to make sure that Gatorbait remained in the shadows, then easily leaped up and out of the pit in the same spot. It was bedlam above. All around her, men who had enjoyed watching the misery of the tortured creatures in the pit now ran in terror themselves, gutless cowards before the hunting hounds. The hounds, eager for the game after their long confinement, chased after them with bared teeth and lolling tongues that looked truly horrible even though they were nothing more than smiles of extreme enjoyment.

Solitaire did not join in on the revelry. She scanned the crowd, but did not see the man she wanted. Fleet may have temporarily disappeared in the chaos, but she was resolved that he wouldn't get away from her tonight. Ignoring the turmoil around her, she slipped, wolf-like, into the night, in pursuit of her chosen victim.

Fleet had not run because he was in terror of the pack. Right off, he had recognized the hounds as Anna's and knew that he would be in no danger from them. But the Welsely people would not be far behind their dogs, he was sure. He thought the boys could probably run them off, but he had no desire to be caught by his former boss at the scene of the dogfights.

He reached the boys' van, in which the last supply of beer had been delivered along with Solitaire, and climbed into the driver's seat. He started to reach into his pocket for the keys before he remembered that Bobby had taken them from him to bring the van out here. Cursing, he began to rummage around in the cab in case Earl kept a set hidden somewhere. When he probed beneath his seat, his hand came across the smooth butt of a shotgun.

"Trust those boys to never leave home without one," he mumbled irritably.

At the moment he lowered his head to check under the dash, Fleet realized that, in his panic, he had overlooked the obvious place. The keys were dangling from the ignition slot right in front of his eyes. Relieved, Fleet started the van's engine and turned on the lights. He was adjusting the side mirror, ready to reverse out of there, when he noticed the frothy white chest and forelegs of the Akita bitch reflected brightly in it. He wanted to keep going, knew it was the wisest move, but he couldn't resist this opportunity.

"Well, tonight might be my lucky night after all," he whispered huskily, as he shut down the engine and reached for the shotgun he had found below the seat. "At least there's one piece of business I'll be able to finish." He left the van's lights on and slowly opened the door.

Solitaire took note of Fleet's furtive manner and backed off a bit until she could figure out what he was going to do. She was ready to face him, but wisely wanted to know the method he would use before devising her own plan.

When Fleet saw what he thought was the Akita bitch getting ready to run from him, he reached back into the van and yanked the keys from the ignition. He wanted to be sure he wouldn't be left behind should the boys try to take the vehicle before he got back. Then he followed Solitaire into the thicket.

Solitaire was unafraid when she saw the stick in Fleet's hands. It wasn't anywhere near as big as the one Earl Kell had beaten her with and she had survived that attack. Still, she would be careful to avoid any more of that type of punishment if she could. She waited behind the only wide tree trunk in the thicket, another dark spot in the shadows.

Fleet knew he was close on the Akita's heels. Cautiously, his rifle at the ready, he walked on. He listened as well as he could and strained his eyes, but a man in the dark is no match for a canine.

Solitaire could scarcely believe her good fortune when he walked within a whisker's breadth of her hiding place. She kept her breathing even while she tensed for the attack.

The full weight of the Akita impacted heavily on Fleet's back, forcing him to fall face-first in the field. He screamed as he went down, but the sound was lost in the general hubbub of the evening. He had stupidly dropped the shotgun to save himself in the fall and now had only his bare hands with which to fend off his attacker. Rolling under Solitaire's massive body, he held those useless weapons over his face in abject terror. A feeling of déjà vu came over Fleet, except this time he knew there wouldn't be anyone to help him.

But Solitaire did not bite him or tear at him as she had before. She only snarled corrosively while she rose slowly to her feet, then stood above him, threatening surely, but not murderous. Unbelieving of his luck, Fleet nevertheless took this chance to stretch his hand in the direction of the shotgun. The Akita continued to back off, her growl still thunderous in Fleet's ears.

Foolish human! You are no match for me in physical combat. And have I not soundly beaten the best canine challenger you can offer? Be glad that I am a 'Competent' of the Teachings, dishonorable one. Through them, I have come to know that it is unseemly for any dog to hate humankind as I have done. With the support of my friends, I have put personal revenge out of my thoughts forever. Although you may not deserve it, you will be the first beneficiary of my forgiveness.

Fleet had no idea what miracle had kept the Akita bitch from tearing him apart, but no such marvel would save her now that he had the shotgun securely in his grasp. He raised it to eye-level and pulled the trigger.

***

One-eyed Jack had followed the hounds into the clearing from a safe distance behind, though he still arrived well ahead of the men. One look at the mad free-for-all told him that the silly hounds had already forgotten their primary purpose for being here. As usual, it was going to be up to him to save the day. The pack was creating quite a diversion, though, which he would take advantage of to look for Solitaire.

Straight into the midst of the fray he pranced, unafraid now that the pack was having too much fun haranguing their bigger targets to be worried about him. He was purposely making his way across the clearing to check out some crates on the outside perimeter when he was confronted by a familiar-looking pair of dusty work boots that would not allow him to slip by. Disgruntled, he backed up to see who it was bothering him. Earl's meaty visage appeared over his protruding belly as he grinned down at the terrier.

"I shoulda knowed y'all'd be here, pipsqueak," he slurred drunkenly. "Ever' time there's trouble around here, seems you show up. But this time, y'all ain't gettin' away!"

Jack hastily reversed away from the big man's hands, but there was nowhere to go. The crowd had them hemmed in. With a quick swipe, Earl lifted the little dog high into the air. He held him tightly around the middle, laughing as Jack's skinny legs flailed the air helplessly. Then he turned serious.

"Gatorbait's hungry," he said flatly. "He got cheated outta his rightful dinner."

He stomped over to the wall of the pit, just above where the gray mongrel still sulked. Leaning far out over the metal barricade, he called to the animal.

"Here, ya mangy critter! See if'n y'all kin best this teeny 'un! I hope t'hell ya choke on 'im!"

As he moved to toss Jack into the pit, the metal Earl was leaning on gave way with a crash, so that the two rolled down the wall together. Gatorbait, scared already, cowered further into the side of the pit.

One-eyed Jack had managed to jump free when Earl fell and now shook himself off, unhurt but in a terrible temper! How dare that awful man lay his stinking hands on him! He was getting pretty peeved off by the way the humans around here took him for a toy! Still in a huff, Jack turned to scramble back up the embankment that had been newly exposed by the fallen tin. A familiar whistling growl behind him stopped the little dog in his tracks. Rabbit-like, he rotated his ears in the direction of the sound, then slowly followed through with his head until he was face to face with Gatorbait. The creature's yellow serpentine eyes glowed eerily in the pale artificial light, turning Jack rigid with trepidation.

But Gatorbait's stare went beyond Jack to the fallen lump that was Earl Kell. He had been apprehensive as long as Earl didn't move, but now that the man was coming to and struggling feebly to get up, Gatorbait began his stalk.

Jack got out of there in a hurry, running up the nearly vertical wall like a small, hairy bug, and left the two grim brutes to face each other. He gave only a passing thought to wondering which one would prove the more savage.

But how was he going to find Solitaire in this havoc? The smells around here were too strong and diversified for him to track his friend, and Anna's hounds were too busy chasing anyone who ran from them to help him out again.

He became more hopeful, observing how quickly the local men were bolting into their pickups and heading back across the bumpy fields. No one was taking any dogs with them, so if he just waited a short while, the clearing would be empty except for canines, and then he would be able to ask them about his friend.

While Jack waited, he noticed an amazing thing. Lola and her pack were working together to single out the dark strangers who had been staying at Kell's place and chasing them into the protection of the only van still parked beside the pit. Why were they doing that? His moist little nose twitched as he realized the exciting implications. Lola must have memorized the men's strong odors from the site of Johnny's imprisonment and was leading her pack in a police action to round the guilty devils up! Jack was pleased to find that he had misjudged the old girl again!

The best part for Jack came when, after all the men had crowded into the back of the van and slammed the doors, they realized that the keys were missing from the ignition. There was a great uproar inside the van, and it shook fiercely until one of them seemed to remember something useful. He reached beneath the front seat, but came up empty, and once again, there was a great deal of swearing and groaning from inside the vehicle.

When Ken, Johnny and the elder Wales arrived on the scene, Lola and her pack were still jumping at the windows and baying good-naturedly at their 'treed' captives!

The Welsely men looked around them in confusion. Except for distant headlights that looked like erratic fireflies in the dark, there was no sign that any locals had been here at all.

"Blast!" Ken spit angrily. "We should have kept better control of the dogs until the sheriff got here!"

"Who'd have figured that big a group could scatter that quickly?" Wales offered in solace, though he was just as angry.

"There's some guys in that van over there," Johnny said as he wandered toward it, calling Lola to 'Off!' His surprise turned to jubilation when he opened the door and recognized the prisoners, but he wasn't so overcome that he forgot to raise his shotgun.

"Pa! Mr. Lorch! Come quick!"

When the older men arrived, Johnny explained that these were the men who had taken him captive at Kell's, most of them, anyway.

Hearing his son's story, Wales raised his shotgun and aimed it at the closest man's chest.

"You swine hurt my son, and I would love for you to give me an excuse to unload a round or two into you." He glared into each of their faces, finding it difficult to control his need to punish them for hurting his child. Through clenched teeth, he growled, "So be smart and stay quiet in there. The sheriff's on his way." He slammed the door with a bang.

The bang was echoed by the even louder percussion of a shotgun.

Johnny and his father exchanged wondering glances before Ken shouted, "It came from over there!"

There was silence as each person in the clearing spent the next few seconds worrying about his own private disaster scenario. For Johnny, the worst thing he could think of was Fleet's threat to destroy Solitaire.

"Oh God," he prayed through gritted teeth, "please don't let him win! Don't let her be dead!"

Before they could move, they heard Fleet's voice floating thinly on the night air.

"Johnny! Help! Johnny, come pull this bitch off me!"

Johnny pushed in front of his father and ran in the direction of the sound. He didn't know whether it was worse for Fleet to have killed Solitaire or for the Akita to have mauled him again. If Solitaire couldn't be controlled, she would have to be put down, anyway.

The senior Wales threw his shotgun to Ken with orders to keep it trained on the van and followed his son into the murky shadows of the thicket.

Johnny stopped to listen for Fleet's shout again, confused in the dark, until Jack whizzed past him. Johnny followed, confident that the terrier's dedication to his Akita friend would lead them right to her.

He heard Jack's little excited yips long before he could make out the form of Solitaire in the dark. The Akita was lying very still in the field, making no effort to shield her face from Jack's anxious pawing. She lay on her left side, her breathing ragged. Johnny dropped to his knees in front of her. Even in the dark, he could see the gaping tear on her hip.

"Oh Solitaire," he sobbed. "What's happened to you?"

Solitaire made an effort to welcome him with a jerk of her tail that was more like the limp movement of a man's wrist than a real tailwag.

Sure that Fleet was responsible for her injury, Johnny was filled with anger. He looked about for the foreman, fervently wishing he would find him in even worse condition than the Akita. But then Solitaire did something she had only done once before. She raised her head and licked him, politely, on the tip of his nose. Johnny was confused. Vicious fighting dogs that eat people don't normally lick noses.

When his father broke through the bushes near him, Johnny called out, "Fleet's got to be somewhere around here. I don't think she hurt him. Don't let him get away, Pa!"

Solitaire looked quizzically at the boy.

Of course I didn't hurt him. The scum is beneath my reproach. I simply kept him from leaving until you arrived.

Johnny stared at her, open-mouthed, so she turned her muzzle heavenward to point out the dark shape of a man clinging to the trunk about eight feet up in a nearby tree.

One-eyed Jack flew to the base of the tree and began jumping against it and barking as ferociously as if he was the one responsible for Fleet's ridiculous position.

"Please, Johnny," Fleet pleaded when he realized he had been discovered. "Call her off and I'll come down peaceably. I already dropped my rifle. Just don't let her get at me again!"

***

Solitaire's head laid heavily on Johnny's knee while Doc finished examining her injured hind leg. When he pronounced the wound the result of a dog bite, not the misfired shot from Fleet's rifle, Anna beamed from her seat atop a pile of broken scaffolding. She had arrived late, but she had still been in time to enjoy Fleet's predicament before he climbed down out of the tree and she had been heckling him about it ever since.

"Well, Fleet," she called over to him, "I guess that's proof positive that you used this dog for fightin', too. I believe that's a few more years in prison to look forward to."

Fleet's expression was bleak as he sat chained with a dog's leash to a substantial tree at the edge of the clearing.

Anna counted on her fingers, "Let's see.... That's dog fightin', animal abuse, stealin' from me, sellin' animals illegally, sellin' *my* animals illegally, falsifyin' paperwork, kidnappin'..."

"I didn't have anything to do with that!" Fleet countered. "I didn't know the kid was even missing."

"Tell it to the judge!" Anna cackled, pleased that she had gotten a rise out of him.

They were waiting for the sheriff to finish interviewing the local men his deputies had rounded up at Kell's front gate. Ken was down there, as well, having taken Welsely's pickup to guide the sheriff back to the clearing whenever he was ready.

One of the deputies had followed Anna in, with Doc as his passenger. They both had a chuckle when they saw Welsely's hunting pack lying in different attitudes of repose all around the van that still held the sorry refugees from Carolina. Anna was immensely proud of her hounds, and didn't think it was necessary to tell the captives that neither Lola nor any of her brood had ever bitten a human being in their life.

"The guilty always expect the same treatment from others that they would have given if the situation was reversed. Those fellas won't move outta there as long as my hounds're around for fear we'll sic 'em up!" she had confided to the deputy.

Jack was curled up beside Solitaire, careful not to disturb, but needing to be close, while Johnny and his father talked with Doc.

"There's a lot of sorry-looking animals in those cages," Doc was saying. "I believe that most of the poor buggers will have to be put down, but it's possible that we can save some of the youngsters. A dog's nature can be pretty forgiving."

"That old blue hound-cross that we found in the pit didn't look too forgiving," said Johnny's father. "The guy he mauled is gonna need a few well-placed stitches, that's for sure."

When Johnny and his father had returned to the clearing, they had heard shouts of distress coming from the other direction, from the dog pit, itself. The man they found hiding there was so obese that he wasn't able to climb out on his own, and he was being stalked by a nasty-looking brute of a dog. It took all three of the Welsely men to pull him out, the big dog worrying the back of the man's jeans the whole time. Then they had shored up the fallen areas of the pit wall so that the crazed dog couldn't escape. They had all had a laugh when the man was loaded into the deputy's car to go for medical attention; he hadn't been able to sit, so he had to ride to town on all fours in the back seat of the police car.

"That was Earl Kell, Pa. He's lucky that dog didn't kill him. And rightly so. That was the one that he kept in the shed where you found me. And wait until you see the way he was caged!"

Doc shook his gray head, disgusted by the numerous stories he had heard this night. "Well, it looks like I've got my work cut out for me for a while, helping the county vet sort that mess out, too. Even the healthy dogs, if there are any, are going to be a big problem."

He looked up, beseeching the others for answers he knew they didn't have.

"Where in heaven are we going to place all of those dogs?"

"I need a new dog around the place, Doc."

Johnny looked at his father in surprise.

"With my son's help, I'm willin' to take a chance on workin' through any social problems one of those fellas might have. Johnny's real good with the dogs, you know."

Johnny grinned, pleased by his father's compliment.

Anna called out, "Maybe Solitaire can help with the socializin', too. She's proved herself by me, that's for sure. The way I figure it, she coulda chewed old Fleet to bits after his rifle locked up, but she didn't. She seems to be over that terrible mad-on she had when she got here, thank the Lord!"

The pain of Solitaire's injuries were fading as Doc's injection relaxed her to sleep. She felt secure and happy for the first time since her puppies were taken from her. With her head resting on Johnny's knee, she took comfort in a favorite dream she had first had long ago when she was a young pup in Japan. In this dream, she foresaw the encounter she would have one day with the God-like creature she would willingly call 'Master'. He had always appeared to her from very far away, though she imagined he had raven hair and slanted eyes. Now, as she dreamed, the Master came closer, arms spread wide to welcome her and give her succor in her hour of need. As he walked slowly toward her, his appearance altered slightly with each step. One step, his legs grew longer; two steps, his skin became darker, more tanned; three steps, his hair lost its deep blue tones and changed slowly to dusky gold; four steps, his eyes became more rounded and Solitaire found her adoring stare was being returned by eyes as clear and blue as – Johnny's!

CHAPTER 33

Topeka! Johnny was excited to have made it all the way to the state capital, though he didn't expect to be doing much sightseeing while he was here. He and Mr. Lorch would have their hands full showing six of Welsely's dogs in four different Groups during this weekend's shows. Yesterday morning they had packed the excited dogs into individual crates inside Ken's motorhome and traveled to the show grounds. Ken had wanted to arrive early, so that they could get a close spot in the exhibitors' parking lot for their setup. Doc was along to watch their 'camp' and helped as best he could with last-minute grooming while the two handlers ran from ring to ring with the dogs. The three made a cheerful party.

Johnny had needed to spend some of his hard-earned money on a new shirt and sport coat for the show. Though both Anna and his father had volunteered to fund his purchase, he had welcomed this first opportunity to demonstrate his independence.

The dark blazer he bought fit his slim, broad-shouldered body well, and he was proud of how old it made him look. Each morning, when he faced the mirror to pull his blonde hair, clean and shiny, into a tight ponytail for the show, he checked to see if he needed to use the razor his father had given him for his fifteenth birthday yet.

Johnny wished his father could have come. Since the night of the dogfights, the two had spent more quality time together and their relationship was improving. The elder Wales was developing a keen interest in his son's work. In fact, he had ended up adopting three dogs from Kell's old kennel. Hunting breeds all, the dogs had quickly forgotten the abuses of their previous life and gaily led their new master along the path of relaxation, if not rest, whenever he wasn't working.

Anna would have liked to be there to watch one of Lola's daughter,

Maude, being shown for the first time, but someone had to stay on the farm to help Abel. Besides Jack, that was, who was also staying back because it had been agreed that the terrier's antisocial attitudes toward foreigners (anybody he hadn't seen before) and unfair imprisonment (his) made his attendance on the crowded showgrounds an impossibility. Johnny had defended the Aussie, saying he would certainly liven up the show hall, but the others had seriously questioned the wisdom of that.

Everyone had been disappointed when Ken had made the last-minute decision to pull Solitaire from the competition. Her leg had healed cleanly, thanks to Doc's and Johnny's careful ministrations; even the scar would soon be completely hidden by dark hair. But she still favored it when she was tired, so Ken thought it wise to give her a little more time to recoup before stressing the leg. Seeing Johnny's downcast eyes, he had quickly added that he would still like to bring her along in order to reintroduce her to the feel of a dog show and get her used to crowds of new people and dogs. Not surprisingly, Johnny had been enthusiastic about that idea.

Johnny and the Akita had been inseparable over the last few weeks, with Ken's blessing. Johnny's innocent warmth had infused Solitaire with a contentment that would not have seemed possible only a short time ago, while her gracious dignity had rubbed off on the boy, giving him an air of composure seldom seen in one so young.

Late in the afternoon of the first day at the Topeka shows, Johnny returned to put away the last of their 'open' dogs to be shown in the Breed competitions and was surprised to see a new face sitting on the picnic bench beside the RV, a young girl so intent on her copy of the show catalogue that she started when Johnny asked her where Doc was. She introduced herself as 'just Karen' and explained that she was with the family next door. None of their dogs had made it to the Group competition, so she had been willing when Doc had asked her to watch over Ken's motorhome for a little while.

Mr. Lorch was always saying how all of the exhibitors become friends during the show circuit, so Johnny smiled his thanks before making sure the other dogs were secure in their kennels and had plenty of water. Then he slipped a light show lead over Solitaire's head and trotted her back to the hall.

Since dogs that are not entered in the exhibition are not normally welcome on the show grounds, Johnny felt a little like a cheater when he slipped Solitaire's unused number into his armband and walked past the steward and into the building.

The show rings were located inside the large hall. Each numbered ring was actually a large square drawn by low expandable fence borders. This morning, numerous dogs of the same breed or group had been gaited by their handlers along black rubber mats and carefully stacked for the judge's perusal. At this hour, most of the rings were empty except for a few people practicing with their more inexperienced entries, but the hall was still so crowded that Johnny fretted about how he was going to make his way through the throng to the grander concourses in the back on time.

In fact, he was pleasantly surprised by how easily he navigated the jostling crowd with the gigantic Akita by his side. The crowd parted like a field of wheat before the wind when they saw Solitaire. One handler hurrying past took one glance at Solitaire and swung his dog, a Pekingese flowing with coat, high above his head, where he balanced it on one hand. The Pekingese seemed well used to this mode of transport and perched quite comfortably above the crowd, his long tail hanging limply down the front of the handler's face.

As he walked, Johnny thought about the girl taking care of the RV. She had seemed familiar and now he remembered seeing her earlier showing one of the terrier breeds – a Norfolk, he thought. He remembered her because her dog had had such an incredulous look on his face when he didn't get chosen by the judge.

"Seems like all terriers have monster egos like our Jack!" he said to no one in particular.

Welsely's had done well that day. Their Brittany Spaniel had taken Winners Dog in his Breed competition, giving him the championship points; but he hadn't gone on to win Best of Breed, so would not be competing in the Sporting Group finals tonight.

"Next time," was Ken's only comment, his high spirits not dampened in the least.

The best news of the day was young Maude's win. She had behaved astonishingly well and was rewarded the points as Winners Bitch. Then she had gone on to surprise even Ken by winning Best of Breed from the Puppy class! They had called Anna from ringside to share the news and had laughed out loud to hear her excited whoops broadcast through Ken's cell phone.

In just moments, Maude was going to make her debut in the big ring and Johnny didn't want to miss that performance. He was sure he would find Doc at ringside, too.

"Johnny! Over here!" Ken waved to catch his wide-eyed apprentice's attention and called him. Sitting sprawl-legged beside her handler, Maude didn't look much like a champion in the making. She looked more like a tired, sorry youngster who had had just about enough of all this jostle.

Johnny knelt down to comfort the big puppy, rubbing the short hair of her head and chest. "Don't worry, Maudie, it'll all be over with soon. Just one last time in the ring..," he looked up at Ken, mischief in his eyes, "...or maybe two more times if you win!"

Ken chuckled nervously, "I'll be happy with a Group placement, thank you. It is her first time, after all!"

The ring steward called the numbers and the best hounds of each breed gaited across the large ring while an announcer introduced them and gave a short history of each type. Johnny felt a thrill when the crowd applauded their favorites. One of the loudest outbursts was for the young Maude, who seemed happy to be able to move again and stretched into the smooth ground-eating gate typical of her race.

Ken had to move quickly to keep up with Maude's long gait. He made it look effortless, but it was a big ring and Johnny thought Ken looked quite flushed by the time the two got to their appointed spot in the line of hounds. Watching him help Maude to find the proper stacking position to show off to the judge, Johnny thought he had never seen his boss looking so happy.

This morning, Johnny had been confounded by how anyone could pick out one outstanding specimen of each breed to place higher than all of the other remarkable animals. Now that the Group judging had begun, he appreciated how much more difficult the judge's job was when those winners from the Breed competitions went up against each other for the honor in the Group classification. By the last hour of the show, Ken had told him, the hundreds of dogs he had seen this morning would be whittled down to just seven, one from each of the AKC Groups – and then the seemingly impossible feat of judging Best In Show would begin.

Group 2nd!

Ken was obviously over the moon with the judge's decision and playfully chucked the hound under the chin to let her know she had done her job well. The whole audience laughed appreciatively when Maude morphed back into her puppy self to jump all over him. More than ever, Johnny wanted to own the ring like Mr. Lorch did one day.

You will, young one. One day you will challenge your Mr. Lorch and you will come out the winner!

Johnny looked down into the laughing face of the Akita standing next to him and felt the familiar completeness that helped him to remain patient these days. Growing up takes a lot of time and he still had a lot to learn, as he was always being told. Still, one day…

"Okay, the Working Group comes next and the people from the Japanese kennel are supposed to meet us here. Are you sure you want Solitaire here?" Ken surprised Johnny with his quick return from the ring.

"She's fine," he replied when he had had time to put his dream aside and return to reality.

Ken studied the boy's face to make sure there was no hesitation there. He had already explained to his apprentice that it might not be a good idea to force Solitaire into a situation where she might revert to the angry animal she was when she first arrived.

But Johnny was resolute. "She proved herself by letting Fleet go that night, didn't she? We can't keep being nervous of her temperament. Besides, they asked to see her."

Ken nodded. He seemed about to say something else, but instead laid his hand on Johnny's shoulder.

"I took a moment this morning to watch the Shih Tzu in the Puppy Sweepstakes," he offered, changing from the more uncomfortable subject. "I wanted to see them because Anna has been suggesting, in that roundabout way of hers, that we keep The Pussycat's whole litter to help replace the breeding stock we lost. I think that we may do even more than that.

"Before we came, I checked up on The Pussycat's pedigree. It's impressive, to say the least. I sure can't figure out how she ever ended up at Welsely's. Anyway, I think we ought to keep the whole passel for a few more months, then see if there are any show prospects in the lot. What do you think, son?"

Johnny liked the way he was being asked what he thought lately, and that his boss insisted he call him by his first name, like an equal. He and Solitaire exchanged knowing glances before he spoke out.

"I think that's a great idea, Ken! I've been teaching The Pussycat's pups how to stand already and they're all pretty good at it. But the male – I call him 'Sunny' because he's so bright – he's really got pizazz! And he loves to show it off, too!"

Ken grinned when he realized that he had been 'double-teamed' on this issue by Anna and Johnny. Well, he didn't mind them ganging up on him if it meant that their dedication to improving the dogs at Welsely's was as strong as his.

"It's a lot of grooming, which we're not really set up to do, but Doc says he's found a young lady who would be willing to come out to Welsely's and help out. We need more people and he says she's pretty experienced – did you meet her when you went back to the RV for Solitaire?"

He didn't wait for an answer, but looked at his watch and around for Doc, who was still nowhere to be seen. "Where is Doc, anyway?"

The best of each breed in the Working Group were already standing in the ring to be judged. There were nineteen near-perfect specimens, each one carefully stacked and watching intently for his or her handler's next signal.

In the front of the line was a male Akita. He was a compact, powerful-looking animal with an even larger head for his size than Solitaire. His forelegs were like tree stumps and his chest broad and well-muscled. The dog's main colors were large, clear gold patches on a background of white. The inky black outlining his eyes, ears and mouth served to make his lighter colors look even more brilliant.

In his reading, Johnny had discovered that the Japanese prefer more white on their dogs than the Americans do. He wondered if it was possible that this was the dog from Solitaire's old kennel. The man handling him was not Japanese, but you couldn't tell from that as many of the dogs in the show were with professional handlers.

That is a dog of the Hachi line. Your assumptions are well thought-out, young master.

"You think it's a Japanese dog, too, huh Solitaire? You like his looks?"

You're getting better at this. Solitaire let Johnny know she was proud of him before turning her attention back to the comely male. *Hmmm. Very interesting!*

Her intensity as she watched the dog so impressed Johnny that he elbowed Ken to bring it to his attention. Ken was intrigued as well, knowing from experience how difficult it is to impress a female of the Akita breed.

"Hey, I hope we get some answers about Solitaire's temperament before too long. She looks like she's interested in a boyfriend," he joked.

Abruptly, Solitaire's mental mood changed from sublime fascination to jagged consternation. Johnny felt it immediately and dropped to his knees beside her.

"What is it, girl?" he asked. "We were only kidding you."

Solitaire didn't take her gaze from the ring to acknowledge Johnny. Her hackles rose slowly and adjusted themselves in solid lines across her shoulders and down her back. The coarser hairs in these areas stood straight out, away from her body, the flesh beneath them tensely knotted. The long muscles of her back legs quivered ever so slightly, stretched taut as bowstrings, ready to propel the Akita forward.

Johnny followed her black stare back to the male – no! – it was the *handler* of the male Akita that she was staring at.

The Group Judge had just asked the contestants to circle counterclockwise so that she could see the dogs' gaits again. In this direction, the dogs were on the inside. On the outside of the circle, and coming straight at them, was the Akita's handler.

Johnny tightened his grip on Solitaire's lead while he examined the man who seemed to be upsetting her. He was tall and thin, with sandy blonde hair slicked back in a ponytail. Except for that ponytail and the nice clothes, Johnny thought, he could pass for Fleet. No wonder Solitaire was upset!

"It's okay, girl. That's not Fleet," he said, "though he looks enough like him to be his brother! Don't you think so, Mr... I mean, Ken?"

Ken was pensive for a moment as he studied the Akita and the object of her scrutiny. Then he jerked reflexively and pulled his show program out from under his arm. He leafed through until he found a few promotional photos. When he found the one he wanted, he drew a deep breath and let it out again through flared nostrils, as though he smelled something bad. He turned the program around so that Johnny could see it.

The letters of the heading were large:

MR. L. TRIDENT HANDLING IMPORT TO AMERICAN CHAMPIONSHIP

The crowd around them erupted into loud applause as the judge pointed her finger at 1st, 2nd, 3rd, 4th place – the Akita, the Giant Schnauzer, the Siberian Husky and the Newfoundland. All were fine examples of their breed, but the imported Japanese Akita was obviously a crowd pleaser.

Right then, Doc arrived ringside followed by a small party of Asian people. After exchanging meaningful glances with one of the Japanese men, Doc motioned to someone in the crowd, catching Johnny's eye as well. He turned to see a uniformed policeman and another official-looking man in plain clothes come forward. The officer waited outside the ring while the dogs and handlers collected their rosettes and had quick words with the Group judge. When all but Trident had exited, he stepped forward to block the way.

Trident seemed bewildered as he handed the male Akita's lead to one of the Japanese men. After listening to the man in plain clothes read something to him, he visibly paled and looked around questioningly. When he saw Solitaire, the corners of his mouth twitched and turned down. His steel blue eyes followed the line of her lead to Johnny's face and then Ken's and Doc's.

Suddenly, the civil scene erupted in violence as Trident pushed the uniformed officer out of his way then punched the other man, sending him sprawling on the floor. He ran straight into the crowd of bystanders, bulldozing them out of his way. People began screaming hysterically as he ran up the bleachers toward the exit doors.

Free me, Johnny!

Without thinking, Johnny reached down and slid Solitaire's lead over her head. With a whoosh, she was gone, following in Trident's wake through the sea of people. Where he had to jump from bench to bench, the huge dog was able to bound two at a time. Trident leaped from the topmost seat, his long legs flying as he made for the exit door. Solitaire lengthened her stride, ignoring the pinch in the area of her old injury. She flew from the last bench straight onto Trident's broad shoulders. Due to the lingering weakness in her hindquarters, her leap didn't have the force needed to propel her victim forward, but she clung stubbornly to his shoulders for several seconds until he became unbalanced and fell over backward. The man's weight knocked the wind out of Solitaire, giving him the time he needed to turn over and hold her down by the loose skin on each side of her throat. He raised his right hand to deliver a heavy blow to the side of the stunned Akita's head.

"No!" Johnny jumped on Trident's arm, dragging it down before he could deliver that blow. Behind him, Ken fell on the agent's other arm, incapacitating the man. Between the two of them, they held Trident until they were joined by the breathless police officer holding a .38.

Solitaire rose slowly. Her hip had been twisted in the fall and was causing her some slight pain again, but her great canine heart was filled with emotional gratification – her young handler had risked his own life to save hers! She walked stiffly to Johnny and rose slowly and decorously to place her huge forepaws on his shoulders, pushing him back against the wall. Her face was almost on a level with his as her triangular black eyes peered deeply into his round blue ones.

Thee, I love! My soul is yours and I would follow you to the ends of the earth, for you are a noble human being. I choose you for my Master!

The surprise left Johnny's face and he folded his arms around Solitaire's heavy torso in complete happiness. He knew he was one of the very lucky ones to have won the love of an Akita!

***

On the drive back to Welsely's, the mood inside the motorhome was joyous. Doc was repeating the story of how his work with the Japanese kennel to coordinate the police action against Trident had been faltering until the kennel manager, Asaki, had broken down and told the true story of what had happened to Solitaire. Once they had the proof of Trident's wrongdoing, their only problem was how to make him leave the Netherlands, where he wasn't charged with any crime, and travel to another country from which he couldn't escape prosecution. He seemed to have gotten wind of some investigations going on and hadn't been traveling in recent months.

Shibuya had been happy to provide the perfect solution; he forced Asaki, who Trident still trusted, to hire the agent to handle his star Akita on the American show circuit, starting with the all-breed show in Topeka, Kansas. He had sweetened the deal enough that Trident wouldn't be able to refuse. Though they both had felt reticent about it, Ken and Doc had promised to bring Solitaire to the scene as a special witness.

"I sure hadn't figured on her being the arresting officer, though!" Doc concluded, jubilantly. He had relished his role in helping to accomplish something really important, after so many years of feeling insignificant.

Ken Lorch couldn't feel better, either. Welsely's dogs had done reasonably well at the show and Anna's hound puppy, Maude, was returning home with two blue rosettes after winning her Breed on Sunday, as well.

He had been able to hire new, experienced help for the specials kennel, too. It seemed that the neighbors' girl, Karen – or 'Just Karen' as Johnny insisted on teasing her - was eager to be out on her own and was looking forward to helping out at Welsely's. She would be moving into the farmhouse with Anna at the end of the month.

Best of all, his old colleagues had welcomed him at the show with open arms, wondering what he had been up to for the past six months. There hadn't been a whisper about any wrongdoings of his; only that an old rival of his had been kicked out of the kennel club recently for threatening to blackmail two other handlers with exaggerated rumors about poor grooming practices. This was news that Ken had had difficulty absorbing without emotion. He was free again to do whatever he wanted – he could return to his old handling position without fear.

Ken exchanged a brief look with Doc, who had become a close friend after all the two had gone through together, and realized that he was already doing what he wanted. Anna, Doc, Johnny – and all of the dogs at Welsely's Kennel needed him to stay where he was. It was a good feeling.

***

Johnny sat in the back of the motorhome with Solitaire, listening to the lively conversation between the two men in the front seats. He had enjoyed the big show, but was tired and looked forward to getting home where he had the next generation of Welsely showdogs to take care of. It surprised him how much he had missed One-eyed Jack on this trip.

He will be waiting. As will all the others. You have earned a place in their hearts, Johnny.

Solitaire sat up to look over the back of their seat – the tenth time in an hour, Johnny noted wryly.

Hmm. Will you be kenneling the new dog in the run next to mine?

Johnny laughed at Solitaire's dreamy expression before turning, himself, to admire the handsome Akita dog in his travel crate. 'Sanjiro' was returning with them to Welsely's while he finished his American championship, and Ken had hinted that it might be for longer, if he fit in.

After a while, the conversation up front faded. In the back seat, Johnny laid his head on Solitaire's plush hip and joined her in relaxed sleep.

For the first time, Solitaire's puppy dreams brought no pain with them. She allowed her visions of happy Akita puppies tumbling together under her loving gaze to be shared by the young man to whom she had devoted her life. In their sleep, both boy and dog smiled.

IF YOU'RE INTERESTED…

I was born a long time ago in a land far, far away – 1950 in Canada.

Very early in life, I developed the precept I would live by; namely that if I could catch it, I would take it home! Though there were six children in my family, the care of our pets was almost always left up to me.

I guess it was no surprise that my first part-time job would be cleaning kennels for a veterinarian. From there, I advanced my position to small animal groomer, then veterinary technician. At various times, I have also worked as a professional dog trainer and – yes – bred Shih Tzu for the showring.

I have lived a few places in the world, been married once or twice, but have always had my beloved Shih Tzu dogs by my side!

My experience with Akitas is more limited, but I consider myself lucky to have owned two ladies of the American type, which are much larger than the original Japanese Akitas. I understand that the two types are now considered separate breeds in many kennel clubs around the world, but I make no difference here. Both the American and Japanese Akita-Inu have my vote for the most beautiful and noble of all dog breeds!

The underlying subject of this book is one I am very familiar with and feel strongly about. I have made every effort not to preach while I told this story, and have tried to explain both sides of the puppy mill controversy; but my hope is that when people read about the sad plight of dogs bred in these conditions, they will no longer support the industry.

See what you think…   andalucandy@gmail.com

Candice L. Martin   www.facebook.com/solitaireadogstory

Made in the USA
Middletown, DE
02 December 2016